Praise for *Deadly Exploits*

Janet Boydell's novel is taut and engaging, unfolding step-by-step in a delicate, well-balanced narrative that demands attention. There's drama here, mixed with mythology, murder, and passion, carried forward by a host of characters who interact seamlessly to draw the reader into an atmospheric tale that harkens back to the best of noir fiction. Well written, immersive, and original, *Deadly Exploits* honors any bookshelf.

—Greg Fields, author of *The Bright Freight of Memory,* American Writing Award Winner, Literary Fiction, and Southern California Book Festival Book of the Year

Deadly Exploits is a must-read for those who love a story rich with complexity, danger, and romance that is also loaded with twists and turns and leaves you wanting more. Janet Boydell's book is a riveting story of malevolent schemes created for the entertainment of a bloodthirsty few.

—C.V. Alba, author of the award-winning *Mat Briscoe Mysteries*

Deadly Exploits is a thrilling ride that crosses continents and the worlds of antiquity dealers, archaeologists, and New York City cops. It's a love story that explores the supernatural and delves into questions of evil, obsession, and the excesses of wealth. Consider *Deadly Exploits* for your next vacation or beach read!

—Denise Frost, author of *A Punishing Breed*

When a string of billionaires turns up dead under chillingly inexplicable circumstances, New York City's police detectives are on it. Their mission: uncover the truth behind a series of murders that defy science. *Deadly Exploits* offers a world where wealth offers no protection, secrets cut deep, and desire simmers dangerously beneath the surface. But the closer they get to the truth, the more they realize they may be the next targets of a power far older and more vengeful than they imagined. Blending myth and modernity, *Deadly Exploits* is a pulse-pounding thriller where curiosity kills.

—Jeff F. Tanner, author and co-author of numerous fiction and nonfiction books, scientific articles, and more

An intelligent, fast-paced crime drama with stolen artifacts, untimely deaths, and a race against the clock, Janet Boydell's *Deadly Exploits* does not disappoint.

—Deanna Nese, author of *The Snowy Plover Inn Mystery Series* and *Yellow Slicker*

Deadly Exploits, written by Janet Boydell, transports the reader into the lives of devious and greedy individuals willing to compromise their values to get what they want. Set in New York City, this thriller crosses international lines, encounters wealth and power, and reveals the price of moral corruption. Janet created a suspenseful story with twists and turns that will keep the reader wondering what could happen next. Just when you think you know, you are once again met with the unexpected.

—Brad Remillard, co-author: *You're NOT the Person I Hired!*

DEADLY EXPLOITS

JANET BOYDELL

BERRY
POWELL
PRESS

Deadly Exploits

First paperback edition September 2025
Cover Design by: Kay McConnaughey
Interior Design: Carolyn Rafferty

Photograph by: Diane Gabriel Photography
at www.dianegabrielphotography.com

Published by Berry Powell Press
Glendora, California
www.berrypowellpress.com
ISBN: 978-1-957321-02-8(Paperback)
ISBN: 978-1-957321-03-5 (eBook)
Library of Congress Control Number: 2025915802

Dedication
For my children and my grandchildren:
You are more loved and adored than you can possibly know.

Contents

Acknowledgments...vii

Prologue – Two Years Ago...ix

FRIDAY (Present Day)

Chapter 1: Bridget Murphy - London 1

Chapter 2: Adama Baptiste - NYC 5

Chapter 3: Bodies in the Hudson..11

SATURDAY

Chapter 4: Dr. Betty Pearson, Chief Medical Examiner (CME).....17

Chapter 5: Professor Colin Taylor, PhD...............................21

Chapter 6: The Millers 27

Chapter 7: Cloak and Dagger...35

Chapter 8: Sorry, We're Closed...41

Chapter 9: No Peeking..45

Chapter 10: Home Again...49

Chapter 11: A Special Event...53

Chapter 12: Caviar and Champagne.....................................59

Chapter 13: The Jewelry Box..65

Chapter 14: No Loose Ends 69

SUNDAY

Chapter 15: William Vanhorn...77

Chapter 16: Captain Ricci 85

Chapter 17: What Case?...89

Chapter 18: 911 93

Chapter 19: Jacqueline Miller 101

Chapter 20: Daisy Hunter...107

Chapter 21: Past Butterflies 117

Chapter 22: The Price of Silence.......................................127

Chapter 23: The Cellphone 133

Chapter 24: Bridget's Dilemma...139

MONDAY

Chapter 25: The Consultant..147

Chapter 26: The Special Task Force...................................151

Chapter 27: Three Bodies..159

Chapter 28: The Paper Bag 167

Chapter 29: Dumbstruck 173
Chapter 30: Please, Let It Go 181
Chapter 31: Dick Betrug 187
Chapter 32: That's the Guy! 193
TUESDAY
Chapter 33: The Favor 201
Chapter 34: She's Not Coming 205
Chapter 35: The London Murders 211
Chapter 36: The Hidden Camera 217
Chapter 37: Late-Night Meeting 225
Chapter 38: It's Graphic 233
WEDNESDAY
Chapter 39: The Banimaya 243
Chapter 40: The Kanijugu 249
Chapter 41: Triggered 255
Chapter 42: The Cart 261
Chapter 43: Apologies 269
THURSDAY
Chapter 44: Eat Me 275
Chapter 45: Stop! 281
Chapter 46: Stuck On E. 70th 289
Chapter 47: Are We Good? 297
Chapter 48: Gunter Maximilian 301
TWO WEEKS LATER
Chapter 49: Reunion 311
Chapter 50: Bakary Baptiste 317
Chapter 51: Carnage 321
Chapter 52: A City Restored 331
Chapter 53: The Ultimatum 335
Chapter 54: LeGalére 341
Chapter 55: Past and Future Exploits 345
Chapter 56: Heart to Heart 351

About the Author 361
Note From the Publisher 363

Acknowledgments

I'm deeply grateful to Berry Powell Press and its exceptional team, especially Carmen Berry for her editorial magic, and Valeri Mills Barnes, my writing coach and editor, who nurtured my growth as a storyteller with boundless patience and remarkable insight. Kay McConnaughey, I gave you a symbol, and you gave me an amazing cover.

To Mark, my devoted partner, who embodies patience and endurance, thank you for helping me stay grounded. My talented daughter, Courtney, my favorite artist, for our playful "what if" scenarios, you are a mother's best friend. To my son Burke, of whom I could not be prouder, your fierce loyalty, devotion, and logic challenged me to elevate my writing skills and rediscover language. And to Anthony, my son-in-law, whose presence in my life is a gift.

In New York City: Catherine and Mark, my nephew, and his wife, who not only opened their New York City apartment (Adama's fictional home) but also guided me through the city I grew to love; the NYPD detectives who talked with me at their precinct; and the NYC taxi drivers who shared their experiences and love for America.

Special thanks to those who shared their expertise: Beth, my niece, whose EMT knowledge provided authentic insights; Leslie Bristow, whose graphic art talents consistently challenged my "source of light"; Christine Edick, my former executive coach who steered me when I needed direction most; Conrad Burnham for his developmental wisdom; and Anne George, thank you for being my lifelong friend and guru—we are and shall always be.

Finally, to my anchors—my true north—my brothers and sisters: Jimmy, Ricky, Bevi, and Gina—without you, I would be adrift. My love for you transcends words. We *are* family—IU.

Prologue – Two Years Ago
Senegal, West Africa

In his dream state, Bakary Baptiste surrendered to the gentle sway of a blissful sea of tall green grasses swaying in the gentle breeze. He reached out to touch the swirling movement, mesmerized by it like couples gliding around a grand ballroom. "Not yet," he murmured, clinging to the ethereal beauty. "Just a moment longer."

Dawn stole the moon's last remnants of silver light. Streaks of illumination aimed to penetrate his closed eyelids. The cool, damp air gave him goosebumps as he shivered. Bakary stirred. *Oh well, it was a nice dream.*

Still unwilling to open his eyes, he nudged his wife, Saruba. "Honey, we left the window open; it rained." Sensing she was asleep, Bakary gently lifted her arm off his chest. He felt the heaviness of her body lying next to him. *She's cold too.*

Bakary's skull throbbed. Instinctively, he touched his temple on the left but recoiled—the flesh was too tender. Flies buzzed around his damp face, and there was a strange, tacky feeling all over his body. His right arm ached as he struggled to lift the covers, and his lower extremities felt void of any sensation. *What's going on?*

A thick, gooey substance had sealed his eyes. Bakary blinked repeatedly to clear the gunk. When that did not work, his trembling fingers cleared most of the crust. Bakary's vision improved, and he stared in disbelief at the crimson color smeared on his fingers. "Is this? Oh my god, blood!"

Consciousness crashed over Bakary like a prank bucket of ice water, jarring his senses. He looked around and realized this was no dream. This place was not his home, and his wife was not by his side. Instead, he was surrounded by morning mist, which hung around him like heavy chains. He struggled to make sense of the seashells, tall grasses, and tangled brush. There were no buildings, no landmarks, and no sign of civilization. Bakary felt weakened by pain in his head and right arm. As he looked around, his mind raced to comprehend the spectacle surrounding him. Instinctively, he cried out, "Help! Help me! Anybody, help!"

Panic set in. Bakary's mind worked backward. Now, he understood the weight, the stickiness, the flies, and the blood. He was buried in a pile of dead bodies. A wave of dizziness washed over him. Repulsed, he smelled the blood and bodily discharges. It was pungent, like the inside of a chicken coop that reeked of ammonia and the rank smell of raw sewage in the streets after heavy rain. The open wounds attracted thousands of buzzing flies.

Like a trapped animal, Bakary frantically peeled, pushed, and rolled bodies away to liberate himself. The extra space enabled him to scoot backward until he rolled onto his stomach. Clawing in the dirt with hands and elbows, he dragged his body forward, flipped over, and sat upright. He stared at the dead bodies and blood-soaked clothing. Bakary's eyes filled with tears. He wept at the sight of a dozen dead friends and neighbors.

Bakary's bullet-grazed right arm throbbed beneath crusted blood. The weight of his friends' bodies had stopped the bleeding and saved his life. Despite numb legs, he quickly stood and stared at the full extent of the massacre—a mound of bloodied bodies. A surge of adrenaline triggered nausea. Bakary doubled over and retched. He spat out the bitter taste of stomach acid and used his sleeve to wipe his mouth.

Pape? "Pape? Pape! Where are you?" Bakary's memory had returned. Ignoring his pain, he frantically searched the pile of bodies. He pulled the men's limp arms one way and dragged their legs the other. He dug impatiently, yanking and rolling dead weight. One was a friend from work, another a neighbor down the street, and then his mailman. He simultaneously felt terror and mercy after failing to find Pape. For a split second, Bakary felt relief. *Thank god, he's not here!* Then his memory crashed over him like a rogue wave. "Run, Pape. Run!" he had screamed the night before.

He whipped his head around.

Bakary ran in the direction he had last seen Pape. While desperately searching, he zigzagged through the tall grasses, bushes, and trees. He called out, "Pape! Where are you?" His voice got louder. "Pape, answer me!" Twenty yards out, his world stopped. Time and space crystallized as he stared in disbelief. "No. No. No!" He ran to Pape, lying face down on the ground. The boy's favorite jacket was soaked in blood from the gunshot he had taken in the back.

Weakness turned Bakary's legs to jelly; they buckled, and he dropped to his knees. "Pape!" The name cracked in his throat as he frantically scooped up the body of his twelve-year-old son. "I'm here." Bakary pulled his boy close to his chest, clutching him, feeling the familiarity of holding his firstborn child. He wept inconsolably. "Papa is here." Bakary sobbed as he rocked the lifeless body of his son. He looked skyward through blurred vision and pleaded. "No, god, please no."

For several minutes, Bakary felt numb. Pape's long, thin arms lay limp, his skinny torso twisted by his father's clutch. Bakary's teardrops fell onto his son's soft brown cheeks. "Oh, Pape, I'm so sorry." He gently caressed his son's face. *How will I tell your mother?* The thought took his breath away and caused his chest to constrict. *She'll be devastated.*

A crackling noise caused Bakary to freeze. He listened, his heartbeat thundering in his ears. *Oh my god, are the killers still here?* He lay low to the ground, cradling his son. The misty fog and tall grasses helped camouflage them. The noise grew louder. Bakary stiffened and waited for them to appear.

"Oh, pour l'amour du ciel, for heaven's sake!" Bakary said when a pig poked its nose through the brush. He flicked his hand. "Partez, partez!" The scolded pig scampered away.

He knew the area might be unsafe. Bakary gently released his son, stood up cautiously, and looked around. With no one in sight, he whispered, "We must be very quiet. I'm taking you home now." He repositioned Pape, picked him up, and carried him through the brush to a pathway. Moving slowly and deliberately, his eyes darted back and forth, searching for signs of danger.

Bakary knew they were on Impie Island, which was known to be forbidden by the locals. It was an isolated location blanketed in millions of clam shells that had accumulated over thousands of years. It was linked to Shell Island, which was connected to the West Coast of St. Pierre, Senegal. To reach the mainland, Bakary needed to cross two bridges. He quickened his pace. *Just a little more to go.* He stepped onto the wobbly slats of the first bridge that stretched outward for thirty yards. Bakary reached Shell Island, which was also covered in millions of clam shells. It was larger and had become a tourist attraction because of its history. The locals served tourists in the outdoor markets.

Based on the night's events, Bakary trusted no one. The killers had left him for dead, but now he was a witness to the savagery he, his son, and his friends suffered. Bakary stayed in the shadows, thankful for the morning mist as he skirted along the edges of the shops. *Now or never.* The second bridge lay a few yards ahead.

Although small for his age, Pape's body was heavy. Bakary shifted his son for better balance. "We're almost there. We must be quiet." His arms shook and ached from the gunshot wound, and his head pounded. Bakary cautiously walked out of the shadows toward the opening of the mainland bridge.

French and English were two common languages in the region. The locals put up an arched sign that read "Merci" and "Thank you." Under a cover of fog, Bakary stepped beneath the sign and onto the creaky wooden planks. Soft voices echoed from behind; the locals were stirring. He quickened his stride to cross thirty yards of boards, finally stepping onto Africa's beautiful red earth.

Bakary scanned the area. To his left were parking slots, and to his right was a small restaurant. Inside, the lights glowed like bright yellow halos. One person moved inside. As Bakary approached, a truck passed and parked in front of the restaurant. The driver had spotted Bakary carrying the boy and rushed over.

"What happened? Is he all right? Are you? Should I call for help?"

Bakary ignored the driver's questions and went to the truck's passenger side. The driver opened the door and helped lift Pape onto the front seat. Bakary got in and clenched his son. The older model truck sputtered as it started, and the gears ground as the driver backed up and pulled away from the restaurant. They drove in silence onto Main Street.

"Which way?"

"St. Pierre. 28 Joal Street." Bakary's response was barely audible.

Tears rolled down Bakary's cheeks, leaving crooked streams in the dust and blood. He wished it were all a dream. Trying to hold back his tears, he prayed. *Oh god, please help me.* Twenty minutes later, the truck pulled up to the house. Bakary got out to carry his son up the cobbled path to his modest home.

"Let me help." The driver's arms were outstretched. Bakary shook his head. "No." The driver lowered his arms and watched in silence. From inside the house, Saruba heard the vehicle pull up. She and her sister had been up all night wondering why her husband and son had not returned. As she pulled back the curtain, she saw Bakary and bolted outside, screaming hysterically at the sight of her husband, covered in blood, carrying their dead son.

"No! No!" Together, Bakary and Saruba collapsed to the ground, weeping as they held Pape, their beloved son. The rest of the family ran outside and gathered around them, crying and holding each other.

The driver of the truck stood helplessly nearby and watched the family wail in pain. There was nothing more he could do. There was nothing he could say. The sight overwhelmed him. He got into his truck, put his hands on the steering wheel, leaned forward, and rested his forehead on the steering wheel.

He, too, wept.

FRIDAY

(Present Day)

Chapter 1: Bridget Murphy – London

For Bridget Murphy, the London fog and rain made a perfect cocktail of misery and sorrow. Bridget stepped from one of London's famous black cabs onto rain-slicked cobblestones. Her long, curly, reddish-blonde hair whipped across her face in the wind. Bridget picked at the strands to free her eyesight. She momentarily glanced at the storefront. Her umbrella sprang open at the very moment her throat constricted with raw emotion.

With a heavy heart, Bridget approached the Colin Taylor Antiquities gallery. The tattered remnants of the yellow crime scene tape flapped against the brass door handle. Tears welled in her eyes. With silent reverence, she ceremoniously pressed her palm onto the cold glass panel of the wooden door, holding it there—a gesture of respect, love, and a forever goodbye.

Later that afternoon, Bridget stared at the case files on her desk in the Fraud and Protection Unit of New Scotland Yard. Ten days of investigating the deaths of three people at the gallery had proved fruitless. This case was unique and painful for Bridget—one of the victims was her friend, colleague, and former professor, Colin Taylor, whom she cherished deeply.

Carter Jones, director of the fraud unit, entered Bridget's office with a Peterson Rathbone pipe hanging from his mouth. The familiar scent had announced his arrival before he appeared in the doorway.

"I understand you are displeased with the Yard's findings about the Taylor case," he said in his Yorkshire dialect. "While we appreciate your unique skill set and spunk, sometimes the obvious must be considered."

"Don't patronize me, Carter. I'm in no mood. You and I both know there's more to this case. It should remain open."

"Yes, well, it seems the Yard agrees with *me* this time, not you." Carter looked as smug as a sixth grader who won first place in a spelling bee. "Thanks ever so much. Do have a good trip back across the pond."

Hoping to appease him, Bridget diminished her tone. Even though sidelined, she felt a powerful desire to protect her friend Colin and spare his wife, Margaret, the undignified label of a murder-suicide.

"Carter, please. What if it wasn't a murder-suicide? What if it were meant to appear like one? Or what if it was a setup—Colin may have been a target? Or …?" Bridget stopped talking when she saw Carter's dismissive hand wave. "What?" she asked, annoyed.

"Bridget, best not to dwell on what-ifs."

"And another thing, since when am I denied access to the gallery's internal security video? That video will show exactly what happened to everyone *inside* the gallery. Police photos and videos taken after an incident aren't as helpful."

"That video is no longer accessible. Even I was refused access."

"That's exactly my point. Don't you think that's strange?" Her eyes turned glassy. "I truly feel we're missing something crucial. Come on, Carter, you've been around long enough to know when a case is going sideways. Don't you feel it too?" She searched his face for agreement.

Carter puffed on his pipe, considering her comments. Bridget thought he might concede. It was fleeting.

"No. I'm sorry, Bridget. As of this morning, this case is closed." Carter turned to leave.

Bridget murmured, "Chicken shit."

Carter spun around. "What was that?" He glared like a grand inquisitor.

"Cheating isn't something Colin would do. He couldn't have an affair, any more than … well, you and me." Bridget scrunched her nose. "Which would be disgusting."

"There's no need to be rude, Bridget."

"Carter, I guarantee you something sinister is happening here—we should keep digging."

"Sinister, Bridget?" he scoffed. "You Americans—like a dog with a bone. Other intelligent investigators worked this case. Might I suggest your imagination is as lively as ever."

Steam came out of Bridget's ears. "My imagination enhances my ability to think out of the box. And has successfully served this unit and the Yard for fifteen years. Something sorely lacking with you."

"I think that's quite enough," Carter said.

Quietly seething, Bridget's jaw tightened, fingers flexed and curled. Bridget regained her composure and tried again.

"Okay, but, bottom line, we need to find that person in the hat from the exterior surveillance camera. He's the only one who walked out of that gallery alive. I feel in my gut that he's involved in Colin's death."

"Bridget, evidence solves cases, not feelings. Might I suggest this case has become far too personal for you? Perhaps your objectivity is in question?"

Bridget jumped up. "Fuck you, Carter." All five feet seven, one hundred fifty pounds of her stood ready for battle.

"And as ever, your vulgar language does not amuse." Carter was visibly annoyed as he walked to the door. "And by the way, if the Yard can't find someone, they're gone. Pack your belongings and send your invoice. Goodbye, Bridget." Carter cleared his throat and left in a huff.

After he left, Bridget fumed and stuffed documents into her satchel. *His PhD must have been a prize in a Cracker Jacks box. Pompous ass.* It was the first time a case had been taken away from her. *I have to fix this. Colin deserves for the world to know the truth. And what do I tell poor Margaret? She'll be devastated.* Clearing her desk, she felt newly resolved. *Fuck him! I'll go home and figure this out myself.*

That afternoon, Bridget went back to her hotel, ate dinner, and packed. The next day, she would be on an airplane home to Boston, Massachusetts.

Chapter 2: Adama Baptiste — NYC

Friday evening, Adama Baptiste climbed to the fourth floor of his charming French-style walk-up on the Upper West Side. He tossed his keys into a small wooden bowl on the kitchen table. After an arduous day at NYPD headquarters, he checked his watch. *Plenty of time for a jog.*

In his bedroom, Adama opened a gun case and secured his Glock 19. He swapped his suit for tactical-style sweatpants and a long-sleeved shirt. He tucked his ID and badge into an armband, placing his phone and wallet into zippered pockets. Adama holstered a sub-compact pistol into his hidden belly holster with practiced efficiency.

Reaching for his NYPD baseball cap, his hand froze mid-air at the familiar reflection from the closet mirror. *Hey Dad.* A familiar ache of loss melted into a warm feeling as he admired his hero and father, Alain Baptiste. Adama's strong features bridged two continents—his father's French heritage met his mother's Senegalese ancestry. His warm honey complexion perfectly complemented his brown eyes, flecked with streaks of golden amber.

At forty-one and six feet three, his powerfully sculpted frame was a testament to years of disciplined exercise. He moved with the agility of an athlete, tempered by the confident stride of a savvy business-man. Although naturally charismatic, Adama's exterior leaned toward the serious. His smile and gaze held genuine warmth, drawing people in and often derailing conversations.

Honoring his father, Adama nodded at himself then slipped his cap over his close-cropped hair. He grabbed his keys and stepped outside to find his neighbor, Mark Dawson, coming up the stairs. They lived across from each other and had become friends. Dawson was an ambitious investigative reporter for the Manhattan Gazette.

"Hey, Adama, how's it going?"

"Great, Mark. And you?"

"Good." Dawson noticed Adama's sweatpants. "Heads up, the Riverwalk is full of people."

"Thanks. What are you up to?"

"Catherine and I are going to the Village to meet friends at Café Wha. Ever been?"

"Sure, they've got a great house band and atmosphere. Tell Catherine I said hello. Enjoy."

"Thanks, see ya later." Mark unlocked his door and went into his apartment.

Outside, Adama stretched, then headed toward the Hudson River Greenway. While jogging, he tried not to think about work. He savored the cool salty air as the day's stress dissolved. His pace was steady with intermittent intervals that sped up and then backed off to increase his heart rate.

The reflection of the city lights danced on the Hudson. He glanced at the river's blackness and dozens of ships moored at Jersey docks. A massive container vessel carved its way out to sea, triggering a twenty-year-old memory. He and his brother, Bakary, had hitchhiked from St. Pierre to Dakar, hearts full of desperate hope to find work on a ship like that. A better life lay elsewhere.

Adama recalled their conversation while riding in a dirty pickup truck.

"If hired, we'll work six days a week and spend six months at sea. Vous devez être courageux," Adama told his brother. "Be brave, you are strong."

"I know. Je sais. I can do it." Bakary convinced himself.

"We'll work hard and follow orders. Think about the exciting cities we will see—Lisbon, Calais, Hamburg, Liverpool, and New York City. Just think, America!" Adama traced their journey with his finger across his worn map.

"Oui, America!" Bakary's face lit up. "I can't wait."

At the Port of Dakar, Adama marveled at the large ships and the determined men desperate for work. He led Bakary through a restless crowd toward the front gate. Fights broke out. Bakary was pushed to the ground. Tall and strong for his age, Adama quickly shielded his brother.

"Hey! Arrêt! Leave him be," Adama commanded.

"Or what?" The biggest man stepped forward.

"We don't want to fight." Adama stood his ground.

Onlookers encircled Adama and the three bullies. Bakary watched as the largest man squared off against his brother. The stranger threw a punch, but Adama's reflexes were quick. He ducked, and the man staggered forward, losing his footing. Adama punched him in the face, breaking his nose. He went down, dizzy and bleeding. A second man approached in a classic boxing stance.

"Quittez-nous," Adama warned him. "Leave us!"

"Non! Little boy." His grin was playful, revealing several missing teeth.

Prepared, Adama waited for the first strike. The man danced counterclockwise, swung, and missed. Stunned, he bobbed and weaved, faked a left, and threw a punch that whizzed by Adama's face. With fixed eyes and calculated force, Adama delivered an uppercut to the man's abdomen—he went down hard, gasping for air. The third man stared in disbelief.

"Toi aussi?" Adama challenged.

"Non, pas moi." The third man backed off, and the circle of onlookers dispersed.

"Come on, brother, get up." Adama helped him stand and brushed him off.

"I can take care of myself." Bakary was embarrassed but grateful.

"I know." Adama put his arm around his younger brother, and they continued forward.

Salt-tinged air swirled the dock's gated parking lot, where Adama and Bakary waited among a hundred other hopeful men. Seagulls circled above as crew members in faded yellow vests and hard hats processed applicants. Instructions were bellowed via bullhorn. "Go to a table and wait until you are called to sit down."

After three hours of shifting anxiously from foot to foot, Adama was finally called forward. He presented his passport, answered questions, and watched the emotionless faces of the two employees who would decide his fate. The sound of the metal stamp's punch echoed in his ears. "You're hired, go to that hangar for processing." One man pointed and yelled. "Next!"

Relief surged through Adama's body. He would now be able to support his widowed mother. His father, a respected police captain, was killed during a robbery. At fifteen, Adama had been thrust into the role of man-of-the-house, juggling high school with part-time work until graduation. The hard truth was that he had to leave home to find a good-paying job, and now he had achieved his goal. He felt proud. *I made it, Papa. I can take care of them now.* His father's broad smile flashed in his mind.

Finding his brother, Adama asked, "Bakary, what did they say?"

"They told me to come back after I turn eighteen." He looked dejected.

Feeling his brother's pain, Adama hugged him. "I'm sorry, brother."

"What about you?" He searched Adama's face and saw the answer.

"They hired me. I have to go over there to be processed." Adama pointed to a structure.

"Oh, wow, that's amazing." Bakary grabbed Adama in celebration, but his jubilance quickly faded. They had never been separated before today. Bakary became distressed. "But we were supposed to go together."

"I know. But I'll work and send money. You'll take my place at home and go to college. You must tell Mama I love her, Grandmother, Auntie, and sister, Binta, too. I'll miss you all very much."

"Of course." Tears formed in Bakary's eyes. "Je t'aime, mon frère," Bakary said.

Adama tried to smile. "Practice your English. I love you, brother. And I'll write to you all." Adama's heart was heavy with the impending separation. "Be strong!"

The two boys hugged and kissed each other on the cheeks. "I have to go now." Adama patted his younger brother's head, picked up his duffle bag, and strode away.

Bakary stood beside the exit gate; a tear rolled down his brown cheek. He watched and waited for his older brother and best friend to turn around, but Adama raised his left arm and waved. They both pondered when they would see each other again.

—◆—

As he jogged along the Hudson River, Adama thought about the last twenty years—all the changes and opportunities he had experienced. In a stroke of luck, he won the Diversity Visa Lottery, which led to his citizenship in the United States, one of his proudest days. After connecting with other African immigrants, he quit his job with the container company to remain in New York City.

Adama moved into a two-bedroom apartment in the Bronx, which he shared with eight other men. He worked multiple odd jobs day and night. He started as a dishwasher at a local café, then bussed tables, and eventually learned how to be a cook. Eventually, he was hired to drive a cab at night and attended college during the day, which ultimately led to a career with the NYPD.

Adama finished at the top of his class at the Police Academy. His impressive work ethic, respect for authority, investigative skills, and leadership qualities resulted in several promotions. After he earned a master's degree in criminal justice, he worked his way up from detective to sergeant, then lieutenant, police captain, and, finally, deputy chief.

For years, Adama sent money home to his family. Hundreds of letters and pictures flowed back and forth. His sweet mother always asked, "When are you coming home, my son?" It tugged at Adama's heart, but he loved New York and had no intention of leaving. Although separated by thousands of miles, Adama's love for his family remained deep and resolute.

Jogging steadily, Adama remembered the tears on his younger brother's face as they parted twenty years earlier. *Je t'aime, mon frère, I love you, my brother.* He steeled himself, picked up the pace, and sprinted harder to shake off the pain of missing Bakary and his family in St. Pierre, Senegal.

Chapter 3: Bodies in the Hudson

Pier 84 was a major tourist site off the Hudson River and the half-way point for Adama's routine run. His reverie about family was disrupted by the yellow crime scene tape blocking the pathway. Adama slowed to a fast walk as he approached.

"Excuse me, sir, this is a closed crime scene," the rookie policeman said.

Adama tugged at his armband and flipped open his deputy chief badge.

"I'm sorry, sir. We have a situation. We're fishing it out of the water." He noticed Adama's jogging suit. "Are you on duty, sir?"

"I'm always on duty. What's your name, officer?"

"Miles Torres, sir."

"Well, Officer Torres, what is the situation, and what are you fishing out of the water?"

"Deputy Chief, we have a body in the water, sir."

"Really? Did anyone call the Harbor Unit?"

"They're already here, sir."

"Good. Who's in charge?"

"I was, Deputy Chief, until you got here," a voice called from a few yards away.

Adama looked beyond the rookie to see Detective Second Grade, Richard "Ricky" Burke. He was six feet two inches tall, with short, sandy brown hair and blue eyes. Adama respected Burke's intellect and dedication. He came from a distinguished line of police officers and was a dedicated husband and father.

"Hey, Ricky, how are Sandy and the boys?" They greeted each other with handshakes.

"All good." Burke eyed his boss. "How did you catch this? And in a jogging suit no less."

"I jog this stretch from my place to the last pier and back. What have you got here?"

"One floater, male. Harbor Unit's pulling him out of the river now."

"Witnesses?"

"Possibly two, a wife and husband, they called 911. They're being questioned."

"Deputy Chief? Detective? Now there are two bodies!" Officer Torres exclaimed.

"Two bodies?" Burke asked.

Holding the yellow tape high, Burke and Adama ducked under. Twenty feet away, one man lay face up on a large black tarp on the pavement. Divers brought another body up the embankment and laid it next to the first. Both Black and well-built, they appeared to be in their early twenties.

"Looks like they were nearly decapitated," Burke said.

Both victims wore orange, elbow-length sleeved jumpsuits with zippers in the front, a yellow vest with reflective gray stripes, and black steel-toed boots.

"Looks like they came from a container ship," Adama said.

"I'll contact Port Authority and get a list of the ships that docked this past week." Burke pulled out a pocket notepad.

"Good. Got an extra pair of gloves, Ricky?" Detective Burke handed him a pair. "Let's check their pockets for IDs."

"Empty pockets on this one," Burke said.

"Same here," Adama said.

"Well, if they worked on a ship, these men would have ID badges," Burke said. "Which means someone took them, or they're in the river."

"Right, either way, our job just got tougher. We need to find our crime scene fast. After you get the list of all the ships, get their manifests, including a crew list," Adama instructed.

"And we need to figure out how long they've been in the water," Burke said. "I'll get the Tide Charts and Times for the Hudson, let's see how far upstream they were dumped."

"Good. And have a forensic tech pull prints. Their fingers are swollen, but maybe we'll get lucky." Adama stood and glared.

Burke noticed Adama lingering. "What's up? Don't tell me you recognize these guys."

"I don't, but I think they may be from a region in West Africa."

"What makes you think that?" Burke asked.

"See their right forearms, the lion's head?" Adama pointed at both arms. "Those are scarification patterns caused by the deliberate cutting or burning of skin. It leaves a particular type of wound in the flesh. And after it heals, it leaves a permanent scar."

"Are they important?" Burke was intrigued.

"To them, yes. These scars are Mandinka. A lion's head pattern is a significant and culturally important symbol. It's supposed to ward off evil spirits. They both have the same scar. My guess is they're from West Africa, possibly Senegal, The Gambia, or Sierra Leone."

"Really? How do you know that?" Burke was impressed.

"Long story. Let's get the crime scene unit out here and set up a thirty-foot grid down to the embankment. Have the river searched for five miles on both sides and alert Jersey's Harbor Patrol."

"Will do, and I'll pull surveillance from the entire area."

"Has anyone called the medical examiner?" Adama asked.

"On the way." Burke watched Adama check the gash on one body. "How long do you think they've been dead?"

"Hard to tell; the river didn't leave us much to work with. The killer knew what he was doing. Clean cuts. Looks like a jagged blade, ear to ear, from left to right. Our killer is right-handed. Another thing is that these guys were young and strong. I'd like to know how they got taken down without a struggle. There aren't any restraint marks."

"More than one killer, or they could have known their assailant," Burke suggested.

"Right. We'll know more after the autopsies and forensic reports. We don't have much time. Let's see if we can catch their ship before it hits the twelve-mile marker."

"On it." Burke took out his phone and pointed at a van. "CSU is here. I'm going to check on our two witnesses." He walked away.

Adama glanced over his shoulder to see two forensic technicians. He recognized one, Jimmy Quinn, a fresh-faced recruit out of the academy, with copper-red hair and green eyes. He was a smart kid with a master's degree, hired by the NYPD and assigned to the Office of the Medical Examiner and Adama's special unit. Adama stood, removed his gloves, and waited as the technicians approached.

"Hello, Jimmy," Adama said. He nodded at the other technician.

"Hello, Deputy Chief," Quinn said.

"We need prints asap."

Quinn nodded, looked at the two bodies, and set his case down. He put on gloves and checked the hands of the victims.

"They're pretty swollen, but I'll do my best."

"Thanks, kid."

Detective Burke approached Adama. "Our witnesses didn't see anything. They looked down at the water and spotted a body under the pier. The woman screamed, and the man called 911."

Both detectives heard the beeping noise as the coroner's van backed up near the two bodies.

"I'll visit with the Chief Medical Examiner in the morning. I'm going home."

"Night, Deputy Chief," Burke said.

Adama looked at the young men on the pavement and felt a sense of sadness. *Poor guys—so young. What a waste.* He walked toward the river walk, breathed in the sea air, stretched, and jogged home.

SATURDAY

Chapter 4: Dr. Betty Pearson, Chief Medical Examiner (CME)

Adama woke early on Saturday morning and made a pot of coffee. Within minutes, an aromatic scent filled his apartment. He opened the French doors to peruse his neighborhood. The weather was clear. The sounds of the city filtered through—cars, dogs barking, and the never-ending two-tone pitch of sirens wailing in the distance.

Although hungry, Adama waited to eat after going to the Office of the Medical Examiner (OME). He wanted to view the bodies of the two men pulled from the Hudson and question the medical examiner. Adama got dressed and headed to the morgue.

As the door to the lab opened, Dr. Betty Pearson peered over her signature red rhinestone-studded eyeglasses, tracking Adama's entrance with her characteristic precision. New York City's Chief Medical Examiner (CME) had built her stellar reputation based on ruthless attention to detail. In this realm, facts weren't just reported; they were rigorously verified and proven before being released from the OME.

At fifty-three, Dr. Pearson wore her brown hair in a practical crop that suited her no-nonsense approach, yet her flashy glasses hinted at a subtle defiance of the austere stereotype of her profession. Her compact five-foot-three frame belied her commanding presence—even the most seasoned detectives knew better than to press her for preliminary findings before she was ready. She waited silently, smiling as Adama approached.

"Good morning, Doc. Thanks for the early morning review."

"Hello, Adama, I've got them ready for you," she said.

Dr. Pearson's footsteps echoed on the sterile white tiled floor of the cold storage area. It was a large room, with stainless steel lockers, stacked three high. Dr. Pearson searched the name cards and pulled out two drawers. Each man lay face up, covered from head to toe.

"This is what I wanted you to see." She pulled down the sheet and tilted the head of one of the bodies. "Each victim has two taser holes on the back of his neck."

Adama leaned closer for a better view. Dr. Pearson gently laid the head down, went to the next man, and tilted his head, revealing the same taser marks in the same place.

"So that's how they did it," Adama said.

"Did what?"

"These guys were young, big, and strong, but no visible signs of a struggle. I wondered how one or even two assailants could subdue them, let alone kill them without a struggle. But they must have known their assailants. I didn't see any defensive wounds or ligature marks on their wrists or legs from being restrained."

"Good eye. The perpetrator used a taser gun, administering millions of volts. The gun shocked the lower neck area for an extended period, causing neuromuscular incapacitation, total mental confusion, and disorientation. These two went down without a fight. And the extended taser time burned completely through their jumpsuits. Whoever did this got close and wanted them unconscious for an extended time."

"Any idea about the time of death?"

"Still undetermined," Dr. Pearson replied. "Rigor came and went. We're using other methods to determine TOD."

"And the cause of death?"

"Both had severed carotid arteries. They would have bled out in minutes. Most likely, they were rendered unconscious, killed, and then deposited into the river. But we still need to finish the autopsies, and we're waiting on lab results."

"Thanks," Adama said. "Can you tell how long they'd been in the water or where they entered?"

"Possibly. The autopsies will show us if any fluid was in their lungs or food in their stomachs. We'll analyze the contents. As for where they came from, we'll check the tides and currents on the Hudson to retrace how they ended up at Pier 84. That area of the Hudson is a salt-front location, and the water is cold, which explains why they were floating."

"And fingerprints?" Adama hoped someone had run them through the Integrated Automated Fingerprint Identification System. "Their fingers were swollen, but we got two good sets. They're being run through the IAFIS fingerprint system."

Bingo. "When will you have the autopsies done?"

"Hopefully by tomorrow. I'll review the findings and call you."

Adama nodded and smiled. "Okay, great. Our team is also checking with immigration. We're coordinating with Homeland Security because these two would have needed visas to leave their ship. I'm headed to the office. Thanks for showing me the taser marks, Doc."

He nodded again and left.

"You're welcome." Dr. Pearson watched as Adama navigated his way through her lab. She carefully rewrapped each man and closed the drawers.

Chapter 5: Professor Colin Taylor, PhD

It had been raining all day when Bridget Murphy boarded the British Airways Airbus at Heathrow Airport. She found her seat by the window and settled in for the seven-hour flight home to Massachusetts. Bridget snapped her seatbelt and stared out the window.

A woman in a dark blue suit stopped in the aisle to check her seat number. Bridget recognized her from the waiting area. Her analytical brain kicked in—*early forties, government, attorney, maybe law enforcement.* The woman had short brown hair that slightly flipped at the ends, light makeup, and wore small, emerald-green button-style earrings. She sat down, nodded once at Bridget, and opened her book.

A few minutes later, Bridget felt the vibrations of the engines, whining and roaring, as the aircraft raced down the runway. She instinctively gave her seatbelt one more tug and smiled inwardly. *Who am I kidding? If this plane goes down, we're all toast.*

Within minutes, they had reached cruising altitude. Bridget looked out the window at the clear blue sky and fluffy white clouds below. She set up her laptop and began working on the Colin Taylor case. Her mind wandered, recalling her first meeting with Colin after arriving as a graduate student at Cheikh Anta Diop University in Dakar, Senegal. He was her advisor and on sabbatical from Oxford, where he chaired the Centre for the Study of Ancient History and Classical Archaeology. *Has it really been nineteen years?*

As she settled into the memory, she fondly recalled being twenty-one, single, and as her mother put it, "full of piss and vinegar."

Running late, Bridget checked her watch. She shifted from a fast walk to a full run down the hallway to her advisor's office. It was the last door on the left in the Department of Anthropology. The sign outside read "Professor Colin E. Taylor, PhD."

Standing outside, Bridget quickly composed herself and gently tapped on the door.

"Come in," a voice said.

Upon entering, Bridget saw a middle-aged man, forty-one years old, who appeared youthful, dressed in an off-white shirt and a blue blazer, sitting behind a wooden teak desk. He had a full beard and brown hair with a touch of gray at both temples. He wore wire-rimmed spectacles that creased the bridge of his nose.

Bridget was out of breath, and her hair was mussed. She adjusted the dark blue backpack slung over one shoulder, hesitantly smiled, and approached the desk.

"Good morning, Professor Taylor. I'm Bridget Murphy."

Without hesitation, the professor's strong British accent chastised her. "You're late, Miss Murphy. You must never be late. That includes your work, meetings, reports, research, dig sites, and presentations. Do you understand?"

"Yes, Professor. It won't happen again." Feeling embarrassed and relieved, Bridget exhaled loudly as she dropped into the chair across his desk.

"And do sit down."

"Oh! I'm so sorry." Bridget jumped up.

"Please sit." His hand gestured downward. "Let's start over. Bienvenue, Miss Murphy."

"Uh, thank you." Bridget looked puzzled.

"Bienvenue. It means welcome in French. You'll want to learn French and Wolof, the other most widely spoken language in Senegal. That is, if you want to assimilate."

"Of course, thank you, Professor." Paying close attention, Bridget sat tall in her chair.

"I've been reviewing your resume, and it's quite impressive. Two undergraduate degrees from Boston University, summa cum laude. One in archaeology and one in art history. Your references are impeccable. And now you're here to earn your master's in anthropology." Professor Taylor looked at her over the rim of his glasses.

"Yes, Professor. I look forward to participating in your program because Africa is rich with ancient dig sites. I've been fascinated by

Africa and love studying its past civilizations, tribal histories, folklore, customs, and languages. Being here in West Africa means I'll finally get the excavation site experience I've longed for."

"That, you shall and more. However, it won't be easy. You'll work long hours, learn, and teach others. Are you ready to begin your journey?"

"I am." Her tone was confident.

"Very well. Acquaint yourself with the others—they're waiting in the library. It's the next building over. Exit to your right. I'll meet you there."

"Thank you, Professor." Bridget's voice was soft and humble.

As Bridget fumbled with her backpack, she noticed several framed pictures of Professor Taylor with a woman. Feeling flustered, she stepped out the door and looked down the long hallway. *That was awkward. His British accent is cool, though. And his wife is beautiful. Now, where is the library?*

———◆———

A week later, Bridget's first encounter with Professor Taylor's wife, Margaret, left a lasting impression. They met at the Student Community Center. Bridget felt an immediate connection to her.

"My dear Bridget. I've heard so much about you. I hear you're from America?"

"Yes. I'm from Boston, Massachusetts. Do you know it?"

"Of course! We've visited America several times. The last time was New York City. Colin had a conference there, but we visited all the tourist sites. I loved Hell's Kitchen and the charming bars of Greenwich Village. American nightlife is so delightful."

"Yes, well, New York City is unique and one of my favorite places." Bridget hesitantly added, "You know, some people find Americans a bit arrogant or rude. I'm glad you didn't experience that."

"On the contrary, my dear, we received the full Monty of American arrogance and rudeness." Margaret let out a gregarious laugh.

"Oh, wow, I'm so sorry." Bridget was mortified.

"My dear, the expression on your face is worth a thousand words. I'm having a laugh with you. Not to worry. We had a marvelous time."

"Oh." Bridget visibly sighed. "That's good to hear."

"Bridget, dearest, you must learn to relax. Come, we'll drink to our meeting." Margaret wrapped her hands around Bridget's arm and pulled her toward the concession stand.

"Okay, but I don't drink. I hate the taste of alcohol." Bridget suddenly felt self-conscious.

"Oh, my dear, your honesty is refreshing." Margaret moved closer to her husband. "Colin, darling, I adore Bridget. Let's adopt her."

Margaret turned her attention back to Bridget. "Don't you worry, my dear. There is no alcohol here. We are very respectful of this country and its culture." Margaret blew Colin a kiss, and the two women walked away.

Usually, Bridget felt uncomfortable when touched by strangers. However, she felt remarkably at ease with Margaret hanging onto her arm. *She's so cool. So self-assured.*

———◆———

The university years flew by in a blur. Bridget earned her master's degree in anthropology within eighteen months. She immersed herself in fieldwork and progressed to site director over numerous excavations across West Africa. Her undergraduate students dubbed her "truth digger," a nickname that embodied Professor Taylor's statement, "There is neither good nor bad. Ours is a science; we follow a process, we analyze without judgment. No dig is complete until we uncover all the facts."

Bridget's uncanny ability to sniff out the truth became the hallmark of her reputation. Her research included nearby countries, such as Senegal, The Gambia, Guinea, and Sierra Leone. Bridget loved Africa, its people, the digs, her students, and learning under the guidance of Professor Taylor. She fully embraced West Africa's indigenous people, submerged herself in the local customs and festivities, and knew enough French and Wolof to be accepted by the locals.

The university offered Bridget a professorship in the anthropology department the week before graduation. During her tenure, Bridget transformed her thesis into a book on West African culture and ancient mythology. Over the next four years, she happily collaborated with her mentor and friend, Professor Colin Taylor.

The plane shuddered, bringing Bridget out of her reminiscing, and seemed to mimic her grief as tears welled in her eyes. She turned toward the window. *Oh, Colin, I'm so sorry that I failed you. I promise you and Margaret that I will solve your case.*

Chapter 6: The Millers

The prestigious Miller Antiquities gallery was located on W. 56th Street, around the corner from 5th Avenue's luxury corridor, not far from Central Park. The building's Art Deco architecture reflected New York's golden era. Adorning the entrance was a shiny brass name plate exhibiting the inscription "Est. 1981" in embossed lettering.

Twin mahogany doors with beveled glass panels and polished brass doorknobs welcomed guests to the gallery. The establishment maintained its exclusivity and security through a "By Appointment Only" policy and a bulletproof double-door foyer.

The owners were Henry Miller, a seventy-year-old widower, and his beautiful thirty-nine-year-old daughter Jacqueline. Both were expert curators and notable authenticators of antiquities. However, Miller's son, Thomas, had no interest in the gallery. Instead, he spent most of his time at the Aqueduct Racetrack—his gallery of ponies. Occasionally, Miller Sr. reluctantly paid his son's gambling debts, causing a father-son rift between them.

Three years ago, Violet Miller passed away suddenly. Jacqueline and Thomas grew closer after their mother's death. Unfortunately, Jacqueline had assumed the role of mediator between her father and brother, but she was deadlocked in a personal war. Henry Miller saw his son as weak and aimless, needing guidance and structure. At the same time, Thomas craved autonomy from a judgmental and controlling father. Family dinners became unpleasant, with Jacqueline's elusive search for the white flag that would bring a truce for the two people she loved dearly.

As a drifter with no ambitions, Thomas had no job, no steady relationship, and resented his father for being overbearing. Feeling hopelessly suffocated, Thomas, in an act of total rebellion, announced he had changed his last name from Miller to Chevalier—his mother's maiden name. Cruelly, Thomas announced his decision on the third anniversary of his mother's death, at dinner. Henry Miller's heart felt like Thomas drove a stake through it, but he remained composed.

"Your mother would be very disappointed," Miller said. He dabbed his mouth with a napkin.

"No, Father. Mother would understand. That was the difference between you two."

Angry, Thomas stood and threw his napkin onto the table. As he passed by Jacqueline, he lightly touched her shoulder as she reached out to him. "Don't go, Tommy."

In that singular moment, wounded by his son's defiance, Miller experienced a profound revelation. He knew Thomas was right about his late wife. She possessed the ability to accept without judgment. Miller realized he must accept his son, with all his flaws, foibles, lack of ambition, alcoholism, and drug addiction, or lose him forever. Henry Miller had just been beaten, not by his son, but rather by his shortcomings.

Jacqueline had watched her father's unconditional surrender with the release of his white linen napkin that gently floated to the floor. Miller's love for his son left him completely vulnerable. From that day forward, he would spoil his son with money and an apartment on the Upper East Side—to keep him close.

———◆———

Three Weeks Earlier

Thomas Chevalier, a handsome thirty-five-year-old with wavy dark hair and a mustache, swaggered through the foyer of the Miller gallery in his Gucci leather jacket, Rolex, and diamond pinky ring. He moved past miniature busts of Nefertiti and Julius Caesar, glanced at cases of ancient jewelry and ornaments, then paused at his favorite piece—a six-inch rhinoceros, made from Nero Porto marble, and valued at six hundred thousand dollars. A Texas oil heiress, Miss Daisy Hunter, offered the piece for sale at Miller's exclusive antiquities gallery.

Once a month, Thomas visited the gallery to pick up his monthly allowance. Upon arrival, he hung his jacket on the coat tree and happily greeted his sister.

"Hey, Jacquie. How's it goin'?"

"Hey Tommy!" Jacqueline smiled at her younger brother. A second later, the desk phone rang. She pushed the speaker button. Thomas folded his arms, leaned against the doorway, and listened. He loved his older sister and was impressed with her grace, impeccable education, and expertise.

"Good morning, Miller Antiquities." She winked at Thomas.

"Hello. May I speak with the owner of the gallery?" A distinctive English voice asked.

"I'm one of the owners, Jacqueline. How may I help you?"

"I am a private broker in possession of several artifacts from West Africa. I need to host a private showing, and I was referred to your gallery."

"Our gallery is available for private events. May I ask who referred you?"

"Yes, Miss Daisy Hunter kindly directed me. She knows the founder, Henry Miller."

"Of course, we cherish Miss Hunter. That was very kind of her." Always concerned about security and discretion, Jacqueline relaxed upon hearing a name she recognized. "Whom do I have the pleasure of speaking with?"

"You may call me Dr. Jeeves."

"Thank you. Dr. Jeeves. When would you like to host your event?"

"I do apologize for the short notice; I need your gallery on a Saturday, in three weeks."

"Of course, let me check the date." Jacqueline opened her calendar. "Oh, I'm so sorry, Dr. Jeeves, we're unavailable that weekend."

"Would Mr. Miller be available to assist me?"

"I'm afraid not, sir." Jacqueline thought about her father, bedridden from his heart attack two weeks earlier.

"That is unfortunate." He paused. "My benefactor is offering a ten-million-dollar commission. Does that help with your decision?"

"That is very generous, however, I must be elsewhere that weekend. Again, I'm sorry."

"Thank you for your time, my dear."

"Of course. Good luck to you, sir." Jacqueline hung up the phone. She looked at Thomas, who had a shocked look on his face. "What?"

"Wow, ten million dollars just to *host* an event. Sis, that's incredible." Thomas pondered the amount—*ten million bucks, what a payday.*

"Yes, it is. Bad timing, though. Still, I must remember to thank Miss Hunter for the referral."

Jacqueline flipped her long raven hair over her shoulder and adjusted her string of pearls. At five-six, her slender physique fit snugly into her silk dress. She prided herself on looking elegant, yet modest—a throwback to a sophisticated Grace Kelly era of poise and confidence. She texted her limousine driver. Thomas carried her luxurious Hermes coat and walked to the front door with Jacqueline.

"Tommy, I'm going to visit Dad. He needs the company, and we can have lunch. Can you join us?"

"No, I just ate." He paused. "Sis, are you sure about passing on the ten million bucks?"

"Yes. I'm sure." She touched his arm and pleaded. "Tommy, come with me, let's all spend some time together as a family."

"No thanks. I'm here to pick up my check, and I have some errands to attend to. Tell Father I said hello."

"Okay. Your check is in the top drawer of the desk. Lock up when you leave."

"I will. See you later." They hugged and kissed each other on the cheek.

Jacqueline left in the limousine, and Thomas walked back to the office. He found the envelope and looked inside. It was his regular monthly allowance of $60,000. *Shit. This barely covers what I owe my bookie.* He put the envelope in his shirt pocket.

Thomas glanced at the desk phone and thought about the $10 million. An idea was formulated in his mind. *Why can't I host the event? Would Jacquie let me? I wonder what Father would say ... probably wouldn't trust me. Hell, there's no harm in talking with the guy.*

A pang of guilt swelled up in his throat, which he quickly swallowed. He continued to justify his actions. "Why do Father and Jacquie need to know?" Thomas said aloud. "It's just a meeting. And if it doesn't work out, who cares? I can talk with her about it later."

Thomas hesitated, looked at the phone, then pushed the redial button.

Thomas left a message. "Hello, Dr. Jeeves. This is Thomas, the son of Henry Miller. I'm calling to let you know I can host your event. Please return my call. Thank you." Thomas left his cellphone number.

His stomach turned. *What if I get caught going behind their backs? Jacquie would be so disappointed. And Father, well ... oh fuck it, this could be my ticket out of here.*

Twenty minutes later, Thomas's phone rang.

"May I please speak with Thomas Miller?"

"Hello, Dr. Jeeves. Thank you for returning my call."

"I'm delighted you called. I just spoke with Miss Daisy Hunter. She informed me of your father's heart attack. I'm so sorry."

"Thank you, he's getting better," Thomas said. "If you're still interested, I can arrange a private showing of our gallery."

"Wonderful. Miss Hunter assured me the Miller gallery best suits our clients' needs. Would you be available tomorrow morning?"

"Tomorrow?" Thomas reviewed the calendar. He was relieved to see that Jacquie had plans for the day. "Yes, tomorrow is perfect. How about ten o'clock?"

"Marvelous. I'll be there. Also, I shall come through the alley door."

"Um, sure, if that's what you want." Thomas thought that was an odd request.

"Excellent, Thomas. I shall see you tomorrow at ten sharp."

"Great. Thank you, Dr. Jeeves." Thomas winced as his stomach burned.

Thomas walked the gallery, confirming Dr. Jeeves would be pleased. The gallery showcased exquisite antiquities spanning over two millennia, featuring ancient works from Rome, Greece, Egypt, and Mesopotamia. Although Thomas did not care about art or antiquities, he knew that Miller Antiquities distinguished itself through objects of exceptional historical significance, aesthetic refinement, and inherent beauty. *This is a no-brainer.*

His nerves shot, Thomas retrieved a silver monogrammed flask from his coat. The bourbon calmed him.

———◆———

Thomas waited nervously at his father's antique cherrywood desk the following day. Bored, he traced the leather top and inlaid design of swirling vines and leaves with his finger. His father's chair, with its brass studs, wooden base, and cast-iron wheels, reminded him of happier days. Feeling nostalgic, he took a quick spin as he had done as a child.

Playing a video game on his phone, Thomas noticed movements on the security monitor. At precisely ten o'clock, a dark town car had arrived in the alley. Thomas punched a code into the security pad, unlocked the deadbolts, and opened the back door. The man wore a black cape and a large black hat, carried a leather binder, and used an ornate cane to steady himself.

"Dr. Jeeves?"

"Yes, Thomas. Are we alone?"

"Yes, we're the only ones here."

"Excellent. I shan't take too much of your time. I should like to peruse your gallery and discuss my requirements and conditions."

The chauffeur helped the man up the steps. Thomas led him into the gallery, where he slowly turned about the room. Thomas was surprised at how old the man appeared to be. His face was weathered, with pronounced wrinkles around his eyes and deep creases around his mouth. His lips were thin, and his cheeks blotched with large brown spots. *Jesus, he's old. I hope he doesn't collapse.*

"Would you like to sit down? Can I take your coat and hat?"

"That won't be necessary. Is there a private screening room?"

"Yes, it's down the hall, first door on the left. The door is open."

Dr. Jeeves peered inside and marveled at the elegance. A hand-crafted mahogany table commanded the center, flanked by six high-backed Pellegrino leather executive chairs that whispered of affluent and savvy negotiations. Against one brick wall stood a temperature-controlled wine cabinet masquerading as a sideboard buffet.

"Well, what do you think?" Thomas nervously listened for agreement.

"This will do nicely, my boy. Shall we discuss the terms and conditions?"

"Sure. We can sit here." He pointed at the table and chairs.

Dr. Jeeves placed his binder on the table, pulled out a white hanky, coughed, and wiped his mouth. Sitting, Dr. Jeeves's gloved hands trembled as he opened his binder. He withdrew a cellphone from his pocket. "First, all communications shall be exclusive to this phone. No paperwork whatsoever," He extended it to Thomas. "Are we clear?"

"Yeah, sure. Not a problem." Thomas examined the phone. "What else?"

"My clients require absolute anonymity; you are not to engage with them. Furthermore, at no time shall you look at or touch any of the artifacts brought inside. Is that understood?" Dr. Jeeves looked solemnly at Thomas.

"Yes, I understand." Thomas only cared about the money.

By the end of their discussion, Thomas had taken copious notes and agreed to host the event in three weeks on a Saturday, from seven to nine, with a four-hour window beforehand to allow for setup by Dr. Jeeves' crew members.

Thomas knew Jacqueline would attend a gala in Washington, D.C., that weekend. He also confirmed the ten-million-dollar commission with conditions of his own.

"Dr. Jeeves, I've agreed to your terms and have one of my own. I want the commission paid directly to me, and I want one million paid up front, to hold your reservation, and the balance thereafter." He sat tall and resolute.

Dr. Jeeves laid his pen on top of his binder. His beady eyes squinted as the left corner of his mouth slowly curled upward, making Thomas uneasy. "Well done, Thomas."

The acquiescence surprised Thomas but left him feeling powerful. "Good. I'll open an account in Grand Cayman and text you the account number."

"Very good, Thomas." He looked at his antique pocket watch and reached for his cane. "And now I shall take my leave."

Dr. Jeeves coughed; it sounded heavily congested. Thomas winced at the sound of phlegm being expelled. The older man used his cane to walk toward the alley. Thomas opened the door to find the limousine driver ready to help his passenger down the steps and into the vehicle.

"See you in three weeks." Thomas waved. *That is, if you don't die first.*

Thomas locked the back door, clapped his hands together, and danced a jig down the hallway. "Oh yeah, baby! Ten million bucks!" he said to the walls. He decided to celebrate at his favorite bar down the street. But first, business before pleasure. He pulled out his personal cellphone and dialed his bookie. Their conversation consisted of a few cryptic words—a bank name and a banker's direct line in Grand Cayman. Thomas saved the contact information. At last, his father's suffocating financial reign would come to an end. He conducted a final check of the gallery, set the deadbolt locks and the alarm system, and stepped into the hazy midday air where each breath tasted of sweet freedom.

Chapter 7: Cloak and Dagger

The flight from London to Boston was smooth enough. Bridget Murphy drummed her fingers on the tray table while thinking about the Taylor gallery deaths. After consulting on hundreds of antiquities cases for fifteen years, a pattern emerged: the majority involved inside jobs. She had learned to follow the money, squeeze dealers, and pressure known fences and their illegal trafficking. She enjoyed watching it all fall like dominoes. But Bridget's instincts told her the Taylor case was an exception; everything about it contradicted the usual pattern.

The investigation revealed troubling inconsistencies: the gallery should have been closed with no scheduled deliveries, yet surveillance captured two men delivering a large box, followed by a man in a black hat and cape walking with a cane. Three victims were found: the owner, Colin Taylor, an assistant, Susan Baker, and billionaire Ahmed Senusret, but no paperwork explained his presence.

Nothing added up for Bridget. She found no direct link suggesting a love triangle between the victims, beyond their presence at the gallery, as determined by New Scotland Yard. The inconsistencies of the three deaths were striking.

Bridget's heart ached about Colin's death. She stared out the window, recalling her visit to the grand opening of his gallery. Colin retired from Oxford five years ago and hung up his traveling pants. No more teaching. No more digging in the dirt. No more sabbaticals. He decided to honor a lifelong dream and open his own antiquities gallery. It had taken years for Colin to accumulate a number of the rarest ancient artifacts: small statues, busts, jewelry, animal figurines, vessels, and his prized acquisition, a five-foot statue of Nemesis, the Goddess of Retribution. The majority of the items were from his personal collection, while other pieces were for sale by private patrons. It was a modest but successful beginning.

When Bridget arrived, two guards stood outside Colin Taylor Antiquities, located on St. James Street, just around the corner from Christie's Auction House in the heart of London. Bridget presented her embossed invitation at the door and handed her coat to a valet.

"Bridget! How lovely to see you." Colin hugged her. "We have your favorite prosecco." Colin waved at a waiter who brought her a glass.

"May I have a glass of ice, please?"

"Same old Bridget, diluting her prosecco with ice. You haven't changed."

"Yeah, well, the ice helps dilute the alcohol. I know, I'm weird."

"My dear, you are unique. Let's find Margaret—she's dying to see you."

"Yes! It's been too long." They moved into the gallery where dozens of people mingled. "I see you've got the who's who of the antiquities world here."

"Yes, we're quite pleased."

"And you named your gallery Colin Taylor Antiquities." She winked.

"Well, I lack your brilliant imagination, Bridget. Do tell, what would you suggest?"

"Well…" Bridget thought seriously. "You know what, Colin? It's perfect. After all, your name is synonymous with antiquities."

"You mean I'm old, dug up from a two-thousand-year-old excavation, and ancient history. Haha! You flatter me!"

"Well, yes, of sorts. You are a rare find. And you do have amazing historical significance." She grinned. "Besides, we all want to be you."

"Clever recovery, my dear." Colin beamed. "We're so glad you came."

"I wouldn't have missed it for the world. I'm very happy for you and Margaret."

Waving outstretched arms, Margaret rushed over.

"My dear Bridget, how lovely to see you. We've missed you so."
They hugged tightly.

"And I've missed you. My favorite bohemian and beautiful guru."

"Thank you, my darling," Margaret said. "I understand you're, what do the Americans call it? A big shot lecturer and criminal investigator now."

"Well, I wouldn't go that far." Bridget blushed.

"I'm sure you're being modest, my dear." Margaret moved over to Colin and wrapped her hands around his arm. He pulled her close to him. "Who are you consulting with now?"

"Well, last year, the NYPD and the Met, and this year, the Louvre, thanks to Colin, the Petrie Museum of Egyptian Archaeology here in London."

"Bridget's being modest," Colin said. "She's also helped dozens of universities and private patrons. All praising her brilliance."

"Well, of course they do, Bridget is one of the best antiquities sleuths on the planet. Right up there with our Sherlock Holmes. They're lucky to have you, dear." Margaret glanced at her watch. "Colin, love, time for your speech."

"Already? Okay. Bridget, don't go anywhere." Colin pecked her on the cheek.

"Dearest, we'll catch up afterward." Margaret kissed Bridget on the cheek and pulled Colin toward the lectern.

Bridget watched in awe as Colin spoke. She was thankful for his recommendations to New Scotland Yard, the NYPD, the Paris Police Préfecture, and dozens of museums, universities, governments, and wealthy patrons. "Your name and reputation will be second-to-none as an antiquities investigator. You have an uncanny ability to solve puzzles. You know the stories, folklore, and cultures surrounding antiquities better than anyone. You see what others miss. All your education, experience, and knowledge will be used well. The world needs your help to resolve antiquities fraud."

Bridget sipped her prosecco. *Was that really fifteen years ago?* Colin wrapped up his speech. She clapped for her friend with a strong feeling of gratitude. *He's such a kind and generous man. I owe my career as a criminal investigator to him.*

———————

As the aircraft descended, Bridget felt pressure in her ears. Her watch indicated fifteen minutes until touchdown. She became agitated about the Yard denying her request to view Colin's internal video footage. Bridget knew the gallery security feed would show the truth about what happened at her dear friend's gallery.

"Damn it, I need to see that video feed," Bridget said aloud to no one.

"Excuse me?" the woman seated next to her asked. "Did you say something to me?"

"What? Uh, oh, no, sorry."

"You know what they say, all work and no play, dot, dot, dot."

"What?" Bridget asked, irritated.

"Let me guess. You're a detective working on a case that has you stumped."

"Well, that's quite a leap."

"I'm Jane Evans." She closed her book. "Sometimes it helps to talk, to see things more clearly."

"Is that right?" Bridget was somewhat annoyed at Jane's unsolicited opinion. "And are you an expert at that?"

"Well, observation is an occupational hazard. I work in law enforcement, but you already knew that."

"Did I?" Bridget acted surprised.

"You know you did. You had me judged before I sat down."

Bridget was dealing with a savvy individual. "Okay, I'll bite. What branch are you in?"

"Let's just call it law enforcement."

Bridget didn't care for the woman's evasiveness; she used an assumptive close. "I see. So, as an FBI agent, did you think you'd help me out?"

"FBI? No, not quite." Jane snickered. "But I did glimpse your crime scene photos."

"You weren't supposed to see those. What's your agenda here, Jane?"

"What makes you think I have an agenda?"

"Well, for starters, you arranged to sit next to me." Bridget pointed across the aisle. "You asked that woman to exchange seats with a bullshit story about vertigo and an aisle seat. Why?"

"Well, aren't you clever?"

"And you're trying desperately to hide your British accent. Who do you work for? The Yard? Ministry of Defense? A specialty branch? Tell me."

"As I said, clever girl. Okay, Bridget Murphy, I'll share, New Scotland Yard, CID, the Criminal Investigation Department."

"I know what it stands for." Bridget glared. "How do you know my name? And, what's the Yard doing on a plane to Boston?"

"We know quite a lot about you, actually."

"Really? You obviously have me at a disadvantage, Jane. Or is that a pseudonym?

"That is my name. Let's just say I believe we can help each other."

"How's that?"

"I have information about your Taylor case," Jane said haughtily. Bridget was flabbergasted. "What? Colin? What information?"

"Your working theory about certain international acts and un-solved murders tied to antiquities is more accurate than you realize. We know the Yard intentionally shut you down."

"You know about my working theory? How, and who's *we*?"

"Not so fast, Bridget. My goal was to introduce myself. I have a partner in London. After he arrives, we'll all meet. We've been track-ing several mysterious events for two years. Events you've been in-volved with, but haven't solved, like your Taylor case. We believe Mr. Taylor was, and you are on to something much bigger than the London gallery murders."

"You're confirming that Colin was murdered?" Bridget became anxious.

"Keep your voice down," Jane warned. "You must be patient."

"Patience isn't exactly my strong suit. And this sucks, you had the entire flight, but you waited until wheels down to tell me this?" Bridget was angry. "Look, Jane, I don't know who you are, but I don't work with strangers."

"Well, that's your choice. I understand you have doubts—we thought you might like some answers. But I can't go into it, not here." Jane handed her a card. "I'll call you this week."

Bridget took it and reached into her satchel. "Here's mine."

"I have your number. But I'll take it." She put Bridget's card into her jacket pocket. Jane scanned the passengers in their section.

Bridget felt unnerved by Jane's control tactics and hated being in the dark. She examined Jane's business card. It showed New Scotland Yard and "Jane Evans, Special Investigations." No cell number or email. Jane was still looking around the cabin.

"Jane, what's with the cloak-and-dagger routine?"

"Purely precautionary."

"Why, are you in danger?"

"No." She leaned into Bridget. "But you could be, so watch your back."

"Whoa! Are you fucking kidding me? I'm in danger?"

"Shh. You'll be fine."

The aircraft's hydraulic landing gear whined as it dropped into place. Bridget's pulse raced, and she felt nauseous. She closed her eyes and tugged on her seatbelt. *What the hell? Colin was murdered, and we're both onto something. I need to watch my back! And how does she know about my working theory?*

The plane jolted when the landing gear hit the runway. The engines roared, and the lights flickered inside the fuselage. Bridget fought the urge to jump up and run out. *It's just a mild panic attack.* She opened her phone to a picture of her mother, remembering her soothing voice. "It's okay, sweetie, just breathe. You'll be okay." Bridget took slow, deep breaths. A minute later, she felt calm again.

Chapter 8: Sorry, We're Closed

Thomas Chevalier nodded at Maurice, the doorman at his luxury Park Avenue residence. Two blocks away, the manager at Via Quadronno escorted him to his reserved seat by the window. A chilled glass of prosecco and freshly squeezed orange juice materialized without being ordered.

It was Saturday morning, the day of the special event at the Miller gallery. While waiting for breakfast, Thomas checked the burner phone and reviewed the day's meticulous timeline. Success hinged on one crucial element—absolute control over his father and sister's whereabouts throughout the day.

With his father bedridden from his heart attack, Thomas knew he wouldn't be a problem. He would visit him after breakfast, then ensure that his sister, Jacqueline, left for Washington, D.C. It would be a busy but exciting day; he was in good spirits but had no time to dawdle.

Thomas walked to his father's duplex, overlooking Central Park on 5th Avenue. Built in 1927, it was bright and tastefully decorated. Thomas cherished his childhood home, but after his mother passed away, he only visited on birthdays and special occasions, or when Jacqueline was present. Thomas made a mental note to stop by the kitchen to say hello to Gertrude, the family's long-time cook.

During the past month, Thomas's visits increased dramatically. After Henry Miller's massive heart attack and open-heart surgery, he remained in the hospital for two weeks due to complications. One week ago, Miller came home with two full-time nurses. Thomas stood in his parents' bedroom doorway, watching two nurses check his father's vitals and bandages.

Waiting patiently, Thomas glanced around the room. Above his father's bed hung a large oil painting of his mother. It captured her kind eyes and warm smile. For a moment, she seemed to glow. *God, I miss you, Mom. You were the only one who understood me.* Since her passing, his father had transformed their bedroom into a memorial—their wedding day, family vacations, lots of precious moments in silver-plated frames, crowding available surfaces. Thomas believed his father truly loved her and missed her as well.

Thomas announced himself. "Hello, Father, how are you feeling today?"

"Thomas! Well, I'm still here." The nurses left the bedroom. "It's nice to see you. Are you working at the gallery today?" he asked.

"Yes, but I wanted to check on you first."

"Thank you, Thomas." He took a raspy breath. "I have something important to ask you."

"What's that?"

"As you know, I can't return to work for another month. Jacqueline and I appreciate your help and wondered if you could increase your hours. You would continue the same duties but work every day."

"Why? What's going on?"

"Jacqueline is overworked and needs help." Henry's concern shifted to a business deal. "Of course, I would increase your allowance for the additional hours."

Thomas's happy mood evaporated. Just once, he wished his father would look at him and see more than a money-hungry disappointment.

"Sure, Father, when do you need me to start?"

"Right away. Can you let Jacqueline know?" He coughed and wheezed.

"Yeah, sure, I'll tell her this morning."

"Thank you, Thomas. I'm so relieved. And please tell her I said to enjoy the gala this evening." Henry coughed again, and his face turned beet red.

"Hey, take it easy. NURSE!"

Both nurses rushed into the room. Thomas felt queasy and moved out of the way.

"Well, I'd better go. Jacquie's waiting for me." Thomas slowly backed away. "I'll uh, I'll come again tomorrow, Father."

Miller reached out his frail hand, fingers beckoning. Thomas moved forward, took his father's hand, and leaned in.

With teary eyes, Henry whispered, "Goodbye, son, and thank you." His weak smile was warm and genuine.

"Goodbye, Dad. I hope you feel better. Rest now." Thomas returned the smile, patted his father's hand, released it, and walked away.

As the elevator descended, Thomas's sadness rose. Seeing his once invincible father lying helpless, with tubes slung across his torso and monitors beeping, unsettled him. And his father's raw emotion moved him. Thomas had learned to protect himself against his father's tough and demanding demeanor. But his father's affection threatened to unravel his plans.

Once on the street, Thomas gave himself a pep talk. *Nothing has changed. Don't get sucked into his vulnerability. He'll be back to his old asshole nature soon enough.* Thomas turned his thoughts to the evening's agenda. *I'll need my tuxedo, shoes, and toiletries.*

Back home, Thomas gathered his garment bag and placed it on the front seat of his Porsche 911 Carrera convertible. It was a beautiful, sunny day, and with the top down and music blaring, he drove down 5th Avenue toward W. 56th Street.

Thomas called Jacqueline about the conversation with their father. She was thankful. Thomas whipped his Porsche into an open spot in front of the gallery, closed the convertible top, and ran up the steps to find Jacqueline inside the foyer. Wearing a chic black and beige sweater set, flared jeans, boots, and a Dior handbag, she exuded a model-like appearance.

"Hey there, Tommy, right on time. My limousine will be here shortly."

"You look nice." He kissed her on the cheek. "Have you got everything?"

"Yes, all set. My flight to D.C. leaves in three hours."

"Father hopes you enjoy the antiquities gala."

"It will be different without him. Many friends and colleagues will miss him."

"What time is your flight back tomorrow?" Thomas asked.

"Nine-forty-five. I'll come straight here from the airport."

"So, about eleven? Okay. I'll be here. And don't worry, everything will be fine."

"I know, Tommy, you've been a big help these past weeks."

"Thanks, Jacquie. I'm always happy to help you, you know that."

"I know, I love you." Jacqueline looked outside. "Ah, there's my limo."

"Let me." Thomas reached for her Louis Vuitton suitcase and carried it down the steps.

Jacqueline gave Thomas a big hug. He kissed her on the cheek, opened the passenger door, and helped her into the back seat.

"Love you. Have a good trip, Sis. See you tomorrow." He closed the door and waved.

Jacqueline waved back. Thomas waited one more minute before retrieving the garment bag from his car. He hung a "Sorry, We're Closed" sign on the door, ensuring no uninvited visitors. He set a reminder to remove the sign at six-thirty.

In the office, Thomas hung his garment bag on the coat tree and strolled around the exclusive gallery, viewing the pieces and talking to himself aloud.

"I gotta admit, the gallery is awe-inspiring. But I'll never understand what Father and Jacquie see in all this stuff. Anyway, it won't be my problem after tonight. I can taste freedom. Come Monday, I'll be on my way to white sandy beaches and complete autonomy."

He suddenly felt shame about betraying his sister. He shoved it down, determined to ignore the feelings. *I have to believe she'll forgive me. Right now, I need to stay focused and get through tonight.*

Chapter 9: No Peeking

Thomas checked the time on his Rolex; he was bored and hungry. He ate at his favorite bar and restaurant, the Whitby Hotel, three minutes from the gallery. After a hearty lunch and double bourbon, Thomas headed back to the gallery, whistling as he unlocked the front door and strutted into the office. Thomas sat in his father's comfortable leather chair and reviewed the schedule for the evening's event.

The burner phone that Dr. Jeeves had given him vibrated in his pocket.

"Hello."

"Hello, Thomas. Are you ready to receive the items?"

"Yes, Dr. Jeeves, all set. And I turned off the cameras in the alleyway, as requested."

"Well done. Remember, each delivery crew knows exactly what to do, and you're not to touch anything after they've gone."

"Yes, I understand."

"Good. I shall arrive at precisely six-fifteen to inspect the premises."

"I underst—" *Jeez, not even a goodbye.*

At precisely three o'clock, the alleyway doorbell rang. Thomas peered through the peephole at the back door, punched a code into the alarm system, and unlocked three deadbolts. When he opened the door, two white vans and four men wearing black baseball caps, black gloves, and plain gray jumpsuits with no logos or visible insignias were there.

"Hello, I'm Thomas."

"We have the items. Show us," one man demanded, clipboard in hand.

"Oh, sure," Thomas said, holding the door open.

The men walked inside the facility, perusing the private screening room, the gallery, the kitchen, and the storage room. Working efficiently, they relocated all the furniture from the private screening room to storage. They retrieved white velvet chairs, end tables, a lectern, red velvet curtains, and specialized lighting from the van. After drilling holes to mount curtain rods, hanging their curtains, securing spotlights on the brick wall, and furniture placement, they transformed the private screening room into a premium mock theatre.

Next, the men brought in and expertly arranged three high-top tables with linen tablecloths, candles, and fresh-cut flowers within the open space inside the gallery. Elegant bone China was neatly laid next to Reed & Barton gold-plated flatware. Two silver ice buckets were placed on the sideboard buffet. The candles were lit, creating a warm ambiance. One man stocked the refrigerator with champagne and trays of assorted delicacies wrapped in cellophane. Another workman arranged champagne glasses in an alternating pattern on the buffet table.

"At exactly six-forty-five, remove one tray of each food item and place it on the sideboard. Open two bottles of champagne and put them into the ice buckets. Keep everything stocked and looking pristine," the man instructed.

"I understand," Thomas said.

Without a word, all four men finished cleaning up, packed up their tools, and quickly departed. Thomas locked up after them and returned to inspect their work. *It looks great. Even Jacquie would approve.* Thomas glanced at his watch. "One more delivery with Dr. Jeeves, and the party begins."

Thomas ceremoniously dressed in his Brioni tuxedo. The black shirt studs stood out against his crisp white linen shirt's pleats, and the black silk bow tie felt like butter as he executed the perfect symmetrical knot. He wrapped the cummerbund around his waist and retrieved the final adornment from a small wooden box—onyx and diamond cufflinks, his mother had given him on his thirtieth birthday. He studied himself in the mirror, adjusted his French cuffs, smoothed down the hand-stitched lapels, and smiled. *I'm ready.*

Thomas emerged from the bathroom transformed. *I feel like a million, strike that, like ten million bucks!* In the office, he hung the garment bag on the coat rack, unzipped it, and removed a small case containing two vials of cocaine. He made two lines on a mirror and sniffed both. He placed his wallet in his right backside pocket, then noticed an airplane ticket still resting on the desk. "Damn, I can't leave this out." He folded it and placed it into the left inside pocket of his tuxedo jacket.

At exactly six-fifteen, the doorbell rang. Thomas saw Dr. Jeeves standing at the back door, accompanied by a briefcase, a town car, and an unmarked van parked in the alley.

"Hello, Thomas. My, don't we look dapper."

"Hello, Dr. Jeeves. Thanks." Thomas saw two men in gray jumpsuits.

"We have one more delivery. Please show these gentlemen the screening room?"

"Of course, this way." Thomas led them down the hallway.

Returning to their van, they carefully brought in a large box. Thomas stayed out of the way. *It must be really heavy.* He was intrigued but remembered the "no peeking" rules set by Dr. Jeeves—it was forbidden to look at or touch the artifacts brought inside.

The six-thirty alarm on his cellphone chimed. Thomas retrieved the "Sorry, We're Closed" sign from the front door. Meanwhile, in the screening room, Dr. Jeeves set his briefcase down next to the lectern and tracked the movements of his workmen as they brought five more mahogany boxes into the space.

When Thomas later entered the room, Dr. Jeeves pivoted sharply. His beady eyes locked onto Thomas. "Go into the office and wait for me there, NOW." His voice dropped an octave.

Thomas recoiled. "Okay." *Whoops, conditions.* He retreated quickly.

Dr. Jeeves heard the office door close, then instructed the men. "Hang one box securely onto the wall. Open and secure the lid, then adjust the lights to illuminate it. Arrange the other five boxes against the wall and close the curtains."

A half hour later, Dr. Jeeves found Thomas sitting at the desk.

"You may come out now."

By six-forty-five, Thomas had arranged a symphony of silver trays along the buffet with assorted delectable canapés, colorful fruit platters, caviar, duck pâté, clams on the half shell, artisan breads, and an assortment of tiered desserts. With champagne chilling in silver ice buckets, Thomas looked around the Miller gallery and admired his handiwork.

Chapter 10: Home Again

The British Airways plane landed at Boston Logan at six-fifty-two p.m. on Saturday. Bridget looked out the window; the sun hung low on the horizon. She was tired, both emotionally and physically, and was glad to be home.

After customs, Jane suggested they separate. "Take care, Bridget." She put distance between them.

"Sure thing." Bridget watched Jane disappear into the crowd. *Friggin' cloak and dagger.*

Bridget hailed a taxi. "Brookline, 25 Warrick Road," she said, getting inside.

Outside her apartment building, two vintage streetlights cast shadows onto the sidewalk. Built in 1915, it featured charming characteristics, including bay windows, domed accent awnings, flower boxes, and a tree-lined street of Red Maples forming a perfectly contoured canopy.

Upon entering her apartment, Bridget wrinkled her nose at the musty smell. It had been closed up for ten days. She looked down at dozens of mail pieces scattered on the floor. She had forgotten to stop mail delivery. She scooped them up and noticed a letter from her attorney. She carried the mail into her kitchen and dropped it on the table.

She liked her quaint apartment, decorated in mid-century modern elegance with versatile furniture in warm colors of taupe and white, accentuated by big pops of forest green and gray. However, it was a far cry from her former brownstone in one of Boston's Paris-inspired upscale neighborhoods in Cambridge.

In the kitchen, she turned on a fan to circulate the air. The clock above the refrigerator read nine p.m. She calculated the time change and decided to stay up until eleven p.m.

Bridget checked her phone, but there was nothing from Jane. Disappointed, she made tea and plugged in her laptop. While sitting at the kitchen table, the letter from her attorney stuck out like a sore thumb. Though she didn't want to deal with it, the envelope triggered memories from four years ago.

While on assignment in Lyon, France, Bridget was swept off her feet by Antoine Tricheuse, a charming French detective. After a whirlwind romance, they were joined in wedlock by Lyon's mayor. Everything was great until the honeymoon phase rapidly faded. The distance, separation, and busy work schedules created cracks that became a chasm. Bridget was shocked when she discovered that Antoine had a mistress.

Not one to turn a blind eye, she called to confront him. "Antoine, we've only been married for three months, and you're cheating? My source is reliable, so don't deny it."

"I wasn't going to. My chéri, I am a Frenchman; it's part of our culture." Antoine's voice softened to velvet, emphasizing his accent. "My sweet Bridget, I promise, in time you'll understand. You are my wife, my love. I'll make you happy, you'll see." He paused and whispered softly, "I adore you. Come to Lyon this weekend. I'll make it up to you."

His disarming and manipulative charm coiled around her like a boa constrictor. Her resolve swelled. "Antoine, your sweet talk sounds like a broken record. So, here's my promise, *darling,* I will never understand. I'm filing for divorce."

"What? You're behaving like a spoiled child—grow up. Besides, I won't allow it." Antoine seethed. "You'll regret it. Have you forgotten that my father is the Directeur Général, one of the highest-ranking officers in France? You'll never work here again, and your reputation will be ruined. So, you can't divorce me."

"Oh yeah?" The corner of her mouth lifted; a smile combined with contempt. "Watch me, asshole." Bridget hung up.

Within a month, Antoine received divorce documents, triggering a malicious response. He threatened to destroy her reputation and strip her of everything she owned. Their legal battle ensued and dragged on for three years. Antoine's shifting demands dragged out the filings and proceedings.

Bridget was still processing the news of Antoine's unexpected death from a month ago. *I can't believe he's dead, and from a skiing accident of all things.* After three years of disputes, his death ended the lawsuit. The balance of a trust had been refunded, everything she'd given up to be free: the proceeds from her Cambridge home, her 401(k), her mother's inheritance, all her savings, even an alimony settlement. *It was all for nothing.*

The finality struck her. *And now he's gone. Fate has a strange way of resolving things. But it's finally over.* She sighed deeply. She stared at the letter and decided it could remain unopened until the next day.

——◆——

Bridget's laptop startled her when the low-battery indicator beeped. *What?* She found the plug on the floor and reset it. *That's it. I'm done.*

Bridget closed the Taylor file and shut down her laptop. She checked her phone, and there were no messages from Jane Evans. "Time for bed," she said aloud.

The bed felt cool and comfortable as she slipped between the sheets. She glanced at photos on her phone. Feeling melancholy, she touched the pictures of her parents, warmed by her mother's enduring smile. Then she searched for photos of Adama Baptiste and sighed heavily. *He's got the best smile, the best kisses, and the best hugs. God, I miss him.*

Their happy faces told the whole world they were in love. Bridget kissed the screen before closing it. Scooting down in her bed, she felt glad to be home. *I think I'll go for a run and treat myself to brunch tomorrow morning. Then I need to figure out a way back into Adama's heart.*

Chapter 11: A Special Event

It was Saturday evening. Century-old stone steps led up to the Miller Antiquities gallery. As visitors passed the two Grecian-style vases resting at the base, the fragrant aroma of azaleas and jasmine flowers filled the air. Antique brass lamps cast a warm glow over the stoop. Entering the foyer was like stepping back in time by two millennia. Everything was ready for an elegant soiree. Thomas Chevalier stood ready with Dr. Jeeves, who glanced at his pocket watch.

"It's time to receive our guests, Thomas. One crucial note—there will be a lady present, Miss Daisy Hunter, and she must be referred to as 'madam.' Do you remember your greeting lines?"

"Of course, I've got this."

"I shall retire to the screening room."

Thomas moved into position at the top of the stoop to wait. He felt handsome in his black tuxedo. *And here they come.* Thomas rubbed his sweaty palms and watched each limousine pull to the curb.

William Vanhorn was the first guest to arrive. He was a sixty-four-year-old, slender-framed man with brown eyes and brown-gray streaked hair that he wore in a ponytail. Vanhorn dressed casually in loose, striped lounging pants and a button-down, flowery shirt, covered by a sky-blue hoodie. The former pastor revolutionized televised sermons. He authored several best-selling books and established the Vanhorn Foundation. However, the board of directors fired him due to scandals involving teenagers and indictments for two counts of rape. His net worth exceeded a billion. Vanhorn sailed from Florida on his superyacht, now moored in Brooklyn, where several young women awaited his return.

Dick Betrug arrived next. The boisterous sixty-two-year-old emerged wearing a loud Hawaiian shirt and tan slacks, subtly hiding an arthritic limp. Tall and heavy-set with a rounded middle section, he had a long, tanned face with a slight mustache. He combed his thinning, dyed-brown hair straight back. The former two-term senator from Alabama, a shrewd businessman, owned several companies. His chemical manufacturing firm faced investigation for dumping hazardous waste, while his attorneys battled class action lawsuits from cancer-stricken downstream residents. He was reportedly worth $12 billion. Betrug was divorced twice as a result of extramarital affairs. Cheating was his favorite pastime, especially on the golf course. Next in line were women, then cigars and gambling.

Gerald Decker emerged from his custom stretch limousine. He was a forty-year-old playboy and the son of a wealthy real estate developer. He wore an open-faced Gucci button-down shirt and navy slacks. His wavy black hair shaped his boyish face with large curls that fell around his forehead, ears, and neck. A large diamond-studded gold cross hung around his neck, highlighting the thick hair on his chest. Decker's normally bloodshot brown eyes gleamed white from eye drops. Decker owned and lived at the luxurious Vincent Hotel on the Upper East Side. His favorite pastime was Manhattan's nightlife, where he pursued gorgeous women, never spending a night alone. Decker's first love was drugs, which he used and sold. And he considered himself a savvy entrepreneur, running a successful drug business that catered to an elite clientele. His trust fund was worth $4 billion.

Ling Chen arrived next. He was a forty-eight-year-old banker who immigrated from Hong Kong. He wore a black silk suit and a white silk shirt, the top three buttons of which were undone. Chen was a slender, five-foot-eight man with a clean-shaven face and jet-black dyed hair. A diamond-studded, solid gold chain hung around his neck, and a five-carat diamond ring dominated his left ring finger. Chen opened ten successful merchant banks along the East Coast, laundering and lending money for real estate development, manufacturing, and shipping conglomerates. Chen paid thirty-three million for a private residence at the Plaza and owned property in Beijing,

Paris, London, and Buenos Aires. Chen owned a private jet, enjoyed gambling, and played golf weekly at exclusive country clubs. His net worth was approximately three billion.

Gunter Maximilian showed up right on time. He was a dapper sixty-three-year-old investment banker who founded GM Wall Street Investments. Maximilian was tall and slender, with thick, sandy-blond hair parted on the side. His large, dark blue eyes drew attention away from the large nose that dominated his face. He dressed in a white long-sleeved shirt and black slacks. Maximilian was a reserved and shrewd businessman. He was considered the luckiest guy on Wall Street, seemingly immune to stock crashes. The Securities and Exchange Commission (SEC) was investigating him for insider trading and fraud. His primary residence was on the Upper East Side, where he lived with his wife. And he supported two mistresses in their nearby townhomes. Maximilian owned several nefarious businesses through shell corporations in the Cayman Islands. His favorite pastime was linebreeding racehorses in Upstate New York. His net worth was three billion.

Daisy Hunter was the last guest to arrive. She was sixty-five and the wealthiest of the group, with twenty-four billion in net assets. She was an unscrupulous oil tycoon who defied OSHA, which resulted in the injuries and deaths of dozens of oil rig derrickmen. She paid millions to ruthless attorneys and fixers who intimidated OSHA inspectors and the victims' relatives. Daisy Hunter stayed at the luxurious Le Chandelier Hotel near Central Park. She had been married and divorced four times and lived in a mansion outside Dallas, Texas. Daisy had a passion for antiquities and was a sucker for Egyptian artifacts. She always traveled with her three spoiled Pomeranians, was a closet eater who over-medicated, and delighted in getting people fired.

Although he recognized the billionaires, Thomas was instructed not to speak with the guests, including Daisy Hunter, a good friend of his father. Thomas used a rehearsed statement as he welcomed each guest to the gallery.

"Welcome, we are very pleased to have you join us this evening. Please make yourself comfortable in the gallery." As Thomas cheerfully greeted the guests, they snubbed him.

Thomas watched the first five limousines arrive like clockwork. However, the pattern changed when Daisy Hunter's vehicle pulled to the curb. No one emerged from the car. Thomas waited patiently at the top of the stoop. At last, the driver stepped out and opened the passenger door. A heavy-set woman swung her legs outside. Her driver attempted to assist her.

"I don't need your help." Daisy slapped his hand and struggled to lift herself out of the seat. "Well? Help me, you idiot!" The driver extended his hand and braced himself with a wide stance for leverage. They interlinked their hands, and the driver pulled as she stood upright.

Daisy looked at the steps and sighed heavily. "Assholes." She assessed the handrail for stability, clutching it with both hands, and slowly ascended the stairs, limping with each step. Thomas became concerned about her wide body fitting through the one open, narrow door. He quietly unlatched the second door. Daisy wheezed loudly as she approached the entrance.

"Get out of my way, you moron," she said, waving him off.

"Yes, madam. I am so sorry." Thomas stepped backward. He was insulted that she didn't recognize him.

"You damn well should be!"

Daisy Hunter offered her hand to Thomas, who aided her in stepping over the door sill. With a scowl on her face, she clenched his hand tightly. Thomas felt a sudden sharp pain as Daisy forcefully pinched his forearm. *Ouch! What the...?* Thomas jerked his arm away. He wanted to yell at her. *Be cool. Ten million, ten million.* He rubbed his forearm and closed the doors.

The five men mingled around the high-top tables. As soon as Daisy Hunter entered the room, she was met with clapping cheers and a chorus of respectful greetings and effusive compliments from each man. Vanhorn poured her a glass of champagne while Maximilian took her coat. Betrug offered to bring her something to eat. But when

Daisy saw the buffet table filled with an assortment of delectable treats, she motioned for him to follow her.

As Daisy inspected the buffet line, she sampled various petit fours, spitting out whatever displeased her. Chen followed behind, cleaning up her mess. Miss Hunter pointed at multiple items, while Betrug and Decker filled two plates with her selections. They carried the plates into the gallery and pretended not to notice as she hungrily attacked the food.

Standing outside the office door, Thomas witnessed the unnerving display of submissive behavior toward Daisy Hunter. He wondered why those men, with so much power and wealth, were subservient to her.

She must have the goods on every one of those snobby bastards.

Chapter 12: Caviar and Champagne

Thomas Chevalier observed the guests devour the assorted hors d'oeuvres. He was vigilant to ensure an ample supply of caviar and champagne. He retrieved another platter of food and three more bottles of Dom Perignon Oenotheque Champagne Rose 1988 from the kitchen. Thomas had looked up the online price—the champagne was worth more than $6,000 per bottle.

As instructed, Thomas maintained his distance from outside the office. He put his earbuds in and listened to music on his cellphone while watching the guests mingle. The billionaires talked amongst themselves—joked, laughed, ate, and drank. All the while, Thomas remained inconspicuous, which suited him perfectly. They did not know him nor care about him. *Hear no evil, see no evil, speak no evil.*

Gerald Decker conversed with Gunter Maximilian regarding his insider trading lawsuits and ways to circumvent the Securities and Exchange Act.

"The director owes me a favor; I'll get him to drop the charges, or he can forget about any more insider tips." Maximilian winked at Decker, whose smile broadened.

"Thanks. I need to discuss laundering more money with Chen. I'm running out of storage space for my stinking cash." Decker looked for Chen.

Daisy Hunter teased William Vanhorn about his indictments for rape and twelve sexual harassment lawsuits.

"You must learn to keep it in your pants, you bad boy," Daisy said. "I practically gave you that damn yacht. For crying out loud, take them out to sea and past the twelve-mile marker."

Vanhorn hung his head in shame. "I just can't seem to help my-self."

"Yes, well, we all have our demons." Daisy looked at the fourth plate of food in front of her.

Betrug meandered over to Daisy and begged her to use her political powers. "Can you get all the RICO charges dismissed, and threaten that piss-ant prosecutor in Alabama to squash my illegal waste disposal indictments?" He wasn't sure what she would say. Racketeer Influenced and Corrupt Organizations Act charges were hard to beat.

"Consider it done, for a favor. I'll call you next week." She winked at Betrug.

"Thank you, madam, and may I say you look lovely as always."

Daisy nodded at the compliment and smiled when she saw Decker approaching.

Dick Betrug ventured over to chat with Ling Chen about his chief financial officer's suggestion of obtaining a low-interest loan to relocate his manufacturing company offshore.

"My CFO is very creative; you shouldn't have any problem getting it approved," Betrug said.

"Sounds good. Just make sure it looks like you're paying something other than zero taxes this time. Fucking board just changed again. They're a bunch of tight asses," Chen said.

"Fuck them and fix it, you owe me." Betrug gave Chen a hard stare.

"Don't worry about it. Your money is safe with me."

They switched topics to their favorite subject, golf.

"So, played any great courses lately?" Betrug asked.

"I'm playing at my new club—the Cardinal Lakes Country Club on Long Island," Chen said.

"Never heard of it." Betrug tilted his head back and slurped a clam on a half shell.

"It's relatively new. Tony Corazon, the former PGA champion, designed it. He bought the land three years ago. The grand opening was last summer. The course is beautiful, with tree-lined fairways, pristine greens, four lakes, and a tremendous signature hole. It's a challenge and has some of the deepest bunkers ever seen. The eighteenth hole comes into an incredible clubhouse. It's fantastic."

"Tony Corazon," Betrug said slowly. "Didn't he win The Masters?"

"Yes, twice. And he won the Players. He's a phenomenal golfer."

"And you financed him. Did he give you a membership?" Betrug asked.

"What do you think?" Chen winked.

"You sleazy bastard. Any chance I can play?"

"Yeah, we're playing Wednesday," Chen said. "I'll text you the tee-time and address."

"Outstanding. I'll be there."

"Great. I'll let Tony know." Chen grinned.

———◆———

At precisely seven-thirty p.m., Thomas rang the small silver bell from its dedicated table three times. Without speaking, everyone obediently turned their gaze towards Thomas.

"If you please, follow me into the screening room."

Thomas led the way, entered a dimly lit room, and stood behind the lectern. He motioned for them to be seated in the wingback velvet chairs. Each billionaire took a seat.

"Madam and gentlemen, I am pleased to introduce your host for this evening, Dr. Jeeves."

Thomas clapped his hands along with the others. As previously instructed, he immediately left the room. Feeling dejected and envious, he closed the door behind him.

Dr. Jeeves cleared his throat from behind the red velvet curtains. It was the signal they had all been waiting for. The six billionaires quickly settled down and fixated on the curtains. Dr. Jeeves appeared and surveyed the room. He could feel their anticipation and delighted in their enthusiasm, like dogs salivating at the sight of red meat. Dr. Jeeves approached the lectern and pulled the chain on the green banker's lamp.

"Welcome. It is marvelous to see you all once again. As you are aware, I represent a small group of benefactors who extend their warmest regards and deeply appreciate your patronage. I must say, each of you men takes masculinity to its finest, and to my dearest

Miss Hunter, we are all graced by your presence, and you never looked lovelier." Dr. Jeeves bowed to Daisy, who pompously nodded her appreciation. The men clapped for her.

Dr. Jeeves slowly opened the brown leather binder on the lectern with careful precision. He put on a pair of vintage eyeglasses and turned the first page.

"Let us begin."

The six participants sat obediently, like kindergartners listening on a rug during story time. Their heart rates increased, pupils dilated, and mouths watered. Each one eagerly craved the rush, vitality, and feeling of aliveness they expected during and after these exclusive presentations. No one imagined the content Dr. Jeeves was about to deliver. This would be a one-of-a-kind story, like nothing they had ever experienced. They sat quietly, mesmerized in their chairs.

"I'm pleased to provide an incredible story of intrigue, danger, and conspiracy. I promise this shall be a narrative like no other. You'll delight in the history, culture, and utter devastation, intricately intertwined with the ancient artifacts to be presented this evening."

"Our story begins in West Africa, and we journey northward by cargo ships to Europe, London, and ultimately America."

Dr. Jeeves shared details about the lives of the people involved in obtaining the artifacts. The tale unfolded the extent of the misery, toil, deaths, and grief shared by dozens of people. With all eyes fixated on Dr. Jeeves, nothing could divert their attention. Captivated by the horror, goosebumps formed on their arms. Wide-eyed and spellbound, they ate cocktail appetizers, like moviegoers savoring individual bites of popcorn.

As the outlandish saga continued, Decker, Vanhorn, Chen, and Betrug smoked their expensive cigars, momentarily holding and slowly releasing the smoke. The white mist billowed upward and hung in the air. Daisy and Maximilian sipped champagne. Occasionally, one or more billionaires would gasp, smile devilishly, or snicker during the presentation. After forty-five minutes of reading, Dr. Jeeves closed his notebook.

"We sincerely hope you embrace the knowledge that each artifact we've handpicked for you is but a token for an enduring experience.

Your special piece was acquired under the direst of circumstances, fulfilling your voracious appetites with a feeling and connection principally unique to you."

The doctor turned off the lectern's lamp and walked to the red velvet curtains.

"Madam and gentlemen, may I present one of the most unique and exquisite antique keepsakes you'll ever possess? Consider your prize an enduring icon that will thrill you at its sight and touch for years."

Dr. Jeeves opened both of the red velvet curtains. Spotlights illuminated a spectacular display. Each billionaire gasped with delight. Their eyes were fixed on the object hanging from the hook. Each person was eager to touch it, but no one dared to move. The doctor returned to the lectern and pulled the chain on the lamp. "Allow me to continue," he said.

The six billionaires salivated over the distinctive events associated with the object. Each incident made them feel giddy with a sense of aliveness. Every person experienced a rare opportunity to partake in multiple outrageous events they could never have encountered alone. The price tag of twenty million dollars was minuscule for these six people compared to a priceless story.

When Dr. Jeeves closed the binder, signifying completion, the room erupted with cheers. Dr. Jeeves bowed with reverence to their standing ovation.

Chapter 13: The Jewelry Box

Hidden in the gallery office, Thomas Chevalier played video games on his phone. Upon hearing a loud commotion from the hall, he removed his earbuds to listen to the cheers and clapping. He noted the time; it was eight-fifteen.

Thomas felt alone and jealous while everyone else gathered in the screening room. He made a mental note to break one of the "conditions" by peeking at whatever was in those boxes. He strolled into the gallery and helped himself to champagne and a plate of food, pretending to be a guest. Back in the office, Thomas retrieved a case that held two vials of cocaine from his garment bag. Making sure no one was looking, he quickly made two lines and sniffed them, instantly feeling better.

Meanwhile, Dr. Jeeves concluded his presentation. "Thank you all ever so much for being our guests this evening. I have one more gift for you." He removed six small, handmade wooden jewelry boxes, each with a red satin ribbon, from his briefcase.

"For you, Madam Hunter." Jeeves presented the first box.

"It's got my initials on it!" Daisy exclaimed.

Dr. Jeeves repeated the process and then returned to the lectern.

"Each jewelry box contains a unique key to unlock the two vintage padlocks on your mahogany box. Please safeguard it; there are no replacements. One more thing—your item shall be delivered to you before midnight. Please take possession immediately."

Dr. Jeeves folded his hands on the lectern and gave his closing remarks.

"We hope you relish the intriguing events we've created on your behalf. Enjoy your new prize and the incredible events that took place for your pleasure. And of course, cherish the thought of making a remarkable investment. Once again, we value your devoted patronage. As you know, our services require a caveat of utter secrecy and rely on your discretion."

Each billionaire glanced at the others, nodding in agreement.

"Then I shall take my leave. Good evening, madam and gentlemen."

Dr. Jeeves stepped away from the lectern and waited as each person approached him.

"Magnificent! You never disappoint," Betrug said with a cigar in his mouth. He shook Dr. Jeeves' hand as if he were the pope or a king.

"You've outdone every other event this time." Vanhorn gently shook the doctor's hand.

"I find myself remarkably satisfied, which rarely happens. You masterfully executed this event. It won't go unnoticed," Daisy Hunter said. She was beaming. She reached for the doctor's hand and tried to curtsy; her knees cracked, and they both pretended not to notice.

"My pleasure, madam." Dr. Jeeves kissed the back of her hand. "However, you deserve full credit for hosting a magnificent event. I look forward to working with you in the future." A round of applause filled the room as the five billionaires expressed their appreciation and approval of Daisy Hunter.

The rest of the billionaires personally thanked Dr. Jeeves and marveled at the beauty of the mahogany wood and elegant latches, also engraved with initials. No boxes were opened. Instead, each person stared upward, transfixed and compelled to touch the suspended artifact. They knew their box contained something similar. Dr. Jeeves allowed them a moment and closed the red velvet curtains.

After several minutes, each took turns shaking hands, confirming future meetings.

"So, Chen, I'll see you at the golf course on Wednesday," Betrug said.

"Yes, Wednesday. Enjoy the rest of your weekend." Chen shook Betrug's hand and turned to Decker. "You sure you won't join us? We need a fourth."

"Sorry, I'm going to the Hamptons. Next time," Decker said. Then he approached Dr. Jeeves. "Man, that was worth every penny."

He pursed his lips, bunched his fingers on one hand near his mouth, then splayed them as his hand blossomed outward. "Magnifique!" Dr. Jeeves smiled.

Decker texted his driver: "Done. Meet me in five."

The other billionaires also texted their drivers. At eight fifty-five p.m., Thomas watched the group meander out of the screening room, each billionaire carrying a small wooden jewelry box. Each guest strolled out the front door to their waiting limousines.

Thomas followed the last person, Daisy Hunter. He stayed clear and waited until she was down the steps before he closed and locked the front doors. He found Dr. Jeeves donning his cape and hat in the screening room. "They all left," Thomas said as they entered the office.

"Yes, I know. Thomas, would you mind getting that?" Dr. Jeeves asked.

"Getting what?" Thomas asked, confused until hearing a knock at the alley door.

"How did you know there was someone there?" Thomas asked.

Dr. Jeeves ignored his question and pointed his cane. Thomas opened the alley door. Without saying a word, the men removed one box and loaded it into the limousine. The driver left. The men came back inside and began removing the remaining boxes.

Chapter 14: No Loose Ends

Thomas Chevalier glanced at his watch—nine-thirty. His anticipation heightened as the evening drew close, and freedom surged through his veins. All six billionaires had departed in their shiny limousines, Dr. Jeeves' men had loaded all but one of the mysterious boxes into the van, and a black town car arrived in the alley. Thomas observed Dr. Jeeves' slow trek to the restroom. The opportunity he had waited for presented itself. *Now or never.*

Thomas briskly walked to the alley door to see the men busy loading a crate. He hoofed it back to the screening room and carefully approached the last box. It was unlocked and resting against the wall. Heart thundering, he glanced back at the door. It was safe. Thomas tugged at the heavy lid—there it was, the mystery object nestled inside its red satin cradle.

Wow, magnificent. So, this is what all the secrecy was about. Thomas stood momentarily spellbound. Like a moth drawn to a flame, he inexplicably leaned forward and outstretched his hand—six inches, three inches—almost there.

"STOP!"

Thomas jerked upright and spun around to see Dr. Jeeves coming forward with his cane held high, and two men framed in the doorway, hardened sentries.

"Oh, I'm sorry. It's just that I wanted to see it." His eyes darted back and forth at their alarm and fury. He felt his transgression was unforgivable.

"Get out, NOW!"

Ashamed and embarrassed, Thomas immediately shuffled toward the door, regretting his actions. He squeezed past their stony stares. Dr. Jeeves eyed Thomas while the two men moved in, closed the box, and took it to the van.

Dr. Jeeves approached as Thomas paced back and forth in the office, his ear pressed against his cellphone. Thomas caught the last of his words.

"Yes, I understand. I'll take care of it." Dr. Jeeves pocketed his phone and stepped into the office, expressionless.

"Dr. Jeeves, I'm so sorry. My curiosity got the best of me. I mean, all the preparation, the famous billionaires, I just had to see what all the fuss was about. Please don't be angry."

"Yes, well, perfectly understandable." Dr. Jeeves tried to smile, but his mind was preoccupied.

The cool reaction surprised Thomas, but he let it go and changed the subject.

"I was wondering, when will your men clean everything up?"

"Soon, Thomas. May I have my phone back?" Dr. Jeeves held out his palm.

"Oh, sure." Thomas reached into his pocket and handed it over. "Here you go."

"Thank you." Dr. Jeeves put the phone in his pocket.

"Now, may I see your personal cellphone?"

"*My* phone? What for?"

"Please." Dr. Jeeves stood motionless with his palm extended.

Thomas frowned and handed his iPhone over hesitantly. He watched silently as Dr. Jeeves scrolled through his recent calls, voicemails, and text messages.

"What are you doing?"

"Insurance, my boy."

"Insurance? For what?"

"Loose ends."

"I did as you instructed. I only used the burner phone. And I didn't save any of our calls or texts on my cellphone."

"One can never be too careful." Dr. Jeeves returned the phone to Thomas.

Thomas was about to put it away when it vibrated. Startled, he looked at the caller ID; it was his sister Jacqueline. Thomas grimaced.

"Sorry. I have to take this." He put his index finger up to his closed lips. "Shh." Thomas walked into the gallery.

"Hello, Jacquie. What's up?"

"Hello, Tommy. I thought I'd check to see how your day went."

"Oh. Everything was just great."

"How is Dad doing?"

"He's fine. I checked on him earlier. And I told him we'd both see him tomorrow."

"Excellent. Well, everything went well here. A few of us are going for dinner. I wish Dad could be here. So many of his friends are concerned about him. I'll tell him about it tomorrow."

Occupied with his call, Thomas paid no attention to Dr. Jeeves, who had entered the gallery to retrieve two empty glasses and a bottle of champagne. He walked back to the office. While Thomas was busy, Dr. Jeeves filled one fluted vessel with champagne and the other half full of it. Then he twisted the raven's body off the top of his walking cane and removed a small vial filled with white powder. With Thomas distracted, Dr. Jeeves delicately tapped and emptied the entire contents of the vial into the glass.

Dr. Jeeves put the empty vial in his pocket and screwed the raven's head back onto his cane. He used a nearby pencil to stir and dissolve the white powder and then shoved it into his pocket.

Thomas returned to the office and saw Dr. Jeeves holding two glasses of champagne. He quickly wrapped up his conversation with Jacqueline.

"I'm glad your gala went well, Sis. I'm going to dinner too. Let's talk when you get in tomorrow. Okay?"

"Absolutely. Hey Tommy, thanks for being so great. I love you, good night."

"No problem. I love you too, Jacquie. Gotta run."

Thomas closed his cellphone. "I'm sorry. I needed to take that call."

With a slight tremor, Dr. Jeeves handed Thomas the tainted glass of champagne.

"That's quite all right, my boy. A toast to you for a job well done."

"Oh, no, thank you. I've had plenty. You enjoy it, though." Thomas was more interested in cocaine than alcohol.

"Do you mean to turn me down, Thomas?"

"Oh, I don't mean to be rude. It's just that I'm excited about the next steps."

"Let's have a toast, and we'll discuss your monetary favors. I've got good news."

Thomas was already high and feeling good from the cocaine. Not wanting to insult Dr. Jeeves, he reluctantly took the glass and sipped. *Funky shit.*

"I thought everything went like clockwork, didn't you? I heard clapping and cheering. Those objects must be very special."

"Yes, Thomas, very special indeed." Dr. Jeeves put two of his gloved fingers under Thomas's glass. "Drink up. Then we shall talk." Dr. Jeeves monitored Thomas as he swallowed the last of his champagne.

"What's the good news?" Thomas asked.

"The balance of your money has been wired and shall be available Monday morning."

"Really! That is good news." A heavy burden was lifted from Thomas's shoulders.

"Now, then, I must remind you that you signed a confidentiality agreement. It is critical that you honor our agreement. Do you understand?"

"Of course." Thomas coughed to clear his throat.

"I heard you speak with Miss Miller. What have you told her, Thomas?"

"Who, Jacquie? Oh, nothing. She doesn't know anything about this." His words slurred.

"Nothing about me or the guests? You're quite sure?"

"Yeah, I'm sure. Shit, you can trust me." Thomas looked glassy-eyed.

"I believe you, Thomas." Dr. Jeeves nonchalantly wiped his champagne glass with a paper napkin. "Now I must take my leave." They walked down the hallway.

The limousine driver helped Dr. Jeeves into the town car. Feeling tipsy in the night air, Thomas closed the door and lowered the two security bars, but forgot to set the alarm and deadbolts. *I don't feel so good. Fucking alcohol. How long do I have to wait for the cleaners to arrive?* Feeling woozy, Thomas sat in his father's chair, leaned back, and blissfully thought about the money. Even though his father was wealthy and he would receive an enormous inheritance, Thomas wanted to be his own man. His joyful thoughts were interrupted by the buzzing of his cellphone. The caller ID showed "Father."

"Hello, Father. Is everything all right?" Thomas leaned on the desk to stand.

"Hello, Thomas. I'm feeling better and restless. How was your day? How is the gallery? I wish I could be there to help with Jacqueline gone."

"Everything's fine, Father. You don't need to worry about the gallery."

"I'm not worried, Thomas. You've been a good son, and we appreciate your assistance. Especially while Jacqueline's in Washington."

"It's no big deal. Besides, she'll be back tomorrow. You should focus on your health. Listen, I'm going out to dinner. Get some rest, and I'll come by tomorrow."

"That would be nice." There was a pause. "Thomas? I know I don't show it, but I want you to know I love you. And these past few weeks, you've made me very proud." Henry stumbled but sounded sincere.

"Um, well, thank you, Father." Thomas was stunned at his father's compliments. "I–I love you, too, Dad."

"Thank you, Thomas. I appreciate that." Henry's voice cracked. "See you tomorrow, son."

"Yes, tomorrow. Good night, Dad." Thomas hung up. Feeling heavy pressure in his chest, he took Rolaids out of his pocket and hurriedly chewed two tablets.

He set his iPhone on the desk. *Wow, I didn't see that coming. I guess his heart attack has him thinking about loose ends. Nothing like a near-death experience to bring someone to their senses.* Thomas felt happy and appreciated his father's words for the first time in years.

He rubbed his temples as he thought about the mess in the gallery. He looked at his wristwatch and adjusted himself in his father's chair.

My god, this is the worst heartburn. He popped two more antacid tablets into his mouth. *Come on, guys, where are you? I want to go home.*

The pressure in Thomas's chest got worse. He tried to stand, but his knees buckled as a sharp pain consumed his upper body. *What's happening? My god, it feels like I'm being crushed. Am I having a heart attack?* Terrorizing fear set in as he clutched at his chest. With erratic and shallow breathing, he gasped. He fumbled with his cellphone and dialed 911. His thumb moved toward the green send button.

He murmured, "Mom … Jacquie … Dad."

Thomas collapsed face down on his father's desk, the cellphone clutched in his left hand.

Ten minutes later, a gray unmarked van pulled up outside the alley door. Two men approached, and one pushed the doorbell. They waited. The other man pushed the doorbell. They waited. Five minutes later, one man made a phone call and nodded as he listened. He hung up, said something to the other man, then got into the van and pulled away.

SUNDAY

Chapter 15: William Vanhorn

Adama Baptiste dragged himself out of bed early Sunday morning after a fitful night's sleep. Saturday night's blind date left him feeling unsettled. However, his troubled mind had nothing to do with the lady; she was captivating and gracious.

Beverly Jackson had met him at the Fiat Café in the Village. She was an attractive and lively defense attorney from Brooklyn. Their encounter was pleasant, but ultimately reopened a wound Adama had bandaged poorly.

Their conversation included familiar topics, beginning with the ever-popular work and careers, followed by ambitious yet unfulfilled travel plans, and, of course, family dynamics, always good for a chuckle. And then, with a couple of drinks and relaxed inhibitions, it surfaced, like a shark circling in warm waters. The main course, waiting to be devoured, is the taboo subject of past relationships and breakups.

Beverly shared about her new divorce proceedings, which immediately triggered feelings of déjà vu and regret in Adama. The latter snagged Adama like a treacherous undertow, churning suppressed feelings of heartache and pain. As his heart pounded, the current threatened to drag him under with unresolved grief. He fought to maintain his composure, resurfaced, and silently caught his breath. Beverly's perceptive gaze understood.

"Oh my god, you're *still* in love with her." Her words reverberated through every fiber of his being. She had inadvertently called him out, and he was guilty as charged.

Adama politely redirected the conversation. They took a short walk after he paid the check, both acknowledging he wasn't ready to date. He hailed a cab, and she kissed him on the cheek.

"You're amazing. If things change, you can reach me at this number. Good luck to you, Adama." She compassionately touched his cheek. Adama thanked her and paid the cab fare for her ride back to Brooklyn. Beverly waved as the taxi merged into traffic.

On his solitary drive home, memories of Bridget Murphy flooded his thoughts—their first meeting and the notorious case that took them to Paris. The "City of Lights" illuminated an intense connection that electrified them both. After solving the case, they returned home and became inseparable. He believed she was *the one*. But four months prior, Bridget abruptly severed their relationship, claiming she needed time and space, no questions asked. The breakup was life-changing for Adama, leaving him bewildered, doubtful, and torn.

While Adama mechanically dressed for jogging, he allowed himself to go there again. *I wonder how she's doing? Is she still in France?*

Saturday evening forced him to confront the depth of his feelings about his lost love and the need to let go. He did not realize how much resentment he harbored toward Bridget, and his hurt turned to anger.

"Enough!" He said aloud, breaking the silence as he laced up his black running shoes. "I need to stop feeling sorry for myself and find a way forward without Bridget. And maybe blind dates aren't so bad after all. Beverly is right, everything works out for the best. Time to put some joy in my life."

———◆———

The air was cool and crisp, and the sun had peeked over the horizon in the eastern sky. Adama stretched and headed out for his jog along the Hudson. He breathed deeply, felt energized, and the rhythm steadied his thoughts. As he approached the halfway point near Pier 84, Adama stopped where the Harbor Unit had pulled two young men from the river on Friday night. Adama untangled the yellow crime scene tape remnants bound to a "No Parking" sign. He tossed it into a trash can along with an empty water bottle lying on the ground.

"Such a shame," Adama said aloud as he walked around the area. He knew firsthand what it meant to be fortunate enough to get a job on a container ship.

Why kill those two men? What had they gotten themselves into, and why can't I shake the feeling that something is off about their case? By now, their ship was somewhere in the Atlantic Ocean. Adama knew the chances of finding the killers were slim.

At home, Adama showered, dressed, and sat down to breakfast when his cell phone rang.

"Hey Ricky, what's up?"

"We've got a dead billionaire."

"Really? Who?"

"The vic's name is William Vanhorn."

"Who's that?"

"Someone with a lot of money and the biggest yacht I've ever been on. Listen, we may have a shitstorm on our hands. Are you busy? Cause we could use your help."

"Sure," Adama said. "Are you at the Columbia 33 Marina in Brooklyn?"

"That's the one, we're at slip twenty-nine."

"I'm on my way." Adama grabbed his keys and left.

After the forty-minute drive, Adama advanced toward the superyacht. Removing his sunglasses, he tried not to be impressed. The name, "Wild One," was painted on the ship's side. Adama found Detective Burke talking with a police officer near the yacht's entrance.

"Hey, Ricky. What have you got?"

"Good morning. A press nightmare. Let's go inside."

Burke and Adama ducked under the yellow crime scene tape. Adama saw crew members lined up along the sides of the yacht.

"Amazing, isn't it? Wait till you see the inside." Ricky motioned to follow.

"Have you taken any statements?"

"We just started. Officers are meeting with the crew."

"How many people on board?" Adama asked.

"I have a count of seven crew and ten guests."

"That's a lot of people. Did you call the medical examiner?"

"She's on the way," Ricky said.

Burke guided Adama onto a canopy-covered main deck with exquisite Siebensee outdoor lounging furniture. The open-air feeling
and vista were stunning. An extended patio allowed guests to wander,
lounge, or sit in a hot tub.

"This way. Watch your head and step." Ricky pointed up and
down. Both men ducked and stepped over the sliding rail into the
main living room. A Steinway grand piano dominated the entryway.
Nearby was a large, crescent-shaped, sea-green couch and a marble
coffee table with fresh-cut roses in a crystal vase. They walked past
a grouping of four designer armchairs and a formal dining room that
seated eight.

Burke led Adama down a spiral staircase, where they descended
in single file. Adama looked around, making sure they were alone.

"What do you know about Vanhorn?" Adama asked.

"William Vanhorn was sixty-four years old, divorced twice, and
worth over a billion. He owns several properties, with a main house
in Palm Beach, Florida. He sailed up a couple of nights ago. He was
a famous televised evangelical minister, forced to resign due to a
dozen pending sexual harassment cases. And last month, he was arrested for two counts of statutory rape and seven counts of drug possession for using Rohypnol. He was out on bail." Burke turned down
a hallway on the port side of the ship.

"What's he doing up here?" Adama asked. "Anything else?"

"Yes. The man liked to party with young women and was with
four last night."

"Are they still here?"

"Yup. The captain said the ship was locked down after midnight,
and everyone was present and accounted for. And we've secured the
scene for Dr. Pearson."

"Good work, Ricky."

"Thanks." Ricky pointed. "Vanhorn is in here."

A uniformed police officer stepped aside upon seeing the two detectives. Burke used a master passkey to gain entry. He pushed and
held the door open while Adama stood in the doorway. His eyes
worked counterclockwise, taking it all in as he observed. Both men
used booties to cover their shoes and stepped into the bedroom.

"Who called it in?" Adama asked, gloves snapping.

"The captain. Vanhorn was supposed to leave for a meeting by seven-thirty but never showed for breakfast. When they buzzed him, he didn't respond. The captain was notified and found the body."

"Okay. Who was the last person seen with Vanhorn last night?"

"It was four young ladies. From what we've pieced together, Vanhorn was up top with the ladies from nine-thirty to twelve-thirty. They all left the jacuzzi together and came in here. Then Vanhorn got angry, kicked three out immediately, kept one, and kicked her out about ten minutes later."

"And their alibis?"

"They all vouched for each other."

"Of course they did." Adama looked around the bedroom. "Okay, set me up with the captain first, then the *last* woman. Get the ladies' statements, Ricky, and bring in more people to manage the crew and guests. Nothing gets out. The last thing we need is a press nightmare."

"Got it." Ricky paused. "You coming?"

"I need the room for a minute."

Adama preferred to walk crime scenes alone. His staff called it "magic time" because he was skilled at figuring out what had happened, observing what was right or wrong, and identifying what was missing or out of place. Burke had worked on many homicides with numerous detectives, but none were as intuitive as Adama. The entire team envied Adama's sixth sense.

"Magic time?"

Adama gave him a side glance. "You guys need to let that go. It's not magic. It's observation and deduction. Besides, I like the quiet."

"I'll go find the captain." Burke left.

The room was tastefully decorated in a classical deco style with panoramic windows. The sun cast shadows around the room. The plush white carpet looked like it had just been vacuumed, except where distinct footprints made deep impressions.

The king-size bed rested on a platform, making it the room's centerpiece, with two end tables on either side. The left end table displayed an array of items: a full pillbox, an unopened four-pack of

Viagra, several condoms, four small vials of cocaine, a mirror, and a plastic card.

Adama walked carefully, avoiding obvious prints on the carpet. A circular-shaped mirror hung over the bed, drawing his eyes upward, where he saw the reflection of Vanhorn's twisted naked torso. He thought it would be the crime scene investigator's dream situation. Adama glanced down at Vanhorn's body. Reaching for a tape recorder, he noted the time and pushed the "record" button.

"Deputy Chief Baptiste. Sunday, May seventh, eight-thirty a.m. No CME or CSI team on site yet. Several footprints led to the bed's left side and extended onto the platform. Two sets of trails lead to the windows, one smaller, the other larger, perhaps Vanhorn and one of the ladies. A sheet, comforter, man's robe, swimming trunks, and men's slippers lay beside the bed."

Adama pushed pause and approached the king-size bed. He resumed recording, describing the possible sadism and masochism spectacle before him.

"On the bed, one deceased male. The victim's head is covered with a clear plastic bag, secured by a belt at the neck. The deceased's body rests in a seated position, back against the headboard. The victim's head and upper torso lean slightly to the left. Both arms outstretched across the headboard, like a seated crucifix. Both hands were snared by leather handcuffs, with straps attached to vertical bars on bedposts. The victim's feet are snared by handcuffs attached to a wooden bar approximately three feet long with spikes on the ends. Indications of an S&M sex game gone wrong. Was this an accident or a murder?" He paused the recorder.

Adama tracked a distinct set of footprints toward the right side of the bed, leading to the nightstand, which was empty except for a small desk phone. Adama opened the nightstand to see a small piece of paper taped to the inside. He looked sideways and read, "R6, L21, R3, L11." He closed the drawer and restarted his recorder.

"A large set of bare footprints steps off the platform, goes to the closet, and returns to the bed. The smaller set was definitely made by someone wearing shoes. That set comes in from the door, walks around the end of the bed, stops at the end table, then turns around and returns to the door." *Hmm, now who might you be?*

"Questions: Did they touch Vanhorn, remove something from the nightstand, and leave? Was Vanhorn alive or dead? Did they kill Vanhorn?"

Adama paused the recorder. From where he stood, he could see Vanhorn's cuffed left hand dangling from the restraint. He restarted the recorder.

"Blood stains on the victim's left wrist and hand, blood smears on the cuffs, headboard, and sheets. The victim's left wrist appears to be twisted and mangled. Looks like Vanhorn struggled. The right wrist appears to demonstrate the same."

A bright flash made Adama squint. He paused the recorder and turned to see a mahogany box on the couch—seven feet long, two feet wide, six inches deep, with a satin finish. Two vintage locks lay on the sofa beside it, along with a smaller jewelry box bearing the initials "WV" on a brass plate; it was empty. A glint on the carpet caught his eye—a skeleton key, unexpectedly heavy in his gloved hand, its handle studded with seven diamonds. Adama assumed it opened the vintage locks. *What's in there?* He reached out to open the lid of the mahogany box, but three quick knocks interrupted him. The bedroom door opened.

"Excuse me, Deputy Chief, the CME is here," Ricky said.

"Thanks." Adama put the key back where he found it on the carpet. "Hey, Ricky, did you walk around to the right-hand side of the bed or near the closet?"

"No, why?"

"Just a hunch."

On his way out, Adama put his recorder in his pocket. He saw Dr. Pearson with two forensic technicians, dressed in white coveralls, knee pads, gloves, hairnets, and booties. Each carried a duffle bag with a crime scene kit.

"Didn't think I'd see you again so soon," Dr. Pearson said. She glanced into the room. "Oh my. *What* have we got here?"

"Listen, Doc, there are lots of footprints in here, including two clean sets on the right side of the bed. They're not mine or Ricky's. I need to know who they belong to."

"We'll take care of it." Dr. Pearson motioned for her assistants to follow.

"I'll leave you to it and check in later." Adama went to find Burke.

"Hey, Ricky, I didn't see a cellphone in the room. Did you?"

"Come to think of it, no. I'll find out if he had one and trace it."

"Thanks. Let's go find the captain."

"She's waiting for you in the library. It's this way."

Detective Burke and Adama left Vanhorn's bedroom and walked single file up the spiral staircase to the main deck. Four young women engaged in conversation were distracted as Adama and Burke walked into the room. Their eyes tracked them, watchful and nervous as cats, until they both stepped through a sliding door to the yacht's starboard side.

Chapter 16: Captain Ricci

The library was a cozy space, with wall-to-wall bookcases. Brass bars held the books in place. A large old-world floor globe rested in one corner. There were several pieces of furniture: one loveseat, two green and white striped wingback chairs, and a small library table. The ship captain was perusing a book about sailing and looked up when Burke and Adama stepped into the room. Burke made the introductions.

"Captain Ricci, this is Deputy Chief Baptiste."

The captain set the book down and greeted Adama. He was surprised to see a woman standing before him. She was attractive, maybe forty years old, with olive skin, almond-shaped eyes, dark eyeliner, mauve lipstick, and sculpted eyebrows. She stood five feet seven inches tall with long black hair twisted around a large comb. Her uniform consisted of a short-sleeved white shirt with two front pockets, black slacks, and black shoes. Her name tag read "Captain Ricci." Each shoulder held an embroidered epaulette with four gold stripes, signifying her rank as captain.

"Uh, nice to meet you, Captain."

"I get that a lot." Captain Ricci's accent was Italian.

"What's that?" Adama reached inside his jacket for his badge.

"Most people are surprised when they meet a woman captain."

"I'll bet." He displayed his badge. "I understand you found the body."

"Yes. That's correct."

"Was the door locked or unlocked?"

"It was locked. I knocked but got no answer," Captain Ricci said. "I used my master key to open the door."

"Who else has a key to Mr. Vanhorn's bedroom?"

"Me, Mr. Vanhorn, my second officer. And now your detective."
She looked at Burke.

"Was your second officer in the bedroom?"

"No. He remained at the helm while I came to Mr. Vanhorn's
room. After I called the bridge for help, I locked Mr. Vanhorn's door.
I posted a crew member to stand guard with instructions that no one
would enter until the police arrived."

"Very efficient of you," Adama said. "Was Mr. Vanhorn onboard
the yacht the entire time?"

"No, Mr. Vanhorn went out Saturday evening at six o'clock."

"Do you know where he went?"

"No. But his limousine driver should be able to give you an address."

"Right." Adama glanced at Burke, who nodded.

"What time did Mr. Vanhorn come back to the yacht?"

"Mr. Vanhorn's limousine returned at nine-thirty last night. My
crew and I mustered to welcome him aboard."

"Was he alone? And did anything unusual happen afterwards?"

"Yes, he was alone and told me to expect a special delivery. Two
men arrived with a large wooden box a couple of hours later. I notified Mr. Vanhorn, and he escorted them to his bedroom. They left
five minutes later. It's in our log."

"Did you see or speak to Mr. Vanhorn after the two men left?"

"Yes. He was on deck with the guests all evening. We maintain
an accurate log of each person who comes and goes. Everyone was
present and accounted for. I gave a copy of our manifest to your detective."

"Thank you. Captain, when was the last time you spoke with Mr.
Vanhorn?"

"Mr. Vanhorn called me at twelve-forty-five a.m. He asked not
to be disturbed for the rest of the evening. He also said he'd be down
for breakfast at seven."

"Did you touch him or anything in the room?"

"Well, yes, I saw him on the bed, and he wasn't moving. His lips
were blue. I couldn't get to his neck, so I checked his wrist for a pulse;

there wasn't one. I used Mr. Vanhorn's room phone to notify the bridge; they called the police."

"What about his cellphone? Our team hasn't found one yet."

"Oh, I don't know, he usually carried it with him."

"Okay. Does everyone on board have a passport?" Adama asked.

"Yes, we have detailed information on the crew and our guests," she replied.

"Okay, thanks, you've been very helpful. We'll need to take your fingerprints and shoes."

"Why do you need those?"

"It's procedure, so we can identify where you walked and what you touched."

"Oh, I see."

"Also, this entire ship and the dock area are considered a crime scene, which means no one is allowed to leave."

"Of course, I understand," Captain Ricci said.

Adama and Burke watched her leave.

"What do you think?" Ricky asked.

"I think she's hiding something. I want to speak with the woman now. And Ricky, check all the passports and find Vanhorn's phone."

"Will do. The ladies are back this way." Ricky led Adama away from the library and into the main cabin.

Chapter 17: What Case?

Adama and Detective Burke entered the main cabin and saw four young ladies. Three of them sat together, but the fourth young woman sat by herself, curled up in a chair.

"They look like babies," Adama said, concern evident in his voice.

"We have their statements. All four are under eighteen." Ricky's eyebrows raised.

"Seriously? Under eighteen?" Adama scoffed. "Well, Captain Ricci, you've got some explaining to do."

"Yeah, and Vanhorn was a real scumbag," Ricky agreed. "What do you want to do?"

Adama thought for a moment. "Nothing yet. We don't know who was involved. And I don't want the captain spooked. We don't need a Coast Guard chase on our hands. So, we'll hold them all here," Adama said. "Who was the last one with Vanhorn?"

"The girl sitting in the chair. Her name is Cheryl Parker."

"Thanks, Ricky." Adama approached the young woman.

"Hello, Cheryl, I'm Deputy Chief Baptiste. I have a few questions." Adama showed his badge. "Please follow me to the library."

Cheryl was seventeen years old. She wore a cute white pants outfit that flattered her slender body. Her face was narrow, with blue eyes, and minimal makeup. Her body posture revealed a frightened young woman. Once inside the library, Cheryl slouched in a wingback chair and folded her arms across her narrow chest.

"I already told that other guy everything I know." She sulked.

"Yes, I'm aware, and thank you. Please describe Mr. Vanhorn's behavior last night."

"Well, Billy was in a good mood all night. Laughing and joking. But as soon as we walked into the bedroom, he changed. He started acting weird. He yelled for us to get out, but grabbed me." Cheryl instinctively rubbed her right arm.

"Then what?"

"Then nothing. He got quiet and looked a bit sad. We just sat at the end of his bed. That's when I saw that big box and asked what it was. Billy jumped up and said it was beautiful, and there was a story that made it priceless. So, I asked if I could see it. He seemed happy again and opened the lid."

"What was in the box?" Adama recalled wanting a peek himself.

"Um, some kinda rock, I think. I tried to touch it, but he yelled and told me to leave. He scared me."

"What time was that?"

"I don't know, a few minutes later."

"Five? Ten minutes? How long?"

"I guess it was about ten minutes."

"Okay, you're doing fine, Cheryl. Now, tell me about sex toys."

Cheryl's mouth dropped open. Adama repeated the question. She reluctantly answered.

"Well, sometimes we used them." Cheryl's voice was low, and she quickly added, "But not last night."

"What about the other ladies?"

"Not that I know of. Billy said no one knew about them except me. Billy was paranoid and said his reputation would be ruined if anyone found out. But we didn't use them last night. They weren't even out of their case."

"What case?"

"Inside his closet. It has a combination lock, and he's the only one who knows it."

"Okay, thank you." Adama recalled the four numbers he had read inside the nightstand. "Cheryl, does Mr. Vanhorn have a cellphone?"

"Yeah, he's on it all the time."

"Did you see him with it last night?"

She looked down, thinking. "Um, yeah, I saw him put it on the nightstand by the closet."

Adama carefully observed her face and asked, "Cheryl, did you take his cellphone or anything else from the room?"

She reacted immediately. "What? No. He practically pushed me out the door."

Adama believed her. He handed her one of his cards.

"Am I done? Am I in trouble?" Tears dropped onto Cheryl's cheeks.

Adama stood up and tried to reassure her. "You're fine. Try to get some rest." He felt sorry for her and the other girls. He had seen too many young women exploited by men with nefarious intentions.

Adama left the library to find Burke waiting in the main cabin. They walked back toward Vanhorn's bedroom.

"Well, what do you think? Did she spill?" Ricky asked.

Adama shook his head. "She didn't kill him. Vanhorn kicked all the ladies out by twelve-forty. The captain said Vanhorn called her at twelve-forty-five. The timeline works if we can verify his phone call."

"I've already asked for the phone logs," Ricky said.

"Good. I noticed security cameras onboard. Get the digital files so we can verify everyone's whereabouts. Have a forensics team search Vanhorn's bedroom for hidden cameras. And tell them to find out what's inside the locked case in the closet. The combination is written on a piece of paper inside the right-hand nightstand."

"No kidding. Anything else?" Ricky asked as they walked down the spiral staircase.

"Yeah, and you'll love this. Cheryl saw Vanhorn's cellphone on the nightstand."

"No way! So, someone took it. Okay, I'll have our mobile tech team track it down."

"Good. Let's go talk with Dr. Pearson."

"We can't. She got another call about a death at a gallery in midtown. Her team finished their work here and packed up Vanhorn's body and anything that wasn't tied down. But the forensic team will stay on site until the end. Dr. Pearson told me to tell you that she's going to the morgue with Vanhorn, and one of her assistant medical examiners will manage the gallery case."

"Which gallery?"

"Miller Antiquities, on W. 56th."

"Who's on scene over there?"

"Bobby Gates is on his way."

"Good. I'll head over there. You stay here and wrap up."

"Sounds good."

"Oh, hey, Ricky?"

"Yeah, I know, find Vanhorn's phone."

"Well, yes. But I was going to say, good job."

"Thanks, boss."

Adama walked to his car, got in, and checked his phone for messages. A minute later, a car pulled up and parked nearby. A young man got out, leaned against his car, and looked at his phone. Thirty seconds later, a second car pulled alongside; the driver got out. Adama recognized both men; the first was Mark Dawson, his neighbor, the reporter. And the second man was Jason Walker, known by every detective in Manhattan as Mr. Cut-Throat from the Manhattan Gazette.

Adama said aloud, "Well, well, looks like the press knows about Vanhorn. That didn't take long. And look who hit the big time—good for you, Mark." Adama called Ricky Burke as he started the car and pulled away.

"Did you forget something?" Ricky asked.

"No. Heads up, the press is here. They're coming to you."

"Already! Okay, I'll manage it. Thanks."

"Later."

Detective Burke was great at managing the press. Adama knew he would ensure the captain posted a sentry by the gate to keep reporters away from the yacht.

Chapter 18: 911

Jacqueline Miller caught her rescheduled flight from Washington, D.C., to New York City at seven a.m. After landing at JFK, she took a limousine straight to the gallery. She punched in the security code—no change in color or sound. *Tommy must be here.* Opening the second security door, her senses were bombarded by the putrid stench of dead fish.

Ugh, what is that? She immediately called out, "Hello? Tommy, are you here?"

Jacqueline listened for a moment and walked into the gallery. She noticed the high-top tables, empty champagne bottles, wilted flowers, burnt-out candles, a buffet table loaded with stale hors d'oeuvres, bowls of shrimp cocktail, and half-eaten caviar floating in water.

"Oh, Thomas, what did you do?" Jacqueline walked to the office. When she reached the doorway, she saw Thomas lying face down on the desk and thought he was sleeping.

"Tommy, wake up." She raised her voice. "Thomas!"

Jacqueline walked over and nudged his arm. He did not move. She knew something was wrong. Her purse and keys slipped through her fingers to the floor.

"Oh my god! Tommy! Are you all right? Tommy, wake up!"

Her instincts told her that he was dead, but she refused to believe it. After calling 911, the operator asked several questions and gave instructions about how to check for a pulse. Jacqueline confirmed that Thomas was dead. The operator told her the police were on the way and not to touch anything.

Jacqueline barely reached the foyer before her legs gave way and she collapsed onto a nearby chair. She crossed her arms around her body and rocked back and forth to comfort herself. "Oh Tommy, dear

Tommy." Guttural sobs emanated from her weakened body. Jacqueline looked outside, searching, desperately hoping the police would arrive.

The tables, covered in half-eaten food and empty champagne bottles, caught her attention, all evidence of an unsanctioned event. *Oh god, Tommy, what happened?* She stood and stared out the front door, "Come on! Where are you?" she said aloud, waiting for the police.

Six minutes later, two police officers knocked on the door. Jacqueline let them inside. They took a quick look around the gallery area. The first officer took control of the questioning while the second officer stood nearby, scanning the gallery.

"Hello, ma'am. Did you call the police?"

"Yes, it's my brother. I think he's dead, please help him." Jacqueline sobbed.

"What's your name, ma'am?"

"Jacqueline Miller."

"Where is your brother?"

"He's in the office. God, I can't believe this is happening." She pointed.

The second officer entered the office, found Thomas, and checked his neck and wrist.

"No pulse. I'm calling it in." He spoke into his shoulder radio to call for backup and a medical examiner. He conducted a cursory review of the office for weapons and other items.

"Is anyone else on site?" the first officer asked Jacqueline.

"Uh, I don't know. I didn't check."

"Ma'am, I need you to stay here until I return."

The first officer called out to his partner. "We need to clear the scene."

The two officers joined up and conducted a standard search of the premises. Once secured, the first officer asked Jacqueline questions and obtained her complete statement.

"A detective is on the way to speak with you. This officer will stay with you." He pointed to a woman police officer who had arrived on site. She identified herself and stood protectively. Jacqueline acknowledged her.

Jimmy Quinn was the first forensic technician to arrive. He wore traditional attire to preserve the premises. He stood in the office doorway and observed Thomas's upper torso slumped over the desk. He set his crime scene kit down and retrieved his camera. Working counterclockwise, Quinn took meticulous photos of the office, the coat rack, pictures, and furniture in the room. He took photographs of Thomas's body hunched over the desk, still clutching a cellphone in his left hand. Quinn repeated the process with a digital video camera.

When finished, Quinn laid out a black tarp and retrieved several items from his bag.

"Did anyone touch the body?" Quinn asked the officer standing outside the door.

"Yes. My partner checked his neck, and so did the owner, Jacqueline Miller. And she used the desk phone to call it in."

"Okay, I'll need her fingerprints and her shoes. Has anyone heard from the CME?"

"We called. She's at another crime scene. An assistant medical examiner is on the way."

"Okay, I'll get started."

Outside the gallery, Detective Robert "Bobby" Gates arrived. He signed in, pulled gloves and booties out of a box, and put them on. He perused the gallery, observing the setup for the special event. "Someone had a good time," He said to no one. An officer nodded and guided him to the office.

Detective Gates was thoughtful, carefully viewing the gallery and the party atmosphere as he walked through. He was forty, had short black hair, brown eyes, and was physically fit. He lived in Brooklyn with his wife and three sons. Gates and Quinn acknowledged each other.

"What have we got?" Gates asked.

"One male, approximately thirty-five to forty years old, was found face down. No blood, no weapons, no signs of a struggle."

"Okay, thanks. Are you finished with pictures and videos?"

"Yes, he's all yours." Quinn put his camera in its pouch.

"Okay, let's see what we've got."

Gates walked over to Thomas to observe his lifeless body and the desk.

"Is that his cellphone?" Gates pointed.

"Don't know. That's how I found it. I didn't touch it. I need to bag it."

Gates tried to remove the phone from Thomas's left hand, but it was stuck—rigor mortis was firmly set. Gates knew that Thomas's fingers could break if he used force. Suddenly, the blackened phone screen lit up.

"Well, look at that, the vic tried to call 911, but he didn't push the send button. That's a shame. Whatever got him came on fast and hard. Hey Quinn, get a photo of this, please."

Quinn brought his camera over and took several photographs from different angles, capturing the 911 numbers displayed on the phone.

"You're gonna need to figure out how to get that phone into an evidence bag so it doesn't get lost," Gates said.

"I'll wait for the assistant ME. She'll probably want me to bag his hands with the phone intact."

"Good thought. Okay, let's see what he's got in his pockets."

Gates patted Thomas's pants and reached inside. He found a wallet, opened it, and found two driver's licenses.

"Interesting, our victim lives in Manhattan and has two licenses, one current, under the name of Thomas Chevalier, and one expired under the name of Thomas Miller. He's also got a couple of credit cards and a nice wad of cash."

Gates took several hundred-dollar bills out of the wallet. He counted the cash and placed each bill on the desk with the credit cards and the driver's license.

"It's a thousand dollars. Take a picture of the bills and the other items for me. And don't forget the vic's Rolex wristwatch and diamond pinky ring. Take a picture of that package of Rolaids next to his hand and bag it too."

Quinn took photographs while Gates removed the watch and put it into an evidence bag. The pinky finger was curled rigorously, so

Gates left the diamond ring alone. He put the wallet and its contents into separate evidence bags and tagged them.

Next, Gates checked the pockets of Thomas's tuxedo jacket. The outside pockets were both empty. Checking the inside pockets proved challenging. Thomas's body was hunched over. Gates kneeled and reached into the inside pockets. One was empty, and the other had a folded paper sticking out. Gates removed it and saw an airplane ticket.

"Well, it looks like our guy was going to the Cayman Islands. It's for a Monday flight, first class no less. Huh, that's interesting, it's only one-way."

Gates placed the ticket on the desk, and Jimmy took a photograph. The ticket was placed in an evidence bag. Gates searched the desk drawers, lifted papers, looked under the organizers, and opened a couple of notebooks. He didn't see anything worth mentioning.

"Hey, Jimmy, make sure all these items are bagged and tagged."

"Will do." Quinn noticed a co-worker standing in the doorway. "Hello, Doctor Robinson."

Detective Gates looked up to see Beth Robinson, M.D., an assistant medical examiner. She was a plus-size woman who filled out her white coveralls. She wore gloves, a mask, knee pads, booties, and a hair net.

"How many people have walked all over my crime scene?" Dr. Robinson asked.

"A few," Gates offered.

"What have we got?" She said as she carefully entered the room and set her bag down.

"You tell us, and we'll know our next move," Gates said.

"Do we have an ID?"

"Yes. Thomas Chevalier or Thomas Miller, depending on which license he's using at the time."

"Has anyone touched the body?"

"Yours truly. I searched the pockets. And two others, the first officer on scene and the owner, checked for a pulse."

"Uh-huh." She moved toward the victim. "Excuse me, detective."

Detective Gates stepped aside as Dr. Robinson approached Thomas's body. She examined the head, neck, and back for signs of foul play; no cuts, no bruises, or puncture marks were evident. She pressed her fingers into the face, eyelids, cheeks, and jawbone to assess rigor mortis.

Dr. Robinson removed Thomas's left shoe and sock, revealing the bluish-purple discoloration of lividity—blood pooling in the lower extremities. The right shoe remained untouched. She had the information needed to evaluate Thomas's postmortem state.

"He's been dead for at least twelve hours—we've got full rigor and lividity. There are no external signs of a struggle, no ligature marks, no obvious puncture wounds. He's young, we'll need an autopsy and labs to determine the cause of death."

She observed the chair where Thomas sat.

"Good, he's sitting on castor wheels. Quinn and Gates, help me roll the chair away to examine his chest area."

"Um, Doc, there's a phone in his hand," Gates said.

"Did you try to take it?"

"Yes, it's stuck."

"Right. It's not going anywhere. Now, carefully hold and simultaneously push the body away from the desk."

Quinn and Gates worked together. They held Thomas up and intact while the doctor knelt to examine the front of his torso.

"Okay, thanks. No blood, no wounds, no obvious signs of foul play. Let's return him to the desk and get him ready to be moved to our lab stat."

"So, no foul play here?" Gates asked. "You think a heart attack?"

"No idea. A heart attack seems unlikely given his age. We'll know more after tests."

"Well, something killed him. Drugs?" Gates asked.

"Were any drugs or drug paraphernalia found here?" she asked.

"Nothing on the desk or floor when I got here," Quinn said.

"I didn't find anything in his pockets. And there's nothing in the drawers. However, we still need to complete our search of the premises. Does this make his death suspicious?"

"Why, detective, what is so suspicious about a seemingly healthy young man, with no visible signs of foul play, found dead for no apparent reason?"

"Well, when you put it that way. But it's weird. Right?"

"Yes, Gates, it seems suspicious." She turned to Quinn. "Jimmy, bag the hands for me. I also want hair samples." She firmly addressed Gates' concerns.

"So, detective, I know you want answers. When I know the cause of death, you'll know. That's all I've got for you. Let us finish here."

"Okay." Gates took the hint. He left the office to see Adama walking into the gallery.

"Hey, Deputy Chief."

"Hey Bobby, how are you? How's the family?"

"All good, thanks."

"What have you got here?"

"One male, deceased, two driver's licenses, two names. One says he's Thomas Chevalier, and the other, expired, says Thomas Miller, thirty-six years of age. No apparent cause of death. No signs of foul play. Looks like the vic died here last night. For now, the assistant ME is calling it suspicious.

"Two different last names, huh. And one matches this gallery?"

"Oh, he had a one-way ticket to the Caymans, leaving this Monday."

"One-way? That's interesting." Adama looked around the gallery arena. "Looks like they had a nice event here. What do we know about the attendees? Do we know if anything is missing?"

"Unknown. I asked the gallery owner, Jacqueline Miller, for a list of party attendees, but she stated no event was scheduled. So, we'll need to figure out who was here. She's also the victim's sister. We put her in a squad car outside."

When Adama first arrived, he noticed surveillance cameras on the street and several cameras throughout the gallery area.

"Hey, Bobby, there's an inside closed-circuit system in the gallery and at least two outside surveillance cameras on the street. Can you get the feeds from both systems?"

"Already on that. Hopefully, we'll see who came and went in the last twenty-four hours," Gates said.

Adama approached the office and saw Quinn and the Assistant ME working.

"Hey, everyone, how's it going?" Adama asked.

"Hello, Deputy Chief," Quinn said. "I called my boss, but she isn't picking up."

"Your boss is on her way to the morgue."

Hearing a familiar voice, Dr. Robinson stopped work and raised her head. "Good morning, Adama." Her smile lit up the office.

"Hello, Dr. Robinson. I hear you're calling this case suspicious."

"Yes, and we're preparing the victim for transport to the lab."

"Okay. Did Gates get what we need for now?"

"Yes." She leaned forward slightly. "But if you want, I'll share more information with you."

"That's okay. We'll come by the lab later today or tomorrow."

"Great. And it's nice to see you again, Adama." Her voice lifted, hoping for some interaction.

"You, too, Doctor Robinson." Adama's tone was neutral. He scanned the office rather than meet her gaze.

Quinn saw the doctor grinning like an infatuated teenager with a schoolgirl crush. It was no secret at the medical examiner's office that Dr. Robinson was sweet on Adama. She looked like a love-sick puppy every time he came around. However, Adama was only interested in a professional working relationship. He was careful not to encourage any special attention.

Adama noticed the coat rack. "Has anyone gone through this garment bag?"

"I'll work that next," Quinn said.

"Okay, I'll leave you to it." Adama walked away.

"See you later, Adama," Dr. Robinson called out.

Quinn put on new gloves and unzipped the garment bag. He searched the pockets and cataloged each item, including a flask of bourbon, a half-used roll of Tums antacid, and two vials of cocaine, one full, one empty.

Chapter 19: Jacqueline Miller

A woman officer stood nearby while Jacqueline Miller sat quietly in the squad car's back seat with the door open. She watched all the commotion from law enforcement officers and medical personnel as they came and went from her gallery. A technician approached the vehicle.

"Miss Miller, we need to take your fingerprints," the woman technician said.

"Okay, but I own the gallery. My prints will be everywhere."

"It's standard procedure and won't take long," she assured her.

Gates stood outside under the awning on the stoop. He pulled a package of gum out of his pocket and put a piece into his mouth. He watched Miss Miller cooperate with the technician. Crime scene tape sectioned off a thirty-foot perimeter outside the gallery. Crowds had gathered on both sides of the street.

Adama stepped outside and asked Gates about the gallery owner.

"Is Miss Miller still here, Bobby?" Adama asked.

"Yes, she's in that squad car; they're getting her prints." Gates pointed at the car parked behind Thomas's Porsche.

"Tell me what you know about her."

Detective Gates provided an overview of Jacqueline's identity, including her brother's location, her whereabouts, and when she returned to the gallery.

"An officer took her statement. I've got someone checking her alibi about her trip to D.C. When we asked about possible perpetrators, she mentioned the victim liked to gamble and that their father occasionally paid off his debts. We're checking with local bookies to determine if he owed any money. Also, she confirmed that our victim is the son of Henry Miller, the other gallery owner."

"I know of Henry Miller. Where is he?" Adama asked.

"According to Miss Miller, he had a massive heart attack three weeks ago and has been bedridden at home with full-time nurses."

"Has he been notified about his son's death?"

"Not yet. Miss Miller is concerned and wants to be with him. She's pretty shaken up."

"Right. Well, the crowd is growing larger. This will hit the news soon. After I speak with her, ensure she gets to her father before he hears about his son on television."

"I'll take care of it," Gates said.

"Does the victim have any financial interest in the gallery?" Adama asked.

"None that we could find. Henry Miller and his daughter Jacqueline have been partners since 1992. Miss Miller mentioned that our vic spends most of his time with the ponies."

Adama and Gates started down the steps. Jacqueline saw them coming. She dabbed her eyes with a tissue and cleared her throat. She stood up as Gates introduced them.

On approach, Adama showed his badge. "I'm very sorry for your loss, Miss Miller. I'll be brief so you can spend time with your father. Did anything unusual happen with Thomas recently?"

"Not really. Tommy has seemed happy over the past few weeks. He's been helping me manage the gallery while our father has been ill." Jacqueline looked down at the sidewalk.

"Is there something else?" Adama observed her expression.

"Well …" she hesitated, wringing her hands. "It's probably nothing, but I received an unusual call a couple of weeks ago. A broker wanted to use our gallery for a private event. I turned him down because the date didn't work, so it can't be him."

Gates and Adama looked at each other. Adama thought about how naïve Jacqueline was.

"Do you recall his name?" Adama leaned in.

"Yes. It stuck with me because it sounded like a movie character—Dr. Jeeves."

"What did he want?" Adama asked.

"He had antiquities from Africa requiring an exclusive viewing space. I never heard of him, but he mentioned being referred by our most significant patron."

"Who was that?"

"Miss Daisy Hunter." Jacqueline's eyes looked red and tired. "That's all I remember."

Adama gave Gates that look. "I'll check them both out," Gates said.

"You stated that you weren't aware of the event last night. Did your father, Henry Miller, know about it?"

"I don't think so. He never mentioned it to me. Why?" she asked.

"Thank you, Miss Miller. That's all we need for now. Here's my card if you think of anything else. A squad car will take you to your father now. Again, we're very sorry for your loss."

"Thank you, Deputy Chief." Jacqueline shook Adama's hand and watched as he headed back up the stairs to the gallery.

Gates saw that Jacqueline, like many other women, was somewhat taken with Adama. Gates once asked his wife, "Do you think Adama looks good?" Her reaction was immediate. "Are you kidding? He's a hunk!" Gates relented. *He's got the magic touch.* Then he refocused.

"Miss Miller? Is your internal security system working?"

"It should be. Why?"

"We'll need to view the digital videos for the past few days. Is there a password to your computer?"

"Yes, it's written on a card in the desk's top drawer."

"Thanks, I'll find it. If you're ready, we'll take you to your father's home now."

"Thank you very much." Jacqueline became emotional when she looked up to see medical personnel carrying the gurney with Thomas's body out the front door. She broke down crying as she followed a woman police officer and a person from the Liaison Unit to a squad car.

Gates was going to check the security videos when Adama approached, looking concerned.

"Hey, what's going on?" Gates asked.

"There's been a death at Le Chandelier Hotel—another billionaire, Miss Daisy Hunter." Adama saw Detective Burke's mouth drop open.

"What the ... no way! Who's on site over there?"

"Detective Sanchez and the CME are on their way. Listen, Bobby, you finish here; I'll head to the hotel. Bring Quinn with you when you've wrapped up here."

"Okay. Hey, Deputy Chief, why didn't you ask Miss Miller about Thomas's one-way ticket to the Caymans?"

"Have we verified it yet?"

"Not that I'm aware of."

"Well, there you go. Could you please check to see if Thomas Miller or Thomas Chevalier has an account in the Grand Cayman? And check out Miller Sr.—discreetly. I'll see you later."

"Will do." Gates admired his boss's strategic mindset. Adama once told him that asking questions also reveals information. And once admitted, it can be manipulated. Adama liked having aces up his sleeves, ready when needed. Gates turned his attention to the desktop computer.

———◆———

Forty minutes later, Jacqueline Miller and the NYPD liaison arrived at her father's home. In the elevator, Jacqueline wondered how she would tell her father about Thomas. When she walked into the bedroom, her father's eyes lit up. Henry Miller smiled, raised his hand, and waved. He looked happier and better than he had the day before. But his smile quickly faded when he saw her tears. He knew something was wrong as she rushed to his bedside.

"Jacquie? What's wrong?" he asked.

"Oh my god, Daddy, I don't know how to tell you." Jacqueline sobbed uncontrollably.

"What's wrong? Are you all right?" Miller patted his daughter's hand to calm her.

"It's Tommy. He's ... oh god, Tommy's gone, he's dead. I found him this morning."

104

"What? He's what? No! It can't be, I spoke with him last night. He's coming over today." The blood pressure monitor began beeping. "I don't believe it. He was fine. What happened?"

"Daddy, they don't know. They won't tell me anything. I returned from D.C. this morning and found Tommy in the office." Jacqueline sat in a chair by the bed and lay her head down. Miller stroked her hair to soothe her, while his heart pounded wildly.

"What do you mean they won't tell you. They have to tell us what happened to him!" Miller tried to sit up. "Where is my son? What did they do with my son, Thom—" He abruptly stopped talking, groaned, and clutched his chest.

"Daddy? Oh, Jesus, Daddy, what's wrong?" Jacqueline screamed, "Nurse! Nurse! What's happening?" she yelled.

Two nurses rushed into the room, which was filled with obnoxious noises from multiple monitors.

"Do something!" Jacqueline screamed. She watched the color drain from his face.

One nurse pushed Jacqueline aside to check Miller's vitals. He was in full cardiac arrest and was not breathing. The male nurse hopped onto the bed and began CPR. The other nurse called 911 for an ambulance, then readied the crash cart. The nurse yelled "clear" and used the defibrillator on Miller. After two shock sessions, Miller's heart stabilized. They continued to monitor him until the ambulance arrived. Jacqueline paced nearby, wringing her hands. The NYPD liaison tried to comfort her.

Within minutes, two paramedics rushed in, quickly moved Miller to the gurney, hooked up the portable drips, and pushed him to the elevator. Jacqueline and the two nurses followed behind. In the ambulance to Mt. Sinai Medical Center, Jacqueline clutched her father's hand.

"Daddy, it's going to be all right. We're going to Mt. Sinai, we're almost there. Hang on, Daddy, it's going to be okay."

By the time they arrived at the hospital, Miller had opened his eyes and smiled at his daughter. He tried to speak but lost consciousness.

Chapter 20: Daisy Hunter

Adama Baptiste arrived at Le Chandelier Hotel at noon. Walking into the foyer, his eyes were drawn to the spectrum of colors that shimmered throughout the entrance. The hotel was one of a kind, with a French-style theme running throughout. True to its name, two large, magnificent chandeliers adorned the entrance. Adama approached the front desk, showed his badge, and requested to speak with the manager. While waiting, he texted Detective Luis Sanchez.

"I'm here. Where are you?"

"Penthouse. You need an escort."

Adama saw an attractive woman in a blue suit coming toward him. "Good morning, my name is Sophie Matisse. I am the manager and owner. How may I be of assistance?" She extended her hand and was drawn into Adama's warm eyes. Her French accent was pleasing to him. Adama showed his badge.

"I'm Deputy Chief Baptiste. I need to go to the penthouse. Can you take me, madame?"

"Oui. This way." Matisse led Adama to the express elevators.

Matisse felt comfortable being with him, enjoyed the slight hint of his musky aftershave, and glanced at his left hand to see if he was wearing a wedding ring. The elevator music was pleasant and evoked a nostalgic feeling. Adama recognized the song, "Hymne À L'amour" by Edith Piaf. It was his mother's favorite song.

"Monsieur, as you can imagine, we're all upset about Miss Hunter. My family and I would appreciate your discretion in this matter."

"Pas de promesses, Madame. But we'll do our best," Adama said.

Miss Matisse smiled, knowing instantly that Adama was fluent in French. She found him even more appealing. However, his comment about "no promises" unnerved her. The elevator doors opened to an elegant foyer.

"This way, monsieur." Matisse unlocked the penthouse door.

Upon entering, Adama felt as though he had been transported back in time. It was a spacious area with high ceilings. The furniture was traditional, featuring King Louis XIV's gold tones and a Baroque-style, complete with all the classical elements of a French castle. To the right sat an Erard French Baroque-style grand piano; to the left, an ornate cabinet made of oak veneer, brass, ebony, and bronze figurines. Adama marveled at the intricacies and opulence of the furnishings. Miss Matisse proudly let him take it all in.

"The master bedroom is this way, monsieur."

"Thank you, Ms. Matisse. Would you please wait in the living room?"

Adama waited until the manager walked away, then opened the door to the bedroom. The noise caused Detective Luis Sanchez to stop writing in his notepad and glance up. Dr. Pearson, who hunched over Daisy Hunter's body, stopped her examination to look around.

"Hey, Deputy Chief," Sanchez said.

"Hey, Luis. How's it going?" Adama asked as he nodded at Dr. Pearson.

"In a word, strangely. Doc and I got here about ten minutes ago. Her staff is due anytime, so we need to make sure they can get up here."

"Right. Well, the hotel manager is in the living room. Let her know what you need."

Detective Sanchez was forty years old, with dark black hair, a full mustache, and a tall, slender build. He joined the force fifteen years earlier and quickly rose to the rank of Detective First Grade. Sanchez was fluent in Spanish. He lived in Brooklyn with his wife, four children, and a plethora of animals—dogs, cats, parakeets, hamsters, and goldfish. Sanchez was well-known for his sense of humor and street smarts.

Adama's eyes swept the chamber. It was another extravagantly designed room. The four-poster bed, where Miss Daisy Hunter lay, was a lavish gold Baroque frame. The canopy featured swooping gold satin curtains, each adorned with hundreds of tassels. Hand-tufted wool rugs covered the parquet wood flooring. The wallpaper was gold-striped with a navy-blue fleur-de-lis design.

About to ask for an update, Adama became distracted by a large wooden box resting on the couch. It looked identical to the one found on Vanhorn's yacht. Intrigued, Adama put booties over his shoes and walked over to Sanchez.

"It's beautiful, isn't it? I've never seen anything like it." Sanchez continued to look it over.

"Yeah, do me a favor," Adama said. "Don't touch it and make sure no one else does."

"Okay," Sanchez said.

"Is there a problem?" Dr. Pearson asked.

"I'm not sure. But Vanhorn had one just like this, so let's be cautious," Adama said.

"Interesting. Same contents?" Dr. Pearson asked.

"Vanhorn's box was closed. I didn't think anything of it at the time, but now there are two dead billionaires, and both have these large mahogany boxes. It can't be a coincidence."

"It looks ancient. Like something you'd see in a museum," Sanchez noted.

Adama stared and became intrigued. "Yes, and … uh, it looks a little familiar." Adama stopped staring at the object and turned to Sanchez. "Tell me what you know about our vic."

"Her name is Daisy Hunter, and she's from Texas. I found her passport in a purse over on the bureau. She's sixty-five years old. By all accounts, she arrived by limousine at three o'clock on Saturday. And—"

Adama put his hand up to stop Sanchez.

"I'm sorry, Luis, but where is that yapping noise coming from?"

"There are three dogs in the bathroom. Evidently, Miss Hunter never leaves home without 'em. They haven't shut up since we put them in there."

"Oh, please continue." Adama tried to ignore the noise.

"Like I was saying, she got in yesterday. One of the valets said she's unpleasant."

"How's that?"

"Well, the three dogs attacked a valet, but Miss Hunter blamed him and threatened to have him fired."

"Three, huh?"

"Oh no, we're talking three, fat, spoiled, and very mean Pomeranians. They've got teeth sharper than a barracuda's. Take a look." Sanchez showed off multiple bite marks on his hands.

"Geez. You should get those looked at. You don't want rabies."

"Seriously? I doubt those spoiled mutts have rabies. They probably have better health care than you and me."

"Still. Just do it."

"Okay," Sanchez said. "Anyway, we've got the security camera from the entrance to the hotel and the foyer. And it has sound. I can play it if you like."

"In a few minutes. Let me talk to Dr. Pearson first."

Adama walked toward the bed. Sanchez remained near the couch.

"Hello, Betty."

"Hello, Adama. Long time no see. Is it a full moon, or what?"

"I know—strange day. I know you just got here. What can you tell me?"

"I can tell you she's dead." Her tone was curt, and she stayed hunched over the victim.

"Are you okay?" Adama was taken aback by her sharp retort.

"Sorry. I haven't eaten, I'm premenopausal, and I was bitten by those nasty little dogs, who may be the only witnesses."

"I'm so sorry," Adama said.

When Dr. Pearson stood upright and turned around, Adama saw specs of blood and what looked to be bits and pieces of mushy particles on her white coveralls. She raised her face shield, removed her gloves, and walked to a dressing room area where she dug inside her medical bag. The doctor came back to Adama carrying a tube of lotion.

"Little shits. Bit right through my gloves."

Her comment prompted Sanchez to come over and display his bite marks.

"Those bites look bad; you should both see your doctors," Adama said.

Dr. Pearson gave him a contemptuous look. "I *am* a doctor."

"Of course, I didn't mean ... never mind." Adama let it go.

"We'll both need tetanus shots and god only knows what transferred from their mouths to our bodies, including her blood." She nodded at Daisy.

"Oh crap, that's right." Sanchez sounded panicked. "Doc, shouldn't we take something?"

"You'll be all right. We'll both get tested. Here, use some of this." Dr. Pearson squeezed a small amount of the analgesic onto her hands and offered the tube to Sanchez. They both rubbed the soothing lotion onto their hands and forearms. Adama impatiently watched. After the doctor put the lotion away, he pressed her.

"Do you have any idea about the cause of death?" Adama glanced over Dr. Pearson's shoulder at Daisy's bed.

"At first blush, I have to say asphyxiation," Dr. Pearson said.

"How? Was she strangled?"

"No. It's not like that." Dr. Pearson shook her head. "What I meant was she may have choked to death, but not by someone else. There is no petechial hemorrhaging. And Daisy's hyoid bone was not broken—the free-floating bone at the top of the neck just below the jaw." She pointed at Daisy's chin.

Adama looked around the room at all the food dishes. "So, you're saying she choked on all this food? That's what happened here?"

"Well, sort of," she said.

Dr. Pearson looked at Sanchez, who was shaking his head with a scrunched-up nose and a look of disgust on his face. He slowly approached his boss.

"What do you mean, sort of?" Adama asked.

"It's gross, boss. I mean, really disgusting. I never want to see it again."

"See what, Sanchez?"

"I got here a minute before Doc. The hotel manager brought me to the room, and I stood in the doorway. I couldn't believe what I saw.

Then Dr. Pearson showed up. And we both saw it." Sanchez stopped talking.

"Saw what?" Adama was growing impatient.

Dr. Pearson looked at Sanchez. "Go ahead, tell him."

"Um. Well, we saw all three dogs, with the victim," Sanchez said.

"Of course. We know dogs don't leave their master," Adama said.

"Well, this was different." Sanchez grimaced. "They were eating."

"Eating? Okay, so?" Adama shook his head.

"Yup, eating—all three dogs, but not from a bowl." Dr. Pearson bit her lip.

The vagueness exasperated Adama. "Okay. What am I missing here? And why is this so difficult? Just tell me what you both saw." Adama glanced back and forth between them.

"Oh, for fuck's sake. The dogs were eating out of *her* mouth!" Sanchez pointed at the bed.

"Picture it!" Dr. Pearson said. "All three of them were ravenous. *She* was the bowl!"

"What!" Adama jerked backward. "What did you say?"

"Right out of her mouth." Dr. Pearson nonchalantly snapped on more gloves. "And they were gnawing at her face."

Adama stared at Daisy Hunter on the bed. He heard the dogs yapping and looked toward the bathroom. He was speechless.

"More like assaulted her face," Sanchez said. "For small dogs, they're ferocious. They snarled and snapped at each other while digging into her mouth, nose, and ears. Her ears!" His voice elevated. "And when we came toward the bed, they hunched together in attack mode—growling with lips curled back, threatening us with their sharp teeth, red from blood. There's bloody food and body parts everywhere! Get the picture?" Sanchez's voice got louder and louder.

"Okay! Okay! I get it!" Adama raised his hand. "Just let me think—and take a closer look." Adama approached the bed.

"Be careful where you walk," Dr. Pearson said.

Daisy Hunter's three-hundred-pound body dwarfed the king-size bed. Centered in the middle, she lay face up with both arms and legs outstretched, staged, like a snow angel. She wore a short, custom-made pink nightgown and silk bed jacket with pink pom-pom slippers dangling from her feet. A carpeted ramp had been attached for the dogs at the foot of the bed. The damage made it difficult for Adama to discern some of what he inspected. Daisy Hunter's nose was disfigured. Part of her right cheek was torn from being chewed, and her left ear lobe was missing. Blood was on the pillowcases, the sheets, and the comforter. There were bits and pieces of food, and other non-descript scraps, scattered on the bed and all over Daisy's neck and chest. Dr. Pearson approached.

"We'll need to collect every scrap. The pieces are either food, parts of her face, or her tongue, which is missing, along with her upper and lower dentures."

My god. Adama was disturbed by the gruesome scene. He glanced at the bathroom door.

Dr. Pearson's phone buzzed. "Good. Two of my forensic techs are on the way."

Like a buffet, several food dishes were lined up on the bed and the floor. A three-tiered food cart sat nearby with desserts, meats, cheeses, nuts, sauces, and dog food. Melted ice cream dripped down the sides of the bowls, and chewed pizza lay on the floor.

"Why is there so much food? Was someone else here? Doc, do you have any idea how much food she ate?" Adama asked.

"Hard to tell," Dr. Pearson replied. "It was a lot from the scraps and what I found in her throat, nose, and ears. It's packed in there pretty tightly. An autopsy will tell us how much food is in the stomach, windpipe, and the nasal and ear cavities. And there's no telling how much the dogs ate. All three must have their stomachs pumped and feces collected for inspection."

"You said there is also food in her nose and ears? Why? And how did it get there?"

"Unknown." Dr. Pearson lowered her face shield and resumed her work on Daisy Hunter. She tried to ignore the yapping and scratching at the bathroom door.

"Well, she wouldn't have done that to herself. Right? Are there any indications that someone forced the food into her?" Adama tried to comprehend the scene.

"Normally, there would be some indication of forced feeding, with cuts and bruising around the mouth and nose. But the dogs destroyed any evidence of that. There are no defensive wounds, no ligature marks on her wrists or ankles, no marks on her neck, no bruises on her arms, no cuts, nothing to indicate someone else was involved. We'll scrape her fingernails for DNA, food, and other substances."

"Okay, for the sake of argument, let's say she did this to herself. Is that even possible?"

"Hey, in my line of work, anything is possible. But to answer your question, it would be tough for a person to do this to themselves. The gag reflex would kick in. And from what I can tell, there is no vomit anywhere."

"What else could cause this?" Adama asked.

"Well, there are other ways for a person to aspirate. She could have had a seizure, loss of muscle tone or coordination, a reaction to meds, a neck injury, or even cancer. I won't know until I do the autopsy."

"Okay. Lots of variables. Any idea about the time of death?" Adama asked.

"I'd say she expired during the past hour, definitely less than two. Rigor just started."

"Really? Less than two hours?" Adama's mind worked backwards. "Daisy Hunter may have been saved if someone had been with her. That's incredible," Adama said.

"It is incredible." Dr. Pearson nodded as she worked.

"Okay, thanks, Betty. We'll be back." Adama turned to Sanchez. It was obvious that he wasn't feeling well. "You okay, Luis?"

"I'm good." Sanchez turned toward the bathroom and the incessant barking. "SHUT. THE. FUCK. UP!" Sanchez touched his holster. "Can I shoot 'em? Please?"

The statement surprised Adama, who bit his lips to hold back a smile. And Dr. Pearson's head bobbed up and down, indicating, "Yes, let him." Adama knew Sanchez was joking. With three dogs and a

114

house full of pets, everyone knew Sanchez loved animals. Considering the situation, Adama knew the behavior was a way to blow off steam. Nevertheless, he needed to maintain decorum.

"All right, that'll do. You're okay. Tell me, who found the body?"

"A housekeeper. She said the dogs went nuts when she approached the body. So, she called the butler, who approached, but the dogs lunged at him, so he called the manager."

"Uh-huh. By the way, Luis, how did you get the dogs into the bathroom?"

"Well, Doc and I couldn't get near the body, so I called Animal Control. But Doc was worried about preserving evidence. You know…because they were eating it."

"Yeah, I get it." Adama winced.

"So, I went to the bathroom and grabbed some towels."

"That was good thinking, Luis."

"Yeah, thanks. Doc and I took turns covering one dog at a time and pulling them off the body. That's how we got bit."

"Well, you managed it well. Have you interviewed anyone yet?"

"No time, Deputy Chief. Doc and I spent all our time in the bedroom."

"All right, get statements from everyone. When Burke and Gates arrive, have them take statements from the rest of the group. There's a housekeeper, chef, valet, doctor, and anyone else with access to her suite. And don't forget the limo driver."

"On it," Sanchez said.

"Okay. I'll talk with the manager. See you later."

Sanchez left to take statements from the hotel staff, and Adama went to find the hotel manager to ask her about the box on Daisy Hunter's couch.

Chapter 21: Past Butterflies

Sunday morning, Bridget Murphy woke refreshed from her trip to London. She dressed in sweats, went to her gym, had brunch, and ran errands. Several times that morning, Bridget checked her phone for calls from Jane Evans. *When will she call me about Colin?*

Home again, her cellphone chimed with Passacaglia. The caller ID displayed Xavier Prawda, the Police Commissioner of New York City.

"Sir, hello, this is Bridget."

"How fast can you get to New York?"

"Uh, tonight, if you want. What's going on?"

"You haven't heard the news? We have two dead billionaires." Prawda paused, and his voice cracked. "And ... my best friend's son, Thomas, was found dead at the Miller Antiquities gallery." He cleared his throat. "Do you know it?"

"Yes, I'm so sorry, sir. Did the billionaires die at the gallery as well?"

"No, they were found at different locations, but all three victims may be connected to the gallery. We've established a special task force, and the mayor has requested your assistance. Please arrive as soon as possible. We need these cases solved asap."

"Yes, sir, I'll fly down tonight."

"Good. We'll put you up at Gild Hall, which is conveniently located near headquarters. I'll see you there first thing Monday morning."

"Yes, commissioner. Thank you." The line went dead.

Bridget quickly grabbed the remote and turned on the television. The news filled the airwaves. She watched the pundits speculate about the two dead billionaires. Manhattan Mayor Gryffin Tait gave a reassuring speech about the NYPD's special task force and the extraordinary qualifications of its new director, Adama Baptiste.

"Holy shit!" Bridget's hands cupped her mouth. Her heart raced as she stared at the screen. As fast as Adama appeared on screen, he was gone. "That's who I'll be working with?" Her anxiety level shot through the roof. She paced around her living room, thinking about Adama and their past, and being face-to-face with him again.

"Oh my god," she said to no one. Bridget turned off the television and sat on the couch. All at once, she was elated, nervous, excited, anxious, happy, and queasy. She reflected on the last year, how they met, fell in love, and how she abruptly ended it due to her complicated divorce.

They met a year ago when the NYPD hired Bridget as an antiquities consultant to work with Adama Baptiste, a lead detective at the 19th Precinct. Despite initial doubts about Bridget, he soon came to appreciate her problem-solving skills. For months, they collaborated on an antiquity fraud and murder case at a local Manhattan gallery.

The stolen antiquities led them to France. Along the way, they discovered three more deaths tied to the curator of the New York gallery. By the time they identified all the perpetrators and stolen items, they had grown close enough to finish each other's sentences.

While in France, they enjoyed long dinners and shared personal details. Nothing seemed out of bounds. Their late-night talks seemed to go on forever, never running out of things to say. Bridget clearly recalled bits of their conversations.

"Where were you born, Bridget? I detect a Boston accent."

"I am from Boston, and a huge Irish family. And you? I hear a French accent."

"I'm from a small French township, St. Pierre. It's in Senegal, Africa. Je parle français. I'm also fluent."

"Ah, impressionante," she said. "They have the best white beaches. And I can't believe you're from St. Pierre. I earned my master's in anthropology from Cheikh Anta Diop University in Dakar. I spent five years learning and teaching in the region. But the best part was listening to the stories by people in the region. It made me realize how vastly similar humans are, regardless of their origin. I also

learned enough French and Wolof to get by. I truly loved it there."
God, he's good-looking.
"That's incredible. And here we are working for the NYPD. It's truly a small world." Adama marveled at Bridget's spirit for life. *She's unbelievably gorgeous.*
"I'd say this is quite a coincidence, except ..." Bridget hesitated.
"You don't believe in coincidence. Neither do I." He smiled broadly.
Eventually, the subject of love relationships came up.
"So, are you married?" Bridget asked.
"Not anymore, but I was married for five years. It turns out that being an ambitious detective didn't sit well with her. Too many late nights and not enough partying time."
"I'm sorry." She hesitated but asked, "Was it difficult for you?"
"Yes, it was tough, sad, and heartbreaking in fact. I was blindsided. I knew she was unhappy about my schedule, but I figured we'd work through it. I came home one night to an envelope full of divorce papers and a nearly empty closet—all of her clothes were gone."
"Oh, that sounds terrible."
"It was. But it's been three years. I've accepted it and moved on. She remarried and lives upstate, expecting a baby. I'm happy for her."
"Oh, that's nice. I guess." Bridget searched Adama's eyes for lingering pain. He had motioned for the waiter and asked for another round of drinks.
"How about you?" Adama looked into her eyes and mused about her beauty. He longed to touch her strawberry blonde hair to see if it was as soft as it looked.
"Me? Oh, well, my love life is boring, not much to tell." Bridget looked away.
"I find that hard to believe." Adama sensed something more.
"Do you have children?" She asked, changing the subject.
"Ah, no. We talked about it, but we were too busy with our careers. In hindsight, I'm glad we didn't have kids. And you? Are you married? Got any kids?"
"No kids." Bridget took a sip of her drink.

Adama watched her body language. Clearly, she was uncomfortable. She shifted in her chair, looked at her watch, and fidgeted with her napkin. Her evasiveness intrigued him. It was an occupational hazard, asking questions, listening to the answers, reading the body language, and looking for a "tell" like a poker player in a high-stakes game. Her avoidance made him more curious.

"You're a very private person, aren't you?"

"Yes, I'm sorry about being evasive, and I owe you an answer. I filed for divorce over three years ago. We're legally separated. He lives here, in France. It's been a messy and complicated divorce process. I'm hoping this next round of appeals brings closure."

"I'm sorry you're having to deal with that. The emotional aspect and drama can wear one out. Hopefully, it'll be over soon." *The guy must be an idiot to lose her.* "How long were you together?"

"Not very long." She felt embarrassed. "Just three months. Then I filed for divorce."

"Really? That's unusual." Adama tried not to look surprised.

"Long story, short...I discovered he had a mistress. He basically told me to grow up and accept it. But I'm not built that way, so it's over."

"That's rough. If it makes you feel any better, I think he's a fool." Adama smiled.

"Thanks." She returned the smile, soaking in his full lips and the brightness of his eyes, an unusual, amber-streaked color.

"Why don't we change the subject?" he offered.

"Great idea, so how about them Yankees?"

They both laughed. Adama was enamored with Bridget. Her aloofness was very attractive, and her spirit was enduring. She was charming, incredibly smart, direct, and genuine. He had never met anyone like her and wanted to get closer to her. He had more questions but decided to be respectful and not pry. At least not tonight.

Adama walked Bridget to her hotel room on their last evening in Paris. They lingered outside her door. He moved closer as they stared into each other's eyes, both leaning in, wanting. Bridget could barely keep her desire from showing, while Adama waited for an invitation into her room.

But they were interrupted by a floor security guard making the rounds. The man's uniform was a stark reminder that they were in Paris to work.

"Well, goodnight, sleep tight, love." Adama kissed her lightly on the cheek.

"And you as well." Bridget's heart sang. *Good night, love.*
After the French investigation ended, they returned to New York and maintained a professional relationship. But the sexual tension between them was palpable. They flirted discreetly with an occasional brush of the arm, lingering stares, and standing closer than necessary. Bridget was positive that people at the precinct suspected and pretended not to notice their mutual attraction. Knowing she would be leaving soon, she tried to remain detached, for Adama's sake. He picked up on her vibe and reluctantly decided it would be best to leave her alone, for both their sakes.

After the case was closed, Bridget finalized her documentation with the NYPD. She prepared for a midnight flight to Boston, having been summoned by New Scotland Yard for an antiquities fraud case. Bridget could not stop thinking about Adama and their time in Paris; she called him one last time.

"I thought I'd call to say goodbye, again. It was great working with you."

"And you. Your instincts are amazing, thank you for the help."

"My pleasure. What's that noise I hear in the background?"

"I'm at a café on the West Side," he said.

"I'm sorry, I didn't mean to interrupt your dinner."

"You didn't." He paused. "Would you like to join me?"

"I would." Her heart fluttered. "Where are you?"

"Serafina's, on W. 55th and Broadway. I'll wait for you." *She's coming!*

"Okay, I'll see you soon." She felt giddy.

Adama smiled at the sight of Bridget exiting a cab. He waved. She hurriedly crossed the street. Adama stood and greeted her with a kiss on the cheek.

Serafina's was a cozy Italian restaurant on the Upper West Side. Its lively atmosphere, delicious food, and selection of wines made it a hot spot for locals and tourists. Adama ordered a glass of Chardonnay and, remembering her preference for sparkling wine, ordered a prosecco with ice for Bridget. They drank, talked about the case, ate, drank, and told stories that made the other laugh.

With longing in their eyes, Adama took a chance. He slowly placed his hand upright on the table, palm open and fingers outstretched, reaching, beckoning Bridget. She did not hesitate; she put her hand in his, and their fingers intertwined. That was all he needed—a simple gesture confirmed that it was Paris all over again.

Bridget couldn't help herself. *I'll never forget his warm hand reaching for mine. No one has ever made me feel so wanted that way.* Sitting on the couch in her living room, Bridget recalled the hugs and playfulness as cherished memories, bathing her with feelings of love and longing, just as fresh as they were a year ago. *He was so sweet.* What happened next was like a playful, sexy scene from a romantic film.

"I live a few blocks north of here, and my car is parked nearby. Feel like a nightcap?" Adama gazed into Bridget's blue eyes.

"Absolutely." Her body hummed with restrained longing.

It was a short ride to his apartment. He parked the car and led Bridget to his building.

"Ready for some exercise? I'm on the fourth floor."

Bridget stared upward and felt Adama take her hand. She felt a sudden rush of butterflies in her belly. Reaching his apartment, he unlocked the door; she ducked under his arm. It was awkward at first, wondering who would make the first move. Bridget looked at pictures on the walls, dragged her finger across the fireplace, and stared out the French doors. Adama tossed his keys on the table, watching her meander around his living room. He burned with the need to draw closer.

"Have you lived here long?" She asked aimlessly as she brushed by a second time.

"A couple of years." He adored her coyness.

With the next brush, Bridget got within reach, and Adama gently coaxed her with an alluring look. She stopped, looked into his eyes, moved closer, and touched his chest.

"Took you long enough." He bent down and kissed her. She dissolved into his muscular arms as he pulled her close.

After a few intense kisses, they ended up on the couch. Clothes were removed and thrown away heatedly. Adama stood and reached for Bridget's hand to lead her into the bedroom. More kissing, more touching, more desire. They eagerly removed the last of their clothing. He scooped her up and gently laid her down on the bed.

Bridget's breath was taken away as his warm, brown, sculpted body moved on top of her. The feeling of being consumed excited her. She arched her back and pressed against him, while he moved her hands upward and held them over her head. All their pent-up sexual tension exploded with heavy moaning and writhing. A while later, as they lay in each other's arms, exhausted, Adama brushed the hair away from her face and kissed her forehead.

"Thirsty?" Adama got up and walked to the kitchen.

"Yes." Bridget smiled at his naked body. "You've got a great butt."

"So do you, love," Adama said.

He returned with two glasses of water.

"God, that tastes great." Bridget drank half the glass.

"Not as good as you." He winked.

Bridget felt herself blushing slightly. She put the glass on the nightstand, lay back, tossed her arms over her head, closed her eyes, and sighed, satisfied.

"Thank you," Bridget said softly.

Adama lay on his side with his head in his hand, admiring her beauty. He caressed her neck with his fingers, trailing the curve of her collarbone downward between her breasts. "For what?"

"I can't remember the last time I felt so relaxed." She turned to face him. "You're great."

"So are you."

Bridget saw the clock on the nightstand. "Whoa, I've got to go." She jumped up and stood naked next to the bed.

"What? Stay, let's have breakfast."

"Oh, I'd love to, but I can't." Bridget searched for her clothes. "I've got a midnight flight to Boston, and I'm on a plane to London at eight in the morning." Bridget pulled up her underwear and fumbled with her bra.

"Oh, I didn't know." Adama was disappointed. "When did this happen, uh, when do you get back?"

"I'm not sure. I expect to be there a while. I'm consulting on three cases of antiquities fraud. Could be weeks." She found her jeans and blouse in the living room. He followed her.

"So, this was a one-nighter?" Adama pulled a T-shirt over his head.

She snickered. "I'm afraid tonight is. I wish I could stay."

"Me too." He found his sweatpants on the kitchen floor and pulled them on. "Well, at least let me call you a cab."

"Okay, thanks." Bridget buttoned her blouse and found her shoes.

Adama called for a taxi while Bridget grabbed her purse and went to the bathroom.

Adama called out to her. "You've got about fifteen minutes before the cab arrives. They'll honk."

"Perfect!"

In the meantime, Adama sat on the couch, surprised by feeling dejected. He heard the toilet flush and the water running in the sink. Bridget came out of the bathroom, brushing her hair. It was obvious that Adama was disappointed. She sat next to him on the couch.

"I'm sorry. Our case was wrapping up, so I agreed to take a new case, and they booked my flights. If I'd known there was a chance for us to spend time together, I would have waited a few days." Bridget kissed Adama on the cheek. "Thank you, though, for a lovely evening. I enjoy being with you. I knew we would be great. Of course, you know how much I wanted you in Paris."

"Me too." He put his arm around her. "You're one of a kind, Bridget."

"I feel funny leaving." She rested her head on his shoulder.

"Well, you know where I am." He hugged her. "I have to admit, I'm disappointed."

"I feel the same way. I wish I could stay."

"We can fix that when you get back." Adama pulled away to look at her. "Okay?"

"Perfect." They kissed and held each other until a horn honked. "Ah, gotta go." Bridget stood up. "I can call and text you from Paris— is that okay?" Bridget asked.

"Yeah, sure. That works. And we'll get together." Adama looked around. "Hang on, I'll get my shoes and walk you down."

"That's okay, I've gotta run. But thanks."

Bridget found her purse and jacket. Adama grabbed her around the waist and pulled her into him. She acquiesced, giving in to the pull, feeling that itch, and feeling *him* again as he pressed against her. She let out a sigh.

"Listen, we'll both be busy, but feel free to call or text anytime. I hope you have a good trip."

They kissed a long, lingering kiss goodbye. Bridget pulled away and opened the door. She gave him a big smile.

"See ya." She stepped into the hallway.

"I hope so. Otherwise, I'll feel cheap."

They both laughed. Adama followed her through the doorway. Bridget lingered before letting go of his hand. She walked toward the stairs. Adama admired her finely sculpted rear end.

"Hey, Bridget?"

"Yeah?" She turned around.

"You walk like music."

Bridget's heart melted. "Oh my." She blushed. "Why, thank you, sir."

She blew him a kiss as she started down the stairs. Adama had leaned on the railing as he watched her go. Bridget had glanced up to see him smiling, and a warm feeling consumed her.

———◆———

Bridget's heartfelt trip down memory lane was interrupted by a loud buzzer from her clothes dryer. She turned on her laptop, searched for a flight to New York, and texted the information to the commissioner. She spent the next few hours doing laundry and packing a suitcase and her satchel. *These damn butterflies. Does he know I'm coming?*

How will he react? How will I respond? Come Monday morning, I guess, I'll find out.

Chapter 22: The Price of Silence

Adama Baptiste strode confidently into the flamboyant living room of Daisy Hunter's penthouse suite. Ms. Matisse, the stylish Manager of Le Chandelier Hotel, was patiently waiting on a Louis XIV silk chaise lounge. As Adama approached, her heart fluttered, and she flushed at his handsomeness.

"Deputy Chief." She stood and primped, straightening her skirt and adjusting her jacket, pulling it a bit lower in the front. "Monsieur, how may I be of service?" Mesmerized, she unconsciously batted her eyelashes.

No stranger to women's reactions, his genuine smile put her at ease. "Ms. Matisse, I wonder if you could tell me about that big box in Daisy Hunter's bedroom?"

"Oui. Miss Hunter informed me there would be a late delivery. About an hour later, I observed two men come into the lobby. They were struggling with a heavy wooden box. I called Miss Hunter, and she instructed me to escort them to the penthouse personally. Is there a problem?"

"No problem. What time was that? And did you see Daisy Hunter?"

"It was eleven o'clock. And yes, she opened the door. I was told to wait here." She motioned around the chaise. "Miss Hunter led the two men with the box to her bedroom. A minute later, they all returned, and I escorted the men back to the lobby. That's all."

"I see. And how did Miss Hunter seem to you?"

"She seemed...delighted and pleased." Her eyes looked down and away. *Not her usual grumpy self.* Ms. Matisse kept her snarky thoughts to herself.

"Okay. Thank you. I'd like to see the video feed from the front of the hotel during that time. And I need the names of anyone who had access to Miss Hunter's suite."

"Certainly, I can arrange that. Is there anything else I can do for you?" Ms. Matisse's face signaled a willingness to stick around.

"No, thank you. You've been very helpful." Adama's cellphone buzzed. It was Detective Luis Sanchez.

"Hey, Sanchez. Where are you?"

"I just finished taking statements from the valets. I'm on my way up."

"First, I need you to get the security footage of the valet area between ten and twelve last night."

"Okay, what am I looking for on the video?"

"A van, two men, and a big box. Ms. Matisse, the hotel manager, is on her way down; she can give that list of names and the videos." He acknowledged Ms. Matisse, who nodded back. They both walked in different directions.

"Got it. By the way, there's a lot of press downstairs, and the news about Vanhorn is out."

"Yes, I know. I'm going back to see Doc and then to HQ. Gotta go."

Adama hung up and walked to Daisy Hunter's bedroom. The medical examiner's team was busy working the scene. Adama noticed the barking had stopped, and the bathroom door was open—animal control had collected the dogs. The CME was preparing Daisy's body for transport to the morgue.

"How's it going, Doc?"

"We're about done here. I got a call from the mayor. The proverbial shit has hit the fan."

"I know, he wants containment. I'm meeting with him in an hour." Adama glanced at the couch. "Has that big box been processed?" Adama pointed.

"Not yet. One of the forensic techs will get to it shortly."

"I want to take another look at it." He put on gloves and moved closer to the couch.

"We've been wondering what that *thing* is?" Dr. Pearson saw how engrossed Adama was with the box. "Why the curiosity?" She stopped to watch him.

Adama ignored her question and removed a pen from his pocket. He used it to poke around the object, which was serenely nestled on a red satin sheet. As Adama lifted one corner of the sheet, he saw a Styrofoam mold holding the object securely in place.

"It looks like it's made of stone—probably granite," Adama said to no one.

He observed the rough texture with variegated colors of gray and a creamy, pale pink, with flecks of shiny gold and silver embedded over its surface. Tiny veins of what looked to be charcoal ran through the stone. Adama shifted his focus to the unique design, deeply carved into the top. He was about to trace his finger around the carved-out area, but suddenly gasped.

"Oh my god! Oh no!" Adama cried out.

His memory shaken, Adama suddenly recognized the object in the box. He froze and stared in silence. A mild state of traumatic shock ensued. Adama's heart rate increased, followed by rapid, shallow breathing, shakiness, and slight nausea. He did not move but felt as though he was floating and suspended in time.

"Adama? What's wrong?" Dr. Pearson got no response. She shook his arm. "Adama?"

Dr. Pearson's words gradually got louder as Adama's awareness slowly returned. "What?" he asked, shaking his head to clear his mind.

"Are you all right?" she asked. "You look like you've seen a ghost."

"Oh. Uh, I'm fine. I need to..." He pointed at the door. "I'll be back." Adama abruptly exited the bedroom.

"What the hell?" In all the years Dr. Pearson had known and worked with Adama, she had never seen him stunned, heard him gasp, or behave catatonic. She watched with concern as he bolted out the door. Dr. Pearson removed her face shield and gloves and went to find him.

———◆———

A few minutes later, Adama exited the hallway bathroom, blotting his forehead with a paper towel. He was surprised to see Dr. Pearson waiting with her arms folded across her chest. He crumpled and tossed the paper towel into a nearby wastebasket.

"You, okay?"

"Uh, yeah, I'm fine." He saw the concerned look on her face. "Doc ... Betty, I'm good. Nothing to worry about."

"Really? You could've fooled me."

"Let's just get back to work."

"No way, you were in a mild state of dissociation, that's traumatic shock," Dr. Pearson said. "I've seen it before. What happened?"

"Bad dreams and old memories. I'd rather not go into it." Adama was still visibly shaken.

"Okay, if that's how you want to play it. Mind if I take your blood pressure?"

"What? No, I just needed a minute." He used the back of his hand to wipe beads of sweat off his forehead. "Uh, Betty, mind if we keep this between us? " He gave her that pleading face.

"Who am I going to tell?" Dr. Pearson smiled matter-of-factly and took a stethoscope out of her pocket. "But *this* is the price of silence." She dangled the long black hose in front of him.

"Ahh, fine, get it over with," he grumbled.

Adama took off his jacket, sat in a nearby chair, and rolled up his left sleeve. Dr. Pearson wrapped the black pressure cuff around his arm.

"One-forty over ninety. That's elevated. We'll recheck it in five minutes." She checked his eyes and held the stethoscope up to his back. "Take a deep breath. And another. Thank you." She put the instrument into her coat pocket.

"So, Doc, am I going to live?"

"You'll live. You sure you don't want to tell me what happened back there?"

"Some other time, huh?" Adama rolled his sleeve back down and put on his jacket.

"Typical. Okay, but I've got my eye on you."

"I wouldn't have it any other way." He gave her a broad smile. "Shall we?" Adama motioned for her to go down the hallway.

More people had arrived by the time Adama and Dr. Pearson got back into Daisy Hunter's bedroom. Jimmy Quinn had joined the other technicians, and Detective Burke was busy analyzing the scene. Adama immediately went to the box on the couch and closed its lid. He approached Burke.

"Hey, Ricky, is everything okay at the yacht?"

"All wrapped up."

"Thanks, we need everyone on deck today."

Adama brought Burke up to speed and instructed him to coordinate with Sanchez about getting witness statements and updates.

"I'm especially interested to know how Daisy Hunter seemed. You know the drill."

"Sure," Burke said. "Are you okay? You don't look so good?"

"I'm fine. I'm going to headquarters. You're in charge. Call Gates and have him come over as soon as he's finished at the Miller gallery. And Ricky, this is critical, make sure the lid on that box remains closed and that no one touches the object inside. Keep eyes on, make sure it's properly sealed and sent straight to the morgue." Adama pointed at the couch.

"Hey, isn't that the same kind of box we found on Vanhorn's yacht?"

"Yes. Same protocol for Vanhorn's box, please have it transferred to the morgue asap." Adama gave Burke a hard stare. "Ricky, remember, *no one* touches the objects inside."

"I'll take care of it. Get something to eat. I'll be in touch."

"Thanks, Ricky, see you later."

Adama left the suite and took the elevator down. At the hotel entrance, he saw three news vans and their crews, including his neighbor, Mark Dawson from the Manhattan Gazette. Adama walked behind the trucks to get away unnoticed. Within minutes, he was on his way back to headquarters.

Chapter 23: The Cellphone

A dama Baptiste had finished meeting with Xavier Prawda, the NYPD Police Commissioner, and his direct boss, Police Chief John Ballantine. It had been a long day, and most of his staff had returned from all three crime scenes. In the bullpen, Adama reviewed the large whiteboard for updates, then addressed his team.

"First, I'd like to thank each of you for working so diligently. The deaths of two billionaires and the son of a prominent gallery owner are unprecedented. We're the official task force. All eyes are on us. Let's hear updates. Burke?"

"I worked the William Vanhorn case at the marina. The CME stated the TOD is somewhere between twelve forty-five and one-thirty a.m. on Sunday. Dr. Pearson labeled the death as suspicious until she completes the autopsy. And we've taken statements from all crew members and guests."

"What about Vanhorn's phone?" Adama asked.

"Our mobile forensic team traced Vanhorn's last call at eight-fifty-five p.m. in the vicinity of 5th Avenue and W. 56th Street. They say the cellphone is on or near the yacht. I suggest we go back with a search team. And we're waiting on forensics regarding the two footprints on the right side of the bed. We'll see if your hunch paid off." Burke looked at Adama, who nodded.

Detective Gates raised his hand.

"Deputy Chief, I worked the Thomas Miller-Chevalier case. He's the son of Henry Miller, co-owner of Miller Antiquities. The assistant ME on site called the death suspicious. TOD was Saturday night between nine and midnight. The focus is on toxicology, as no obvious signs of foul play are present. We got the gallery's internal security videos, and I forwarded that file to you. Interesting note: The gallery is located on 5th Avenue and W. 56th Street. That coincides with the pings from Vanhorn's cellphone at or near the gallery on Saturday night."

Detective Luis Sanchez raised his hand and referred to his notes. "I worked the Daisy Hunter case at Le Chandelier Hotel. The CME has listed TOD between ten a.m. and noon today. Notably, the last call made from her cellphone was at eight-fifty-five last night, also in the vicinity of 5th Avenue and W. 56th. That connects her to the gallery as well."

"So, we have a direct connection between all three victims and the gallery," Adama said. "In addition, two of our billionaires had a large mahogany box in their possession. Let's confirm whether those two objects came from the Miller gallery and our deceased host. We need the names of everyone who attended last night's gallery event."

Adama looked at Julie Flynn, a new technician.

"Sir, we reviewed the feeds from the street, which show six limousines pulled up at seven p.m., and six people walked into the Miller gallery. At nine p.m., the same six people left by limousine. We're running facial recognition and should have results soon. Also, Thomas Chevalier was last seen standing on the stoop at nine p.m." Julie Flynn closed her notebook.

"Good job. Keep Burke posted about the facial recognition results of those six guests. Listen, while we wait for the autopsy and test results, our job is to get into every aspect of our victims' lives. Who were they? Who did they meet before and after the event? Cellphone records, financials, and who benefits from their deaths? That's all, thank you."

The team went back to work. Adama and Burke spoke as they left the room.

"When do you want to go talk with Captain Ricci?" Burke asked.

"In a few minutes. Do me a favor and call Dr. Pearson to find out if she has analyzed the footprints from Vanhorn's bedroom. Get us a warrant for the cellphone search. I'll update the chief and be back in fifteen minutes."

After his meeting, Adama met with Burke, and they headed to the parking lot.

"I've got the search team on standby. The warrant should be ready by the time we get there." Burke's phone buzzed. "It's from the CME about the footprints." Burke showed Adama the text, and they both smiled. "Nice hunch, boss."

They crossed the Brooklyn Bridge and pulled into the marina parking lot. As the detectives approached the yacht, Captain Ricci met them on the dock.

"Hello, gentlemen. Are you here to tell us we can return to Palm Beach?" she asked.

"Unfortunately, no. May we come aboard and speak with you privately?"

"Sure, follow me."

Captain Ricci led them to the library, where they all took a seat. Adama never took his eyes off the captain. It made her uncomfortable, as he intended.

"What can I do for you?" she asked.

"We're here to find Mr. Vanhorn's cellphone," Burke said.

"Oh, you think it's on the yacht?" she asked.

"Our mobile forensic team is excellent. If they say it's here, it's here." Burke's smile reflected quiet confidence.

"Well, my crew searched, but couldn't find it," Captain Ricci said.

Adama knew she was lying. *Carefully chosen words on her part.* He leaned forward, rested his forearms on his knees, interlaced his fingers, and confronted the captain.

"Captain Ricci, that's twice you lied to me. First, when I asked you about Mr. Vanhorn's cellphone, which you took off the nightstand. And the second time was just now, again interfering with our investigation," Adama said.

"Why would you think that?" Captain Ricci's right eye twitched, clearly unnerved.

Adama stood. "Burke?" His height and close distance intimidated the captain.

"All too easy. Two distinct sets of prints were on the right side of Mr. Vanhorn's bed. One barefoot—Vanhorn's. And the other?" Burke paused for effect. "A set of ladies' Cobalts, size eight. Identical to what you're wearing now." The corner of Burke's mouth formed a micro expression of contempt.

Collectively, all eyes dropped to her shoes. Caught red-handed, Captain Ricci's posture slumped ever so slightly in the chair. Her silence spoke volumes.

"After finding him dead, you walked to the nightstand and took his cellphone before calling for help. Didn't you, Captain Ricci?" Adama leveled the acquisition with confidence.

What was left of Captain Ricci's professional demeanor crumbled. She pleaded her case while demonstrating a show of authority.

"Okay, you're right. But you don't understand. Bill ... I mean, Mr. Vanhorn gave me explicit instructions to take his cellphone if anything happened to him. I didn't have a choice."

"Oh, you had a choice," Adama said. "You chose to interfere in a possible murder investigation. Making false statements is a crime, as I'm sure you know. Before I bring a search team on board, *where's* the cellphone?"

With a mixed look of shame and disdain, Captain Ricci stood to accept defeat. She withdrew a cellphone from her pocket and displayed it in her open palm, like a peace offering. Burke pulled on gloves and took custody of the cellphone with practiced efficiency.

"Are you hiding anything else from us?" Adama asked.

"No," Ricci responded.

"Is there a password?" Burke waved the phone at her.

"Uh, yes. It's 'Wild One' but all one word, capitalize the 'W' and the 'O,' replace the 'e' with the numeral '3' and add an exclamation point at the end."

Burke entered the password. It read 'WildOn3!'. "Like this?"

Upon confirmation, Burke tapped "Enter." Vanhorn's cellphone displayed a selfie of him and four naked young women in a jacuzzi.

"Did you tamper with this phone?" Burke asked.

"What do you mean?" Ricci asked innocently.

"You know what he means. Think carefully before you answer, Captain," Adama warned.

Ricci nodded. "Yes, I erased a few photos." She collapsed into her chair.

"You did *what*?" Burke scoffed with disbelief.

"Mr. Vanhorn instructed me to delete certain photographs in the event of his death."

"That's willful obstruction." Adama glared. "It's not looking good for you, Captain."

"They were … of a compromising nature." Her voice was barely audible.

"I take it the photos included Vanhorn and someone else?" Adama asked.

"Me." The word dropped like an anchor.

"You?" Burke was stunned. *You're just full of surprises.*

"Yes. Bill—Mr. Vanhorn and I had an understanding. For his sake and mine, I couldn't let those pictures get out."

Adama and Burke exchanged glances. It was quiet in the room for a minute.

"Did you kill Mr. Vanhorn?" Adama asked.

"Oh, god no!" Ricci jumped up. "I would never. I just needed to delete those pictures. That's all. I cared for Bill."

"Did you know about the restraints and the case in the closet?" Adama asked.

"Yes. Bill and I had a sexual relationship for a while. But that ended years ago. He prefers younger girls." The captain rolled her eyes. "And he liked to take pictures. It was harmless." She shrugged.

Both detectives' ears perked up. Adama and Burke had the same thought as they looked at each other. *So, you did know they were underage girls.*

"Do you have access to the case in the closet?" Adama asked.

"No, he never let anyone near it, and he was the only person with the combination. Bill was a control freak."

"How do you think he died?" Adama watched her body language.

"I don't know." Her voice was mournful. "It doesn't make sense. He was always careful. We used a safe word, and the restraints had quick-release tabs. It must have been an accident." She hung her head and sank into the chair.

Afraid the captain would flee at the first opportunity, Adama gave a nod to Burke, who approached the captain with cuffs in hand.

"Captain, you're under arrest for aiding and abetting in the commission of a federal crime, under Title 18 U.S. Code Section 2. Based on your knowledge of and assisting William Vanhorn with soliciting and transporting minor girls. You'll be detained at our headquarters until you are turned over to the FBI. In addition, you're under arrest by the State of New York for obstruction and tampering during a police investigation.

"Oh, my god!" she exclaimed. "It wasn't me; it was Vanhorn. I want my attorney!"

"That's one of your rights," Burke said. He read the Miranda rights to the captain and took her into custody.

Adama approached several police officers on duty and told them to secure the yacht and the surrounding premises. "Make sure everyone stays on board for the next few days." Adama turned to Burke. "We're done here, let's go."

As Adama and Burke led Captain Ricci down the dock, the entire crew watched in shock from the railings.

"Ricky, call the Coast Guard for additional help and get a car posted here to ensure no one leaves that boat." Then Adama told another officer to put the captain in the back of his squad car. "Follow us to HQ," Adama said.

Burke called for a squad car to babysit the yacht. Adama stared out the window at the East River as they crossed the Brooklyn Bridge. His mind churned about the victims, the gallery, and the stones inside the boxes. All were pieces of a puzzle to be solved. But he had a nagging feeling there was something more to come. Adama closed his eyes. *What am I missing?* For a split second, the image of the two men dragged from the Hudson flashed before him. His eyes popped open. *My god, could they be part of this?*

Chapter 24: Bridget's Dilemma

Bridget boarded the United Airlines flight to JFK International Airport. She tugged at her seat belt and stared out the window. Melancholy washed over her—a contentious divorce, her father's death, the murder of her long-time friend and mentor, and letting the one man she truly loved slip away. *I hope he can forgive me. I hope he gives me a chance to explain.* She leaned against the window and daydreamed about Adama Baptiste.

Bridget had fallen in love with Adama in Paris. And even though they had not officially said, "I love you" to each other, she knew he loved her too. Bridget had planned to share her feelings, certain he would reciprocate.

While Bridget and Adama grew closer, her estranged husband, Antoine Tricheuse, schemed. For three years, he had demanded everything she owned. Bridget fought, refusing to yield her house and modest fortune to a man she'd been married to for three months. But Antoine was a clever man and cornered her with a vicious call that she was unprepared for.

She recalled his shocking narrative. "I know about your police detective. I hired a PI and have a full dossier about your love affair. Did you actually believe I'd let you go unscathed? You're either naïve or stupid. I'm done with your stubbornness. Meet my demands, or I'll ruin you both. And you can forget about going to the authorities; innuendo is enough to destroy a career. I doubt the NYPD will keep your detective after I release scandalous materials. You have one week. Meanwhile, I'll send you a few of my favorite shots."

At first, Bridget was not intimidated by his hiring of a private investigator and his wild accusations and dismissed Antoine's blackmail threat—until the package arrived. Photographs showed her and

Adama embracing, as well as pictures of where he lived and worked, including the names of his superiors and the names of her clients and work colleagues. The full gravity of the situation created a dilemma for her.

Bridget often thought of reporting Antoine's blackmail threat, knowing it was the right thing to do. But, coming forward meant implications—the police are well aware of bitter accusations and messy divorces. And if they believed her, Antoine had made it clear he would release the photos, leading to Adama's professional downfall. She backed off after realizing she had no recordings, no paper trail, no proof of threats; just lots of pictures that told a true story.

Countless times, Bridget wanted to call Adama. She'd tell him everything, and he'd know what to do. He was more intelligent and resourceful than Antoine; perhaps he could devise a strategy to end the threats. But what of his reaction, bravado, sense of right and wrong? She knew his nature—an unwavering moral compass and stubborn courage. He would fight, wielding the law like armor, possibly sacrificing himself in the process. He would move mountains to protect her and take Antoine down.

On the other hand, was the dossier the only threat? Antoine had proven himself an unstable adversary. She knew the past three years weren't about jealousy; this was about a woman who scorned him. His entitled, self-aggrandizing, and exploitative persona couldn't tolerate rejection. He had to win—but he wasn't just a greedy bully anymore; he had become obsessed with revenge. She worried about how far he would go. The uncertainty gave her chills.

Most of her time was spent thinking about the tenuous situation. Her decision crystallized with painful clarity: Adama's safety above all else—even if it meant losing him forever. Before the deadline arrived, Bridget had devised a calculated plan. She would sever ties with Adama and inform Antoine of their breakup, hopefully deflating his vengeance. It could work if Antoine knew he would get everything and walked away feeling like the victor.

Bridget worked through possible scenarios—Antoine's reactions, their dialogue, and words to appease his ego. Steeling herself, she approached him with a deal: she would relinquish all her wealth, valued at more than five million dollars, in exchange for his surrender of the dossier and promise never to harm Adama. Antoine happily agreed—done deal. Documents would be drawn up, and Bridget would sell her home, forward her wealth, including her mother's inheritance, and agree to alimony—all to save Adama and finally be free.

Bridget's first action would be the agonizing call to Adama. She remembered how happy he sounded.

"Hey there, I was just thinking about you. When does your plane land? I'll pick you up."

"Adama, I'm not coming," Bridget said.

"Oh? Did something happen?"

"Adama, would you do something for me?"

"Anything, love. Name it." His voice was playful.

"It won't be easy."

"What do you need? Tell me."

Bridget swallowed hard and took a deep breath.

"I need some time ... alone, with no questions asked."

"That sounds ominous. Are you all right?"

"Yes."

He waited for more explanation. "Why don't I fly up so that we can talk?"

"No, it's best if we don't see each other for a while."

"Really?" His voice softened. "I didn't expect that. How long a while?"

"I'm not sure. I have to go to France, and it's best if we stay away from each other."

"Bridget, is this about Antoine? Has he done something? Why so mysterious?"

"I know what I'm doing." She sighed loudly, forcing resignation. "Adama, you said you'd do anything for me."

"And I meant it. But am I supposed to walk away, no questions asked?" Being a detective, Adama had to ask. "Bridget, has Antoine threatened you, or harmed you?" A lump formed in his throat as he waited for the answer.

"I can handle Antoine. Please do this for me."

"Love, talk to me. None of this makes sense. Let me help you, I can come to Fran—."

"NO! Please, let it go!" Her outburst surprised them both. "I want you to know that I … that I …" Her voice cracked.

"That you what?"

"That I'll miss you terribly." She sobbed. "I've got to go. I'm so sorry." She hung up.

"Bridget? Hello? Bridget!"

Although that was their last conversation, Adama sent texts and left messages, but there was no reply. Bridget saved them, listening daily to hear his voice. His last voicemail broke her heart.

"Hello, Bridget, I'm in Boston. I'm staying at the Marriott off Old Bridge Road. I'll be here for a couple of days. I drove by your house—it was empty with a 'Sold' sign. I've tried to find you—it's like you've vanished. I don't know what happened. Could you at least tell me if you're safe? I also want you to know that I should have told you how much … well, I miss you very much. Please, love, call me. I need to know you're all right."

Bridget desperately wanted to see him, but summoned the willpower to text him to keep him away. "I'm fine. Go home."

Adama was devastated and flew back to New York. Soon after, Adama sent her one last text, "I don't understand, but I respect your decision. We had something special. I won't bother you again. I wish you well. Goodbye."

Bridget wept over his messages. All she had were the saved photos of their time together, the loving voice messages, and the sweet texts she reviewed daily. She loved him and believed cutting ties had saved his career and possibly his life.

———◆———

The landing was rough, jolting Bridget back to the present. She collected her belongings, found a cab, and arrived at the Gild Hotel. She liked the familiarity of being close to NYPD headquarters. She welcomed the new assignment. She also knew her game face needed to be strong and her focus laser-sharp.

While lying in bed, she second-guessed herself and her decision to keep Adama in the dark, along with everything else that happened. Two weeks after her agreement with Antoine, she learned that Antoine had been killed in a skiing accident in the French Alps. Her divorce became moot; French authorities would return all funds in the trust account. Further documentation would decree that Antoine Tricheuse was deceased and Bridget was a widow.

But Bridget's personal tragedies weren't over. During that time, the unthinkable happened: Bridget's father had a stroke and died. She moved into her parents' home, grieved, sorted through forty years of marriage, had an estate sale, and sold the property. Many aunts, uncles, and cousins grieved with and supported Bridget throughout the process.

Just when Bridget emerged, under a very dark cloud, and returned to work, Margaret Taylor called with unbearable news. She would never forget the call, nor the pain in her voice.

"Oh, my dearest Bridget, I've the most dreadful news. My darling Colin has been killed. I'm so lost."

"What? Oh my god, Margaret. No! It can't be. What happened?"

Margaret gave Bridget all the details. Bridget promised to be on a plane the next day to help her and the Yard with the investigation.

Bridget's world crashed—her husband died, her father passed away, she lost her friend and mentor, and she'd pushed away the one true love of her life. Bridget scanned her pictures of Adama. *I've missed you so much. I know you were so hurt and upset with me. I should have told you about Antoine's threats.* Her heart ached. *Will he forgive me, and how will he react when he sees me? If he sees me. Did the commissioner tell him I'm coming?*

Tired of thinking, Bridget turned out the light, hugged her pillow, and prayed for guidance.

MONDAY

Chapter 25: The Consultant

Adama Baptiste arrived early at NYPD headquarters for a meeting with his detectives about the two dead billionaires and Thomas Miller-Chevalier. Passing the main conference room, he noticed his boss, Police Chief Ballantine, talking with Police Commissioner Xavier Prawda. The chief motioned for Adama to join them.

"Ah, here he is now," the chief said.

Adama opened the door and stepped into the room; they all shook hands.

"Good morning, commissioner. Nice to see you," Adama said.

"Hello, Adama, do you know why I'm here?" Prawda asked.

"Yes, sir," Adama answered, standing tall and resolute.

"Where are you with the investigations of the two dead billionaires and Thomas Miller? The press is having a field day. This morning's goddamn Gazette's headlines were 'GALLERY KILLER ON THE LOOSE.' I hate that little rag. Not to mention they're questioning our competency." The Commissioner's face turned beet red.

Chief Ballantine interjected. "Sir, it's been twenty-four hours. We're still conducting our investigations, and as you know, Adama's team has already ascertained a connection between all three victims with the Miller gallery." Chief Ballantine looked to Adama for reassurance.

"Sir, we're still piecing it all together and have several leads. The medical examiner has prioritized the autopsies. We should have a cause of death today or tomorrow. In the meantime, we're tracking the last movements of all three victims." Adama said.

"Victims? Do you know who Thomas Miller is?" Prawda asked.

"Yes, sir, he's the son of Henry Miller, owner of the gallery," Adama said.

"Really? I'm not sure you fully grasp the situation here, Deputy Chief. Thomas Miller is the son of *my best* friend, Henry Miller, who's back in the hospital after hearing about his son's death. Our friendship dates back years, so this is a personal matter. And we also had two billionaires die in *our* city." Prawda was visibly upset. "I want answers."

"Sir, I understand the implications. We'll conduct thorough investigations and find out what happened, and I'll keep the chief informed."

"You do that. In the meantime, the mayor insisted we bring in extra help. We need to close these cases quickly."

"Help?" Adama glanced back and forth from the commissioner to his chief. "Sir? What do you mean by *help*?"

"The mayor and I have hired an outside consultant," Prawda said. "She's a pro when it comes to high-profile cases. We've used her before."

"Sir, with respect, we have a solid team. Bringing in a consultant could slow us down." Adama looked at his chief for support.

"Just the same, you'll work with the consultant." Prawda looked around the room. "By the way, where is Murphy?"

"Right here, Commissioner," Bridget confidently answered as she strode into the room.

Flabbergasted, Adama's jaw dropped, shocked by her presence. For a brief moment, the highest-ranking men in the NYPD found themselves speechless—completely disarmed by Bridget's striking appearance. Her vibrant blue eyes, full lips, square chin, and slight dimples in her rosy cheeks pierced even the toughest man's armor.

"Ah, Bridget, welcome." Prawda broke the silence and extended his hand.

"Good morning, Commissioner, and hello, Chief Ballantine." Bridget shook their hands, then moved toward Adama.

"Hello, Adama, it's nice to see you again." She casually extended her hand. Externally, she presented a professional demeanor, but internally, her emotions ran off the charts.

"Bridget. It's been a while." Adama grudgingly extended his hand. The warmth of his hand felt familiar, and she did not want to let go. Adama also hesitated, but he gave a light squeeze, released her soft hand, and backed away.

"Thanks for coming on such short notice," the chief said.

Surprised again, Adama glanced at his boss. *So, you knew she was coming?*

Commissioner Prawda took control. "We're all glad you're here. Aren't we?" Prawda glanced at Adama, who immediately reacted.

"Yes, Commissioner." Adama nodded.

"So, you two know each other?" Prawda asked.

"Yes, sir, we worked a case last year," Adama said matter-of-factly.

"Good, then you know that Murphy is an expert criminal investigator regarding high-profile cases." He looked at Adama and Bridget. "Now listen, you two, I don't want to read in the tabloids about some fucking alien sucking the blood out of our billionaires. I want results and regular updates." Prawda pulled his buzzing phone out of his pocket. "Aww, geez. It's the mayor." His look was stone-cold. "Everyone clear?"

"Yes, sir!" Both Adama and Bridget responded simultaneously.

"Good. I'm going to brief the mayor. Walk with me, Chief." Prawda turned to Adama and Bridget. "I expect your very best, don't let me down."

"You can count on us, sir," Adama replied.

"Yes, sir, Commissioner," Bridget said. "And I'm ready to get to work."

Adama raised his index finger and gestured to Bridget to *hold that thought*. He called out.

"Chief? A word?"

"No. I've got a meeting. You and Murphy get to work. That's all." The chief kept walking with the commissioner.

Noticing Adama's frustration and sensing his reluctance to have her involvement, Bridget felt like an unwanted fly buzzing around the room.

"They didn't tell you I was coming, did they?"

"No." Adama felt as though he had just surrendered to the enemy. "Okay, let's get you caught up. We formed a special task force. You'll be working with three of my best detectives. Come on, I'll introduce you."

"Okay. But we may have similar cases, and maybe we can help each other."

"So, you're here for *you*?" His tone was sarcastic.

"Wow, seriously? You sound angry."

"I don't like being blindsided. You could have texted to let me know you were coming. Oh wait! Let me guess—you lost my number." Adama looked away from her.

Bridget was surprised at his hostility and did not care for his tone.

"Hey, that's not fair. And by the way, the commissioner should have told you I was coming. Besides, the last thing I knew, you were working out of the 19th Precinct." She paused and huffed. "Well, we're certainly off to a great start."

They both stopped talking and calmed down.

Adama conceded. "You're right, one of them should have told me."

Bridget changed the subject. "When were you promoted to deputy chief?"

"Two months ago. What, you didn't keep tabs on me?"

"Hmm. Well, congratulations, and you deserve it. Let's leave it at that." Bridget liked hearing his familiar sense of humor.

"Let's go to the bullpen." Adama checked his attitude as he stopped at the door. "Is your case about London?"

"You heard about Colin?"

"Yes. I'm sorry for your loss. I know he meant a lot to you," he said sincerely.

"Thanks, he will be missed."

"Why do you think our cases are linked?"

"Because I don't believe in coincidence."

They left the conference room. Adama shoved his hands in his pants pockets as he and Bridget walked down the hallway.

"Nor do I." He smiled inwardly, recalling how similarly they think.

Chapter 26: The Special Task Force

Adama led Bridget down the hall toward the bullpen, where Adama's staff, consisting of three talented detectives, several forensic technicians, and support staff, waited. He provided a quick overview of his new department.

"The special task force was created specifically to deal with high-profile cases, certain types of corruption, and, more recently, human trafficking due to the increase and sensitive nature. We also handle art and antiquities connected to the city, including those associated with international crimes. I handpicked my detectives and support personnel."

"That's an impressive responsibility," Bridget said.

"Thanks. We've got full jurisdictional authority; however, I'll never forget my roots, so we collaborate between all NYPD precincts and domestic and foreign entities."

"I'm sure you'll make the NYPD proud," Bridget said.

"Well, we just got started, and with these notable deaths, our division will be under an intense spotlight to prove itself."

"You can handle it." Bridget smiled to break the tension.

"Thanks. I'll check in with everyone when we go inside, then introduce you." Adama opened the door to the bullpen. "This is it."

Upon entering, Bridget separated from Adama. Team members noticed the newcomer and watched her as Adama addressed his team.

"As you all know, yesterday was one for the books. We're on point for all three fatality cases. We must proceed cautiously and accurately—no mistakes. And, you may have noticed I didn't come alone. I'll introduce our guest in a few minutes."

Adama walked to a whiteboard on the other side of the room. Pictures of all three victims, the locations of their deaths, critical information, and next of kin were noted under each profile. The board was updated as new details emerged.

"Where are we with identification and notification of next of kin?"

Jimmy Quinn read from an iPad. "Sir, all notifications are complete. Our CME met Thomas Miller's father, although his daughter had already informed him. The coroner in Palm Beach notified William Vanhorn's adult children. And Dallas's CME notified Daisy Hunter's adult children. Dr. Pearson scheduled separate identification meetings for all three families."

"All right. Where are we with forensics, fingerprints, DNA, internal security tapes, facial recognition, witness statements, and alibis?"

Lynda, a crime scene technician, raised her hand. "Sir, we've run all prints collected through the IAFIS system. Several sets of prints were collected from the front entrance and inside the gallery, the hotel, and the yacht. Provided everyone is in the system, we'll have a complete list soon."

"Great," Adama said.

Detective Burke consulted his notebook. "Surveillance cameras and facial recognition helped identify the seven people outside Miller Antiquities on Saturday. Six billionaires, including our two vics and their limo drivers. And Thomas Miller, the son."

"Right. So, we know who attended the event. That's great news. Those individuals are the key to our investigations."

Detective Bobby Gates spoke up. "Statements have been taken, and all alibis have checked out. We've requested triangulations for each cellphone, along with call logs and messages. And forensics is still on scene at all three locations."

"Great. What next?"

Burke leaned over and nudged Gates. He raised his eyes toward Bridget and looked back at Gates questioningly. Gates gave him a "Beats me" look.

Burke raised his index finger. "How do you want the assignments managed for the other attendees at the gallery?"

"We'll use two-person teams. In the meantime, the main focal point is the gallery. We'll work backward from there. I want to receive updates and reports from everyone by the end of the day, along with a comprehensive timeline of events for all parties involved. For now, the CME has labeled all deaths as suspicious. I'm meeting with Doctor Pearson later today. Hopefully, she'll have something for us by this afternoon."

Adama wrote the word "motives" on the whiteboard. "Who benefits? Who were our victims? Get all financial, personal, and business information. Find partners. Search for extended family members and dig up everything about everyone who attended that gallery event. And remember, their families deserve answers."

He turned to Detective Burke, who had raised his hand. "Burke, question?"

"Yes. We still need to meet with the owner of the Miller gallery."

"Right. You go this morning, but see me first. Best to start with Miss Miller. And Ricky, Mr. Miller, was readmitted to the hospital. He's in bad shape."

"Got it, thanks." Burke understood that he needed to be tactful and cautious.

"All right, listen up—we work these by the book. Use your sources, no stone unturned—and one more thing. The press is pushing hard for information. No one speaks to anyone outside this office. The mayor and the commissioner will manage the press—no leaks. Understood?"

Everyone in the room nodded in agreement.

"Good." He motioned to Bridget. "The commissioner, the chief, and I agreed to bring in an outside consultant."

He knew that statement would ensure everyone's attention. They took turns looking at Bridget, then back at Adama.

"This is Bridget Murphy. For those unfamiliar with her reputation, she's an expert criminal investigator specializing in high-profile cases. Bridget is an excellent asset for our particular set of circumstances. Bridget will work within our division. She has security clearance and will have complete access to our files. Please give her your full support."

Everyone in the room looked at her.

Bridget waved. "Good morning. You can call me Bridget or Murphy, your choice." She smiled as she looked around the room.

"We'll save the individual introductions for later," Adama said. "We've got a lot of work to do. Send me regular updates, I'll be reporting to the chief and the commissioner on a daily, if not hourly, basis. Okay, that's it. Thanks, everyone."

Adama motioned for Bridget to follow him to his office. He turned back.

"Ricky, can you join us?"

"Be right there." Ricky gathered his files.

Bridget set her satchel on a glossy round table in Adama's office. Adama stood behind his desk and flipped through the pink slips of messages. He scrunched two and tossed them into a wastebasket. Burke gave a polite knock and entered the room holding four folders.

"Bridget Murphy, this is Richard Burke, our lead detective," Adama said.

"Nice to meet you, Burke," Bridget said.

"Call me Ricky. Nice to meet you. I know you by reputation." They shook hands.

Burke turned to Adama. "I brought the case files on our three vics."

"Good. Bridget will want to review those." Adama continued reviewing messages. "Give Bridget everything we've got so far and set her up in an office. She'll also need a computer, email, and access to all the electronic case files and other docs."

"Sure. There's an empty office across from me," Ricky said.

"Perfect." Adama turned to Bridget. "What else can we do to help you get up to speed?"

"Thank you, Ricky." Bridget turned to Adama. "All that sounds good, but I'd like to see the bodies, visit the crime scenes, talk with the CME, learn about the gallery attendees, and review the Miller invoices and shipping records. Can we do that now? And can I get hard copies of the case files? I'll read them in the car."

Bridget's request surprised Adama. He assumed she would want to settle into an office and read. Adama was reminded about her direct communication style and no-nonsense work ethic.

"Right. Sure, we can do that," Adama said.

"Here, Bridget, these are the three case files." Ricky handed them to her, along with one of his business cards. "My cell number is on that. I'll get our IT department to set up your email account. And I'll forward the electronic files asap." Burke smiled but sensed tension in the air.

"Thanks, Ricky." Bridget took the files.

"Ricky, do you have profiles on the others at the gallery?" Adama asked.

"Right here." Ricky waved the fourth folder.

"Great." Adama quickly reviewed the data and pictures about the other four billionaires who attended the gallery on Saturday. He recognized each person. The fact sheets provided their last known location in the city.

"Here you go." Adama passed Bridget the folder.

"Thanks." Bridget put the files into her satchel; she stood ready to leave.

"Ricky, list the following assignments on the whiteboard." Adama handed him the list. "Bridget and I will go to the morgue first, then meet with Gerald Decker and Dick Betrug. Text me addresses after you confirm their current location."

"Yes, Deputy Chief," Ricky replied. "By the way, I've got a quick update about another case when you have a minute."

"What is it?" Adama asked.

"Detective Gates identified the container ship that brought in our two dead vics from the pier. It's long gone, but the captain is cooperating. Hopefully, we'll have names soon."

"That's great, have Gates send the ship's manifests. I'd like to know where they came from and what they carried."

"Will do," Ricky said.

"Ready, Bridget? I'll bring you up to speed along the way." Adama headed to the door.

Bridget grabbed her bag and followed. Burke stepped aside as they left the office. He fixated on Bridget. *What a looker.* He also detected something between Adama and Bridget. *This should be interesting.*

Once outside, Adama pointed, and they got into his sedan. After settling in, Bridget opened each file, read, and made comments aloud.

"So, Thomas Miller was only thirty-six and died of an apparent heart attack. That's pretty young."

The next case was William Vanhorn. "Possible autoerotic asphyxiation? You don't see many of those. Was he alone?"

"We're still verifying who had access to his bedroom," Adama answered.

Finally, Daisy Hunter. Bridget read the report and scrunched her nose at the pictures. "Daisy Hunter choked to death, and her dogs were eating out of her mouth? That's disgusting." She closed the folder. "What's your take on these deaths?" Bridget asked.

"All three deaths are currently regarded as suspicious. They all attended the same gallery on the same night. We're operating under the theory that all three deaths may be connected to the Miller Antiquities gallery on W. 56th. Do you know it?"

"Yes, and I know the owners, Henry Miller and Jacqueline Miller. I met them both at separate venues. Jacqueline and I met in London last year on a fraud case. She's excellent, by the way. And I was introduced to Henry Miller at the Met during an Egyptian antiquities gala a year ago."

"Right. We've surveillance videos from outside the Miller gallery. All six billionaires arrived separately and left at nine p.m. They all looked healthy getting into their limousines."

"So, six billionaires and a private antiquities event. Sounds intriguing. I wonder what they were viewing or buying."

"No idea—haven't gotten that far."

"What about the cause and time of death for each victim? Are the autopsies done yet?"

"Different times. It looks like Thomas Miller may have died Saturday night, and William Vanhorn and Daisy Hunter died Sunday morning. The CME initiated autopsies last night. Hopefully, we'll know the cause of death today. We'll go there first."

"What did Miller and his daughter have to say about Thomas's death and the other vics?"

"Not much. We had all of two minutes with Henry Miller at the hospital. The man is understandably distraught. His doctor is keeping him sedated. Jacqueline Miller gave us a statement at the gallery. She didn't know about the event, so we assume Thomas Miller scheduled it without their knowledge."

"That's interesting, if true. Perhaps Thomas thought he'd line his pockets with some extra cash on the side. Do our gallery owners have alibis?"

"Rock solid. We confirmed that Miss Miller was at an event in D.C. and flew back Sunday morning. She found Thomas dead in the office on Sunday. And Mr. Miller had a massive heart attack a few weeks back. He is bedridden with two full-time nurses. After hearing about his son's death, he went into cardiac arrest and was readmitted to Mount Sinai on Sunday afternoon."

"I'm sorry to hear about Henry and his son. And poor Jacqueline, finding her brother dead. That's rough."

"Right. A devastating situation for them both. Did you know Henry Miller is a personal friend of the commissioner *and* the mayor?"

"Um. I heard they were all college buddies and even vacationed together. I imagine they're anxious for answers."

"Yes, well, you missed the best part of our meeting this morning. They'll drive us crazy until we get answers."

"Well then, let's get some."

Driving, Adama glanced at Bridget and thought about their relationship. It had been four months since they'd seen each other. He was still reeling from their last encounter, which had been cut off with no questions asked. He spent the previous months hurt, confused, and more recently, angry. He did not want Bridget working the cases for personal reasons, but he admitted she was a capable investigator. *Bringing her in was a good call by the mayor. Damn it.* Bridget felt his eyes and looked over. He nonchalantly turned away and drove in silence. She could sense his anger and wondered if her involvement had been a mistake.

Chapter 27: Three Bodies

Bridget and Adama passed through security upon arrival at the BOME. He led her down the hallway to Dr. Betty Pearson's lab, where she happened to see them through the window of the heavy metal door. The doctor motioned for him to come inside. She was expecting Adama, but not Bridget.

"Good morning," Dr. Pearson said. Her eyes moved to Bridget for an introduction.

"Oh, I'm sorry. This is—"

"I'm Bridget Murphy, a consultant with the NYPD. It's nice to meet you." Bridget extended her hand as she approached Dr. Pearson.

"Oh! And you as well. I'm Doctor Betty Pearson, Chief Medical Examiner." The doctor was aware of Bridget from past cases. "I know you by reputation. You solved that big case in Paris last year. I heard it was a tricky one." Dr. Pearson shook Bridget's hand.

"I had a good team, we got lucky," Bridget said.

"I doubt that." Dr. Pearson adjusted her rhinestone glasses. "Please, call me Betty or Doc."

"Thanks." Bridget liked her.

Adama watched their interaction and listened to their discussion about work experiences and famous cases. He felt left out of the conversation. He admired both women and watched the positive body language between them. After a few minutes, Adama cut in.

"Excuse me, I hate to interrupt." He turned to Dr. Pearson. "Betty, what can you tell us about the victims?"

"Only preliminaries. Follow me."

Dr. Pearson walked slightly ahead and next to Bridget. She led them into the examination room where three bodies lay on separate tables. A white sheet covered each body. Dr. Pearson pulled back the sheet to expose Thomas Miller's head and chest area. Adama and Bridget stared at the Y-shaped incision and stitches on his chest.

"We finished the autopsy on Thomas Miller-Chevalier this morning." Betty read selected excerpts from Thomas's results. "Thirty-six years old; heart showed signs of a slight coronary aneurysm forming, other organs showed signs of deterioration from chronic drug and alcohol abuse. Alcohol, cannabis, and cocaine were all found in his system through saliva and hair tests."

"Enough to kill him?" Adama asked.

"No." Betty shook her head.

"What then?" Adama asked.

Betty placed the clipboard on a tray next to Thomas's body. "We also found traces of a controlled substance—carfentanil, an extremely potent opioid. The blood work will determine the quantity and whether or not it was lethal. We also found undigested food and alcohol in his stomach, indicating he died shortly after ingesting both."

"Do you think this was an overdose or foul play?" Bridget's voice slowed at the mention of the last scenario.

"Inconclusive at this time."

"What about the rest of the food and champagne bottles—was anything found in them?" Adama asked.

"We brought those back with us, as well as the glasses. My forensic pathologist ran tests for drugs and chemicals. We should have results later today. Dusting showed multiple fingerprints on each champagne bottle and the glasses. However, it looks like someone attempted to wipe one glass clean." The doctor pointed to a single glass resting on a shelf.

"Wiped clean? That's an odd thing to do at a gallery event," Bridget noted.

"Maybe the person wore gloves," Adama said to Bridget.

"That's possible. However, our tests revealed tiny fragments of tissue, similar to those found on a Kleenex or a napkin, around a small scratch on the stem of the glass. Someone tried to wipe away tell-tale signs that they touched or drank from that glass." Dr. Pearson was, as always, concise.

"Now we're getting somewhere. What about DNA?" Adama asked.

"In the works. We evaluated all of the gallery's glasses, bottles, and surfaces for foreign substances, poisons, and toxins." Dr. Pearson pulled on gloves.

"How long will that take?" Adama asked.

"A day, maybe two. These victims take priority," Dr. Pearson replied.

"So, best guess about cause of death?" Adama asked.

"Guess, no. Cardiac arrest—his heart stopped."

"And what can you tell us about the other victims? Any similarities?" Bridget asked.

The doctor walked over to Daisy Hunter and pulled back the sheet covering her large body. The doctor exposed Miss Hunter's face and neck. Her mouth was open, and her nose, cheeks, and ears showed scratches and torn or missing flesh. Adama and Bridget approached.

"What caused the damage to her face?" Bridget asked.

"Preliminary findings indicate her dogs are responsible." Dr. Pearson looked at Adama sheepishly, recalling her attempt to explain what those dogs did to their owner.

Bridget scrunched her nose and gagged at the sight and smell. She put her index finger under her nose. Dr. Pearson offered Bridget a breath mint from her pocket. Bridget took it.

"We're still removing the food from her mouth, esophagus, and lungs. It's in her ears and up her nasal cavities. We've collected more than eighty ounces of food." The doctor pointed to four glass beakers filled with food particles. "The contents found in her orifices consisted of chicken, duck liver pâté, crackers, olives, cake, pork sausage, a variety of cheeses, cookies, and assorted candy and nuts," Dr. Pearson explained.

"That's bizarre," Adama said.

"It is, and more interesting, the food was tightly compressed. A technician is at the hotel searching for any implement that may have been used to pancake it there."

"So, cause of death?" Adama asked.

"We won't know for sure until the autopsy is complete. But my initial findings show that Miss Hunter had an impaired gag reflex, as well as gastroesophageal reflux disease. Hypoxemia is present based on the amount of food lodged in her airway."

"Meaning?" Adama was becoming impatient.

"Asphyxiation," Bridget interjected. Dr. Pearson nodded in agreement.

"Could this have been self-induced?" Adama asked.

"No determination yet."

"Come on, Doc, you know what I'm asking." Adama was insistent.

"Yes, Adama, I do. Was she murdered?" Now, Dr. Pearson was annoyed.

"Right."

"Perhaps," she said. "It's difficult to comprehend how anyone could self-inflict or ingest that much food into their mouth and other orifices, especially within such a condensed period of time. But, food was under her fingernails and squished between her fingers, indicating she may have participated in the act."

Adama and Bridget stared at Daisy Hunter's shredded face. They wondered how her actions were physically and mentally possible.

"How long did it take for her to die from asphyxiation?" Bridget asked.

"Definitely within five minutes. Nothing was digested," Dr. Pearson said.

"So, suspicious circumstances?" Adama asked.

"For now, yes," Dr. Pearson relented. "We've taken tissue samples from her face, nose, mouth, and ears to check for DNA. Keep in mind, there are no defensive wounds. No bruises, no cuts on her hands or arms. If someone else were involved, she didn't fight back."

"Could she have already been dead, and someone did this afterward?" Bridget asked.

"As some perverse act? Perhaps. What do you think, Adama?" She and Bridget looked at him.

"Based on timing, witness statements, and videos of people coming and going from her suite, she was alone during the last hour of her life." He paused. "What about Vanhorn?"

Dr. Pearson went to William Vanhorn's table and pulled back the sheet to expose his face and neck areas. Adama and Bridget stood nearby.

"We've just started his autopsy. Death was caused by a restriction of oxygen to the brain. Based on how we found his body, erotic asphyxiation appears to be the culprit."

"Any indications that someone else caused his death?" Adama asked.

"Perhaps. His hands and feet showed deep ligature marks. He struggled to free himself from the restraints, especially his hands. His wrists were bloody from tugging, and his left wrist was broken. We'll check for foreign DNA."

"A broken wrist? That sounds like he wanted out," Bridget remarked.

"Indications are that he tried to free himself, both hands and feet," Dr. Pearson said. "We found signs that he thrashed about on the bed, especially with his feet. He could move his legs up and down and slide them from side to side. The bar that held his foot restraints had spikes, and they tore the sheets and dug into the bed."

"In other words, he tried to get out of the cuffs himself?" Bridget confirmed.

"That is a current theory. If a person is conscious, they thrash about while experiencing a lack of oxygen, even if self-imposed. It's an involuntary reflex."

"How long would that take?" Bridget asked.

"About four to six minutes," Dr. Pearson said.

Bridget looked uneasy.

"Could someone have restrained Vanhorn and left him to die?" Adama asked.

"Of course, the restraints were improperly attached. Release tabs on both handcuffs were inaccessible to Vanhorn. He couldn't have freed himself, even if he wanted to."

"The cuffs were put on wrong? Could someone have purposefully arranged them so he couldn't get out?" Adama suspected murder.

"And he broke his wrist trying to free himself. I'd say he wanted to live. Wouldn't you?" Bridget asked.

"It appears as such," Dr. Pearson said. "We're checking for foreign DNA. We took cheek swabs of everyone on board. And we're analyzing the bed linens, his robe, and the restraints. The results will take a while. There were a lot of people in that room." Dr. Pearson stood by Vanhorn's body and listened to Adama and Bridget as they exchanged suppositions.

"Maybe he or she was a novice and didn't know how to use the restraints properly," Bridget said. "Maybe it was an accident, and the person panicked."

Adama envisioned the scenario. "Or Vanhorn could have restrained himself."

"By himself?" Bridget asked.

"It's not completely uncommon," Adama said. "Achieving sexual arousal can be addictive. Even without a partner, people are known to restrain themselves. It's hazardous."

"Is that what you think happened? He set himself up, and it went sideways?" Bridget asked.

Dr. Pearson nodded. "It's possible. I've seen dozens of cases where victims died from self-induced autoerotic asphyxiation. The majority are accidental deaths."

"Okay. So, for now, suspicious circumstances?" Adama confirmed.

"For now," Betty agreed.

"Thanks, Betty. Come on, Bridget, let's get you to the crime scenes."

"Thank you, Doc." Bridget smiled.

"You're welcome, Bridget. It was nice meeting you." They shook hands.

Adama was ready to move forward with the day's agenda. He motioned to Bridget and walked toward the door. Bridget initially followed him but slowed as she approached Daisy Hunter's body.

"Hang on." Bridget stopped. "Help me out. Is it possible *something*, and not *someone*, made Miss Hunter behave in a manner that caused her to ingest all that food in such a short time frame?" Bridget asked.

Adama stopped and turned around. "What are you thinking, Bridget?"

"We all agree that her death is bizarre. Doc, besides Miss Hunter's health issues, could she have eaten or drunk something that made her behavior so bizarre?"

"If Daisy did ingest something that made her, for lack of a better word, go insane, we'll find that in the toxicology. We've run blood panels to look for pathogens, toxins, and drugs on all three victims." Dr. Pearson appreciated Bridget's question with a nod of approval.

"Well, if that's the case, we could hypothesize a similar scenario about Thomas Miller and William Vanhorn," Adama said. "They were all at the gallery together. If Thomas ate or drank something that gave him a heart attack, then Vanhorn could have eaten or drunk something that asphyxiated him, and in Daisy, it could have caused self-induced choking. That would mean we're looking at a whole other ball game." Adama looked to Dr. Pearson for agreement.

"Indeed. But we would need to consider the timing of each death; none were simultaneous," she said. "However, depending upon the substance, bodies react differently."

The three of them silently considered the possibility of such a unique scenario. With a genuine connection between all three deaths, foul play was no longer hypothetical. The possibility of mass murder entered Adama's mind; he knew time was of the essence, putting the other four billionaires at risk.

"Doc, we need those results asap."

"Absolutely," she agreed.

"Great question, Bridget. Bravo." Adama smiled at Bridget for the first time that day.

Bridget brightened up. *How about that, he remembered how to smile.* She happily returned a smile with warmth and acceptance.

Chapter 28: The Paper Bag

A dama caught himself surrendering to Bridget's magnetic smile. *Those dimples are man-eaters.* His relaxed posture stiffened as he doused himself with icy resolve. He scrunched his nose, and his wordless rebuke chastised her. *We're not hunky-dory.*

Disappointed, Bridget's smile dissolved as she backed off. *Message received.*

"Okay, Doc, now that we've talked about the victims, what about the boxes we found with William Vanhorn and Daisy Hunter? Did you find any prints?" Adama asked.

"Yes. There were only two sets of prints on both the large and small boxes. They belong to our two vics."

"Wait. What boxes?" Bridget asked.

"Over there." Adama pointed.

Two large wooden boxes rested on a large metal table. All over the outside of the lids was a whitish residue, left by the aluminum powder that helped lift the oval-shaped fingerprint patterns belonging to William Vanhorn and Daisy Hunter.

"When can we dust and analyze the object inside?" Dr. Pearson asked.

"Not yet. I don't want anyone opening or touching what's inside. Understood?" Adama sought confirmation. Dr. Pearson nodded in agreement. Bridget was intrigued.

"Why? What's inside? And why can't anyone touch it?" Bridget asked.

"Vanhorn and Miss Hunter both had a box in their bedroom. We confirmed each victim received them on Saturday night, *after* attending the Miller gallery event."

"So, the vics attended an event at the Miller gallery, purchased whatever's in the box, and you think there's a connection between the deaths, the gallery, and these boxes?" Bridget asked.

"It's a possibility, although there's no hard evidence yet," Adama said.

"Okay, that sounds plausible. Can I see what's inside?" Bridget asked.

"Uh, sure. I'll open one," Adama said.

Adama put on gloves. He carefully unlatched and lifted the heavy lid of Vanhorn's box. Inside was the stone-like object resting on a red satin sheet. Bridget and the doctor moved closer to view it. The three of them stood in silence, staring at the object.

"It's stunning." Bridget extended her arm, and Adama quickly intercepted.

"Better not," Adama warned.

"Why not?" Bridget asked. "I just want to feel it."

"You and everyone else; it's like a magnet," Dr. Pearson said. "He won't let anyone touch it."

"I think it best to observe for now. We're not sure how it's connected to the victims and possibly their deaths. Better to be cautious." Adama stared at the stone.

"It's unique. How many of these were sold at the event?" Bridget asked.

"According to the owners of the gallery, none. We think Thomas Miller may have organized a private event." Adama watched Bridget as she examined the stone.

Bridget tilted her head and leaned in. "Huh, you know, it's familiar. Strange, I can't quite place it." She stared at it intently.

Adama studied her face. *Come on, Bridget, do you recognize it?* He waited and listened while Bridget and Dr. Pearson discussed the stone. Enough time had passed with no reaction. Adama looked at his wristwatch.

"Right. Well, we're off. Stay in touch, Doc, and thanks." Adama slowly lowered the lid and engaged the latch. He pulled off his gloves and went toward the door. "Bridget, you coming?"

"Huh? Oh, sure." She turned toward Dr. Pearson. "Goodbye, again. Thanks for your time." Bridget reluctantly walked toward Adama, stopping momentarily. She turned back with a puzzled look on her face. "You know, it's odd, but it kind of looks like the old stones that I—" She suddenly gasped. "Oh my god!" Bridget's eyes widened. In a millisecond, her memory flooded back. She understood everything: what the stone was and what it meant to see it here, lying in a box. "Oh, my god, no!"

Bridget became alarmed and quickly walked back to the boxes. Adama followed her. The look on her face told Adama that she understood what the object represented. Her face expressed profound sadness. She grabbed hold of his arm.

"You know, don't you, Adama? You know what that is, right?" Bridget's voice trembled; each word weighed heavily with an aching melancholy.

"Yes. The same as you," he said. His expression filled with sorrow.

Bridget's breath became short gasps. Her heart pounded in her chest, and her fingers tingled. She felt sick and reached for a nearby table to steady herself.

"I can't, I-um…" Bridget stumbled. "What the fu—?" She turned in circles, holding her forehead with her hands. She was hyperventilating, and her face turned pale.

Adama reached out to steady her. "Bridget, don't faint. Breathe!"

The doctor watched their interaction. "You too? That's the same reaction Adama had in Daisy Hunter's bedroom. What's going on here?" Inquisitively, she watched them turn about in a fitful dance. "Careful, Adama, I think she's losing it."

"Hold it together, Bridget." Adama grabbed her shoulders and, bending down, eye level with her face, commanded, "Breathe!"

"Okay! Ah-shew, Ah-shew." Bridget's lungs struggled to claim oxygen. She slowly inhaled and exhaled with deep breaths, but was becoming light-headed. "I can't brea…" She wobbled and sagged against Adama for support.

Unphased by Bridget's distress, Dr. Pearson calmly pushed a metal caster-wheeled stool over to Bridget. "Sit down and put your head between your legs."

"Have you got a paper bag?" Adama intercepted the rolling stool with his foot. "Sit, Bridget."

He guided her onto the seat. Bridget put her head between her legs while Adama kept one hand on her back. Dr. Pearson went to a cabinet and brought a brown paper bag to Adama.

"Here, Bridget, this will help," Adama said. "Place the bag over your mouth and breathe in and out. You've got this."

With trembling hands, Bridget curled the opening and took a deep inhale. The bag crunched with a brittle staccato sound, and with each panicked breath, it collapsed and expanded like a bellow. Adama continued to steady Bridget on the stool.

"Water?" Adama asked, not taking his eyes off Bridget.

"Not until she's stable. Just keep her breathing into the bag, she'll be fine," Dr. Pearson said.

Bridget's erratic breathing had calmed down. Her lips were no longer blue, and the color was returning to her face.

"You're doing fine, Bridget," Adama said, patting her back. He looked over at Dr. Pearson, who had a scowl on her face.

"What?" he asked.

With arms folded, Dr. Pearson squared off with Adama. "Talk to me." Her statement was razor-sharp. "First, your trauma at the hotel, and now Bridget's panic attack. All because of what's in those boxes?"

"Slow breaths," Adama said. He now had two women to manage.

"Obviously, that *thing* over there is important and means something. I need to know if those objects have anything to do with the victims." Dr. Pearson's voice was tight and controlled.

"Betty, look, I had suspicions about the object in the box, and Bridget confirmed them. I'm not at liberty to discuss it now. We need to verify a few more details." Adama looked into her eyes. "I need a little time. Trust me, please?"

The doctor respected Adama and conceded. "Okay, but you're not blowing me off again. So, if you want any information about these victims, their autopsy reports, DNA, toxicology, or whatever, from my office, you'll tell me what you know first. Agreed?"

"Agreed."

Dr. Pearson approached Bridget. "How are you feeling, dear?"

Bridget gestured with a thumbs-up. The color of her face had returned to a pinkish glow. She felt better but clutched the paper bag like a security blanket.

"Bridget, are you feeling well enough to go? We have a full day ahead." Adama looked in her eyes for reassurance.

"Yes, I'm good." Bridget stood, waved the bag, and followed Adama. "Thanks, Betty."

"You're welcome."

Despite her curiosity, Dr. Pearson heeded Adama's warning not to touch the boxes. Instead, she reverently pulled the sheets over Thomas Miller and Daisy Hunter and resumed work on Vanhorn's autopsy.

Chapter 29: Dumbstruck

Adama and Bridget walked past the security guards and out of the OME's building. He walked Bridget to the passenger side and reached for the door handle.

"I've got it," she said curtly.

Adama backed off with palms in the air. His phone buzzed, and he read a text message from Detective Burke. He got into his car and shared the news.

"We found Gerald Decker. He's at the Vincent Hotel. The guy owns it." Adama snapped his seat belt. "He's one of the billionaires who attended the gallery event. Do you still want to go?"

"Yes." Bridget reached for the file folder and began reading the department notes about Gerald Decker.

While driving northbound on FDR, Adama thought it strange that Bridget was so quiet. *She usually has dozens of questions about a case.* The repetitive tapping of her fingernails on the folder told him something was amiss. They sat in silence for several minutes until Bridget closed the file and tossed it on the seat. She crossed her arms, huffed, and stared out the window. Her passive-aggressive behavior got to him.

"Are you okay? You seem upset."

"You think? What was that, payback or an ambush? Talk about being blindsided."

"What? What are you talking about? It was neither." Adama did a double-take at her.

"Why didn't you tell me about the stones?" Bridget glared at him.

Now he understood. "I wasn't sure and didn't know how to tell you. I'm sorry. Okay?"

"Well, what are we going to do? We can't ignore this." Her voice quavered. "I mean, we have to do something, right?"

"We will. But only when the time is right." Adama's voice was stressed. "There's more here than meets the eye. This just became an international incident. We need to be cautious. A lot of people have died because of those stones. I'm concerned this may lead to a deadly conspiracy. So, this information needs to be managed very carefully."

"No shit. The last thing we need is targets on our backs."

"Right. So, we do our job, solve the cases, and strategize about the boxes later. Agreed?"

"Agreed." Bridget let out a deep sigh. "God, I'm so embarrassed. I almost fainted. And breathing in a paper bag like a schoolgirl?"

"It's okay, Bridget. And completely understandable." Adama felt bad for startling her at the morgue.

"What did Dr. Pearson mean when she said, 'You too?' Did you have the same reaction?"

"Just about. It hit me hard too."

"I can imagine." Knowing something of his past, she empathized with him. She changed the subject.

"Well, anyway, Dr. Pearson is awesome."

"She's one of the best."

"You two work well together. She trusts you, and she likes you."

"We're just friends." He changed the subject. "We're almost to Decker's. Maybe he'll tell us what happened at the gallery. And if he has a box."

Wondering what she looked like, Bridget pulled the visor down and opened the mirror.

"Ugh, I'm a mess." She removed a tube of pink lip gloss from her pocket and dabbed a small amount onto her lips. "Look at me, I'm still shaky." She showed her trembling hands and looked in the mirror. "At least I look normal." Bridget used her fingers to fluff and reshape her hair.

Adama thought she looked beautiful. *You're not even close to looking normal.*

"We're here. You ready?" Adama looked for reassurance.

"I am. Let's do this."

Adama parked at the entrance of the Vincent Hotel. A valet opened Bridget's door, as another valet approached Adama. He flashed his badge.

"Keys are in the ignition. Keep it close, we won't be long."

"Yes, sir," the valet said.

The outside entrance was impressive but paled in comparison to the foyer. Shiny red and white diamond-striped floor tiles created a geometric pattern. A mirrored wall at the far end created the illusion of an endless room. Adama and Bridget approached the front desk.

"Good morning, may we speak with the manager?" He flipped open his badge.

The registration clerk reached for a desk phone. Adama and Bridget wandered over to a round marble table with an extensive array of colorful flowers. Bridget admired their beauty.

"Um, roses, lilies, and carnations. They're real and smell great."

Adama glanced at the flowers and shrugged. He was not impressed. A few minutes later, a short man in his fifties, wearing a black suit and shiny patent leather shoes, approached them.

"Good morning, sir, and madam. I am the manager; may I help you?"

"Yes. I'm Deputy Chief Adama Baptiste, we're with the NYPD." He flashed his badge. "We need to speak with the owner, Gerald Decker."

"Certainly." The manager instructed the registration clerk to inform Decker that detectives were on their way.

"Mr. Decker resides in the penthouse. We'll take his private elevator."

Inside, Bridget thought the space was surprisingly small. The mirrored door showed their reflections. Bridget smiled. *He's even more handsome than the last time we met.* She averted her eyes after Adama caught her spying. The elevator produced a familiar "ding" when it reached the top floor. All three exited and entered an elegant foyer. The manager knocked on Decker's door.

"Yes?" A man in an untied bathrobe, shorts, a T-shirt, and slippers opened the door.

"So sorry to bother you, sir. This gentleman and lady would like a few words with you."

"Oh, yeah? What about?" Decker asked.

"Gerald Decker?" Adama stepped forward. "Are you Gerald Decker?"

"Yes. Who are you?"

Adama was somewhat surprised. He half expected to find Decker dead. He quickly refocused and flashed his badge.

"I'm Adama Baptiste, Deputy Chief with the NYPD, and this is my—"

"And I'm Bridget Murphy, a consultant with the NYPD."

"Do you mind if we come in? We have a few questions to ask you." Adama asked.

"Whatever." No stranger to being questioned by police, he reluctantly opened the door.

Adama thanked the manager and held the door for Bridget. They followed Decker as he swaggered into the formal living room. It was grandiose with floor-to-ceiling windows that wrapped the corner suite in a panoramic embrace of the city. Brazilian walnut flooring flowed throughout; its rich chocolate tones warmed by hidden LED underlighting that traced the perimeter.

Decker sat on the eclectic Marquee black and honey striped Chenille sofa and crossed his legs. A white slipper dangled off his foot. He sat back and stretched his arms across the back of the couch. Decker stared with disdain as Adama and Bridget approached. He hated cops, especially ones with questions.

Gerald Decker was unshaven and slovenly looking. Bridget thought he must have just gotten out of bed. When Decker yawned loudly, she and Adama knew the conversation would be dismissive at best and hostile at worst.

"Mind if we sit?" Adama asked.

Decker pointed at the two chairs across from him. "Sure. What's the saying? Take a load off. Those shoes must be killing you."

And here we go. Bridget had interviewed dozens of condescending guys like him. She gave Decker a smile that unnerved him. *What a stuck-up, pompous ass you are.*

"MacKenzie-Childs Queen Bee Armchairs—very nice." Bridget sat and shifted her weight to get the whole feel of its comfortable, satiny finish. With an air of superiority, she leisurely curled her fingers around the ends of the extravagantly carved armrests. She delighted in mocking Decker, like a queen on her throne.

Everywhere Adama looked, he saw opulence. A designer chandelier cast prismatic light onto accent pieces, imported wool rugs cushioned his step, and expensive artwork proclaimed vast wealth. *My entire apartment could easily fit into this one room.* Adama sat in the empty armchair opposite Decker and opened a notepad.

"Let's get this over with. What do you want?" Decker asked.

"Mr. Decker, where were you Saturday night?" Adama asked.

"Saturday night? Let's see, where was I?" He took his time, rubbing the back of his neck. "Oh, yeah, I went to Duane's. Ever been to Duane's, officer?"

"It's Deputy Chief, and no, I've never been."

"That's too bad. I guess the NYPD doesn't pay you enough to enjoy life."

"What's Duane's?" Bridget knew but wanted to have some fun.

"Oh, you don't know!" He leaned forward. "Well, it's a fun little soiree for a late-night supper. If you understand, I like watching women dance in their scantily clad costumes. It's burlesque, my dear." Decker's eyes wandered all over Bridget's body. "You're a pretty thing, I bet you'd look good dancing there." He leaned forward with a flirtatious look.

Bridget bristled at his misogynistic haughtiness, and she despised narcissistic men.

"And did you also go to Miller Antiquities, *my dear?*" Bridget mocked him.

"I just told you, I went to Duane's. Are you deaf?" Decker glared at her.

"Don't play games with us, Gerry," she scoffed. "We have you on surveillance."

Decker gave her a "fuck you, lady" look, which pleased Bridget. She had pushed the right button.

"Okay, let's all relax. What were you doing at the gallery, sir?" Adama asked.

"Seriously? It's a fucking gallery, what do you think?"

"So, what did you purchase?" Adama wanted him to mention the boxes.

"You came here to find out if I bought something from that dump?" Decker laughed. Seeing the serious look on Adama's face, he answered, "No, I did not buy any of their shit. Okay?" Decker sat back and crossed his legs.

"Did you go alone?" Adama asked.

"Yes. Is that a crime?"

"Did you eat or drink anything?" Bridget asked.

"That's a weird question. Of course, we all did," Decker said. "It was a great spread. The caviar was Russian Volga Reserve. Do you two like caviar?"

"Who were the other attendees?" Adama asked.

"You're the detective. Do your job." Decker's chin went upward in a show of arrogance. He leaned forward, picked up a lit cigar from an ashtray, puffed, and blew smoke into the air. Bridget detested the smell of cigars but acted unfazed. Adama enjoyed a fine cigar on the occasional blue moon. He breathed in the sweet scent.

"Mr. Decker, are you aware that two of the six billionaires who attended the evening with you on Saturday night are dead?" Adama asked.

Both Adama and Bridget watched Decker turn pale. His expressionless face revealed he was dumbstruck. Decker uncrossed his legs and put his cigar into the ashtray. He gave Adama a blank look, then composed himself and cleared his throat.

"Okay. Two people are dead. What of it?"

"Did you know the host is also dead? That's three people, all connected with the gallery. What are the odds, Gerry? By the way, do you still have the box?" Bridget asked.

The question made Adama stiffen in his chair. *Here we go, never a dull moment.*

"Dude, what's she talking about?" Decker addressed Adama.

"Please answer the question, Mr. Decker," Adama said.

Bridget and Adama stared at him, waiting. They both knew how to use silence to make people feel uncomfortable. Almost a minute passed before Decker unraveled.

"What? Stop staring at me," Decker said. "I told you, I don't have any box here."

"Cut the crap, Gerry," Bridget said. "We know all of you billionaires had a box delivered."

Adama grimaced, knowing her statement may not be true. He knew she was fishing.

"So, what, that doesn't mean I have one," Decker said.

"No, but if you have a box, it could mean you're next in line to be a corpse, Gerry. The slabs in the morgue are cold and hard. But you'll have to wait your turn for an autopsy. There's a line." Bridget was unleashed.

"What the fuck, lady!" Decker's face turned beet red. "I think it's time you both leave."

Adama tried to calm him down by changing the subject. "What's the name and contact information of the chauffeur who drove you on Saturday?"

"Why do you need that?" Decker asked.

"Just routine. Is he at the hotel now?" Adama asked.

"No. He has the day off." Decker sensed Adama's impatience. "His name is Danny Garcia, and he lives in Brooklyn. Okay?"

"Thank you." Adama noted the information.

"So, let's see, we've covered where I go, if I eat, a gallery, a killer box, dead people, my chauffeur—what's next, my sex life?" Decker sneered.

"Mr. Decker, we believe the three deaths may be connected," Adama said. "As a precaution, we're trying to locate all the attendees and their boxes."

"Oh, really? Does the boogie man come out of the big wooden box?" Decker laughed.

"You need to take this seriously," Bridget said.

"Mr. Decker, tell us about the event," Adama said.

"Like what?" he asked.

"Like, what was it for? Previews of artifacts? Did anything unusual happen?"

Decker sneered. "Now, I get it, you're fishing. You don't know shit, and you expect me to tell you about the event. Nice try." He laughed and smugly puffed on his cigar.

Bridget was not amused. "Do you mind if we look around?" Bridget asked.

"Yes, as matter of fact, I do mind." Decker slapped both hands on his thighs, leaned forward, and stood up. "We're done. Have fun hunting down your killer boxes." He pointed at the door.

Adama and Bridget stood up. Adama held a business card.

"My number is on this card. Please call me if you'd like to talk. We're here to help."

"Oh, how nice, the police want to help me. Well, no thanks. See yourselves out, now."

Decker stood by the sofa, crossing his arms in protest.

Adama placed his card on the coffee table and tapped it. "Call me."

Decker watched as they left his suite. He looked at Adama's card and talked to himself. "Huh, two dead billionaires. I wonder who? And that stupid gallery guy too? That's weird." He picked up his cigar, puffed, and blew smoke into the air. "Fuck the police."

Chapter 30: Please, Let It Go

Adama and Bridget rode the cramped elevator down from the penthouse suite of the Vincent Hotel. She was still wound up from their encounter with Gerald Decker, while Adama was quiet and agitated about not learning anything new.

"Do you think Decker is dirty?"

"Definitely. He's been busted for dealing and possession. However, he has a great lawyer. Nothing seems to stick."

"No wonder he was so hostile."

The elevator reached the bottom floor, and they walked to Adama's car. The valet handed over Adama's keys.

"Have a nice day, sir."

"Thanks. Excuse me, did you work here Saturday night?"

"Yes, sir. Until midnight."

"Did Mr. Decker have anything delivered here on Saturday, Sunday, or today?"

"I didn't see anything. He goes out every night and usually returns after midnight, after my shift has ended. I haven't seen him since Sunday evening," the valet said.

"Thanks." Adama got into the car.

"What are you thinking?" Bridget was in earshot.

"I'm wondering if the deaths are somehow connected to the boxes being opened. We know that Vanhorn and Daisy opened theirs. Maybe Decker hasn't opened his yet."

"You mean if he has one. Adama, it's weird, but I believed him when he said he didn't have a box."

"Bridget, what he said was, 'I told you; I don't have any box here.' That's a different statement. And he described the 'big wooden box,' which means he's seen or has one. I wonder if he had it delivered somewhere else?"

"Nice catch, Adama." Bridget was impressed.

"And you, with your segue, 'You're next in line to be a corpse.' You get right to the point." Adama was a bit displeased with Bridget's approach.

"Oh, come on, Adama, he's a patronizing asshole, and I saw no reason for pleasantries. But it didn't work."

"No, it didn't, and he's a stupid man. I wonder how long he's got before it kills him too."

"Wow! That's a leap. Is that why you won't let anyone touch the stones inside the boxes? You think people will die?"

"Unfortunately, it's not that simple. But somehow, it's all connected. I need the missing pieces." Adama reached for his phone and called Detective Burke at headquarters. "And we need to find the others before they open their boxes."

"What's up, Deputy Chief?" Burke asked.

"Two things. First, Decker's limo driver is Danny Garcia, who lives in Brooklyn. Find his address and get his statement immediately. Find out if he knows anything about the boxes from Miller Antiquities."

"And the second thing?" Burke asked.

"Did anyone interview all the valets at the Vincent Hotel to find out if Decker had a large box delivered?" Adama asked.

"I believe so. Hang on, I'll check the notes." Ten seconds passed. "Yes. We talked with nine valets, spanning two days and three shifts. Nothing was delivered to him. The only thing they ever saw was Decker getting in and out of his limousine. Why do you ask?"

"His limousine! Of course! Thanks, Ricky." Adama hung up.

"Who's limousine? Decker's?" Bridget figured it out. "Of course! His limo!"

"Right! I'll bet that's where he's got it," Adama said.

"Oh, that sneaky bastard." Bridget reached over and touched Adama's arm. "Hey, I know this is inconvenient, but I need to eat something."

"Okay, but I want to find Dick Betrug and his limo driver. We can't afford to miss these people; they may leave town." He looked over at Bridget. She gave him a soulful look. "And we'll get something to eat on the way. There's a pizza shop nearby. Will that do?"

"Pizza sounds good."

———◆———

From the moment Bridget arrived, there had been tension between her and Adama. He was calm and detached, except for his compassionate behavior at the morgue. Bridget decided to address the elephant in the room.

"Hey, I know it's bad timing, after everything that happened between us. I wondered if we could talk. This morning was a surprise for both of us." Bridget was nervous and fumbled her words. "And, it must be awkward having me here. I've been meaning to call you. I planned to call after I got back from London. I've wanted to ask … to see if we could get together and clear the air, after our …" she hesitated.

"Our what?" He looked ahead.

"Really? Am I that forgettable?"

"Bridget, the last thing you are is forgettable."

"So, you do remember we had an amazing relationship."

"Oh, that. Right." Adama showed no emotion.

"Yeah, that." Bridget watched his face for any form of expression. He did not smile, frown, or flinch. "Well, can we talk about it?"

"I'd rather not."

"Look, I know that I mishandled my need for space. I mistreated you, and I'm very sorry. I hope we can discuss what happened."

"Discuss? What I recall was a unilateral decision, with no questions allowed. I should have been included." Adama paused and took a breath. "You know what, this is not the time or place to have this discussion. We have a job, so let's focus on that."

"But I can explain. There were extenuat—"

"Look, Bridget, it's okay. We had a good time. I don't think we need to rehash."

"Adama, you don't understand. I—"

"Please, let it go." Adama's tone was dismissive.

His words rang a harsh bell, and they were the exact words Bridget had used four months earlier. Adama made a hard right turn and pulled sharply to the curb.

"We're here."

Bridget jerked forward when the car stopped. She sat for a moment, feeling sad and confused. His sharp retorts were uncharacteristic. And his chilliness meant it was worse than she realized.

"Okay." She unbuckled her seatbelt. "Are you coming?"

"No. Can you get me two slices of cheese and a soda?" He opened his cellphone.

"Um, sure." Bridget went inside, ordered four slices of cheese pizza, and looked outside to see Adama on his cellphone. A few minutes later, she brought a pizza box, napkins, and two cans of root beer to his car. "Here you go."

Bridget set the pizza box between them, tossed the napkins onto the dash, and put the sodas in the cup holders. Adama reached for a napkin, opened the lid, and took a slice of the pie. Bridget mimicked him. They ate silently; each bite punctuated the gnawing tension filling the air. Bridget's stomach twisted into knots, and Adama felt guilty for shutting her down.

"If I may, let me say a couple of things," he said. His voice was calm. He looked over for approval. Bridget nodded. "I apologize for being so abrupt. The truth is, I can't focus on solving three potential murders, an impatient mayor, my team, the press, an international conspiracy, and us."

His last word hung in the air with unspoken possibilities.

"I need my wits about me, and so do you. I'm not saying I don't want to talk; let's consider doing that after we've wrapped up these cases. Will that work for you?"

"Yes," she said. She exhaled to calm her stomach. "You're right. Juggling emotions and solving cases doesn't mix. I'm sorry I brought it up. Just promise to hear me out, I've so much to tell you, and I'm sure you do too." Her eyes pleaded for reassurance. *Please say yes. God, I wish we could hug each other.*

"I promise." He was disarmed. Sheer willpower stopped him from grabbing her.

"Thank you." She smiled, her charm and dimples lit up her face. "Wait, I'll put the box in the trash." She got out, sated and full of bounce.

Adama watched, holding his smile. *How am I supposed to defend myself?*

"Okay, let's go find Dick Betrug." Bridget got into the car, eager to work.

Chapter 31: Dick Betrug

When in NYC, Dick Betrug always lodged at the Stetson Hotel on Manhattan's Upper West Side. Famous for its western theme and unique furnishings, it complemented Betrug's rugged persona. After leaving Miller Antiquities on Saturday evening, he had instructed the manager to place an expected package on his dining room table. Then Betrug arranged a rendezvous with a married paramour at her French-inspired Long Island chateau. He spent the weekend there, returning to Manhattan Monday afternoon.

Exhausted, Betrug exited his limousine, ignored the Stetson's valets, and hurried to his suite. He turned on the LIV golf channel to catch the weekend's highlights, poured himself a triple shot of Pappy's fifteen-year-old bourbon, neat, and lit one of his signature cigars. He stepped outside to gaze at the city. Below, Columbus Circle hummed with traffic, to the north, Central Park beckoned, and to the south, the Empire State Building stood sentinel in the distance. Leaning on the rail, he took it all in, puffing on his cigar and sipping his bourbon.

Betrug suddenly remembered his special delivery. He felt giddy. The formal dining room was surrounded by slender columns adorned with pieces of genuine tree bark. Spread a few feet apart, they created the illusion of a forest. The large box rested on the table.

"Let's see what you look like." Betrug felt the smoothness of the rich mahogany grain.

Two vintage locks secured the lid. Betrug remembered he needed a key. He looked around for the small jewelry box with the initials "DB" engraved on the top.

"Shit. What did they do with my key?" he said aloud, feeling a twinge of panic. "Oh, right, I put that damn box in my overnight bag."

He went to the bedroom and retrieved the jeweled skeleton key. Betrug inserted it into the first lock. It clicked open. He set the heavy lock on the table. He put the key into the second lock but froze when he heard a knock on the door. He looked through the keyhole to see the manager, a man and a woman.

"Who is it?" he asked.

"Police." Adama held his badge to the keyhole.

"Just a minute." Betrug quickly took a throw blanket off the couch and covered the box. He opened the front door to see Adama and Bridget. He addressed the manager.

"Since when don't you call me before bringing someone up here?"

"My apologies, sir. We rang twice, but you didn't pick up."

Betrug thought for a moment. "Oh. I was outside on the patio." He turned to Adama. "What do you want, officer?"

"My name is Adama Baptiste, Deputy Chief with the NYPD, and this is Bridget Murphy, CI. May we come in to ask you a few questions?"

"What does CI stand for?" Betrug asked.

"Criminal Investigator," Bridget answered.

Betrug turned to the manager and chastised him. "You can go."

"Thank you, sir." The manager walked away.

"Okay? What's this about?" Betrug fixated on Bridget.

"Sir, we're investigating the deaths of two billionaires and a third victim at the Miller Antiquities gallery. We'd like to ask you a few questions." Adama said.

"Uh, sure." Betrug opened the door. "Did you say two billionaires? Who?"

"William Vanhorn and Daisy Hunter—they both died Sunday. And Thomas Miller died Saturday night. You didn't hear about it?" asked Adama.

"Uh, no." The color went out of Betrug's face. "Let's go in here." He led them to the living room and turned off the TV. "Take a seat." Betrug sat in a wingback made of authentic Zebra hide and Kodiak Bear leather. "How do you like this western theme? Makes me feel like I'm hunting in Wyoming."

"Sir, we've been trying to locate you for two days," Adama and Bridget followed and sat across from Betrug on a Yellowstone Curved Tufted sectional, wrapped in buffalo hide.

"Really? Well, I was out of town, having too much fun to watch the news." He winked at Bridget, picked up his glass of bourbon, and took a sip. The glass was two-thirds empty.

"Were you at the Miller gallery Saturday night?" Adama asked. He extracted a small notepad from his jacket.

"Saturday night? Uh, yes, I did go there. Why?" Betrug's voice sounded wary.

"We're still conducting our investigation. All three deaths are considered suspicious at this time. We're trying to piece together the events of Saturday night."

While Adama and Betrug talked, Bridget surveyed the décor. A massive set of buffalo horns dominated one wall. Artwork included galloping wild mustangs, buffalo herds grazing, and at least two dozen ornate mirrors in woodsy-style frames on the wall behind Betrug's chair. They reflected everything in the living room, including the dining room, directly behind her and Adama. Bridget's gaze was drawn to the corner of a brown box protruding from beneath a blanket on the dining room table. She suddenly stood up.

"May I use your restroom, please?" Bridget's request surprised both men.

"What? Uh, sure. It's down the hall on the left," Betrug said.

"Thanks. You two keep talking." Bridget strode away purposefully.

"Look, detective, I'm unsure how I can help you." Betrug swirled his bourbon, his attention fixed on Bridget's departure. "She's quite attractive. Must be distracting for you."

"Sir? Saturday night?" Adama shifted his position, deliberately blocking Betrug's line of sight. "Did you obtain anything from the gallery?" Adama asked.

"How is that relevant?" Betrug's cooperation was faltering.

"We have reason to believe there is a connection between the deaths and items obtained at the gallery," Adama replied.

Adama's statement unnerved Betrug. He cleared his throat. "That sounds ominous." He chugged the last of his bourbon.

Meanwhile, Bridget quietly exited the bathroom and wandered to the dining room. Seeing the mahogany wood and the size of the box, she knew instantly that Betrug possessed a similar box to Vanhorn's and Miss Hunter's. Her pulse quickened as she returned to the living room. She casually settled next to Adama. Betrug became distracted, ignoring Adama's questions.

"Sir, please answer the question." Adama redirected Betrug.

"Huh, what?" Betrug's speech was slurred.

"Did you receive anything from the gallery, specifically a large box?" Adama asked.

"Ah, nope." Betrug looked away and puffed his cigar.

Adama saw the body language and knew he was lying. "Sir, how long are you staying in the city?"

"A couple more days. Got a big golf game on Wednesday. Want to join me, kitty?" He looked squarely at Bridget.

"I'll pass." Bridget ignored his drunkenness.

"Mr. Betrug, can you tell us what happened at the gallery and what you saw and heard?" Adama asked.

"Murphy, that's Irish. Tell me, do you date the people you interrogate? You're quite the looker."

Adama bristled as Betrug's gaze crawled over Bridget, his manipulation transparent. The man's deplorable lust after Bridget made Adama's jaw tighten.

"Sir, we'll ask the questions." Adama's voice carried a warning edge.

"Oh, come on, it's just a little flirting. She's a big girl, let her speak for herself." Betrug beckoned to Bridget while deflecting Adama's question. "So, tell me, little filly, shall we go for a ride? What do you think?"

"I think you'd give me an STD," Bridget said.

"Ha, saucy, I like that. Let's take a roll in the hay and find out?" Betrug winked.

Bridget took a breath. She'd had enough of his sexual overtones. She leaned forward. "Listen dickhead, I've known lamps with more illumination. Men like you talk big, but that usually means they're compensating for … certain inadequacies. I don't imagine you walk around a locker room without a towel."

"You bitch. Maybe I should take you here and now." He stood, huffing.

"Hey!" Adama was already on his feet, blocking Betrug's advance. "We're done here." Adama's stance and size were menacing.

Adama and Betrug had squared off—young bull, old bull, puffing, ready to charge. Without taking his eyes off Betrug, he commanded. "Bridget—move to the door."

Betrug was a large man, but Adama was younger, faster, and stronger. With resignation in his bloodshot eyes, Betrug backed down. Adama flicked a business card onto the sofa and walked to the door.

"Hey, asshole, what's the big deal with the box, anyway?" Betrug slurred, his bravado safer at a distance.

"Perhaps you'll find out—soon," Bridget said.

"What was that?" Betrug asked.

"Good day, sir." Adama opened the door.

In the elevator, Bridget breathed heavily and exhaled slowly, tension still present in her shoulders.

"What a creep. That guy was three sheets to the wind."

"I don't think alcohol had anything to do with his natural temperament. Even sober, he'd be a jerk." Adama studied Bridget. "I'd ask you if you're okay, but you managed yourself well." His muscles flexed unconsciously. "I wanted to punch his lights out."

"How chivalrous of you." Her smile was filled with gratitude.

Adama waved it off and shifted back to the case. "Could you confirm the box on his dining room table?"

"Yes!" Bridget's eyes lit up. "You saw it too?"

"Yes. But I'm not as clever as you. The restroom bit was brilliant."

"Well, it paid off. What do we do now? Like you said, what if the box or the stones are somehow connected to these deaths? Shouldn't we take the box now?"

"We don't have enough to get a warrant, let alone take anything from anyone. What we know is that he just lied to us. We need evidence that proves the stones are here illegally, connected to an international incident, and that the billionaires knew they were paying for stolen goods. That's how we get them."

Bridget nodded. "You're right. I'll make a few calls and start researching the gravestones, the Senegal murders, and connect the dots."

"That's a start. Let's head over to the gallery. We need to watch their internal video. I'll get Ricky started on their inventory, receipts, and shipments to find the connection between the gallery and the boxes."

The elevator doors opened with a soft chime, revealing the hotel lobby. With tensions eased, Adama and Bridget stepped in sync toward the waiting sedan and headed for W. 56th Street.

Chapter 32: That's The Guy!

Weaving through traffic toward Miller Antiquities, Adama's thoughts turned to loose ends and tying them all together. He needed to be strategic, collecting strong evidence—the stones, videos, documentation, intention, and motive to back his conclusions. He needed proof, beyond a reasonable doubt, that the billionaires and perpetrators committed an international crime, including murder, and it had to hold up in a court of law.

The accusations he was about to level would embarrass the NYPD and set in motion a series of events that could lead to heads rolling. It wasn't just his career on the line.

"We'll meet with Burke, view the security feed, and you can walk the crime scene," Adama said. "Depending on the time, we'll head to Le Chandelier Hotel." Adama looked at his wristwatch. It was after three p.m. "It'll be past seven before we make it to the yacht. We'll go there first thing in the morning."

"Sounds good." Bridget read the file about Thomas Miller.

Adama pulled out his cellphone and called Detective Burke.

"Hey, boss, where are you?" Burke asked.

"We're on our way to the gallery, are you still there?" Adama asked.

"No, I finished meeting with Miss Miller and am on my way to speak with Henry Miller. I have an appointment at the hospital."

"Okay, is there someone at the gallery to let us in?"

"Miss Miller may still be there. If not, an officer will let you in."

"Ricky, did you see the internal security feeds from the gallery?"

"Yes, I forwarded a copy to your email. It shows the six billionaires, Thomas Miller, and one other person."

"What other person?"

Bridget's ears perked up. She leaned toward Adama, who put the call on speaker.

"Ricky, I have you on speaker. Who was the mystery person at the gallery?"

"No idea. The guy dressed like a character out of a fiction novel, with a funky, round hat. And he's smart—he never looks up. The cameras show him entering the office and walking down the hallway, but never through the front door."

Adama felt his right hand being pulled by Bridget.

"Hey Ricky, this is Bridget Murphy. Did the man in the hat also wear a cape and carry a cane?"

"Yeah, how'd you know that?" Burke asked.

"Oh my god." Bridget covered her mouth with her hand.

"Hello? What's going on?" Burke asked. "You there?"

"Thanks, Ricky. I'll call you back." Adama ended the call. "Bridget, how did you know about that guy, and why are you so surprised?"

"Because that sounds like the same man in Colin Taylor's surveillance video."

"Your London case? Are you sure?"

"I will be when I see the video at the Miller gallery."

"Right, we'll be there soon."

Bridget held the four file folders in her lap. All she thought about was the man in the cape and how her instincts suggested both cases were connected.

————◆————

They arrived at Miller Antiquities in time to find Jacqueline Miller exiting the front door.

"Bridget?" Jacqueline said. "Are you assisting with Thomas's case?"

"Hello, Jacqueline. Yes, whatever I can do. I'm very sorry for your loss."

"Thank you." Jacqueline faced Adama. "Hello, Deputy Chief, do you have an update?"

"We're here to view the gallery's security tapes," he said.

"Oh, I see. Let's go inside." Jacqueline led them through the front door. "I apologize for the odor. The food is gone, but it still smells awful." Jacqueline said.

Jacqueline turned on the desktop computer in the office and opened the security systems' files. She demonstrated how to search for the correct dates. Adama politely asked her to wait in the gallery, and she left the room. Adama chose the Saturday video, time-stamped six o'clock, and fast-forwarded until a man in a large black hat appeared walking down the hallway.

"That's the guy!" Bridget said.

"Are you sure?" Adama asked.

"I'm positive. Same clothing, hat, posture, and cane. That's him, Adama!"

"He never goes near the front door. He must have used the alley." Adama searched the videos. "I don't see one. Thomas must have turned it off."

"That makes sense. This guy doesn't want to be identified," Bridget confirmed.

"Well, now we know at least one other person knows what happened here."

"And in London. It has to be connected," Bridget said.

"We'll see."

Adama appreciated her insights but knew better than to allow videos to guide him through an investigation. He wondered how many stolen stones were in New York, London, or elsewhere. And he conceded the possibility of more deaths. Adama closed the files and turned off the computer.

"Do you still want to look around?" he asked.

"Yes, I won't be long."

"I'll go talk with Miss Miller."

Bridget entered the screening room and immediately came out to find Adama. She motioned for him to join her.

"What's up?" Adama asked.

"The chairs and the lectern. The arrangement suggests the perfect setting for a 'show and tell,'" Bridget said. "Why a lectern light unless someone reads in the dark? And these red velvet curtains hid something large that hung on that big hook in the bricks. It was high-lighted right there."

"Bridget, it was a special event. And a large video monitor hung there. It was removed and put in the storage room," Adama explained.

"But that's not what the bright lights were for. No, something else hung on that big hook. Did Miss Miller say when the monitor was removed?"

"I'll ask." Adama went out to the gallery and came back. "Miss Miller said the monitor was hanging there on Saturday morning before she left for D.C."

"Exactly, this room was changed on Saturday after she left town. Another thing is that these lights were hung recently, and there's still brick residue on the floor. Someone did a poor job of cleaning up after themselves."

Bridget sat in one of the white velvet chairs. She perused the room.

"Each person had a perfect view of the lectern and whatever hung on the wall. The whole setup is intentional. Wealthy people love being pampered. I mean, look at these chairs, fit for a king." Bridget went to the lectern. "I'll bet the guy with the hat stood right here, telling those billionaires a whopper of a story." Bridget's hands clutched the sides of the lectern.

"Maybe." Adama inspected the brick wall, the floor, the large hook, the curtains, and the lights. He listened as Bridget continued with her observations.

"The event was very special, with only six guests allowed. That usually indicates a private collection. I've seen this setup with dark art auctions. Sometimes buyers sit in secret rooms and bid; sometimes it's a fancy get-together. I'm inclined to believe the six billionaires came to hear a story about something unusual. And a trophy hung on that hook for all to view."

"And you think it was a box?" Adama asked.

"I do, and after the dog and pony show, each billionaire received their box. I'll bet they paid a boatload of money for those stones."

"Plausible." Adama agreed with her line of thinking. "And it was hosted in an obvious location, free from suspicion. Elegance in plain sight. People feed on dark art and the thrill of owning something precious and illegal. Maybe that's what Thomas hosted here."

"Did Jacqueline and Henry Miller know about the event?" Bridget asked.

"Miss Miller said no. And there's no evidence to the contrary." He reevaluated the room. "Good analysis, Bridget. I didn't make a connection to dark art. But that makes sense."

Adama and Bridget went to the gallery.

"Thank you, Miss Miller. We'll be in touch." Adama shook Jacqueline's hand.

"I'm sorry we had to meet again under these circumstances," Bridget said.

"Me too. Goodbye Bridget. Goodbye, Deputy Chief Baptiste."

On the ride back to HQ, Adama thought about the man in the big hat, the dead billionaires, the stones, and Bridget's instincts about a connection between New York and London.

"Got your London files with you?" he asked.

Bridget nodded. "Everything that I was allowed to take."

"Good. Bring it all to the office tomorrow morning."

"Okay," She said softly and gratefully.

Upon arrival at NYPD headquarters, Bridget and Adama parted ways. He checked for updates from his staff. Burke informed Bridget that her office was set up. He gave her a key fob to gain access to the offices. She thanked him, packed up her files, and headed back to her hotel for the night.

———◆———

On their way home to Brooklyn, Detectives Gates and Sanchez had stopped at the home of Danny Garcia, the limousine driver for Gerald Decker. The white stretch limousine was in the driveway. Garcia cooperated and answered questions about Decker, the gallery, and the box. He allowed them to look inside the limousine. Immediately afterward, Gates called Adama.

"You were right, the box was picked up Saturday night at nine o'clock from the Miller gallery, and it's sitting inside the limo."

"Describe it to me," Adama said.

"The box looked about seven feet long and two feet wide, made of dark hardwood. The lid was closed with two old-fashioned locks on the outside."

"That's it. Assign a squad car with twenty-four/seven surveillance. Have the officer report any movement of the limo, if that box is moved, or if anyone shows up and takes it."

"Got it. Do you need anything else from us?"

"No. Good job, Bobby. Tell Luis I said thanks. Have a good night."

"See you tomorrow." Gates hung up.

TUESDAY

Chapter 33: The Favor

Tuesday morning, at the Gild Hall hotel, Bridget woke just before breakfast was delivered at six a.m. After eating, she took a quick shower, dressed in a black suit, a light blue button-down shirt, and black shoes. She put her hair up in a French twist and added a touch of makeup and lip gloss. She gathered up her London files and placed them into her satchel.

Ten minutes later, Bridget arrived at NYPD headquarters. As she started up the steps, her cellphone rang. No caller ID visible.

"Hello?" Bridget squinted at the sun's reflection off an adjacent building.

"Hello, Bridget, it's Jane Evans." She sounded upbeat.

"Jane! When can we meet?" Bridget wasn't interested in another spy routine.

"You Americans, always straight to the point. It is refreshing."

"I see you found your British accent." Bridget teased her.

"Yes, well. No point trying to fool you."

"Seriously. When can we meet?"

"Today, if you like." Jane's tone shifted to serious.

"I do like. But I'm in New York."

"I'm also in New York."

"Did you follow me here?" Bridget stiffened.

"Of course. I told you we have eyes on."

What.The.Fuck! "Just tell me what you know about the murders and Colin."

"We'll get to that," Jane said. "Shall we meet for lunch at Dottie's Café on 12th Avenue?"

"What time?" Bridget asked.

"How about noon? Does that suit you?"

"I'll be there."

"Good. Looking forward to it. Goodbye, Bridget."

Bridget hung up without saying goodbye. Determined, she entered NYPD's headquarters, cleared security, and took an elevator to the third floor. She stopped outside Adama's office. His door was open. Bridget watched him for a moment. *He's so good-looking.* She observed him seated and reading. She lightly tapped the door.

"Mind if I come in?"

"Bridget." Adama smiled. "Good morning. You're early."

"Well, I need to leave at eleven-thirty for a lunch meeting. I wanted to make sure you knew."

"Of course. Sit down." He motioned to the chairs across from his desk.

"That's okay. So, you're good if I take an early lunch?"

"A meeting about our cases?"

"Well, actually, it's personal." Bridget seemed nervous.

"All right." Adama nodded. "Is everything okay?"

"I hope so. I'll know soon enough."

"Need any help?" Adama sensed Bridget had something serious on her mind.

"No thank—" Bridget paused. "Well, actually, maybe you can help."

"Sure. What's going on?"

"I'm meeting with a woman from New Scotland Yard to discuss my London case. And I—"

Adama looked surprised. Bridget scrambled. "It's not official business for the NYPD."

He nodded and said, "I see. So, Scotland Yard is in New York? That's interesting. I didn't get the memo. Huh." His disapproval was evident. "So much for decorum."

"Oh, uh, look, it's no big deal. Just lunch." Bridget realized the implications.

"Yesterday, we agreed that you'd bring your London files here and we'd compare notes. You're the one who thinks these cases are connected. Does this woman have information about the Colin Taylor lover's triangle?"

"It wasn't a lover's triangle, it was murder." Bridget's voice revealed her frustration. "And I had to leave London before I could prove it. Now she's here with information about Colin, which could prove useful to our cases."

"Why didn't she give you the information in London?"

"Well, that's the million-dollar question."

He watched her body language. "You're suspicious about her."

"Yes. Some things don't add up."

"Then, why not invite her to speak with us? Let's make it official."

"Because I don't want to spook her. This is about London, not New York."

Seeing her frustration, Adama sat back in his chair and crossed his arms. "Okay, Bridget. What do you need?"

"Well. I'm meeting her at noon at Dottie's Café, and I need a favor."

Bridget stared at the floor, tapped her fingers on the door jam, and scrunched her nose.

"Ask, Bridget. What do you need?"

"Well. Frankly, I'd like her followed."

"Followed?" His eyes widened. "I have to say I wasn't expecting that. Why does she need to be followed?"

"Well, something is off. I can't figure out if she wants to help me, or..." She stopped.

"Or what?"

"Uh, well, she told me to watch my back."

"What?" Adama sprang from his chair.

"I'm sure it's nothing. I want to find out who she's working with." She waited. "What do you think?"

"I think I'm coming with you."

"Adama! No, you can't. I know you're concerned. I can take care of myself. Besides, I'll be in broad daylight."

"Oh!" The pen in his hand dropped to the desk. "Well, that certainly makes me feel better. Because, you know, no one *ever* gets killed in broad daylight."

"Okay, that was a dumb thing to say."

"What the hell, Bridget? Why didn't you tell me sooner?"

Bridget did a double-take. "You cursed! Adama, you used a swear word. I don't think, no, I know I have never heard you curse. That's amazing. By the way, why don't you swear?"

"Knock it off. Why didn't you tell me about the threat?"

"I'm sorry. I should have told you." Bridget waited. "So, can you have her followed?"

Bridget watched Adama's face; he was contemplating the request. A long minute went by.

"Yes, Bridget, I'll put a couple of guys on her. Tell me what she looks like. Someone will be in the restaurant before you arrive. They'll follow after she leaves. Does that work for you?"

"Yes. I'll text you a description of her. We're meeting at noon." Bridget turned to leave, stopped, and spun around. "Thanks, Adama. I really appreciate this."

"Sure, but there's just one catch." Adama sat back down in his chair.

"Oh. What's that?"

"You tell me everything she gives you about the London murders—deal?"

"Deal." Bridget walked away happy.

Adama watched her leave. He sighed heavily. *She's so cute.*

He looked at his wristwatch, grabbed his cellphone and notebook, and walked down the hall to meet with the chief and commissioner. And Bridget went to her office to research the stones.

Chapter 34: She's Not Coming

Dottie's Café was a classic 1950s-style diner located across from the West Side piers along the Hudson River. The café boasted a nostalgic décor of red, white, and blue. The waitresses wore red chiffon scarves tied around their necks, flared poodle skirts, and black and white saddleback shoes with white bobby socks. The café was owned and operated by seventy-year-old Dottie Redstone, who grew up in Hell's Kitchen. Locals and tourists enjoyed the homey atmosphere, and Dottie often walked through the café pouring coffee and chatting with the customers.

A cab dropped Bridget off outside the café at exactly eleven-fifty a.m. She stood by the door, shifting her satchel from one shoulder to the other. At noon, the hostess led her to a cozy booth with puffy red Naugahyde seats. Bridget heard one of Elvis Presley's hits, "Heartbreak Hotel," playing on the old-fashioned jukebox. A waitress came over holding a coffee pot.

"Coffee, hon?"

"Yes, please, with cream."

The waitress flipped one of the heavy mugs over and filled it up.

"Cream is on the table. Are you ready to order?"

"Not yet."

Bridget took Jane's business card out of her pocket and tapped it on the table. She looked around the café and spotted two guys sitting in the back of the restaurant. They saw her and did not react. Bridget nonchalantly shook her head as she poured cream into her coffee. *Really? Two undercover guys? A bit overkill, don't ya think, Adama?*

Bridget checked her watch. Ten minutes after twelve. *Where are you, Jane?* Bridget checked her phone for messages. Nothing. She anxiously examined every woman who entered the café. No one looked familiar. Another ten minutes went by. Bridget looked at the "Unknown" number on her phone, dialed it, and got a busy signal. *You're seriously gonna stiff me?* Bridget finished her coffee and took a refill when the waitress came by.

"You waitin' for someone, honey?"

"Yes, she'll be here soon, and then we'll order." She raised her cup. "Good coffee."

The time was now twelve-thirty. She checked for messages. Nothing. *I'm such a fool. What's going on?*

At twelve-forty, the two undercover detectives got up and walked toward Bridget. Her eyes widened as they slowly approached.

"What's going on?" she asked. One detective pointed at the door. Bridget saw Adama coming into the café. He removed his sunglasses, glanced around, and approached her booth.

"What are you doing?" she asked. "You're going to blow this for me?"

"I'm not blowing anything." Adama slid into the booth. "Your contact isn't coming."

"And how would you know that?"

He looked around and spoke softly. "Because she's dead."

"What? She's what?"

"You heard me. The Midtown North Precinct notified us that a woman, fitting the description of your Jane Evans, was found dead in an alley less than a block from here. That was twenty-five minutes ago."

"Well. How do you know it's my Jane Evans?"

"We're sure." Adama pulled out his phone, scrolled through photos, and showed one to Bridget. "Is this your contact?"

The picture showed a woman in a dark blue suit and short brown hair. Her face was pale white, and her throat had been cut. Bridget winced. She recognized the woman and the button-style emerald earrings that Jane wore on the plane.

"That's her." Bridget's voice trailed off. She closed her eyes and hung her head.

Bridget turned away and sat quietly. Adama saw that she was upset.

"Look, I know this is tough." He reached over and patted the back of her hand. "But now we're going back to headquarters, and you'll tell me exactly what you think is happening." Bridget looked away.

"New Scotland Yard, if that's who she worked for, will be all over us. Bridget! I need answers, and I don't care how personal this issue is." Adama stared at Bridget intensely. "Now, tell me that you understand?"

"I understand," she said softly.

Bridget leaned toward him. "Adama, I don't know what's going on. That's why I was meeting with her. She had information about the Colin Taylor gallery murders. The woman acknowledged the three victims had been murdered. And there's more. But I can't talk about that here."

"Well, she's dead now, so we'll never know. Also, you weren't the only one who needed to watch their back. So, we'll be taking precautions with your safety. I'll arrange a security detail for you until the case is solved—around the clock, unless you're with me, one of my detectives, at HQ, or your hotel."

Still dazed, Bridget's head bobbed up and down. "Did they find anything on her? A phone, ID, a notebook, anything?"

"No purse, ID, phone, or keys." Adama scrolled through pictures on his phone and showed them to Bridget. "But, they found your business card in Jane's coat pocket."

"Oh my god." Bridget's eyes widened at the sight of smeared blood.

"Right. Whoever did this was a pro; they took everything, except your business card." Adama looked at Bridget very intently.

"So, it was deliberately left; they wanted us to find it," Bridget said.

"Yes. It's a message, of sorts." He made a move to get up. "We need to leave. Now."

Bridget pulled a ten-dollar bill out of her pocket and left it on the table. They walked to his car. Adama looked around while he held the right passenger door open for a bewildered Bridget. She got in and stared out the windshield. Adama walked around, saw his two detectives across the street, and gave them an "all clear" hand gesture. He got into the car.

"Buckle up, Bridget."

Adama pulled up to the light at the corner and gestured towards Pier 84.

"You know, Friday night we fished two guys out of the Hudson, just over there." He pointed with his right index finger. "Turns out they were crewmembers on an Egyptian container ship. It's in international waters now. Both men had their throats cut. I figured they got caught doing something wrong, were punished, then thrown overboard."

"Wait, did you say Egyptian container ship?"

"Yes, why?"

"The dead billionaire in London owned a Cairo-based shipping and container company."

"But numerous container ships come into New York and New Jersey."

"Fair enough. So, why are you telling me about two dead guys?" Bridget wondered about the connection.

"Because the murderer of Jane Evans has the same MO. Same type of jagged blade and a cut from left to right."

"That sounds like a stretch. A container ship and two dead guys. Jane came from England."

"Right. But then Dr. Pearson told me about the two taser marks on the back of her neck. They're identical to the taser marks found on the two dead crewmen." Adama let the information hang in the air.

"So, you think their cases may be connected?"

"Maybe. I need everything you have on that woman and your London case."

"I have it in my bag." Bridget patted the satchel resting next to her on the seat. She thought for a moment. "You need to run her prints. Jane Evans could be an alias."

"Already in the works. Our forensic technician should have the info from IAFIS by the time we get back to HQ."

Bridget knew that IAFIS was an acronym for Integrated Automated Fingerprint Identification System.

"That's great." Bridget had snapped out of her *I can't believe it* mode, and she was already thinking about the next steps to solve the triple murders in London.

"By the way, you were brought in to help solve NYPD cases. Stay focused."

Bridget did not look at him. *I hate it when he does that—friggin' mind reader.*

"I'd like to see all the bodies—your two dead vics from the Hudson and my Jane."

"Look who's back in the game." Adama smiled with quiet appreciation.

"Well, both cases are connected to art galleries and billionaires. And since neither of us believes in…"

"Coincidence?" Adama had finished her sentence.

"Yes." She cast an adoring glance his way.

Memories of their time in Paris washed over Bridget—how they finished each other's sentences, read each other's minds, and anticipated each other's needs. She smiled inwardly and fought the urge to touch his hand. As if their thoughts had intersected, Adama drove while lost in a parallel reverie, heavy in thought, and with an unwavering desire to be reconnected. Adama sat quietly, weaving through traffic until they arrived back at headquarters.

Chapter 35: The London Murders

Adama pulled his sedan into the parking lot of NYPD headquarters. He and Bridget passed through security and quickly walked toward his office. Bridget carried her satchel, still feeling numb about Jane Evans's murder.

"I need to check on something. I'll meet you in the conference room," Adama said.

"Okay." Bridget set up her laptop and organized her files. A few minutes later, Adama entered and closed the door.

"I have my notes about London. What do you want to review first?"

"Just talk to me about your case." Adama sat across the table from Bridget.

"Okay, I'll fast forward to the murders of Colin Taylor, Susan Baker, and Ahmed Senusret, the three victims. The police told Margaret, Colin's wife, that her husband was engaged in a classic love triangle that ended in a murder-suicide. Which, of course, devastated Margaret. She insisted that none of that makes sense. I knew Colin, and I agree with her."

"Well, that's understandable," Adama said. "No one wants to believe their spouse could be involved in a love triangle. What makes you think it wasn't?"

"Margaret told me Colin wasn't supposed to be at the gallery that morning. And that two days before his death, he planned to call me about something strange, possibly dangerous. And that I was the only person he trusted with the information."

"What was that information?"

"I don't know. And Colin refused to tell Margaret, for her safety."

Adama shook his head dismissively. "Well, that's not evidence." Adama saw the dejected look on Bridget's face. "Okay, what *have* you got that we can work with?"

"You think I don't know this sounds like a far-fetched conspiracy?"

"Bridget, being defensive won't help. Tell me what you know, and we'll figure it out."

"I know that Colin loved his wife more than life. And I know in my gut that someone killed him and probably the other two. And here's the kicker—I think the Yard may have covered it up to make it look like a lover's triangle and a murder-suicide."

"Okay, but to what end?"

Bridget's thoughts drifted to Carter Jones and his dismissive accusations. "You sound like Director Jones at the Yard telling me my imagination is running wild. But I trust my gut."

Adama saw that look again, sadness and doubt creeping in. His expression offered infinite tenderness.

"Bridget, you, of all people, know that we need hard evidence. I trust your instincts. But let's start with the facts and work backward. Have you got surveillance?"

"Yes." Bridget pulled up the digital files on her laptop.

Adama got up and walked around the table to sit next to her. He hoped her emotions were in check, and she wasn't too close to the investigation. No one is immune to clouded judgment. They watched the activities that took place outside the Colin Taylor Antiquities.

Adama recapped. "So, six people come and go. The assistant, and the mystery man in the cape—by the way, he looks like our Miller Antiquities mystery guy. Then two guys bring in a large box and leave within minutes." *The same type of box was found with Vanhorn and Daisy Hunter. That's a connection.* He kept his thoughts to himself.

"Next, Ahmed Senusret shows up, and the mystery man leaves forty minutes later," Bridget said. "And, lastly, Colin arrives. That's the outside activity in a nutshell."

"Okay, tell me about the billionaire."

"Like I said, his name was Ahmed Senusret. He flew in the day before the murders from Cairo. He was sixty-eight years old and worth eleven billion. He owns Senusret International Shipping & Containers near Port Said, Egypt."

"What's your billionaire's connection to the gallery?" Adama stood, walked to the window, and looked at the hazy sky.

"Senusret called the gallery four times over two months. That coincides with Margaret telling me a private dealer contacted Colin about some African artifacts. He was looking for a gallery for a private event to show African artifacts."

Hearing Bridget's last comment, Adama recalled what Jacqueline Miller said—a man called looking for a gallery for a private event to show artifacts from Africa. *Another connection. She may be on to something here.*

"Adama? Did you hear me?" Bridget nudged.

"Yes. It sounds like Colin acted appropriately," Adama answered. "What about Senusret? Is he legit?"

"No way, he's bad news. The Yard confirmed Senusret was engaged in human trafficking, mostly young girls, as well as dark art and other black-market items. His shipping business gave him the perfect conduit for transporting anything, anywhere in the world. And he was arrested in Cairo for beating and raping three women last year."

"What agencies are following this guy?" Adama clenched his fist to hold his rage.

Bridget scrolled through her notes, reading aloud. "Several international agencies were cooperating to prosecute Senusret and his shipping organization for human trafficking, fraud, and other crimes. Among them were the National Center on Sexual Exploitation, INTERPOL, World Without Exploitation, Rights4Girls, and more. All dedicated to ending sex trafficking and the exploitation of women and children. Half the world had Senusret in their sights."

"Show me Taylor's internal security feed? I'd like to see what happened inside the gallery."

"Yeah, well, that's a problem. I can't get my hands on it."

"Really? Why not?" Adama asked.

"Long story short, the Yard wouldn't release it to me. Some BS about my connection to Colin being too personal. They closed the case and sent me packing." Bridget was embarrassed to share that last bit of information.

"What about the Yard's crime scene investigation? Do you have their photos and video?"

"I only have the crime scene photos, but I have a friend at the Yard who owes me a favor. I'll see if she'll send the police video."

The room was quiet. Bridget got up, poured a glass of water, and glanced out the window.

"Jane didn't work for New Scotland Yard," Adama said.

"What?" Bridget spun around. "You got the prints back. Who did she work for?"

"INTERPOL. Jane left New Scotland Yard three years ago. She and her partner had been tracking Senusret for two years. They were close to a formal accusation before Senusret died."

"Well, let's find her partner."

"A hit-and-run driver killed him in London yesterday."

"Oh my god! Unbelievable. Every time I think we're getting somewhere, we fall behind. It feels like someone is always two steps ahead of us. What are we missing?"

Bridget looked despondent. Adama knew precisely how she felt. Over the years, he had plenty of leads that spontaneously dried up.

"Okay, I've seen and heard enough," Adama relented. "Let's consider this a joint investigation until we're told to back off."

"Really? That's great. Wait, are we going to be told to back off?"

"Absolutely," Adama said with confidence.

"But will we?" Bridget asked squeamishly, afraid of the answer.

"Absolutely not." Adama winked at Bridget. "Let the games begin. I've got a meeting. Text me when you get the video file."

Bridget's eyes shone with admiration as she beamed at him. She felt happy and relieved to work with such a force of nature. *If anyone can make it happen, he can.*

———◆———

Bridget's friend at New Scotland Yard came through. An hour later, a digital file arrived via email; she texted Adama. "Got the video. I'm in the conference room."

Adama walked into the room and sat down next to Bridget.

"The video camera begins at the front door and methodically records the entire gallery in a counterclockwise sweep," she explained. The camera captured a scene that revealed utter devastation and violence. Priceless antiquities had been destroyed; the floor was littered with shattered fragments of the past. And when the camera panned to the lifeless body of Colin Taylor, Bridget's stomach turned at the sight of her dear friend lying in a pool of his blood.

"The cause of death was blunt trauma. The forensic pathologist determined Colin's fatal head wound was probably caused by that small Roman bust on the floor next to him." Her heart ached from a profound sense of loss.

The next camera shot looked like a bizarre scene from a horror movie. A pair of fancy black boots protruded under a significant block of marble. The camera revealed that the billionaire, Ahmed Senusret's entire upper torso had been crushed by the weight of the statue Nemesis, the Goddess of Retribution.

"The autopsy report stated the cause of death as exsanguination, or blood loss from an injury. Turns out the statue's protruding hand severed his femoral artery. He didn't stand a chance." Bridget felt no remorse for the man.

The next camera shot showed Susan Baker's body. She had a cord wrapped around her neck and multiple bruises on her face.

"She died from asphyxiation." Bridget stopped the video. "That's it. The rest of the video shows other areas of the gallery. No one else was inside. It's obvious that someone was hell-bent on destroying the gallery and killing everyone inside."

"What assumptions have you drawn?" Adama asked.

"Well, several facts support something nefarious and far-reaching. It's not a coincidence that the man in the black hat shows up at antiquities galleries in both our cities. Next, Jane Evans worked for INTERPOL and was tracking Senusret, which probably led to her murder here in New York. And Colin was working on something dangerous, so he was probably set up and murdered as well. I believe there's something bigger at play here, including an international situation. Someone sure has gone to a lot of trouble orchestrating an elaborate cover-up."

"Nice and plausible, Bridget." Adama pointed to the laptop. "Do me a favor, finish the video so I can see the rest of the gallery."

"Okay." Bridget pushed play. The video panned around the gallery, focusing on the areas near the bodies.

"Stop. Can you zoom in there?"

"What do you see?" Bridget saw it. "Holy shit! I overlooked that before."

"That's because you didn't know what to look for."

"It's one of those big mahogany boxes. So, it's not random."

"Right. We just found a critical link to our cases. Breadcrumbs leading to a more complex spider's web of circumstances. Now, there's no doubt we have an international incident on our hands."

"I knew it!" Bridget's voice revealed a mix of excitement and vindication.

"Let's not get ahead of ourselves," Adama cautioned. "We still need to tie it all together."

"Now what?"

"Now, the shipping manifests. I need to find out where my team is with the container ships and the manifests. Locating where those boxes came from is crucial." He stretched his arms and contemplated all the pieces of the puzzle.

"And who shipped them?" Bridget had dug through her notes and held up the name of Senusret's shipping company.

"Exactly. Looks like your Egyptian billionaire and his shipping company may come into play after all. Good work, Bridget. We'll start there. Let's go find Burke."

Adama assembled his team in the bullpen for updates. Each detective and technician provided updates. Most of the team was writing reports. As the briefing concluded, Adama requested that all reports be submitted by the end of the day. He asked Bridget to be ready to move out within ten minutes.

Chapter 36: The Hidden Camera

Adama and Bridget left the office to visit Le Chandelier Hotel. Bridget viewed Daisy Hunter's penthouse suite. The bedroom had taken on a distinctive odor from a mixture of various types of leftover food. She spoke with Ms. Matisse, the hotel's manager. When finished, Bridget told Adama that she was satisfied and that his team had done a great job.

"I'd like to take another look at the two boxes at the morgue, as well as the two dead crew members and Jane Evans. Can we go there next?"

Adama nodded and called Dr. Betty Pearson to make sure they would be able to view the bodies. Upon arrival at the morgue, Adama asked Bridget for a favor.

"Uh, you may recall that Dr. Pearson insisted on an explanation regarding our *episodes*," Adama said. "I don't want to tell her everything, yet. I need you to follow my lead."

"Okay, I've got your back. Don't worry."

"Thank you. Let's go."

Dr. Pearson saw them through the window and waved them in when they got to the lab.

"Hello, you two. You're both looking much better today. Before I show you anything, Deputy Chief, do you have something to share?" Dr. Pearson was in no mood to barter.

"Right," Adama said.

"And that goes for you, too, Bridget. I know you know what's inside those boxes, so anything you offer would be appreciated."

"Absolutely." Bridget liked Dr. Pearson and wanted to collaborate with her.

"All right then, I'm all ears." She stared at Adama.

"We believe those boxes contain artifacts that may have been stolen during a robbery two years ago. Thirteen gravestones were stolen from a cemetery in Senegal, Africa. When I saw the item in the box, it surprised me." Adama's explanation was truthful and concise.

"That's it? You had a mild shock episode because the items looked familiar?" She turned to Bridget. "And you had a panic attack because you also recognized the stones? Do I have that right?" Dr. Pearson asked.

The doctor put one hand in her pocket and the other up to her chin, musing about the explanation.

"Hmm. A simple and yet reasonable elucidation." She glared and shook her head. "But I'm not buying it."

"Well, there's more to it than that," Adama said.

"You think?" Dr. Pearson smirked. "Enlighten me."

"Several people participated in the robbery and were murdered, including a child. The individuals responsible for the crime were never apprehended, and none of the stones were recovered. Until now, that is," Adama said. He looked at Bridget for help.

"That's right. The items inside the boxes shocked me for the same reason. I heard about that story two years ago. Years ago, I worked in that township and knew the people—it's a tight-knit community. So naturally, it hit me hard. And I never expected to find the stones in New York City. It was a horrendous crime; everyone was devastated, with no justice for them."

The doctor was still suspicious but appeared somewhat satisfied. "Okay. I'll accept that for now. But I insist on being informed immediately if there's more. Understood?" Dr. Pearson asked.

"Yes," Adama and Bridget answered simultaneously.

"Okay, what do you want to see, bodies or boxes?" Dr. Pearson asked.

"The bodies, please," Bridget said.

"Right this way." Dr. Pearson motioned for them to follow her.

The cold body storage area was freezing, causing Bridget to shiver. Dr. Pearson pulled out the two drawers that held the young men pulled from the Hudson and uncovered their faces.

"We still haven't identified them. Were you able to get names from the shipping company?" she asked Adama.

"We're in touch with them. But the ship is on its way to Europe, then to Africa. I'll keep you posted."

"They're so young. Anything unusual?" Bridget asked.

"There are taser marks on the back of their necks. High voltage and excessive, knocking them out for a long time," Dr. Pearson said.

"Official cause of death?" Adama asked.

"Severed carotid artery. They both bled out within five minutes. No water was found in their lungs, so they were dead before being dropped overboard. Another thing, their stomachs were full, they had just eaten rice and chicken, and were killed shortly thereafter."

"Geez. Sounds awful," Bridget said.

"Deputy Chief, how did you know they were from Africa?" Dr. Pearson asked.

"The scarification pattern on their upper forearms," Adama said. "The lion's head is traditional from the Senegal region, or thereabouts. It's special."

Curious, Bridget lifted the sheets to look at the men's forearms while she listened to Adama and the doctor. They both noticed her actions.

"It's on the right forearm, Bridget," Adama said.

"I see it." Bridget walked from one man to the other. "Yes, definitely West Africa. What a shame. These poor souls. They probably have families back home. We need to identify them and let their families know."

"And over here is our Jane Doe." Dr. Pearson motioned for them to follow her to a metal table in the examination room where the outstretched body of a middle-aged white female lay covered with a sheet. The doctor pulled back the edges, exposing the head and neck. Adama and Bridget looked down at the body. It was grayish white with a large gash that stretched from the left to the right side of her throat. Dr. Pearson pointed out the taser marks at the base of the neck.

"We've confirmed her name is Jane Evans," Adama said.

"Okay, we'll make it official. What else do you know about her?" Dr. Pearson asked.

"We're waiting on additional information; we'll relay later. Can we take another look at the two boxes?" Adama asked.

Dr. Pearson gave him a look. "Are you two okay with viewing them again?"

"Yes, we're fine. We know what they are now." Adama glanced at Bridget.

"They're over here." The doctor led the way. "We moved them." The doctor took the spiral key bracelet off her wrist and opened the door. Her phone rang and she excused herself. "Call me if you need me."

"Thanks," Adama said.

Adama approached the box, which had significant white powder fingerprint marks. He knew that the box belonged to William Vanhorn. Adama opened the latch and the lid. Bridget stepped up to peer inside. She was taken aback. Adama sensed her hesitation.

"Are you all right?"

"I'm fine. I can't believe they're here. I want to know how? I want to take it back where it belongs. So many emotions are flooding me right now."

"I get it. But we need to be patient."

"I know." Bridget's voice was solemn.

"Do you want to see Daisy Hunter's stone again?"

"Sure."

"How did you hear about the robbery?" Adama asked as he opened the other box.

"A friend of mine in Dakar emailed me the article in the Senegal Times. We attended university together. She was devastated too. We love Dakar and its people." Bridget added, "I want to find the bastards who did this."

"Me too." Adama loved how passionate Bridget was about justice.

They finished viewing the boxes, and Adama closed and latched the lids. Returning to the lab, Dr. Pearson approached them. "I have something else to show you. I sent two technicians back to Daisy Hunter's room to search for an object that could compress the food into her orifices."

"Yes, what did you find? A murder weapon?" he asked.

"No. But we found a hidden camera in this little stuffed dog." Dr. Pearson held a fluffy white dog with a large black nose. "And it recorded everything that happened in Daisy's bedroom."

"Can we view it?" Adama asked.

"All you have to do is push play." Dr. Pearson pointed at a laptop.

Adama did not hesitate. The first shot was Daisy's face. It filled the screen while she played with the toy dog's controls. Images of the room went in and out of focus—the ceiling, the floor, the lamps, and the bed. The three hundred sixty-degree wide-angle lens captured a disoriented room, tumbling like a weightless spaceship. When Daisy finally centered the camera on the dresser, her nose loomed just inches away, so distorted it looked like it belonged on Mount Rushmore.

A few minutes later, the camera recorded Daisy opening a large box resting on the couch. She caressed and seemed to hug the object inside. She stood up wild-eyed and robotically went to a nearby phone, pushed one button, and spoke to someone. Later, the video showed Daisy dancing around in her short, pink nightgown, which was much too small for her large body. She stopped in front of a large mirror, stuck her tongue out, shook her fist, and appeared to be shrieking at her reflection. Then Daisy looked around, grabbed various items in the room, and threw them at the mirror.

"That explains how the mirror got shattered," Adama said. They all watched in silence.

Shortly afterward, her chef delivered a cart full of food and quickly withdrew from the room. Daisy licked her lips as she meticulously arranged selected dishes across her bed. Her face contorted, and her eyes bulged. Inexplicably, she stuffed handfuls of food into her mouth, devouring and chewing ravenously. It looked strange until it became bizarre—she used the heel of her palm to mash food up her nostrils and packed it into her ears. She squished it between her fingers and down her nightgown. Chocolate sauce dripped from her chin as the feeding frenzy intensified—stuff, chew, gag, stuff again. At her feet, three dogs ran wildly around the room.

The recording showed Daisy wobble and calmly climb into the center of the bed. She coaxed her dogs, each racing up the cloth-covered ramp. She was delighted as they danced over her belly, making it jiggle as they pounced. When they were all around her face, she shoved more food deeper into her mouth, gagged, then opened wide and let the dogs eat from her mouth. With outstretched arms, legs, and open eyes, she lay quietly, in a trance and motionless.

What followed was a scene from a horror movie—the dog's hunger turned feral as they fought and tore at Daisy's face. Out came her top dentures, followed by the lowers. She did not move as they ripped at her tongue until it was shredded. Next, they used their paws, nails, and teeth, tearing at her flesh, nose, and ears.

The video confirmed statements from the housekeeper, the manager, and the doctor while in the room with Daisy. No one was complicit in Daisy's death—except Daisy. The next people seen on the video were the NYPD and medical personnel. Dr. Pearson stopped the video.

"So, self-inflicted," Adama said solemnly. "Now we know what happened to Miss Hunter."

"Now we know. I've adjusted TOD to noon," Dr. Pearson said.

"My god, it's like she went crazy," Bridget said. "If I hadn't seen it, I wouldn't believe it. Have you ever seen anything like this before?" Bridget asked.

"Never. This one is unique and will probably be researched for years," Dr. Pearson said.

Having concluded their visit, Adama and Bridget thanked the doctor and left. It was five-thirty and time for them to get back to headquarters.

"When we get back, I'll meet with the chief and the commissioner. You meet with Burke and let him know what we learned at the morgue."

"Sounds good."

"And Bridget, you did great today—Jane Evans, the London videos, the Miller gallery, your assumptions, connecting the dots between two countries. You provided credible insights." His statement was a core-deep acknowledgment of her value.

"Thanks." She was moved beyond words. "See you tomorrow." *There he is—my sweet Adama. It feels like he's softening toward me.*

Bridget and Adama separated. She found Detective Burke and explained what they had discovered. Bridget called a cab and left feeling content and hopeful.

Chapter 37: Late-Night Meeting

Bridget felt uplifted after a productive day that included solid fact-finding, appreciation, and acknowledgment. It seemed she and Adama had overcome an impasse. Bridget ordered dinner, ate, and got ready for bed. She had just turned on the television when her cell-phone chimed with a text from Adama.

"Can you come to headquarters? Now."

"Yes. What's up?" She texted back.

"See you soon. Bring your London surveillance time log."

Well, that was cryptic. Maybe he found something!

Bridget jumped up, changed into jeans and a sweater, and grabbed her satchel. Ten minutes later, she was in a taxi to headquarters. After clearing security, she headed to Adama's office. He heard her in the hallway.

"In the conference room." Adama led the way.

"What's going on?"

"I obtained the Taylor gallery's proprietary *internal* security footage."

"No way! Adama, that's incredible. How did you get it?"

"I have my sources. Did you bring the Yard's timeline with you?"

"Yes." Bridget patted her satchel. "Have you already watched the video?"

"Let's go." He pointed down the hall.

The conference room was a standard room with a large table in the center, surrounded by twelve chairs. A smartboard hung on the wall, and a credenza sat opposite, with a box of Kleenex and a dozen water bottles. There was an open laptop resting on the table. Adama and Bridget sat side by side. She retrieved a surveillance timeline and placed it on the table. Adama turned to face her. Concerned about proceeding, his expression tightened with reluctance.

"What?" She sensed something was wrong.

"This won't be easy to watch." His voice was gentle and heavy with concern.

"Are you worried I can't take it? You know I've seen plenty of crime scenes, including murders. It's okay. Just show me." Bridget bristled at his hesitation.

"I think you should brace yourself," Adama said. "Colin was your good friend and colleague. I know you're strong, but this video is graphic."

Bridget's demeanor changed from elated to sober. She got it. He was protecting her. She thought for a few seconds, took a deep breath, and threw her shoulders back.

"Murder is always graphic. I can take it."

"Right."

Adama pressed a button on the laptop, and a video file appeared. But he did not press the play button. He gave Bridget an overview.

"There is no sound, so we won't hear the conversations. The gallery's security system included five internal cameras. One camera, mounted over the front door, recorded the reception area. And four wide-angle cameras are strategically placed throughout the gallery, making every inch visible. The feeds from all four cameras have been spliced together based on time and movement within the gallery. And at some points, the video is grainy."

"Understood." Bridget's left leg bounced rapidly under the table.

Adama clicked the mouse and started the video. The first scene showed a young woman coming inside the front door. She walked behind the front desk, sat down, opened a book, and drank from a white disposable coffee cup.

"That's Susan Baker, Colin's assistant." Bridget pointed at the monitor. "So, she opened the gallery that morning. Colin's wife said it was supposed to be closed."

Minutes later, Susan looked up at someone coming into the gallery. The person wore a large black hat, a cape, gloves, and used a walking cane, carrying a briefcase.

"There's our mystery man. Same guy, different locations, he gets around." Bridget continued narrating. "Susan looks happy to see him, that's curious. And he keeps his hat on and head down."

"No face. He's avoiding the cameras. Smart," Adama said.

"Now Susan's holding the door, and here come the two men with the large box we saw on the police video." Bridget pointed at the screen. "The time stamp reads eight-thirty-seven. That coincides with the white van that arrived at eight-thirty-five, and my timeline."

"Right, and that box looks identical to the ones found with Vanhorn and Daisy Hunter," Adama said. "We know of at least one box in London; there may be others."

"Six are unaccounted for. They could be anywhere in the world, being sold at private events, like here in New York. I'll bet this is the work of a syndicate for black-art." Bridget's mind worked overtime with theories.

"Let's focus on the video," Adama said.

"The caped man points his cane and sends the two guys into the gallery. They set the box against a wall. They talk, and the guys leave at eight-forty-five. Then Susan escorts them out." Bridget sat back in her chair, perplexed.

"What's up?" Adama asked and paused the video.

"I'm surprised about Susan's behavior. She was expecting them. My theory of a break-in is falling apart."

"It appears that way." Adama resumed the video.

"Now Susan points at the box, but the caped man shakes his head. She wants to see inside."

"He can't show her—she'd be a witness to stolen property." Adama narrated the next scene. "Not much happens for the next few minutes, then Ahmed Senusret shows up. Susan takes him into the gallery, where both men shake hands."

The video displayed a tall, heavy-set man with dark skin, clean-shaven, and a bald head. He wore dark slacks and a dark jacket buttoned at the waist. He towered over Susan by a foot.

"So, they *all* know each other," Bridget noted. "Well, that rules out several suspicions."

"Right. Now watch Senusret. His body language suggests he's not happy with Susan. He shakes his finger at her and turns to the caped man."

"Yes, the caped man points his cane, sending Susan back to the front desk. She looks disappointed," Bridget said.

"Senusret doesn't want her in the gallery," Adama said.

The video showed the caped man and Senusret engrossed in a conversation near the box. Opening his briefcase, the caped man removed a binder and a small jewelry box, handing the latter to Senusret. The caped man read from the binder while gesturing toward the large box.

"He's explaining something to Senusret. Instructions, maybe?" Adama offered.

"No. It's something more, like storytelling. If you asked me, he's performing," Bridget said.

Adama paused the tape. "What do you mean?"

"Well, the caped guy is using expressive hand movements and gestures at the box. Restart the video."

Adama pushed the play button.

"Look at his posture, how he holds the binder—in a proper, almost regal way. And his hand movements suggest details and description. He's reading from notes but pauses now and again, probably for dramatic effect. And look at Senusret's face; he loves it and is engrossed. It's similar to Miller Antiquities—minus the lectern and the fancy chairs."

Adama nodded, impressed by Bridget's keen eye and ability to capture so much information by observing the body language between the two men.

"You could be right. Our mystery guy points his cane at the box the whole time he talks. Whatever he is saying, it's connected."

"And that little box, with the ribbon—look how Senusret clutches it, like it's a treasure or something." Bridget was thoroughly engaged with the scene.

"Yes, Senusret does appear to be elated. We found jewelry boxes similar to Vanhorn and Daisy Hunter. They held a large key that opened the two locks."

Adama let the video play. The two men talked uninterrupted. The entire exchange took approximately forty minutes. Afterward, the caped man closed his binder and extended his hand in a lordly manner. Senusret took it, bowed, and moved nearer to the box. In the meantime, the caped man walked to the front desk and talked with Susan. She listened and smiled broadly.

"Look at that, Susan just set two glasses on the counter," Bridget said.

"Yes, she's happy, they're celebrating. It must mean their client is happy. Perhaps Susan coordinated the sale of the gravestone." Adama suggested.

"She went behind Colin's back." Bridget's voice held anger. "Where's she going?"

Susan walked outside the camera range of the front desk.

"What's he doing with his cane?" Bridget wished she could take control of the mouse. She leaned in for a closer look.

They watched the caped man as he unscrewed the top of his cane and removed a small vial. The video was grainy, but they both saw the same thing.

"Did you see that?" Bridget pointed. "He poured something into one of the glasses."

"Here comes Susan with champagne," Adama said.

"The caped man filled both glasses and handed her the tainted one. He encourages her to finish. But he never drinks from his glass."

"Right—no DNA left behind." Adama scrutinized the caped man's behavior.

"Stop the video," Bridget said. Adama pushed pause.

She looked intently at Adama. "What do you think he put in Susan's glass? Poison, a sedative?" Bridget thought for a moment. "Is it possible he did that to Thomas Miller?"

"It's possible," Adama answered. "Dr. Pearson found carfentanil in Thomas's bloodstream."

"We need to get Susan's autopsy report." Bridget jotted down a reminder on her notepad. She looked at the screen. "What happened to Senusret?"

"He's still in the gallery. Let's focus on the front desk." He restarted the video.

"Okay. So, the caped guy looks at his pocket watch, picks up his briefcase, waves, and then walks out the front door. That's what I saw on the external video. He was the last one to leave, alive."

Adama stopped the video. "What does your time log say?" Adama tapped Bridget's notebook.

"It says the caped man walked out at nine-fifty a.m. And we know a limo was waiting outside at that same time."

"Did Scotland Yard's forensics team run tests on the glasses and check for fingerprints?"

"They should have," Bridget said. "Maybe I can still log into my account at the Yard and get the toxicology reports."

"Good. We'll look at those later."

They continued watching. The video showed Susan's head hanging low, as if she were reading a book. Something startles her, and she jerks upward. She answers the phone.

"Who called her? Do you have that data, Bridget?"

"Yes, it's the owner of a hat shop across the street. He saw all the activity and thought it strange that Colin wasn't there. He spoke with Susan—she said everything was fine. But the guy called Colin and told him about the delivery van and the strange man in black."

"What time was that?" Adama asked.

"That was ten a.m. exactly. And we have the call going to Colin's cellphone as well."

"Okay. Let's watch what happens after the caped man leaves." Adama restarted the video.

They watched Senusret remove a large key from the jewelry box. He opens two locks and opens the lid.

A new camera angle showed Senusret's face. "He looks mesmerized. It's like a magnet; everyone wants to touch the stone. I did." Bridget added.

"There, he touches it. He's tracing his fingers around the symbol carved at the top."

"Creepy. He's really into it. Oh, here comes Susan. Of course, she wants to see what's inside." Bridget saw her stumble.

"Bridget?" Adama paused the tape. "When you were in London, did you see that box?

"No. I inspected the crime scene at the gallery, but there was no box. The Yard must have removed it." Bridget made a mental note about the Yard, possibly removing a key piece of evidence and closing the case so quickly. "Do you mind if I run to the restroom?" Bridget asked.

"Go ahead," Adama said.

Adama was waiting patiently at the table for Bridget. *I'm glad she's here, but I'm unsure about showing her the rest of this video.*

A few minutes later, Bridget came back into the conference room. *It's so good to be working with him again. I hope he feels the same way.*

Chapter 38: It's Graphic

The clock on the wall in the conference room read ten-forty-five p.m. Adama and Bridget agreed that their cases had many more similarities than differences. Adama asked Bridget if she was ready to continue. He pushed the play button on the laptop video app.

The timestamp on the video showed "10:30 a.m." Ahmed Senusret and Susan Baker stood in the gallery talking. Senusret seemed to point at the foyer and motioned for her to leave. Suddenly, they both turned toward the front door. Colin Taylor walked into the foyer and turned toward the gallery. Another camera recorded Colin approaching the uninvited guest, Senusret, and a very nervous Susan.

"Well, he's not happy. It looks like Colin is yelling at Senusret—waving his arms and pointing at the door," Bridget observed.

"And Senusret looks angry, too, yelling back."

They watched as Susan stepped between Colin and Senusret. She held both hands up and waved. Without warning, Senusret struck Susan across the face, causing her to fall and hit her head on a nearby curio case.

"Oh my god, he hit her." Bridget gasped. "And he's going after her."

Colin's fingers dug into Senusret's muscular arm to subdue him. The two men struggled while Susan crawled away. With fear in her eyes, she watched and held her aching head until she lost consciousness. Colin broke free, raised both arms in surrender, then patted the air downward to quell Senusret's wrath.

"Brace yourself, Bridget." Adama's finger hovered over the pause button.

Instantly, they saw Senusret reach for a small marble bust of Marc Antony. He swung at Colin and missed. Filled with rage, Senusret lunged at Colin, who was too slow to react.

"Oh my god, he hit Colin!" Bridget called out.

Colin stumbled backward, holding the side of his head. Senusret advanced like a predator on weakened prey. A dazed Colin raised a shaking arm to defend himself, but Senusret's actions were swift and brutal. He repeatedly struck Colin with callous disregard for human life.

"Oh god, he's beating him. Stop!" Bridget's voice commanded the violence to stop.

Disoriented, Colin dropped to his knees. Senusret scanned his helpless quarry, raised the bust high, like an executioner with an axe, and crushed Colin's skull with devastating force. Colin's body slumped onto the floor. Senusret mused for a moment and tapped his foot in the black liquid that oozed from his motionless victim. His fingers released Marc Antony's head, landing next to Colin's body.

Bridget looked away. Adama stopped the video. She ran to a wastebasket to throw up. Adama opened a bottle of water and placed it on the table.

"Come sit down, Bridget." He felt powerless as he consoled her.

"Oh my god, poor Colin." She whispered his name while the color drained from her face. Bridget's body shuddered as she pressed her palms hard against her face. Adama brought a box of Kleenex from the credenza as he escorted her back to the table.

"Here, love." He offered a tissue. "I'm sorry you had to see that." Adama cradled her.

"I can't watch anymore. I need some time."

"Of course. Let's take a break. We can deal with this later."

Bridget stood, Adama ensured she was steady, and walked her to the bathroom.

———◆———

Bridget gripped the white porcelain sink in the ladies' room to steady herself. Feeling nauseous, she splashed cold water over her face. Glaring at the mirror, she watched the tap water mix with her streams of tears. Bridget instinctively shook her hands to rid them of excess water. Standing before the mounted paper towel dispenser, she cranked the metal nob. It released an inch-sized piece of brown paper. As she pulled downward, the dispenser's serrated edge nicked her finger. "Damn it!" she muttered and sucked on the small bleeding cut. Bridget tried again, another crank, another pathetic inch of paper, then something snapped. She frantically pulled, yanked, and shredded paper towels in a frenzy. The fury within had swelled upward like hot lava. With curled fists and uncontained rage, she pounded on the dispenser. With each strike, hollow metal reverberations echoed off the walls.

"Everything okay in there?" Adama restrained himself from running inside.

Hearing Adama's voice pulled her back from the brink. "Um, yeah. I'll be out in a sec." Bridget composed herself, rinsed her mouth, gathered the shredded towel pieces, and tossed them into the trash. She opened the bathroom door to find Adama standing there.

"We don't have to finish the video, Bridget."

"Yes, we do. I want to. Just tell me. Have I seen the worst of it?"

"More or less." Adama walked her back into the conference room. "But the next part is also difficult to watch."

"Well, keep it going. It's the least I can do for Colin." She sat down.

Bridget took a deep breath. Out of the corner of her eye, she spotted Adama's clenched fists and instinctively did the same. Bridget hardened herself for more brutality. Adama restarted the video.

The video feed exposed the gallery from a different angle. Senusret stood over Colin's body, still, staring downward. He pressed his palms to his face, massaged it, and dragged his fingers upward across the top of his bald head. The camera captured Senusret's facial expression morphing from a human being to something unholy—an unhinged and feral beast. His eyes darted around the gallery until they fixed on Susan, whose unconscious body lay a few feet from Colin.

Though Susan Baker lay unconscious on the floor, Senusret was seen shaking his finger at her. He nudged, then kicked her legs with his foot, but she did not move. The next kick was to her stomach. Senusret walked in circles around her, spat on her face, drew back his foot, and gave her a swift kick to the head. Senusret went to Colin's office and returned with a lamp. After ripping the cord off, he wrapped it around Susan's neck and strangled her—no resistance, just sheer brutality.

Adama paused the video. He and Bridget sat in silence for a minute.

"That poor girl." Bridget's hands trembled.

"Yes, and now we know the truth. Senusret killed both Colin and Susan."

"And I was wrong. It wasn't the mystery-caped man after all. I've been blaming him."

"Bridget, there isn't much more. Do you want to finish?"

"Yes. Get it over with."

The rest of the events in the video were wild and crazy. Senusret began breaking things. He shattered vases and knocked over pedestals of ancient artifacts. He smashed two curios with his fists, destroying several more than two millennia-old objects.

The large bald billionaire, Ahmed Senusret, halted the carnage when confronted by a woman's figure—Nemesis, the Goddess of Retribution. Though demure in appearance, her unfurled wings stretched outward like dark harbingers of doom. Her right arm extended upward, clutching a long dagger, while her left hand jutted outward, fingers spread wide in a threatening and powerful stance. Senusret walked the whole circumference of the statue.

"Does it look like he's talking to that statue?" Adama asked.

"Yes, but I can't tell what he's saying," Bridget said.

Through the grainy feed, Adama and Bridget saw Senusret yelling and shaking his fist at the marble statue. His movements became animated, his arms flailed wildly, like an angry fan at a sporting event. Senusret bent down and dipped both of his palms into the pooled blood around Colin, smearing it on the statue. He walked behind it and pushed, but it did not budge. He pushed harder until it rocked on its pedestal.

"Well, that explains his bloody fingerprints everywhere. Is he trying to topple the statue? It must weigh over a hundred and fifty pounds."

"One-seventy-five," Adama said.

The entrance to the gallery was adorned with floor-length drapes tied back by long, velvet cords featuring golden tassels. Senusret yanked one set of cords, then the other. It was so aggressive that the drapes and rods crashed to the floor.

"What's he doing?" Bridget wondered aloud.

"Watch. He's going to use them."

Senusret put one set of cords around the neck of the statue and wrapped one set around the wings. He grabbed all four ends and took a step backward.

"My god, he's going to bring it down," Bridget said.

"You might want to look away," Adama warned.

"No way."

Senusret pulled on the ends of the cords. He struggled with the weight of the statue. He wrapped his fists tighter around the cords, put his left foot on the edge of the base for leverage, grabbed hold, used all his weight, and pulled with all his might. Loose from its base, the statue faltered. He yanked harder, all the while screaming at the woman figure.

Two seconds later, Senusret froze. The goddess wobbled and toppled forward. She seemed to come alive, acting on her own volition, smiling. Senusret, momentarily mesmerized, was lucid enough to raise his arms for protection. The gesture was useless. He collapsed under the weight of the statue. The video feed showed a dark liquid flowing from his torso. The screen turned black. Adama pushed the stop button.

"Wow, it's like the guy went nuts," Bridget said. "Like some evil spirit possessed him. Where's the rest of it?"

"That's it. Until the police arrive."

"Show me, please." Bridget was emphatic.

Adama fast-forwarded through stagnant video.

"The police arrived at twelve forty-five. Two minutes later, they called for help. Three ambulances and more police arrived at twelve fifty-five."

"Now I know the truth," Bridget said solemnly.

"Bridget, I'm sorry, but this video confirms why the Yard labeled it a murder-suicide. No one else participated in their deaths. You see that, right?"

"Well, now I have a better understanding of what happened. But I don't think it was a lover's tryst, not with Colin anyway. Maybe Susan and the caped guy had a thing."

Bridget got up and walked around the room.

"Why did Senusret suddenly go crazy? Why kill everyone? And himself?"

"We'll get there. This video was helpful. But now, we need to shift our focus to the Miller gallery and our dead billionaires. After everything we've seen today, I believe there is a connection with our two cases."

"Thank you for seeing that, Adama."

"If we solve one case, we'll solve the other." He'd never seen Bridget look so defeated. "You look exhausted. I'll drive you to the hotel. We'll pick this up in the morning."

"You're right. I've had it." Her body felt heavy and sluggish, as if she were wading through water.

The night had taken its toll. They cleaned up and left the building. Adama pulled up to the entrance of Gild Hall, where they sat silently for a long minute.

"Are you okay?" Adama's voice was gentle, and his face expressed concern.

Bridget removed her seatbelt and whispered, "Do you want to come up?" Her vulnerability emanated with each word.

Adama's loving yet bittersweet smile gave her the answer. "That's probably not a good idea. You've had a rough night—try to get some sleep." He leaned over and tenderly kissed her forehead. "But call if you need anything."

"Yeah, you're right, as usual," she sighed. "Thanks for the lift. See you in the morning." Bridget got out and waved goodbye.

"Sleep well, love." Adama watched Bridget walk up the hotel steps, her movements fluid and graceful. *You still walk like music.* A familiar ache stirred in his chest, and for a split second, he imagined following her inside. But he knew better. Adama waited until Bridget disappeared into the lobby. He reluctantly eased his vehicle onto the dark, empty street.

WEDNESDAY

Chapter 39: The Banimaya

A partly cloudy sky cast dark shadows mixed with brilliant illumination over the buildings and streets of New York City. Bridget and Adama's gazes locked, cast with mixed yet familiar feelings, as their paths converged while going through security at NYPD headquarters.

"How are you feeling this morning?" Concern etched the tiny lines around Adama's eyes.

"Tired. It was a restless night." Bridget's eyes matched her response. "How are you?"

"The same. I worried about you." Adama struggled to look away from her gaze. "Let's check in, get updates, then head out to Vanhorn's yacht."

"Sounds good." She placed her satchel on the security conveyor belt.

In the bullpen, Adama learned that Gates and Sanchez had triangulated Ling Chen's cell phone at or near the Cardinal Lakes Country Club on Long Island. In the meantime, Ricky Burke would remain at headquarters and manage the ongoing investigations. Bridget and Adama would head over to Brooklyn to visit Vanhorn's yacht.

Adama drove while Bridget reviewed the case file. They were two blocks from the Brooklyn Bridge when Adama received a call from Jimmy Quinn, a forensic technician at the morgue.

"Hey Jimmy, did you get the forensics back on all the bodies?"

"Good morning, sir. Not yet. Dr. Pearson found something, let me get her." Adama heard Quinn's muffled voice. "I have the deputy chief on the line." Footsteps echoed, followed by the familiar stretchy snap and pop of gloves being removed.

"Adama?"

"Good morning, Doc. Quinn said you found something?"

As Dr. Pearson spoke, Adama's eyes widened with surprise. He scanned the rearview mirror, and without warning, hit the brakes and wrenched the steering wheel into a sharp U-turn.

"We're coming to you."

"What's going on?" Bridget asked.

"It seems the dead billionaires have something in common after all."

"You mean besides the two wooden boxes?"

"Yes. Hang on, the morgue is a few blocks away." Adama lit up flashing lights and skillfully weaved through the morning traffic. "This could be the break we need."

Bridget cinched her seat belt and reached for the grab handle above her door. She never liked riding in speeding cars, even with an experienced driver at the wheel. When the car stopped in front of the morgue, she let out a gasp.

"Good grief."

"You, okay?" He had already unsnapped his seatbelt. "Let's go!"

Adama hurriedly led the way as they dashed through security, down the hallway, and burst through the metal door.

"What did you find?"

Hearing the commotion, Dr. Pearson and Jimmy Quinn looked up.

"Well, good morning to you too," Dr. Pearson said. "Hello, Bridget."

"Hello, Dr. Pearson. Hello, Jimmy," Bridget said.

"So, Betty, you found a connection between William Vanhorn and Daisy Hunter?"

"Yes. They're over here."

The doctor pulled back the sheet to expose the head and neck of Daisy Hunter and repeated the process on William Vanhorn.

"So, what am I looking at?" Adama studied Vanhorn's body.

Dr. Pearson turned Vanhorn's head to the right. "This." She pulled the hair away from an area behind his left ear and pointed. Adama put on gloves.

"What is that?" Adama asked. "Can we have more light, please?"

The doctor repositioned the overhead lamp, flooding Vanhorn's face and neck with a harsh white light. Adama squinted and gestured to Bridget. "Come take a look." Bridget put on gloves and stepped forward.

"What do you make of it?" Adama asked. "Is that a tattoo?"

"I don't know." Bridget looked bewildered. "Jimmy, have you got a magnifying glass?"

Bridget left Vanhorn and walked over to Daisy Hunter. Adama followed, and Dr. Pearson exposed the same area on Miss Hunter. They took turns studying the same mark behind her left ear.

"When did you find these?" Adama asked.

"This morning, during a final review." Dr. Pearson said. "I don't know how I missed them. It's like they appeared overnight. I measured these marks on both bodies. They're identical—same quarter-inch diameter, same design, both positioned a half inch behind their left ear."

"What about Thomas Miller? Did he have the same mark?" Bridget asked.

"No, I searched his entire body. There was nothing on him."

Bridget's mouth dropped open, her eyes flickered, and her head bobbed—a light bulb went off. She gazed from Adama to Dr. Pearson, to Quinn, and back, with a "duh" look.

"What?" Adama asked.

"Don't you recognize it—it's the same as the symbol on the stones," Bridget said.

Dr. Pearson took the magnifying glass and inspected it closely. "Are you sure?" Her tone was skeptical. "How is that even possible?"

Adama took the magnifying glass while Quinn danced on his tiptoes, waiting for his turn to see the revelation.

"Is she right?" Dr. Pearson asked.

"I think she is," Adama said, straining with the magnifier.

"Go look at the stones." Bridget challenged. "You'll see."

Dr. Pearson grabbed her key ring and headed for the room where the two boxes had been stored.

"I'll open it." Adama followed protectively. Inside, he carefully lifted the lid of Vanhorn's box. Everyone inspected the carved area at the top of the stone. The shape was old and worn, but distinctive.

"She's right." Dr. Pearson conceded. "What else do you know about this, Bridget?"

"Before I was a criminologist, I was a professor of anthropology at Cheikh Anta Diop University in Dakar. I worked on digs in Senegal, Sierra Leone, and other West African countries for five years. I found this symbol on the gravestones in an ancient burial ground, on an island off the coast of St. Pierre, Senegal," Bridget explained.

"I was born and raised in St. Pierre, Senegal," Adama said. "When I was a boy, I saw a similar symbol in an old graveyard—but this symbol is different. This one has a gash in the middle of it."

Bridget was quick to explain the difference. "That's because there are two symbols, with very different meanings. I worked at the dig on Impie Island, which is forbidden to locals and tourists. And that gash is called a "wor"—it means betrayal in Wolof."

"Okay, you two certainly get around. But tell me, why would these marks be on the bodies of Vanhorn and Daisy?" Dr. Pearson asked.

"I have no idea. Unless…" Bridget's face changed from puzzled to shocked.

"Unless what?" Adama asked.

"Let's recheck Vanhorn." They crowded around Vanhorn's body.

Holding the magnifying glass over Vanhorn's quarter-inch symbol, Bridget meticulously described the mark. "Looking closely, you'll see two Fibonacci spirals in the center. A piece between them is called a 'pon,' which means 'bridge' connecting the two spirals."

"Fibonacci spirals?" Quinn asked.

"Yes. It's a geometric pattern that's pervasive throughout nature. The spiral is created by a series of connected quarter circles inside a set of squares sized according to the Fibonacci sequence."

Bridget looked up at the three faces staring at her. They waited for further explanation.

"Oh, come on, surely you recognize the pattern?" Bridget asked.

She delighted in stepping into her former professor's shoes.

"It's related to mathematics. Each number is the sum of the two preceding numbers. For example, zero, one, one, two, three, five, eight, thirteen, and so on. Get it?"

"Math wasn't my strong suit," Quinn confessed.

"I've got it," Dr. Pearson said. "Jimmy, you know what a nautilus looks like, right?"

"Sure. It's one of those cool ancient marine animals that swim backwards," he said.

"Excellent reference, Doc," Bridget said. "Think of a spiral galaxy, sunflowers, and even pinecones have the same golden ratio—it's a pattern. And, Doc, a bisected nautilus is the perfect example."

"I see it now, these marks look similar to seashells and snails," Adama said.

"Now I get it," Quinn said.

"Okay, but there's more," Bridget said. "It's all related to West African mythology."

Dr. Pearson, Adama, and Quinn huddled around Bridget, fascinated by her expertise in West African tribal history, culture, mythology, and folklore.

"Every culture uses mythology to explain its roots, reinforcing cultural identity, who they are, and where they came from. Mythology answers how and why things work in a society, legitimizing social structures and connections to ancestral origins, values, and mores. It explains the meaning of life and death to its people."

"So, what do these marks mean?" Dr. Pearson asked.

"There are two ancient gravesites off the coast of St. Pierre spanning two locations: Impie Island and Shell Island. Both are sacred burial grounds for ancient tribes in the area. There are two significant symbols at play here: one is called Banimaya and the other Kanijugu."

Adama said, "I know about the Banimaya symbol from growing up in St. Pierre. My brother and I visited Shell Island. We crossed a bridge and visited the gravesites there. I heard about the Kanijugu symbol but never saw it. We were forbidden to go to Impie Island—legend says it's cursed."

"Hence the segregation," Bridget said. "Over time, the old rituals and knowledge had been replaced with scary stories, and a legend was born."

"Tell us about the symbols, Bridget." Quinn's interest piqued.

Nearby, Dr. Pearson was quiet and doubtful. As a scientist, it was amusing, at best.

"I'll begin with the Banimaya. It symbolizes the sacred connection between life and the afterlife. You'll notice I didn't say "death" because the ancient ones believed that life was everlasting. The Banimaya symbol serves as a guiding force, ensuring the tribal leader passes into the afterlife with dignity. The Banimaya symbolizes what once was, remains." She pointed to the symbol. "You can see that both spirals are connected and encased within an open circle, representing how life is never complete."

"And the Banimaya is carved at the top of a tribal leader's gravestone," Adama added.

"That's correct, and when a benevolent tribal leader dies, he is honored and treated with grace. Tribal members leave small gifts as a gesture of gratitude. All good leaders were buried together on hallowed land—Shell Island. In addition, the leader's spirit may be called upon to share wisdom, counsel, and assist the current tribal leader and his people."

"But why are there two different symbols?" Quinn asked.

"I'm glad you asked." Bridget's eyes lit up as she returned to her roots in archaeology and anthropology. "Gather round and I'll share the story of a four-hundred-year-old curse."

Chapter 40: The Kanijugu

Adama, Jimmy, and a reluctant Dr. Pearson gathered around Bridget, eager to learn about the ancient symbols. Bridget continued, explaining the crucial differences between the Banimaya and the Kanijugu symbols.

"Jimmy, you asked why there are two symbols. While the Banimaya honors benevolent tribal leaders, the opposite is true for a malevolent, or evil-hearted, leader. After death, that leader is jeered— no gifts offered. The shaman directs the stonecutter to chisel the original Banimaya symbol into a stone. But it's not finished. The shaman then orders the placement of a severe gash—called a wor, which means betrayal. The stonecutter chisels a wor directly through the entire Banimaya symbol. The wor destroys the pon—the sacred link connecting the two spirals. Severing that connection is the gravest punishment for a dead tribal leader. Once marred, the Banimaya is transformed into the Kanijugu—a symbol of evil and corruption. The Kanijugu is 'mal, mauvais and dépravée'."

"What do those words mean?" Quinn asked.

"They're French for evil, bad, and depraved," Adama explained. "The Kanijugu is essentially an evil curse—and the legend says any gravestone marked with the Kanijugu is also condemned."

"Precisely," Bridget continued. "Since the pon connects the worlds of the living and the dead, the wor gash severs that connection, condemning, dishonoring, and banishing the corrupt leader. His transition to the afterlife is blocked, trapping his evil spirit to languish in eternal torment."

"And what exactly constitutes evil, and how is it applied?" Dr. Pearson asked, still skeptical.

"According to folklore, it's based on a person's evil heart or soul. If the person was cruel, had tortured, raped, disfigured, ordered murders, or if he exploited for power and enrichment, that person, or leader will have brought the Kanijugu curse upon himself."

Adama added personal knowledge. "We learned that bad leaders were segregated to a plot of rotten earth, completely isolated from the good leaders with the Banimaya symbol. The separation ensured no transfer or contamination to the living. Because the Kanijugu interred the evil heart's spirit, the rotten earth was also affected by the stone with the Kanijugu symbol. I remember the scary stories that parents told their children about becoming bad men or bad women, and how the evil spirit would invade their hearts and eat their minds, making them 'dof,' meaning crazy."

"That sounds pretty cool," Quinn said.

"It is, and I'm not finished," Bridget agreed. "Doc, you asked about the application. And Adama, the scary stories you heard were meant to teach children lessons. This folklore states that if a *living* person is evil-hearted and touches, disturbs, or exploits a gravestone marked with the Kanijugu symbol, then that person's evil spirit shall be connected with the evil tribal leader and suffer dire consequences."

"What happens to them? What's the connection?" Quinn asked.

"It's physical, Jimmy. Once the condemned stone is touched by any person with a truly evil heart, the Kanijugu curse manifests through a euphoric feeling, then a tingling sensation in the body, indicating an irreversible contamination."

"How would an infected person behave?" Dr. Pearson finally heard something useful.

"At first, the evil person feels euphoric, even invincible, but in reality, they are in an otherworld-like trance. The effect can be immediate or dormant, depending on when the evil-hearted person is *triggered* by something. And that *something* has to be consistent with their evil deeds, or how they lived. The irony is that the cursed person ultimately brings about their own demise. Basically, the person goes crazy and is out of control, all while engaged in a behavior that leads to their death. The next part, however, directly pertains to Vanhorn and Daisy Hunter. According to the curse, that person's body shall be marked with the sign of the Kanijugu, condemning their soul for all eternity." Bridget took a breath after her long explanation. Silence fell as everyone digested thoughts about the West African curse. Even Adama wondered if the curse existed. *Two dead billionaires, two stones, two touches. Did they really go crazy after touching their stones?* It meant both victims were evil-hearted. He did acknowledge that their deaths were linked to how they lived. *And what about the billionaire in London? He touched his stone and went crazy. Is this all possible?*

"So, you're saying an evil person is triggered by their evil deeds, and the Kanijugu causes them to kill themselves with their own evil longings?" Adama asked.

"Yes, that's a good interpretation. For example, if a bad person exploited, badly deceived, cheated, or harmed others, and benefited from those deeds, they would die similarly, based on their evil exploitation of others."

"So, are we talking possession?" Dr. Pearson asked. "Because it sounds like the tribal leader's evil spirit is transferred to an evil-hearted living person."

"It's not a transfer or a possession—think of it as a connection. Evil begets evil, causing contamination." Bridget's simplification of it seemed to help.

"Like 'live by the sword, die by the sword,'" Dr. Pearson said.

"Exactly," Bridget said.

"That's wild," Quinn said. "But, what happens if a good person touches the cursed stone?"

"Great question. No one is perfect, Jimmy. People make mistakes; this curse isn't about lying, stealing candy, or cheating on a spouse—transgressions one would confess to a priest. Nor is it about breaking the Ten Commandments, at least not for normal people. The curse is about crossing that proverbial line—going way outside the norm. However, the curse does have an exception. If a person's heart or spirit is decent, and they touch the Kanijugu cursed stone, they will feel no tingling sensation, no connection occurs, and their life is spared. The curse won't affect them."

"Is that why the men who dug up the stones weren't affected?" Adama asked.

"Well, those men were locals and probably decent people," Bridget said. "And I suppose one or more could have been evil-spirited. Unfortunately, they were all murdered, so the curse didn't have time to affect them. Remember, the effect isn't immediate; the person must be triggered by something connected to them and how they lived their lives."

Adama wondered if any of his staff, people on the yacht, or in Daisy's entourage had touched the stones, either intentionally or accidentally. Everyone was still alive. He had been drawn to touch the stone in Daisy Hunter's bedroom, but was interrupted. He felt a sense of relief and vindication for having sequestered the stones. He realized his hunch had paid off, but not for any reason he could imagine. In his mind, they were a danger to everyone until proven otherwise.

"People don't wear labels; good or evil hearts don't wave a flag. So, how do we protect people from the stones?" Adama asked.

Bridget smiled at him, understanding his protective yet suspicious nature. "I guess any of us could touch those stones and be just fine." She offered a reassuring look. "People know their own hearts. In fact, I'm happy to touch a stone if it'll make you all feel better."

The group exchanged uneasy glances, as common sense and professional composure momentarily cracked under the weight of ancient superstition.

"I believe you. But do me a favor and hold off a little longer," Adama said.

Dr. Pearson, the scientist in the room, had listened thoughtfully, but wasn't ready for a leap of faith.

"Okay, all that aside, how did the symbol appear on our victims?" Dr. Pearson asked. "Based on that mythology, our vics touched an ancient gravestone marked with the Kanijugu, then died shortly afterward under very unusual circumstances."

"Betty, the legend says the mark of the Kanijugu appears on the body. Curses are complex; some people believe in magic, voodoo, bad luck charms, others in witchcraft, including physical manifestations. Mythology is based on cultural tradition or religion; it isn't an exact science. There are many universal forces at work that none of us understands. I don't have a logical explanation." Bridget motioned to the bodies. "And yet, there it is, right in front of us."

Dr. Pearson wasn't buying it. She turned to Adama. "I can't list the Kanijugu curse as a cause of death." Her statement gave everyone pause. "In fact, I don't believe in curses."

"Neither do I." Adama agreed verbally, while feeling a whisper of doubt.

"Well, that's your choice," Bridget said. "But there are thousands of cultures with similar beliefs. And they believe in curses, demons, devils, and evil spirits. For thousands of years, people have lived their lives based on mythology and symbolism, as well as the mystical and spiritual power of the universe. It's taken very seriously. We should be respectful; it could lead us to the truth."

"Doc, you told us the cause of death for both victims was asphyxiation, right?" Adama said.

"That's right. And that's exactly what I'm listing on their death certificates."

"Um, Bridget, I have a question. Have you ever seen this mark or symbol on a person?" Quinn asked.

"No, Jimmy, I've never seen the Banimaya or the Kanijugu symbols outside the West African gravestones. They're no longer used. This curse is ancient. And I need to do more research."

Bridget offered a cautionary look at Adama. He caught it and knew it was code for "not here and not now."

"I get the feeling you two are up to something, again," Dr. Pearson said.

Adama looked through the doctor's pretty red glasses and into her big blue eyes.

"Listen, Betty, Bridget is good at this. She knows more than I do. You've provided us with the first solid connection between these billionaires. Thanks for finishing the autopsies. We'll be in touch. I promise." Adama smiled at her as he turned to leave.

"I'll hold you to that," Dr. Pearson said.

"Understood." Adama blew her a kiss. "Ready, Bridget?"

"Adama, wait. Can I examine the stones now and run some tests?" Dr. Pearson asked.

"All in good time, Doc." Adama waved goodbye and directed Bridget out the door.

Dr. Pearson smiled to herself about Adama. *So, he's from Senegal, Africa. Very interesting.* She understood now how Adama recognized the scarification patterns on the two young men found in the Hudson—they were from West Africa.

"Let's get these bodies back on ice," she told Quinn.

"Yes, ma'am." Quinn smiled at the exchange of warmth he witnessed between Adama and Dr. Pearson. He helped pull the sheets up and put all the victims into their respective drawers for protection.

Chapter 41: Triggered

Adama and Bridget had finished their meeting with Dr. Pearson at the morgue. Seeing the Kanijugu symbol on the two billionaires was eye-opening and meant the investigation may take a different direction. The sun was clawing its way upward in the east. Adama and Bridget were headed to the Brooklyn marina to peruse the crime scene of Vanhorn's superyacht.

"That was good work, Bridget. I wouldn't have connected the marks with the symbols. It's been too many years. Your analysis gives us more context to solve our cases. And we both know there's more to this than two boxes and two dead billionaires." Adama paused. "Tell me, what else is going on in that head of yours?"

"I have a working theory," Bridget said. "But right now, my concern is for anyone with a stone. If I'm right, we don't have much time, and I need to think." Bridget put her arms back over her head and stretched her lean body.

"Why don't we forget the marina, grab breakfast, and talk. Maybe I can help."

"That sounds good. I'm hungry."

Adama drove to La Parisienne Café, two minutes away. The French connection was not lost on Bridget; it warmed her. They sat by the window and ordered lattes and French toast with berries.

"I have the feeling you know more about the murders in St. Pierre. Am I right?" Bridget asked.

"Yes. My brother was shot, and my nephew was killed, along with twelve others." Adama clenched his jaw, gnawing on feelings of pain and anger toward the men responsible for harming his family.

Bridget caught a flash of raw grief etched in Adama's anguished expression.

"Adama, I'm so sorry." She reached over and gently squeezed his hand.

"Thanks. My brother, Bakary, survived. But he and his wife are devastated about their son."

"How awful for them. So, your nephew was the twelve-year-old boy mentioned in the newspaper? I had no idea." Her heart ached for him.

"This is international now. The commissioner and chief need to be updated. They'll get the wheels in motion as soon as possible to help coordinate the stones' return to West Africa."

Bridget agreed and summarized. "Yes, and the special event at the Miller gallery was the end game. It's clearer now. The theft was orchestrated so that twenty gravestones would be dug up and sold as artifacts. Whomever is responsible, picked up the men in St. Pierre, took them to Impie Island, forced them to dig, and afterward, murdered them all."

"Including my twelve-year-old nephew. And only thirteen stones survived the process," Adama said. "The damaged stones were left behind. The local police never solved the crime, and for two years, no one has seen or heard anything about the missing stones."

"Until now. We know at least six landed in New York, and one ended in London." Bridget sipped her latte.

"That leaves six stones unaccounted for, and they could be anywhere," Adama said.

"And two out of six billionaires died from suspicious circumstances. The others may be in danger of a similar fate."

They stopped talking when the waiter brought their two plates of food.

"Well, you said it yourself—it's all connected," Adama said. "We need to find the other boxes as soon as possible. We have probable cause for a warrant to search and seize purchased stolen international goods. Detective Burke is working on getting a judge's signature for the other four billionaires."

"Well, I hate to say it, but I think all those stones with the Kanijugu symbol affected those people." Bridget took a bite of food. "I mean, just look at how those billionaires lived, how they made their money, the lawsuits, their arrogance, exploitation, and more. They are evil people. And we need to review Senusret's case file—he touched the stone and went nuts. I wonder if his autopsy report states a small mark behind his left ear?"

"Good question, you should work on that." He took a bite of hashbrowns and thought about Bridget's hypothesis. "So, you believe the curse will get to all of them if they touch the stone, then they'll kill themselves, consistent with their lifestyle. You believe that?" Adama asked.

"It's not that simple, Adama. I'm following the facts. That's our job. And as far-fetched as it sounds, it looks like the stones with the Kanijugu are linked to the deaths of Vanhorn and Miss Daisy Hunter. Somehow, they were triggered." Bridget sliced her French toast.

"You mentioned being triggered at the morgue. Tell me more about that." Adama said.

"The legend says there may be a delay in the curse's effects until the so-called evil person is triggered by something or someone. I'll start with Vanhorn. He was definitely into kinky sex and had a long history of using and abusing teenagers. And he's been indicted for two rapes and using Rohypnol, and those are the ones we know about. The guy is a major creep."

"No argument there." Adama stabbed two blackberries.

"Okay, stay with me because this will sound far-fetched," Bridget said. "Vanhorn goes to the gallery, returns to the yacht, and his stone is delivered a while later. Let's say he opens the box and touches the stone. Then he hangs out in the hot tub until he and the girls go to his bedroom. Once he gets to the bedroom, he's triggered by his frustration with sex. He's older, the girls are young, he's impotent, feels sorry for himself, gets pissed, and kicks them out. Then he decides to self-gratify, and in the process accidentally kills himself." Bridget sighed loudly.

"That's far-fetched all right," Adama said. He drizzled syrup over his toast. "Besides, the cause of death will be determined by science, not a curse."

"Of course, but that's exactly what the curse does—these people die by their own hand, and in line with how they lived their lives. So, of course, the deaths look natural."

"Okay, what about Daisy Hunter? How do you explain her stuffing all that food into her orifices?" Adama recalled the food in Daisy's mouth and swallowed hard.

"Well, we saw the nanny-cam video. Daisy Hunter was no angel; she was responsible for multiple safety violations and related deaths at her oil fields. And she cheated their families out of millions in settlements because of her political connections. And her case file stated years of therapy for binge eating, anger, and self-loathing. So, like Vanhorn, her box arrives, and she touches the stone, orders food, and sees herself in the mirror. She's triggered—all that self-hate erupts, and she starts shoveling food as fast as she can—it was self-induced asphyxiation by food."

Bridget hungrily dove into her plate of food, while Adama lost his appetite. He thought about Bridget's comments and was confounded by the notion that those two billionaires accidentally killed themselves because a curse triggered their inner evil and demons. He remained quiet for a minute, as did she.

"Okay, Bridget, let's think on that. In the meantime, what other theories do you have rattling around in that brilliant brain?"

"My working theory is that someone or some organization is out there deliberately creating chaos and profiting from it by selling the spoils to billionaires around the world."

"Wow, based on what?" Adama pushed his plate away.

"I've suspected it for a while. In the past few years, there have been several instances of exploitation, death, plundering, and people murdered in connection with ancient artifacts."

"But we know that happens all the time," Adama said. "The cost of fraud runs in the billions worldwide, and includes money laundering, drugs smuggled through cultural objects, thousands of forgeries, thefts, and deaths associated with all of it. I've got stacks of open cases."

"You're right, but the exploitations didn't make sense in several instances." Bridget pointed with her fork. "Are you going to eat those blueberries?"

"No, help yourself." He pushed his plate toward her. "What do you mean?"

"I worked three cases in the last two years where the stolen items weren't that valuable. And look at the Senegal stones. They're four hundred years old, not two thousand years old. And in other instances, it seemed the ensuing chaos was created, like a flashpoint, that dispersed as fast as it occurred. I don't understand it. Not yet anyway."

"Have you told anyone?" Adama asked.

"Who would I tell? It sounds crazy. I have no proof and no one to blame. But if I'm right, this is bigger than we can imagine."

"And therefore, more dangerous." Adama suddenly became more serious. "If you're right, Jane Evans and her partner may have paid the ultimate price pursuing a similar theory."

"And possibly Colin." Bridget sipped her latte.

They discussed her West African research and evidence supporting her mythology theory. They both knew presenting a curse was unfathomable and that people would call them lunatics, destroying both their careers. Nevertheless, they reached a consensus that the correct identification and claim for the six stolen stones would kick off an international investigation involving multiple agencies.

"My brother, Bakary, needs to come to New York so he can provide eyewitness testimony about what happened and provide proof that the stones belong in St. Pierre. But that would mean Bakary must recount the horrific events of two years ago. I don't know if he'll do it." Adama was leery and did not want to cause more hurt for his brother.

"Well, once we get the cases solved, we'll work on repatriating the gravestones," Bridget said. "He may come knowing it will help heal St. Pierre, and in the process help him and his wife. It's worth a try. I want to help." She wiped her mouth with a napkin.

"That's a good approach; I'll think about that. Thanks." He looked at her empty plate and marveled at her appetite. "Full?"

"Hmm, I feel better. Shall we go?"

Adama paid the check, and they left. In the meantime, they agreed to focus on their immediate cases and find the other billionaires connected to the Miller gallery. Adama verified the appropriate warrant had been issued, and he and Bridget drove to the Stetson Hotel to confiscate the gravestone and arrest Dick Betrug.

Chapter 42: The Cart

The manager of the Stetson Hotel revealed that Betrug had left early for Cardinal Lakes Country Club on Long Island. After displaying a warrant, he let Adama and Bridget into Betrug's suite. They checked the dining room table and all the other rooms, but the large wooden box was gone.

Adama and Bridget left the hotel and headed out to arrest Betrug for illegally purchasing and receiving stolen artifacts. Upon arrival at the clubhouse, they saw a fire engine, a captain's truck, an ambulance, three police cars, and a coroner's van. They walked inside the foyer, where dozens of people had gathered. Adama searched for someone in charge.

"I've got a bad feeling about this," Bridget professed softly.

"Yeah, me too." Adama showed his badge to an employee. "I'm Deputy Chief Baptiste, NYPD. I need to speak with the manager."

"Oh, he and the other policemen are at the ninth hole, sir," she said.

"We need an escort there immediately. Who can take us?"

"Um, that guy in the green T-shirt." She pointed.

Their escort stopped at the ninth hole. Adama and Bridget walked to the bunker. Emergency personnel surrounded a body that was twisted under a mangled cart. Two paramedics stood nearby with a black body bag and a gurney. One police officer took pictures of the scene. Other officers took statements from nearby golfers.

"What have you got?" Adama showed his badge to an officer.

"One male, deceased. He rolled the cart off the top of this bunker." They looked up. "The course owner found him." The officer pointed at Tony Corazon.

"Got an identification?" Adama asked.

"Yes. His name is Dick Betrug. Are you in charge now?"

"Yes," Adama said.

He and Bridget moved closer to view Betrug's body. Firefighters attempted to lift the cart, but the legs were twisted in the framework. One said they would need to cut cart sections to free the body. Adama approached the Long Island's Nassau County medical examiner after he stepped away from the scene.

"What's your take on the cause of death?" Adama flashed his badge.

"Hard to say what killed him. Could have been the broken golf shaft that punctured his carotid artery, or his crushed chest, or his broken neck. We'll need forensics."

"Right. Any witnesses?" Adama asked.

"Uh, I think those two, over by that bench." The coroner pointed at Tony Corazon and Ling Chen.

"Thanks." Adama looked over and motioned for Bridget to join him. "You won't believe who that guy is on the bench."

"Who?" Bridget looked.

"Ling Chen." Adama could hardly hold back his delight at the irony.

"Unbelievable." She giggled softly.

Adama called Gates and gave him the news from the golf course.

"No fucking way. Unbelievable!" Gates said. "We're pulling up."

They approached Chen and Corazon.

"Hello, I'm Deputy Chief Baptiste, and this is Bridget Murphy. We're with the NYPD. We want to ask you two some questions about Dick Betrug. But first, what are your names?"

"I'm Tony Corazon. I own the club, and that's Ling Chen, a member."

"Can you tell us what happened here?" Adama asked.

"I can tell you the guy went nuts. He attacked me and then drove his cart over the edge of the bunker. Ask Ling." Corazon pointed at Chen.

"Mr. Chen?" Bridget asked, watching him stare at the ground. "Sir?"

"Yeah, it's true," Chen responded. "He clubbed Tony in the back, tore up the green, then tried to run Tony down with his cart. He tried to kill him."

"Why would he want to kill Tony?" Adama asked.

"I don't know," Chen mumbled.

"Mr. Corazon, walk us through what happened from the beginning," Adama said.

"We were playing the ninth hole. After we all teed off, I told Betrug he needed to leave after we finished the hole," Corazon said.

"Why did you do that?" Bridget asked.

"Because he'd been cheating since the start, and I didn't want to play the back nine with him," Corazon answered.

"How was he cheating?" Adama asked.

"Different ways—calling Mulligans if he didn't like his tee shot, resetting his ball on the green, or calling gimmes, and tossing lost balls into the fairway." Corazon shook his head. "And, the guy cursed, threw balls and clubs. I'd had enough, so I respectfully asked him to leave after we got to the clubhouse."

"What exactly did you say to him?" Bridget asked pensively.

"I told him I wouldn't tolerate his cheating, and he needed to leave." Corazon paused.

"How did he take that?" Adama asked.

"Not good, it never goes well when you call someone out for cheating—but this guy?" Corazon shook his head. "He flipped way out. His face turned red, and I thought his eyes would pop out. It's like someone flipped a switch. I've never seen anything like it."

"What else did he do?" Bridget asked.

"After he cussed, called me a liar, said he'd ruin my club, and spit on me, he flipped me off and nearly ran me over as he sped away. And then came road rage in a golf cart—he ran over bushes, tossed stuff out of his cart, zigzagged, and yelled obscenities—he was unhinged."

"Then what?" Adama asked.

"After we got to the green, Betrug screamed, "I hate this fucking game, and I can cheat if I want to! I hate Chen, and I hate you!" He drove his cart straight toward me. I didn't think he'd run me down, so I stood there until I saw him swinging a golf club. That's when I ran, but he caught up and smacked me in the back. I dropped to the ground." Corazon winced and adjusted his sore back.

"Mind if I take a look at your back?" Adama asked.

"No." Corazon lifted his shirt to reveal a large red welt the size of a softball.

"Would you like a paramedic to look at that?" Adama asked.

"No thanks. I'll live," Corazon said as he pulled his shirt down.

"Okay, what happened after he hit you?" Adama asked. "How did he end up in a bunker?"

"He wasn't paying attention. Just so everyone knows, before teeing off, I warned Betrug and Chen about the bunkers at this hole— one eight feet deep, and the other twelve. I told them to follow the signs, stay on the cart path, and stay clear of the bunkers," Corazon explained.

"So, the course posted warning signs?" Adama asked.

"Of course," he said defensively. "Both bunkers were roped off with warning signs. But Betrug ran over one of the ropes, yelling, 'Yee-haw!' like a cowboy. He spun the cart in circles, tearing up the greens, and ran over the flag. Then he came after me again, waving his club. I scrambled and jumped into the first bunker. He yelled, 'Chicken shit!' narrowly missing me as I fell." Corazon's voice dropped two octaves. "I guess he didn't see the second bunker. I looked up and saw his left rear tire slip off the edge, his cart tumbled downward." Corazon was genuinely despondent.

"Sounds awful," Bridget said.

Corazon saw it all again, in his mind. "Yeah, like a slow-motion crash on TV. The cart teetered, tipped, and flipped, and landed hard on its left side. Betrug screamed, and the cart crumbled as it rolled to a halt. The whole frame twisted. Golf clubs flew into the air, and the cart rolled again. When it stopped, it was upside down and mangled."

"What did you do?" Adama asked.

"I ran over to check on him, then Chen showed up. Betrug's body was twisted inside the cart, and his eyes and mouth were open and full of sand. Blood oozed everywhere." He stopped talking. Corazon's eyes glazed over.

"Mr. Corazon?" Adama saw that he was traumatized. "Mr. Corazon, are you okay?"

Corazon flinched, blinked, and refocused. "Sorry," he mumbled. "I…it was horrible."

"Perfectly understandable. Sit down and take a minute," Adama said.

Corazon cleared his throat. "Where was I? Uh, I called the pro shop and told them to call an ambulance and to notify the starter to clear the course. Then you people showed up." Corazon pointed at all the paramedics, police, and coroner's staff. "The police separated me and Chen and took our statements. We've been waiting here ever since. Can I go now?"

"Soon, we're almost done," Adama said.

"Did either of you see Mr. Betrug on Saturday night?" Adama moved closer to Chen.

"No, I just met him today," Corazon said, head down.

"And you, Mr. Chen? Did you see Mr. Betrug Saturday night?" Bridget asked.

"What has that got to do with anything?" Chen asked.

"Answer the question, sir," Adama instructed.

"Yes. I saw him. That's when I invited him to play golf," Chen said.

Adama turned to Mr. Corazon. "Here's my card. You can go. Thank you."

"So, we can go?" Chen asked as he stood up.

"I said Mr. Corazon can go. But you're going to headquarters. A detective is on the way to take you into custody for the illegal purchase and receipt of stolen goods," Adama said.

Corazon heard Adama's comment, stared at Chen in disgust, and walked toward the clubhouse, shaking his head.

"I want my lawyer," Chen said.

"Of course you do," Bridget said.

"You'll have plenty of time for that at the station," Adama said.

Detective Gates and Sanchez hurriedly walked up. "Hey there, Chen. We've been looking everywhere for you," Gates said.

"Perfect timing, hello detectives." Adama shook their hands.

"Hey, Bridget, how are you?" Gates asked. Sanchez acknowledged her with a nod.

"Hey guys, how … oh my god, he's running away!" Bridget shouted.

All three men noticed Chen running toward the clubhouse.

"Now, where do you suppose he's going?" Gates snickered.

"Shit!" Sanchez took off after Chen.

"Oh, shit!" Gates ran behind Sanchez.

Adama ordered a nearby police officer to assist in catching Chen. The officer took off running.

"Unbelievable! I feel like I'm in a movie. I've never seen a suspect run away," Bridget said.

"It happens all the time, Bridget. They actually think they'll get away. My money is on Sanchez. Let's get in a cart."

Up ahead, Chen saw Corazon and grabbed his arm. "Tony, call my lawyer, please."

"No. And your membership is revoked." Corazon peeled Chen's hand off his arm.

Chen got within yards of the patio when Sanchez forcefully tackled him. Gates and the police officer converged in seconds to help subdue Chen's thrashing while Sanchez cuffed him. Fresh-cut grass stains ruined his shirt and pants. Impressed by the takedown, the patio erupted with cheers from onlookers. Sanchez hauled Chen to his feet and read him his Miranda rights.

Within a minute, Corazon walked onto the patio, thrilled to see Chen in cuffs. Adama and Bridget had pulled up and watched as a police officer escorted Chen to a squad car.

"Good job, guys," Adama said. He and Bridget exited the cart.

"It's just like in the movies, I love it." Bridget grinned with approval.

The detectives had meandered out to the front of the clubhouse where they compared notes about Chen, his arrest, and the golf club. Adama noticed two limousine drivers talking. He left his team and strode over to the drivers—one looked ashen.

"Are you Dick Betrug's chauffeur?" Adama asked.

"Yes, I am … or at least I was," Andrew said.

"I'm Deputy Chief, Baptiste." He opened his badge. "And who do you drive for?" he asked the other.

"I drive for Mr. Chen," he replied.

"Good. I need to ask you both a few questions. Would you mind waiting over there?" Adama pointed, "Don't go far." Chen's driver walked about ten yards away.

"I can't believe he's dead," Andrew said.

"I'm curious, do you have a large box in your limousine?" Andrew looked sheepishly at the ground. "Uh, yes, sir."

"Mind if I take a look at it?" Adama asked.

"I don't know if I'm allowed to do that." He looked nervous.

"Well, if you're worried about your boss..." Adama pointed at the coroner's van.

"Oh, well, I guess it's okay." Andrew led Adama to the limousine.

Gates, Sanchez, and Bridget had observed Adama conversing with the two chauffeurs. After Adama walked away, they trailed by a short distance. Andrew extended a key fob, and the limousine chirped; the doors unlocked. He opened the back passenger door. Adama bent over to peer inside, straightened up, and turned to find his detectives assembled behind him.

"Take a look." Adama gestured.

The detectives took turns to inspect the discovery. Bridget emerged last. "You were right, Betrug took it with him, and it's open."

"Right. Hey Gates, do you have the warrant?

"Got it right here," he patted his coat pocket.

"Please have Betrug's body and that box taken to Dr. Pearson's lab. If the coroner gives you a hard time, have him call me. And Gates, this is important: *no* one touches the object inside. Keep eyes on it."

"Yes, sir." Gates called for a police van. He put on gloves and climbed into the limousine. He carefully closed and latched the lid on the box, then placed several items into evidence bags.

Adama told Sanchez, "Have these two limo drivers taken to headquarters for questioning."

"Yes, sir." Sanchez took charge.

———◆———

Adama and Bridget pulled away from the clubhouse and drove down the long driveway, past the front gate to the golf course. Both quietly processed the day's events. As they merged onto Highway 495 en route to Manhattan, the pair felt satisfied about taking possession of another box.

Chapter 43: Apologies

For three days, the investigations had been going nonstop. Adama and Bridget relished the hum and rhythm of tires on the highway, lulling them into a quiet, peaceful state. After several minutes, Bridget broke the silence.

"Want to talk about Betrug and his behavior?" she asked.

"You mean about his going nuts on the course?"

"Well, it's consistent with the other billionaires. It sounds like he got triggered by being called out for cheating."

"Well, he has a history of that—in business, in marriage, with people, and golf."

"Do you think he'll end up with a symbol behind his left ear?"

Adama glanced at her. "I hate to say it, but I was just wondering the same thing."

"Do you believe it's the curse of the Kanijugu?"

"Let's wait to see what happens." Adama looked straight ahead.

Bridget changed the subject. "Well, that's three boxes down, three to go."

"Right. Gates and Sanchez will confiscate Chen's box from his Plaza residence. And tomorrow we'll find Maximilian, confiscate his box, then rinse and repeat with Decker."

Bridget was still reeling from their meeting on Tuesday night. "Before we return to headquarters, thank you for getting the Taylor gallery security videos. That was no small feat—you must have friends in high places, even in London."

"You're welcome. It proved useful in connecting the dots between the two cases."

"Yes, and I also apologize for my mini breakdown. Watching the raw video feed was just …" Bridget paused, searching for the right words. "I mean, seeing everything unfold in real time was visceral. Police photos tend to be clinical by comparison. But seeing Colin alive one minute and then …" her voice faltered slightly. "Watching how he died was more than I could take."

"It was a brutal thing to watch. Your reaction was understandable."

"You tried to warn me, but I'm headstrong."

"You certainly can be, but in a good way. I'm just sorry you had to witness Colin's death; I know how much he meant to you."

"Thanks," Bridget said. "And I apologize for inviting you to my room last night. That was awkward and unprofessional."

"No, it was heartwarming. But you know I couldn't go up—you were too vulnerable."

"Yeah, I understand," she said.

After crossing the Long Island Expressway, they turned south onto FDR.

"I owe you an apology as well. My reaction to your wanting to talk on Monday wasn't very nice. I've been resentful lately, and I let it get the best of me. Please know that I want us to have *that* talk. We have a lot to discuss, and it would be best to finish this case first. What do you think?"

"I think that's perfect. I've so much to tell you, but I'll wait." Bridget felt hopeful again.

"Great. I'm meeting with the commissioner and the chief when we get back. It could take a while. Do you want me to drop you off at your hotel or headquarters?"

"HQ. I want to review my emails and finish my research about the stones."

"Sounds good."

Adama pulled into the parking lot, and the two headed to their respective offices.

"So, I'll see you in the morning," Adama said.

"Yes, tomorrow morning. Hope your meeting goes well."

Adama took the elevator up to Commissioner Xavier's office, where he found his boss, Chief John Ballantine. Adama briefed both men on the task force's progress. Meanwhile, Bridget settled into her office, immersed in the emails and documents her colleague forwarded from Dakar. Tired, Bridget went to her hotel for the rest of the evening and a much-needed good night's sleep.

THURSDAY

Chapter 44: Eat Me

Daniel Garcia straightened his tie as he prepared for another day as Gerald Decker's personal limousine driver. It was mid-morning, and he would drive to the Upper East Side of Manhattan to pick up his boss. He embraced his wife, Nancy, in the kitchen and kissed her.

"I'm driving Mr. Decker to the Hamptons today. Not sure when I'll be home." He grabbed his chauffeur's cap and jacket from the hook by the back door. "Call if the bank reaches out. Love you."

"Okay. Love you too." Nancy waved a gray thermos. "Hon, your coffee."

"Oh! Thanks, honey." Garcia kissed her again and took the thermos.

Outside, Garcia breathed in the crisp, cool air. He inspected the luxurious ten-passenger limousine, checking the back row and the extra-long curved sofa behind the driver's seat. The interior highlighted premium leather and exotic woods for an opulent touch. It featured state-of-the-art media, a small refrigerator, and the bar was stocked with the finest liquors, Lalique crystal decanters and glasses, as well as various snacks.

Satisfied, he got behind the wheel. After revving the engine, he cautiously backed out of his modest driveway.

Born and raised in Queens, Garcia lived four houses away from his parents. Driving, he spotted his father mowing the lawn. He swelled with pride about the man he admired most.

"Lookin' good, Dad," Garcia called out the window.

"Back at you, Danny boy. Be safe, son." His father waved.

Garcia wondered about his future. *Will I be doing the same thing at seventy? Will my boys think their old man is extraordinary? Hope so.*

An officer in an unmarked police car watched the limousine back out of the driveway. He immediately called Detective Gates.

"What's up?" Gates answered from headquarters.

"The limo just left. Garcia is driving. Should I follow?" the officer said.

"Yeah, keep me posted," Gates said, then called Adama. "Garcia just left in Gerald Decker's limo. The officer will follow him."

"Good. Let me know if he picks up Decker or drops off that box. Bridget and I are on our way back from Vanhorn's yacht. Keep me posted," he said.

"Will do, boss," Gates said.

———◆———

Garcia navigated the streets of Manhattan and wondered about his boss's temperament. He had been Decker's exclusive driver for two years. He didn't like the man, but the money and benefits were too lucrative to abandon. Garcia knew his boss was a volatile drug dealer and addict, prone to mood swings and caustic outbursts. Garcia wanted out. *Someday I'll be my own boss. I need the bank to come through.*

Garcia pulled into an open spot in front of the Vincent Hotel and got out.

"Hey Louis, hey guys. How's it goin'?" Garcia smiled at the head valet and his staff.

"Hey, Garcia," Louis said. The others tipped their hats.

Garcia opened the trunk and waited by the passenger door.

Today, Decker was going to the Hamptons to attend his mother's birthday party. It would be a four-day celebration; an extravaganza with live music, and a who's-who list of celebrities and government officials, including the governor of New York.

Decker and Veronica sauntered out of the hotel with the confident grace of runway models. Decker wore casual but expensive pants, a vibrant shirt, sunglasses, and a Cartier diamond-studded Tank

Française watch. Veronica always turned heads with her long, brown hair, flawless makeup, and Italian sculpted face. Her tall, slender body fit snugly into the slinky, red Valentino gown, which featured a slit up the right side. She carried a beaded purse, a black shawl, and wore black Jimmy Choo Mesh Crystal Pumps. She was eye candy on Decker's arm.

"Good morning, sir, and good morning, miss," Garcia said. With a valet right behind him, he opened the door.

Decker got in, marooning Veronica. "Well, hurry up if you're coming."

Garcia helped Veronica into the limousine. The valet's eyes popped with anticipation as the slit in her dress opened, revealing her long, tanned legs.

"Thank you, Danny," Veronica said.

"You're welcome, miss." Garcia ensured she was comfortable before closing the door.

Two personal attendants passed luggage to the valets, who loaded the trunk. Garcia tipped his hat at Louis and the crew before sliding into the driver's seat and pulling away. Turning left onto 5th Avenue, traffic was heavily congested. He checked his phone—four hours to the Hamptons.

Danny unbuttoned his jacket and settled in for the long drive.

———◆———

The police officer tailing Garcia called to report the limousine had stopped at the Vincent Hotel on E. 77th Street and left with a man and a woman. Gates told the officer to continue following, then called Adama.

"Hi, boss, are you back from the marina?" Gates asked.

"Bridget and I are just entering the city. What's up?"

"Garcia just picked up a man and woman from the Vincent Hotel. What do you want to do?"

"Do we know if it was Decker?"

"Unknown. The officer didn't have a clear view of the passengers."

"Okay, have the officer pull the limo over and detain them. Send me the location, and we'll converge on the limousine together. Call Burke and Sanchez to join us. Also, Decker's got a registered firearm."

"Understood." Gates made the calls and headed out.

———◆———

Garcia turned on the radio and tried to relax. Danny Garcia glanced in the rearview mirror to see Decker drinking from a vodka bottle, then offering it to Veronica.

"No thanks."

"More for me, then." He took another gulp.

Veronica settled in for the long ride. She set her purse and shawl on the seat and removed her shoes. She noticed the large box on the seat behind the driver.

"What's that box doing here? I didn't notice it last night."

"That's because you were wasted. I picked it up a couple of nights ago."

"Can I see inside?" Veronica asked.

"Sure. Why not?" Decker smiled with delight.

Decker crouched his way forward and stroked its smooth reddish-brown surface. Veronica followed. Decker unclasped the jeweled skeleton key from his gold neck chain. He inserted the key into one lock, then the other, while he boasted about his new acquisition.

"Wait until you see this. It cost twenty million, but it'll be worth more than a hundred million in five years."

With a dominant stance, Decker positioned himself over the crate. "Let's open this baby up." He lifted the lid.

"What is that?" Veronica asked.

"*That* is my mother's seventieth birthday present. This one will really get to her." Decker laughed.

"It's beautiful." Veronica eyed the object with its variegated colors and polished yet gritty surface.

Decker was fixated. Compelled by the stone, his fingers traced the unusual symbol embedded at the top and slowly stroked it downward. It felt cool. Within seconds, a strange euphoric feeling overcame Decker, followed by a tingling sensation that shot through his fingers, up his arm, and sent a shiver down his spine. *I should keep this for myself.*

"It's incredible. But the story makes it priceless," he said.

"What story?" Veronica was intrigued.

"A tale out of Hollywood, with lots of blood, guts, and gore. That old fart in his big black hat never disappoints. They outdid themselves this time."

"Who's they?" she asked.

Ignoring her question, Decker crouched back and found his seat. He pushed a nob to open a secret compartment inside the wall panel. A safe had been installed to hide his stash of drugs and cash. He punched in a code, and the door popped open. Veronica was charmed by the stone and glanced backward; Decker was busy, so she reached out to touch the stone.

"Don't touch that!" Decker's voice elevated with displeasure.

Startled and feeling like a kid caught sneaking a cookie, Veronica withdrew her hand. Decker gave her a scornful paternal look and patted the seat beside him.

"Come sit with me."

Decker reached inside the safe, pushed his gun out of the way, and pulled out a leather pouch. The words "Eat Me" were inscribed in gold leaf lettering on the outside. He thought the words were clever and perfect for the contents inside. Decker waved the pouch in the air and teased Veronica.

"Oh, Veronica, we're gonna have a good time riding to the Hamptons."

The pouch contained all his favorites, including pills, cocaine, fentanyl, marijuana, and his special stash of premium heroin. Falling for his stunt, Veronica wanted what he had to offer. Decker always had the best of everything and a reputation for buying and selling the finest drugs.

"Coming, darling," she said.

Veronica carefully maneuvered the length of the limousine, occasionally bending over to steady herself. Decker became aroused when he saw the cowl neckline of her gown flare open. He caught a glimpse of her breasts and smiled.

"Nice rack."

Half-listening from the driver's seat, Garcia knew what was coming. He closed the partition, stopping three inches from the top. He had seen and heard it all before. His cellphone rang.

"Hi, honey, what's up?"

"The bank just called. Our loan was approved!"

"Holy shit, that's fantastic!"

"I'm so happy for you, now you can buy your first limo."

"That's fantastic! Listen, babe, I'm driving. Can you get us an appointment?"

"Already done. We sign the loan docs tomorrow at ten!"

"Fantastic, great job, honey. I'm so relieved."

"I love you, sweetheart!"

"I love you too. See you tonight." Garcia put his cellphone down and smiled as wide as the Grand Canyon.

Whoo-hoo—my own limousine! He glanced at the rearview mirror. *I'll finally be able to walk away from this asshole.*

Chapter 45: Stop!

Riding in the limousine, Decker and Veronica snuggled next to each other as he extracted cocaine from his leather pouch. He prepared two perfect lines on a gold-rimmed mirror with practiced efficiency and snorted both through his carbon straw. Veronica eyed the nose candy with anticipation and watched Decker prepare more, which he quickly snorted.

"Hey, it's my turn!"

"Don't worry, you'll get your fill." *Just another coke whore.*

Decker removed a handful of pills. "Eat me!" He laughed and tossed the pouch to Veronica, who instinctively put her hands out to catch the bag. It landed in her lap.

"Sometimes you can be a real jerk, you know that."

"Oh, lighten up. That was funny. Let's relax and enjoy ourselves."

Decker popped four pills into his mouth and drank from a bottle of Beluga Epicure, Russian vodka, guzzling a third of the bottle. Meanwhile, Veronica formed two lines of cocaine on the mirror and sniffed both, feeling satisfied.

"Hey, baby, tell me the story about that stone."

"The story, yeah, the best, cool guns, special forces, suckers, a great kill shot, like a movie—only real." Decker slurred his words.

"Real? Sounds awful."

"Yeah, well. I got my money's worth." Decker's mouth and tongue were numb. "These drugs are fucking awesome."

Feeling lively, amorous, and possessive, Decker's gaze traveled slowly over Veronica in her sexy crimson dress. He leaned over, squeezed her thigh, and gathered the silk between his fingers, inching the gown upward.

"Come on, baby, straddle me—the sex will be hot."

Desire emanated from him like heat; his hands traced the curves of her lithe body, squeezing the roundness of her firm buttocks. He kissed her hard. "You turn me on," he murmured. "And this dress is so fucking sexy."

Veronica easily succumbed; her body aching with desire, she whispered in his ear, "I want you; I need you."

"Oh, yeah, you're mine." Radiating with lust, he pulled her closer, his hands roamed and squeezed her breasts, and she moaned as he kissed the nape of her neck. He pulled down on her dress straps—one broke. Veronica heard it pop and felt the side of her dress droop, exposing her breast. Decker hungrily dove in.

"Gerald, wait, you've torn my dress."

"So, what, I'll buy you a new one."

Without warning, Decker wrapped his strong arms around her upper torso and pulled her onto the long sofa. He positioned himself above her, moaning and pulsing. Veronica struggled, pushing against his shoulders.

"Gerald, wait. Gerald, STOP!"

Inexplicably, and to her surprise, he got off her.

"What is going on with you today?"

Decker, disheveled and panting, ignored her. He found his drug pouch, removed a bag of white powder, prepared the spoon, and watched the China white bubble. Decker filled a syringe, wrapped a tourniquet around his left arm, and injected himself. Within seconds, he felt the rush of pure ecstasy surge throughout his body.

Veronica sat up and attached the loose dress strap to the other one. It was strong enough to keep her breasts from falling out. She saw Gerald inject himself and knew he would pass out. Decker mumbled incoherently, lay back, closed his eyes, and drifted away to paradise.

"Damn you." Upset, Veronica moved forward toward Garcia. She put her fingers into the opening of the partition and used the glass to steady herself.

"Danny, take me back to the hotel."

"Ma'am?" Garcia was surprised. "You want to go back to the hotel?"

"Yes. I don't want to go to the Hamptons. Please turn around."

Garcia checked his rearview mirror, waiting for Decker's instructions. With his boss unconscious, he welcomed the traffic jam's delay.

Veronica glared at her unconscious lover. *You're not worth all this.* She retreated to the passenger door, tapping her long red fingernails against the handle as she watched pedestrians on 5th Avenue.

"They're moving faster than we are," she announced, ensuring Garcia heard.

The limousine sputtered and shook violently. Concerned, Garcia made a left onto E. 70th—a one-way street—immediately pulled over behind a parked car on the left, and got out to check under the hood, with the engine still running.

Veronica tensed. *What's going on?* Decker jolted awake, sitting upright.

"Gerald, thank god you're awake. Take me back to the hotel."

Decker ignored Veronica's request, found his pouch, swallowed a handful of pills, then washed them down with more vodka. Next came more cocaine.

"Gerald, what are you doing? You can't mix all those drugs."

Within seconds, Decker convulsed. His eyes rolled back, his mouth contorted, and his nose bled. He aimlessly hammered the seats and windows with his fists.

"What am I doing? I'm having fun, that's what!" He snarled, his eyes wild.

Decker seized a crystal vodka carafe, then another, grabbed the backup stock of fifth-sized vodka and bourbon bottles, and hurled them at the windows. They crashed, bounced, and broke. Glass shattered everywhere. He dug into the seat cushions using large shards of glass. Decker put small pieces of the glass into his mouth and chewed; blood dripped from his distorted smile.

Veronica was horrified. She shielded herself from more flying glass. When she saw his contorted expression, she knew he had snapped.

"Oh my god!" Veronica pressed against the door.

"It itches, it burns, ahh! Make it stop!" he screamed.

Decker maniacally tore his shirt open, buttons flying. He raked his nails wildly across his chest, arms, face, and neck until blood oozed from the wounds.

Veronica screamed. "Help! Let me out! Let me out!"

Already alarmed, Garcia yelled, "What's going on back there?"

"He's fucking insane. I want out!" She tried to unlock her door, to no avail.

Decker fell into a quiet trance. Veronica eyed him suspiciously as she cautiously approached the partition.

"Please help me, he's acting bizarre. I'm afraid!"

Garcia climbed back into his seat and tried to lower the partition. Nothing happened. He attempted to unlock all the doors from his door panel, but again, nothing worked. "Go to the passenger door. I'll meet you there."

The limousine jerked, and the engine sputtered to a halt. Veronica heard Garcia and scrambled to the door. Garcia jumped out and went to Veronica's door. He cupped his hands around his eyes to see inside the darkened windows.

"Unlock the door! Pull on the nob!" he shouted.

"It's not working!"

Veronica pounded the window with her fists. Garcia froze—Decker's maniacal face appeared behind her, wild-eyed, possessed, and predatory. He watched helplessly as Decker yanked her away and slammed her onto the floor. Garcia circled the vehicle, trying every door. None opened. The limo's systems had failed—there was no music, air, power windows, or locks.

Garcia returned to the driver's seat as the limousine rocked from the back. Veronica's screams pierced his ears. He pounded the partition, jammed his fingers through the slot at the top, and pushed down hard.

He yelled, "Mr. Decker, what are you doing? Stop now!"

Garcia grabbed his flashlight from the glove box and repeatedly struck the partition. He remembered the lug wrench. After pushing the trunk release button, he ran to it, but it wouldn't open. He pushed up and down using his body weight, hoping to disengage the lock. Desperate, Garcia flagged down a taxi coming up behind him. "Quick, your lug wrench. There's a woman in trouble. Please give it to me before she's killed. Please!"

"Are you crazy? Get the hell outta my way!" He drove right past Garcia.

Returning to the limousine, Garcia noticed everything was quiet. He wondered what had happened. The minutes-long struggle felt eternal. As he slid into the driver's seat, the engine sputtered and all the systems reactivated. The doors unlocked, air surged through the vents, music played, and the partition lowered. Garcia saw Veronica, battered, bloody, and half-naked, on the floor. Decker lay motionless on the sofa.

Veronica became hysterical. "I want out! Let me out of here!"

"I'm coming! Garcia ran to her passenger door. Once open, Veronica burst out, knocking him backwards, and he hit his head hard on the street. Barefoot, Veronica fled screaming around the corner and up 5th Avenue.

"Veronica! Wait! Veronica!" Garcia called out, searching. She had disappeared into a crowd of pedestrians. Dazed, head throbbing and nauseous, Garcia returned to the limousine and froze.

"Oh my god."

Decker lay supine across the long sofa. White foam seeped from his mouth, blood streamed from his nose, face, and chest, as though he had been beaten to death.

"Mr. Decker? Sir?"

Decker was unresponsive. Noticing a couple of bystanders, Garcia closed the passenger door, entered the front seat, and found his cellphone on the floor. He dialed 911. After reporting the emergency and his location, he clutched his throbbing head. In the distance, sirens.

Not a moment too soon.

———◆———

A quarter mile back, the trailing policeman heard the call for help and responded. His red and blue lights flashed, and his siren blared. He phoned Detective Gates about the 911 call.

"We're on our way. Secure the scene," Gates said. He hung up and called Adama.

"What's going on?" Adama asked.

"We found Decker, but a distress call came from his limousine."

"Okay, send us the location, and we'll meet you there."

Bridget checked the location on her phone. "We're about ten minutes out."

Adama turned on his lights and siren.

———————◆———————

Garcia peered at Decker through the partition. Against his better judgment, he decided to check on his boss. Hesitantly, Garcia entered the ravaged back cabin of the limousine. Torn seats, exposed stuffing, broken bottles, and alcohol fumes engulfed his senses. Glass crunched underfoot as he crouched toward Decker. He poked Decker's arm. Nothing. Garcia checked for a pulse, then noticed twitching fingers. *He's alive!*

"Hey, boss. It's okay, I'll call an ambula—"

Decker jerked upward, grabbed Garcia, pulled him off balance, and whipped him around onto the floorboard. With an unforgiving chokehold, Decker's arms squeezed, cutting off Garcia's airway.

"Hey, Danny boy, how does that feel? What did you do with Veronica? I'm gonna kill you, then her, and I'm gonna enjoy it."

Garcia instinctively struggled to be released. He thrusted his fists backward, punching Decker's face.

"You can't stop me. I'm invincible."

Unfazed and stronger, Decker held his quarry in check. Garcia kicked and hit harder without success. *My god, he's going to kill me.*

Decker toyed with his prey, squeezing, releasing, then re-engaging pressure while laughing.

"How about some drugs, Danny boy, we'll make it last."

Seeing broken bottles everywhere, Garcia frantically felt the floor and snatched the neck of a bottle. He thrust the jagged edge repeatedly into the right side of Decker's face. Immediately released by his captor, Garcia stared in horror at the bottle protruding from Decker's head, embedded in his eye, nose, cheek, and ear.

Decker touched it, smiled wickedly, then yanked it out. He screamed as his right eye came with it, dangling by its optic nerve. Blood gushed out of his eye socket, down the front of his shirt, and squirted onto the seats. "That's fuckin' gross," he said, seeing his eye hanging off the bottle's edge.

Wide-eyed at the gory scene, Garcia scrambled backward, glass shards embedding in his hands. Garcia saw a crazed look on his boss's face.

"Hey, man, take it easy," Garcia said. "Please. Don't—"

Without warning, Decker pounced, crushing Garcia beneath him. Garcia felt pain pierce his right side. Decker's body weight crushed him. Immobilized and suffocating, his last thought was for his wife. *I'm sorry, honey—*

Light faded to black as Garcia slipped into unconsciousness.

Chapter 46: Stuck on E. 70th

The police officer following Decker arrived on the scene first. He looked inside the limousine and saw two bodies, one on top of the other. He checked for a pulse on Garcia. It was weak. Next, he checked Decker, but there was no pulse. The officer called for two ambulances. Within minutes, one arrived, followed by the other. The officer called for more help.

Detective Ricky Burke also heard the distress call and headed to the scene. Adama, Bridget, Gates, and Sanchez were within minutes of the location. The police band called out two possible fatalities in a limousine located at 5th and E. 70th Street.

Burke called Adama. "Hey, boss. I'm on scene. Gerald Decker is dead. He's in his limousine. And there's another male in pretty bad shape. The ambulances just got here. Where are you?"

"About two minutes out, same for Gates and Sanchez."

"Okay, I'll secure the scene," Burke said.

Bridget nudged Adama. "What's happening?"

"They've got two males—one is Decker and he's dead, and one unknown in critical condition."

"Shit," Bridget said.

Upon arrival, Adama and Bridget jumped out and approached the crime scene. They joined up with Burke, put on gloves, and peered inside the limousine. The body of Gerald Decker was on the floorboard. Two more police cars, a second ambulance, and a coroner's van had just arrived.

"This is one for the books. Someone went bat-shit crazy," Burke said.

"It looks like a wild animal tore him to shreds. Is that an eyeball?" Bridget asked.

"Where's the driver and the woman passenger?" Adama asked.

"Multiple witnesses reported a woman in a red dress, covered in blood, running northbound on 5th Avenue. The limo driver is in that ambulance." Ricky pointed.

"I'll be right back," Adama said.

Outside one ambulance, Adama showed his badge to the EMT, who closed the back doors. "Is our other victim inside?"

"Yes, sir, unconscious and barely stable," the EMT answered. "Driver's license identifies him as Daniel Garcia, from Queens."

"Open up, I need to see him."

"Sir, he's in terrible shape; he needs a hospital."

"I only need a minute. Open up."

"Yes, sir."

Inside, Adama flashed his badge and observed Garcia—oxygen mask, bloody face, hands, knees, and abdomen. A paramedic had controlled the bleeding from multiple lacerations on Garcia's right side. An IV bag and a bag of blood hung from a hook. The monitor showed a weak heartbeat.

"He's a lucky man," the paramedic said. "We stopped the bleeding."

"How long is he gonna be out?" Adama asked.

"Hard to say. We've got to leave, now."

"Where are you taking him?"

"Mount Sinai, Levy Place."

Adama handed over one of his cards. "Okay, do me a favor. Text me when he wakes up."

"Sure."

Adama stepped out, doors closed, and the ambulance pulled away, flashing lights and sirens blaring.

Gates and Sanchez circled the limousine while Jimmy Quinn photographed the inside. Bridget and Burke examined the interior from opposite doors.

Bridget caught Adama's eye and nodded at the inside. "The box is here—and it's open, like the others. I asked Burke to close and secure it."

"Good." Adama peeked inside. "Hey Quinn, you know the drill, don't touch the stone inside. Have it transported to the morgue immediately."

"Yes, sir," Quinn said.

———◆———

In the ambulance, Garcia woke to wailing sirens. Blinking, he tried to sit up but found himself immobilized from chest to feet. His head was bandaged, and he was wearing a cervical collar neck brace. A paramedic scribbled on a metal clipboard.

"What happened? Where am I?" he mumbled.

Without looking up, the medic answered, "You're in an ambulance, we're taking you to the hospital."

"Am I gonna be okay?" Garcia asked anxiously.

"You may have a concussion; there's a severe laceration on your left side. But the bleeding has stopped."

"Why can't I move? I want to sit up," Garcia said. "Oh my god, my side hurts."

"You're strapped to a backboard, for your safety. I'll give you something for the pain."

The paramedic noted Garcia's grimace and reached for the medication case, steadying against the ambulance's motion. "Do you have any allergies to pain medication?"

"No. Not that I'm aware of." Garcia said, moaning.

After checking the patient's vitals, the paramedic drew the dose of morphine, swabbed the IV port, and administered the medication. "This will help. You'll feel warmth in your arm first." He documented the dose in a file on his clipboard.

"Whoa, that's nice," Garcia said. Almost immediately, his eyes closed, and he drifted away.

The paramedic monitored Garcia's vitals in between medical reports. He found Adama's card and sent a text message. "He's awake." The ambulance's siren abruptly stopped as they approached Mount Sinai, Levy Place.

———◆———

Adama watched the mahogany box be removed from the limousine and loaded into the coroner's van. Quinn found the jewel key hanging around Decker's neck. He bagged and tagged it along with the locks. Other technicians worked the scene, and detectives took witness statements; news vans gathered. Adama received a text that Garcia was awake, and Burke reported on Veronica.

"We just got word that a woman in a red dress and covered in blood was dropped off at the CityMD East 79th Street Urgent Care. She's being treated now."

"Good, let's go talk with her," Adama said. "Then we'll go to Mount Sinai."

The three of them got into Burke's sedan and left the scene. Both the urgent care and the hospital were north of their location. It would take about thirty minutes.

Inside the ER, they found Veronica wearing a traditional hospital gown. She looked woozy. She opened her eyes to see Adama, Bridget, and Burke standing around her bed.

"Who are you?" she asked, startled by their presence.

"I'm Deputy Chief Baptiste. And these are my colleagues, Detective Burke, and Bridget Murphy. We're with the NYPD. We need to ask you questions about what happened inside the limousine." Adama offered a warm smile to help her relax.

"Oh no. Please. It's too awful." She cowered on the clinic bed.

"We understand this is difficult," Adama said, "but, please, tell us what happened."

Veronica took a deep breath. "We were headed to the Hamptons. Gerald started up with the booze and drugs, worse than ever. He went crazy and tried to kill me." Veronica sobbed.

Bridget approached the bed and patted Veronica's hand.

"Veronica, my name is Bridget. I'm sorry about what happened to you. Can you tell me about the large box in the limo?" Bridget hoped to redirect Veronica's angst.

"What? Oh, the box. Gerald showed it to me before he started acting crazy. He took so many drugs, then passed out, and woke up. He started throwing things and attacked me. It was awful." Veronica broke down again. "I tried to get out, but the doors wouldn't open. I was trapped."

"I'm so sorry, Veronica," Bridget said. "Tell me, did you or Gerald touch the object in the box?"

"He did, yes. But, when I tried, he yelled at me."

"You're doing great. Now, think carefully. You said he went crazy, right? Was that before or after he touched the item in the box?"

Veronica thought for a moment. "It was after. He caressed it, mumbled, and said his hands tingled, making him high. It looked like he was in a trance. That's when he went for the drugs and started acting weird." Veronica looked at Bridget. "Do you think that stone made him go crazy?"

"You're doing great, Veronica. Did Gerald say anything about the object?"

"Like what?" Veronica asked.

"Where it came from? Who gave it to him? Anything?" Bridget asked.

"Um, yeah. He got it Saturday night at a gallery. He paid twenty million dollars and said it would be worth a hundred million in five years. All he thinks about is drugs and money. He doesn't give a shit about anyone else but himself."

Adama nodded at Bridget, encouraging her to continue with her questions.

"Was that all?" Bridget asked.

"Um, well, he said it was his mother's birthday gift. Oh! And he said the story was amazing." Veronica wiped her eyes.

"What story? What did he say?" Bridget pressed.

"That some old guy in a big hat told them an amazing story. And it was the best story they ever told, with blood and guts, or something, and he got his money's worth."

"They? Who are they?"

"I don't know. Everything changed after he opened that box. It was like he was possessed. You should have seen his face after he touched that thing. For a second, I thought he was going to have an orgasm." Veronica sighed.

Adama leaned close to her. "Veronica, did Gerald tell you how the box ended up in the limousine?"

"No, just about the story at the gallery." Veronica looked around, frightened. "Where is Gerald?"

"I'm afraid he's dead, I'm sorry." Bridget's voice was kind and comforting.

"Good. That son-of-a-bitch tried to kill me." Tears filled her eyes. "I want to go home." She turned her head away, crying.

"Thank you, Veronia. Get some rest." Bridget patted her arm.

Adama felt sorry for her. "Thank you, Veronica."

The three left the room and walked down the hallway toward the exit.

"Seems we have one more indication that touching the stones adversely affects people," Bridget said.

Burke put his hand on Bridget's arm. "Wait a second. Are you saying these stones hurt people?"

Adama winced and intervened. "We're not sure, Ricky. But we're concerned there may be a connection."

"When were you planning to tell the rest of us?" Burke asked.

"We couldn't. We don't know for sure," Bridget interjected. "This woman is our first confirmation that the victims' behaviors, and possibly their deaths, may be related to the stones. There appears to be a pattern. At least, I think so. And I'm expecting helpful data that may shed more light on these cases."

"I'm beginning to think so too," Adama said, surprising them both.

"Hang on. What's going on?" Burke looked directly at Adama. "Why keep us in the dark?"

"Sorry, Ricky. It's touchy. And there's a lot at stake. Do me a favor and trust us." Adama nodded apologetically. "Hopefully, we'll know more soon."

Burke did trust Adama. He nodded. "Okay, so, now what?"

"Right now, we need to find the other boxes, fast," Adama said. "Four deaths and four boxes. Where are we with the other two billionaires on the list? Do we know where they are?"

"I'll check." Burke made a call.

"Okay, in the meantime, let's visit Danny Garcia at Mount Sinai."
Adama led the way to the parking lot.

———•———

At the hospital. Adama, Bridget, and Burke found Danny Garcia
awake and talking with his wife, Nancy.

"Hello, Mr. Garcia. I'm Adama Baptiste, Deputy Chief. This is
Detective Burke and Bridget Murphy from the NYPD. We'd like to
ask you a few questions."

"Now? He needs rest," Nancy protested.

"We won't take long," Adama said." We need to know what happened inside the limousine."

"Oh man, it was horrible. All I know is the engine shut down.
Nothing worked. Veronica was screaming, so I pulled over. Decker
was beating her. I tried everything, but I couldn't get to her. Poor girl.
I've never felt so helpless in my life." Garcia was embarrassed. "Is
she all right?"

"Yes, she'll be fine. What can you tell us about the box inside the
limo?" Adama asked.

"The box? I picked that up from the Miller Antiquities on W. 56th.
Gerald attended an event there on Saturday. He told me to drive
around to the back of the gallery. Two guys put the box in the limo,
then I went to the front to get Gerald."

"Did you look in the box, Mr. Garcia?" Bridget asked.

"No way. It had locks, so I couldn't even if I wanted to."

"Who were the two men?" Burke asked.

"I don't know. Two guys with a van, no logos, and they didn't
speak to me." Garcia looked at Adama, "How is Mr. Decker?"

"I'm afraid he's dead," Adama answered.

"Oh." He looked at his wife, who patted his hand. "What's the
big deal with the box?" Garcia asked.

"Did Mr. Decker say anything about where the box came from?"
Adama asked.

"No, not that I recall. He never mentioned it before Saturday
night."

"Okay, thank you, and we hope you feel better," Adama said.

Burke dropped his card on the nightstand. "If you think of anything else, please call."

Adama, Bridget, and Burke left the hospital and drove toward headquarters. On the way back, they stopped at a café. Over lunch, they discussed the stones, the statements by Veronica and Garcia, the six billionaires, the gallery, the price paid for each stone, and all the data they'd collected since Sunday.

"Twenty million for a stone? What a waste of money." Burke scoffed and poured mustard over his pastrami sandwich.

"They didn't pay for a stone; they paid to hear a story," Bridget said matter-of-factly. She looked up to see Adama and Burke staring at her.

"What do you mean?" Burke asked. "Who pays twenty million for a story?"

"Wealthy assholes, that's who." Bridget took another bite of her burger.

Adama looked at Bridget with admiration. *Of course, the story.* He realized Bridget had figured out the connection to the gallery, the man in the hat, the billionaires, the money, and the boxes. It was all about a story. He'd wait to discuss it later. Bridget seemed to hear his thoughts and dropped the topic.

"Well, I'm stuffed." Bridget took a sip of soda.

"Me too. I love this place," Burke added.

"Come on, you two, let's go," Adama said.

Adama paid the check at the counter, Bridget used the restroom, and Burke grabbed a few toothpicks from a container. They walked outside, got into Burke's car, and pulled away from the curb.

Chapter 47: Are We Good?

Leaving the restaurant with Adama and Bridget in his vehicle, Burke navigated the heavy traffic back to headquarters. His phone buzzed.

"What's up?" Burke listened for a minute. "Uh-huh, okay, thanks."

"Who was that?" Adama asked.

"Gates and Sanchez just left the docks and got the manifest from a container ship that docked there last Friday," Burke reported. "The shipping company was Senusret International Shipping and Containers, located near Port Said, Egypt. A small container was offloaded Friday and delivered to a marina warehouse. A video showed two men in coveralls unloading six wooden crates into a van."

"Let me guess—our two Africans," Adama said.

"Confirmed by facial recognition," Burke said.

"Well, that explains their involvement—and deaths," Adama said.

"The guys in the morgue with the taser marks?" Bridget asked.

"Yup. All loose ends get tied up in a conspiracy," Adama replied.

"Holy shit, it's all connected—the murders in Senegal, Senusret and the murders in London, your two young men, Jane Evans and her partner, the six boxes here in New York, four dead billionaires, everything—it's an international conspiracy." Bridget glanced at Adama, revealing her fear, anger, and sadness.

"What are you two talking about? What about Senegal and London?" Burke asked.

"Ricky, we've got a lot to tell you." Adama turned to Bridget in the back seat. "You were right," he said. "We need to collect those other boxes asap. When we arrive at HQ, Bridget, please check your email and get Burke up to speed. I'll meet with the chief, and we'll regroup."

Burke talked with the team at headquarters and obtained warrants to search Ling Chen and Gunter Maximilian's homes. Meanwhile, Bridget read emails from her Dakar contact, hoping for past evidence of Kanijugu symbols found on the mummified remains of corpses in Senegal. No such luck. She gave Burke the rundown on her London case, as well as information about the ancient gravesite and murders in Senegal.

———◆———

Adama returned from his meeting. "Warrants? Email? Updates?" Adama asked.

"Nothing new on my end," Bridget answered.

"Got the warrant for Gunter Maximillian," Burke said. "He left his office an hour ago; he plays tennis every Thursday at five o'clock. Hopefully, we'll catch him at home."

"Let's go." Adama grabbed his coat. "We'll hear what Maximilian says and collect his box."

"If he isn't dead," Bridget said glibly.

Burke looked in the rearview mirror. He turned north onto FDR toward the Upper East Side. Traffic was moderate, the tires thumped with each expansion joint, horns honked, and cars maneuvered around them.

"That's a macabre thing to say," Burke said to Bridget.

She erupted. "Well, I'm so sick of these people and the chaos they feed on. They murder, exploit women and children, and destroy our natural resources. They break laws and get away with it, and don't care about anyone but themselves. I hate them."

Bridget's outburst surprised Burke, and Adama became concerned.

"And they should die." Bridget's voice cracked.

"You don't mean that," Burke said.

"Bridget, let's stay focused," Adama said calmly.

"I do—no, I don't. I'm sorry. It's just that these fuckers think they can exploit anything or anyone—all for more money and a thrill from a disgusting story because they're emotionally dead inside?" Her voice elevated. "Margaret lost a husband—Colin and his assistant are dead, Jane and her partner are dead, two young men were murdered, and all those people in St. Pierre, and your nephew! Oh my god, so many deaths." Bridget broke down and sobbed.

Eyes filled with empathy, Adama turned and reached back with an open hand. She took it, finding comfort in its warmth.

Burke noticed their connection. *No doubt, these two got more going than just a working relationship.*

"I need water." Burke swerved to the nearest curb. "I'll be back in ten."

Adama acknowledged his detective as they exited the car. Adama slid into the seat next to Bridget and put his arm around her. She rested her head on his shoulder.

"Bridget, you've been running hard for weeks, and it's taking a toll. And I know you're scared. I won't let anything happen to you."

"It's all too much. Poor Colin, caught up in all of this." Bridget buried her face against his chest and wrapped her arms around him. They held each other for several minutes until she lifted her face. With swollen eyes and sniffling, she wiped her runny nose between her fingers. "I'll be fine."

Spotting Burke's return, Adama warned her. "Burke's coming back. You, okay?"

"Yes, I'm fine." She cleared her throat.

Adama looked around and found a napkin in a cup holder. He gave it to her and surprised her with a light kiss on her lips. "Okay. I'm moving to the front now."

Bridget reluctantly released him, then wiped her fingers and nose with the napkin. "By the way, I spotted your two undercovers a minute after they started tailing me."

"Of course you did." He smiled. "I'd speak to them, but there's no point with your observational skills." Adama moved to the front seat.

"Are we good?" Burke asked, jumping into the driver's seat.

Bridget took a deep breath and exhaled. "I'm good," she announced confidently. Putting on a brave face, she straightened her shoulders and compartmentalized the entire episode. "Let's go get him!" Bridget said. "We've got work to do."

Adama nodded at her resilience. "She's back," he said confidently.

Burke glanced in the rearview mirror to see Bridget smiling at him. He winked. "You got it." He pulled away from the curb, lightening the mood by mimicking a foreign language. "Goonterr, vee arre comingk forr yuuu." They all laughed at his terrible impression.

En route, Adama called Gates and Sanchez and put them on speaker. "We got the warrants. Go to Ling Chen's apartment at the Plaza and confiscate his mahogany box and the skeleton key. Chen is out on bail; if he interferes, arrest him immediately. One more thing, don't open or touch the object in the box. Take it directly to Dr. Pearson; she knows what to do."

"Don't worry, we'll get the box," Gates replied.

"He better not have *dogs!*" Sanchez was heard in the background. Everybody laughed.

"Stay in touch, guys." Adama hung up.

"What time is it? Will Maximilian be home?" Bridget asked.

"As of an hour ago, our mobile techs tracked his phone to his house—tennis anyone?" Burke said.

"Only one way to find out," Adama replied. He called the captain at the 19th Precinct to request backup and a police van at Gunter Maximilian's home on E. 76th Street.

"This ought to be fun." Bridget savored Adama's lingering kiss. *Butterflies.* Meanwhile, Adama hummed with the same electricity, but channeled it toward their mission.

Chapter 48: Gunter Maximilian

Detective Burke used Google Maps to traverse the streets to Maximilian's home address. He turned onto E. 76th Street and parked. Looking up through the windshield, he whistled at the ornate façade of the five-story townhome. "Wow, this guy is loaded."

Burke and Bridget flanked Adama as they crossed the street. Their footsteps echoed off the street and the surrounding buildings. They looked up at the heavy wrought iron gate on the stoop of Maximilian's home and climbed up the steps. To the right, Burke heard a mechanical whine, then a series of rhythmic clicks.

"Hold up, his garage door is opening," Burke said quietly.

"Perfect timing," Adama said.

They waited as the garage door secured at the top. Maximilian was startled at the three dark figures, standing shoulder to shoulder, like 1930s gangsters, ready to take out a rival.

"Can I help you?" Maximilian stood beside the open door of his shiny black Rolls-Royce. He wore white shorts, an aqua-colored polo shirt with a black collar, and tennis shoes. He held a case, snuggling a Wilson Blade 98 Tennis racket.

The detectives stepped into the garage, casting long, eerie shadows that stretched all the way to Maximilian. Each scanned the area. Maximilian was alone.

Flipping his badge open, Adama said, "Deputy Chief Baptiste with the NYPD, and these are my colleagues. Are you Gunter Maximilian?"

"I am. What can I do for you?" He held the tennis case close to his midsection.

"We have questions about your attendance at Miller Antiquities on Saturday night," Adama said.

Maximilian drummed his fingers on his tennis case. "What would you like to know?"

"For starters, where is your large mahogany box?" Bridget levied the question with grit.

Maximilian gave Bridget a dismissive once-over. "I don't know what you're talking about."

"And here we go. Cut the crap, Gunter." Bridget closed in. "Lying is a sign of weakness and a really bad idea. So, spare us the bullshit song and dance and 'fess up, or picture yourself in handcuffs. Now, where is it?"

Burke stiffened; Bridget's conduct surprised him. He looked to Adama for an intervention but received a slight head shake. Adama stepped forward to back up Bridget. Burke quickly followed suit. Three tough guys, looming, a wall of authority. Maximilian swallowed hard.

"We're waiting, sir," Burke said, fully committed.

"Okay, look. I was invited to the event. But I had no intention of—"

"Save it! Where's the box, Gunter?" Bridget sounded angry.

"If I were you, I wouldn't make her ask twice," Adama said.

Maximilian reached for his phone. "You can't do this. I'm calling my lawyer!"

"Bad move, Gunter." Burke dangled his handcuffs.

"We have a warrant to search these premises for stolen property," Adama said. He quickly produced a folded piece of paper and waved it in front of Maximilian.

Burke approached and took the racket case; Bridget searched the garage. She looked up at the rafters and opened several long white cabinets.

"This cabinet is locked." Bridget whipped around. "Where's the key?"

Adama tilted his head at Gunter. Burke was ready with cuffs. Maximilian held up his key ring. Burke took the keys to Bridget, who opened the closet.

"Found it!" Bridget announced.

"Tsk, tsk, Gunter." Burke's tone was mocking as he stood face to face with the liar in their midst.

"Can we talk about this?" Maximilian pleaded.

"Sure, start talking," Adama said.

Maximilian's composure cracked. "Okay, I was at the gallery, and yes, I purchased a rare item. But I swear, I had no idea it was stolen until Saturday."

"I want details. Who was there, what did you buy, everything?" Adama demanded.

"I arrived about seven o'clock. There were six of us; we ate, drank champagne, heard a story, and they delivered the boxes late Saturday night."

"That's not going to cut it. Cuff him, Burke," Adama ordered.

"Wait!" Maximilian held out his arm. "What I'm about to tell you could get me killed. I need police protection for me and my family. Promise me."

"No promises," Adama said. "Tell us everything you know about those boxes, and then I'll speak with the DA."

Maximilian sighed. "There was a man there, and he told us a story."

"We're not here to buy shares in your blue-chip evasiveness. Give us a name, Max," Burke said.

"He goes by Dr. Jeeves," Maximilian said reluctantly.

"Jeeves?" Burke and Adama recognized the name from Jacqueline Miller's statement.

"Wearing a big black hat, cape, and a cane?" Bridget asked.

"Yes. He arranged the event."

"Go on, tell us the story," Adama said.

"It was about ancient gravestones that had been dug up and taken from Africa. Quite a few people were killed in the process, including, well, a boy. The details were gory, I never expected to hear that story—it's not what I paid for." Maximilian stared down. "I thought I was buying a four-hundred-year-old artifact. That's what I was told."

"From two years ago? Impie Island, Senegal, Africa?" Bridget's voice was low.

"Yes. How did you know?" Maximilian asked.

"We're asking the questions," Burke interjected.

"How much did you pay?" Adama asked, containing his rage.

Maximilian was silent and squeamish. Burke jiggled the handcuffs.

"Twenty million," he said. "Each."

"Whew! That's a lot of money for a gravestone."

"But they didn't pay for gravestones. These assholes paid for the *story*." Bridget's eyes penetrated like hot pokers into Maximilian's soul. "Didn't you, Gunter?"

"Well?" Adama wanted to hear him say it. "Is that true?"

"More or less," Maximilian admitted.

Burke was flabbergasted and didn't believe it until he heard it.

"Why that community and why kill all those people? They were poor and took a night job to feed their families." Bridget choked up. "You may have wealth and power, but the blood on your hands can't be washed away with money or status. A twelve-year-old child was gunned down, you sick fuck!"

"Easy, Bridget," Adama cautioned. "Who else was in on this?"

"I don't know." Maximilian saw disbelief on their faces. "Look, these aren't the kind of people who advertise. And when they call, you don't say no."

"But you went. Tell me how you were contacted and by whom?" Adama asked.

"They use secret email addresses. I received a text and logged in," Maximilian said.

Burke shook his head. "For black-market art and antiquities? Tell us the rest."

Maximilian said, "Yes. I was invited under strict secrecy."

"Was it an auction? Did you attend an online bidding site?" Adama asked.

"No, we buy sight unseen, that's how it works. We pay in advance, attend an event, and hear a fantas—" He stopped cold as he caught Bridget's furious expression. "Um, to hear a narrative, connected to an object."

"Have you attended other events? With the same people? Here in the city?" Adama asked.

"I've attended two; I'm a new member. Each event is different— the prize, the people, the location."

"The *Prize*? That's rich. Did you ever have morals?" Bridget was livid.

"So, let me get this straight," Burke said. "You attend these exclusive events, with other wealthy scum, and pay obscene amounts of money to be entertained by detailed accounts of chaos and violence— then you take home a souvenir?"

Maximilian's face dropped. "For the most part."

Adama was incensed at the carpetbagger nature and predator behavior of these oligarchs. He wanted details about the other two events. His city was being used as a playground for people indifferent to human suffering, and his nephew died as a result. No, Adama would not let this man off easy.

Bridget was mortified and repelled at the clarity. Hearing it out loud turned her stomach.

"You sick son-of-a-bitch, you *buy* death and destruction. What kind of emptiness drives a plutocrat to feed off the suffering of others, off twisted, deadly exploits?" Bridget's restraint barely contained; she instinctively made a fist. "I'd punch your lights out if these guys weren't here."

Speechless, Adama, Burke, and Bridget stared at the criminal, stunned by what they had heard. Maximilian withered under their collective gaze. He whimpered as the warmth spread down his leg, darkening his white shorts. He cupped his groin, moaning.

Burke looked down at Maximilian's puddle of shame. Bridget and Adama's gazes followed. The titan of Wall Street had just crumbled before their eyes.

"Read him his rights and take him in," Adama told Burke. "And take his phone."

"Gunter Maximilian, you're under arrest for the purchase, receipt, and possession of illicit and stolen international property." Burke proceeded to read Maximilian his Miranda rights.

"Wait a second! Where's the key to the padlocks?" Bridget asked.

"Inside my car." Maximilian broke down and sobbed as Burke cuffed him. "What about my protection? They'll kill me."

One can only hope. Bridget dared not say it aloud.

"You have a lot of explaining to do. Once you're processed, we'll see about protection," Adama said.

"Jesus, you don't get it. I won't make it to morning," Maximilian said.

His words sent a chill down Adama's spine. A surge of protectiveness washed over him as he glanced at Bridget inside the Rolls-Royce. She came out holding up the key box.

"Got it!" Bridget announced.

She and Burke fumbled with the two vintage locks, carefully opening the lid to ensure the stone was inside. Adama kept an eye on them as they stared at the object. "Lock it up, guys," he ordered. "Burke, bag the key."

They relocked the box, and Burke put the key and jewelry box into evidence bags. Two squad cars and a police van pulled up to the residence, blocking the garage. Adama gave instructions to take Maximilian to their precinct for questioning.

"Officer, I want this man placed into protective custody. Keep him separate, and he doesn't talk to anyone but me. Understood?" Adama asked.

"Yes, sir," the officer replied and led Maximilian away.

Adama addressed another officer and pointed at the open cupboard. "Take that box to the morgue, make sure you give it to Dr. Pearson, CME." He looked him in the eye. "No one opens that box, understood?"

"Yes, sir." The officer motioned for backup.

Adama, Bridget, and Burke watched with satisfaction as Maximilian's head ducked into the squad car while others loaded the box into their van.

"Feel better?" Adama asked Bridget.

"Yes, we got him, the evidence, and a confession." She smiled with satisfaction.

Burke gave her a well-deserved pat on the back. "Geez, Bridget, you don't hold back!" He teased, imitating her with a splash of fun. "'Cut the crap, Guuunnnterrr!'"

"You liked that, huh?" Bridget laughed.

Adama patted her shoulder. "Well done, Bridget."

"Thanks, boss."

They piled into Burke's sedan. It was rush hour, traffic crawled, and horns blared.

"This will take a while," Burke said.

"I'm hungry. Anyone else?" Bridget asked.

"Hell yeah, I could eat," Burke said. "And we can sit out the traffic."

"You two and eating. My mother would say you have hollow legs." Adama laughed.

Burke pulled over to an Italian restaurant. Inside, they ordered drinks. When Bridget asked for ice to go with her prosecco, Burke gave her a look.

"Let it go," Adama said with a smile. *That's my Bridget.*

TWO WEEKS LATER

Chapter 49: Reunion

The flight from Dakar touched down at JFK International on time. Adama waited outside the customs baggage claim for his brother, his excitement mixed with anxiety. Two years had passed since the funeral of his nephew, Pape Baptiste. Since Adama's move to New York, family ties endured the test of time and distance through a steady stream of letters, photographs, and phone calls every month. Adama looked forward to news from home.

As his younger brother, Bakary, cleared customs, Adama waited near the terminal exit. Bakary spotted his brother and held out his arms. Pure joy emanated from Adama's eyes, and his heart raced like a champion thoroughbred at the finish line.

"Bakary!" Adama waved frantically.

"Frère Adama! My dear brother." Dragging his carry-on, Bakary raced to Adama.

The two brothers hugged and kissed each other on both cheeks. They looked each other over and hugged again.

"Mama, Saruba, and Binta say hello. They miss you so much."

"I know. I miss them too. Is that all your luggage?"

"Yes. Just a carry-on."

"Let me take it. Are you hungry?"

"No, we ate on the plane. But I am tired."

"I'll bet. That's a long flight."

Adama and Bakary arrived on the Upper West Side within an hour. Adama carried his brother's suitcase up the four flights to his apartment. Bakary looked around the small place. He noticed there was only one little bedroom.

"I can get a hotel—I don't want to intrude," Bakary offered.

"No, you're fine. Besides, this is New York City; the hotel rooms aren't much bigger."

"Okay, then I'll take the couch. That's all I need."

"Oh, no, you won't. I remember how loud you snore!"

"I remember you throwing shoes at me!" Bakary laughed. "You were a lousy shot."

"Haha, did you know I missed on purpose?"

They both became emotional; memories were still fresh. "It's as if no time has passed, brother," Bakary said.

"Oui, I'm so happy to see you," Adama said. "Want a beer?"

"Yes, that sounds good. But never tell Mama."

Adama opened two beers and handed one to his brother. "Our secret."

They clinked bottles. Bakary opened the French doors, and a cool breeze flowed into the room. The brothers walked out to the balcony and sat. Bakary looked down at the street in both directions. He noticed, but did not mention, the noise, the multitudes of people, and the traffic. He already longed to be back home.

"New York is very different from St. Pierre."

"It is, but I like it." Adama raised his bottle, "À la famille."

Bakary and Adama clinked their beer bottles again.

"The news of the stones has everyone in St. Pierre excited. We've waited two long years to find out what happened to them. The township collected money and paid for my trip. We can't believe the stones are here in New York City."

"Yeah, well, some of them anyway. It's a long way from Africa. And I'd sure like to know what happened to the others."

Adama looked at his brother and sighed. He could see how sad his brother was. Although he did not have a wife and children, he had seen his share of devastated parents dealing with the loss of a child or a loved one.

"How are you? How is Saruba?" Adama's voice turned melancholy.

"Oh, we manage day to day. She's still mourning. Our lives will never be the same." Tears welled, and he wiped his eyes.

"I'm so sorry, Bakary. I wish I could have done more to help."

"No, you helped a lot by coming, working with our police, the calls, and the inquiries on our behalf."

"Yeah, but it didn't do any good. And the stones—it was like they vanished from the face of the earth, along with the guys who did it." Adama held his fury; it felt even worse with everything he'd recently learned.

Bakary took a sip of beer. "At least you found six stones. That's something."

Adama sensed his brother was anxious. "Are you nervous about tomorrow?"

"Yes." Bakary sighed. "I'm afraid I'll let the people of St. Pierre down, and you."

"Not possible. The town leadership needed someone of substance to claim the stones. And you're that person."

"It's just that they desperately want the stones returned. They want closure. And they want justice for their loved ones. And for Saruba and our family, it won't bring Pape back, but at least we'll have some closure. You of all people know the significance of those ancient gravestones. Our friends, neighbors, and part of our heritage were ripped away that night." Bakary shook his head.

"I know all too well."

"The township thinks that our connection will somehow help." Bakary looked to his older brother for reassurance.

"I know. We'll take it one step at a time. First, your statement to the commission. The International Convention Against Illicit Traffic of Cultural Property invited you because you articulated the events of that night so powerfully. Now they need to hear you in person." Adama squeezed his brother's shoulder firmly. "Remember, your testimony will help them prevent future atrocities and the ensuing greed."

"I want that too." Bakary exhaled loudly. "But, what if my story isn't enough? I am scared, big brother." Bakary gave Adama a soulful look. "We never want this to happen again." He touched Adama's arm. "Your support means everything to me, our family, friends, and neighbors. No matter what happens, thank you."

"You're welcome, brother. Just remember, these cases involve complex international paperwork. I'm not the expert, but once the commission approves your case, an international commission will facilitate the return of the stones to St. Pierre. As a witness, your testimony, combined with your knowledge of the cultural history, the stones, and their origins, will help connect all the dots.

"How long will all this take?" Bakary took the last sip of beer.

"Hard to say. It's a process."

"How long do I need to stay? My plane ticket is good for a week."

"Don't worry, we'll deal with that later. You'll give a formal statement tomorrow morning, then we'll wait. Also, I want you to meet Bridget Murphy. She's largely responsible for getting us this far. She's an expert in criminology, anthropology, and archaeology. And she's been involved in dozens of international cases. She's got connections and a personal stake in your case."

"How so?"

"Well, a good friend of hers, a former professor at Cheikh Anta Diop University, was killed in London because of one of the stones. She has history there. She taught at the university and loved living and working in Senegal. She can be trusted." Adama repeated in French, "On peut lui faire confiance." Adama touched his brother's shoulder. "Avoir la foi." He told his brother, "Have faith."

"You mentioned one gravestone in London. How do we get it back?"

"Bridget is coordinating that paperwork. One step at a time, brother."

Bakary hung his head. He put his hand over his eyes to cover his grief. "I still don't understand it all. My son is dead, and for what? Gravestones? Will we ever find those responsible?"

"I'm so sorry, Bakary. I know this is hard."

Bakary touched the left side of his head. He rubbed the scar and indentation where he had been hit with the butt of a rifle the night his son was killed.

"I need to let Saruba know I'm with you. Excuse me for a few minutes." He went inside.

Adama heard the bathroom door close. He waited on the patio, thinking of ways to help. Adama looked at his wristwatch. It was ten-thirty. It had been a long day, and he was tired. Bakary returned to the patio.

"I'm exhausted," Bakary said. "I'd like to shower and turn in, okay?"

"Yes, good idea. Clean towels are in the cupboard."

Adama picked up the two empty beer bottles and walked inside. He watched Bakary go to the bedroom. His cellphone rang. It was Bridget.

"Hello, Bridget."

"Hi. Did your brother get in okay?"

"Yes. He's with me."

"I've got good news. I heard from the government reps in Senegal. All the relevant agencies are cooperating. Your brother's testimony with the commission is the final step. Once the commission consents and all the documents have been submitted, the stones can be returned within weeks."

"That's great news, Bridget. Thank you."

"Absolutely. How is he? This must be awful for him."

"I think the light in my brother's eyes has gone out."

"Of course. I'm so sorry for his loss. And for you."

"So many people died because of those stones. I wish I could find the perpetrators." Adama did not share his true thoughts. *I'd like to kill every one of the motherfuckers involved.*

"What time will you two be at HQ tomorrow?" Bridget asked.

"We'll be there by eight. The proceedings start at nine."

"Okay. I'll see you then. Have a good night, Adama."

"You too, Bridget. Goodnight."

Chapter 50: Bakary Baptiste

Adama and Bakary both had a restless night's sleep and awoke early. Adama dressed in his everyday work attire: a black suit, striped tie, and black dress shoes. He made coffee and set out a couple of bagels, cream cheese, and sliced cantaloupe.

Bakary emerged from the bedroom wearing a traditional Kaftan for formal occasions. Seeing the familiar garb from his homeland made Adama feel nostalgic and homesick. Adama came over to his brother with a broad smile. He held his shoulders.

"You look amazing! So beautiful. It reminds me of Africa's rich, earthy colors."

"Thanks. Saruba picked it out for me." Bakary felt proud.

Made from high-quality damask, the two-piece garment was a loose-fitting design. The Kaftan, or upper part, flowed from the shoulders, past the waist, and stopped short of Bakary's mid-thigh. The color was a deep brown with reddish-orange undertones, and the intricate gold embroidery consisted of geometric patterns stitched down the front. The matching-colored trousers completed his outfit along with his brown loafers.

"Saruba thought showing our traditional dress would be a good idea."

"She's right, it's perfect. You represent St. Pierre and Senegal well."

Adama couldn't help but notice the scar on his brother's left temple from one of the wounds he received when his son was killed. It was a constant reminder to all of their family of their grievous loss.

Silence filled the room like a heavy mist. The two men stood facing each other, their eyes meeting in wordless understanding. Bakary's shoulders rose and fell with a deep sigh that seemed to come from his very core. Adama stepped forward and pulled him into a firm embrace.

"You'll do well, brother," he said softly. His voice carried both strength and gentleness.

They walked downstairs to Adama's car. As they drove toward downtown, Bakary marveled at the hustle and bustle, the crowds of people on the streets, noises from trash trucks, police and ambulance sirens, and the magnitude and number of buildings. It overwhelmed him.

"Your city looks different in daylight," Bakary remarked. "How do you do it?" he asked solemnly.

"Do what?" Adama weaved through the traffic.

"Live in this place. It's so dense, so different from home."

"Yes, it is." Adama nodded. "At first, I was overwhelmed, but after I got my Visa and made a few friends, I got used to it, then I liked it, and now I love it here."

"I can tell. You seem satisfied." Bakary looked over at his brother. "When this is over, I hope we can talk about you and your life. I'd like to know more. I've been selfish."

"No, don't think that. And don't worry, we'll talk."

Adama could tell Bakary was anxious.

"Listen, it's going to be okay. After we get to headquarters, I'll introduce you to a few people. We'll enter a large conference room with an oval-shaped table and a dozen chairs. Others will be present, along with a camera to record the session. The administrator will ask you to read your Statement of Facts; then the commission members will ask you a series of questions. Hold nothing back. Tell them everything that happened."

"Will you be there?" Bakary asked. He nervously rubbed his hands together.

"Yes. I'll be in the room, but I have no official role. Additionally, Bridget has already provided a dossier that includes your statement, along with information about the tribal history of St. Pierre. She lived and worked there. Her experience lends credibility to the culture, mythology, and significance of our ancestors and Impie Island. You'll be fine."

"How long will this take?"

"Most of the day, I imagine. It starts at nine, they'll take short breaks, and stop for lunch. However, if you need a break, please don't hesitate to ask. Remember, they're here to help."

Adama and Bakary arrived and passed through security. They stopped at Bridget's office.

"Good morning," Adama said. He was happy to see her.

"Hello, Adama." Bridget's eyes sparkled at the sight of him. She saw Bakary and smiled warmly.

"Bridget, this is my brother, Bakary Baptiste. Bakary, this is Bridget Murphy."

"Dalal ak jàmm." Bridget welcomed him in Wolof. She held out her hand. "It's very nice to meet you."

Pleasantly surprised, Bakary instantly felt at ease with her. "Yaw nag," Bakary slightly bowed with his "and you" response. "Thank you for everything you've done to help our people."

"It's my pleasure. We all want justice for you, your son, and your people. I'm very sorry for your loss." Bridget paused. "Do you have any questions for me?"

"Uh, no, I'm just nervous," Bakary confessed.

"Understandable. Don't worry, you're in good hands." She nodded at Adama.

"Are you ready?" Adama asked.

"As I'll ever be," Bakary said with a shaky voice.

"Okay, let's go." They walked down the hallway. Along the way, Adama pointed out the restrooms.

Chapter 51: Carnage

The clock on the wall read eight-fifty-five a.m. Adama, Bakary, and Bridget entered a large conference room where others had assembled. A cameraman made last-minute adjustments to his equipment while a court reporter set up her stenography machine.

Adama touched his brother's arm. "Dëgëral."

"I will, brother. I'll be strong." Bakary raised his chin high.

"Water is on the table, and your photographs are cued up. You'll sit across from the administrator," Bridget said.

"Thank you." Bakary nodded and walked to his chair.

A large, well-dressed, bald man hastily entered the room. Like a famous attorney striding into a courtroom, he was intimidating, commanding respect with each confident step. A woman and two men with binders trailed him.

"Good morning. My name is Mathew Fox, and I'm the assigned administrator. I will oversee these proceedings on behalf of the National Stolen Property Act and the International Convention Against Illicit Trafficking in Cultural Property. Will everyone please take their seats? At no time will anyone speak unless I specifically address them. Does everyone understand?"

Adama, Bridget, and seven others sat in chairs around the perimeter of the room. Bakary sat in the lone seat at the large table. Mr. Fox explained the process and asked the court reporter and the cameraman if they were ready to begin. A clerk turned on the small microphone on the table. An open bottle of water and a glass were in front of Bakary.

"We are present to hear testimony from the sole survivor of horrendous acts of violence, exploitation, and the theft of thirteen gravestones from Impie Island, Senegal, Africa. The purpose of this hearing is to determine the circumstances surrounding the event that took place on May 29th two years ago, and the possible repatriation of the stolen property. I shall read the preamble of the Act:

"The National Stolen Property Act is a United States Act of Congress that prohibits the transportation, sale, and receipt of certain illegally obtained property in interstate or international commerce, including stolen goods and forged securities. The definitions for the terms used in the Act are codified at 18 U.S.C. § 2311; the offenses are codified at 18 U.S.C. §§ 2314–2315."

The recorder asked Bakary to state his full name, address, and occupation for the record.

Bakary stood and looked over at Adama, who gave him a reassuring nod.

"My name is Bakary Pape Baptiste. I live at 28 Joal Street, St. Pierre, Senegal, Africa. I am a senior mechanical engineer." Adrenaline surged, causing his mouth and throat to dry out.

"Thank you, Mr. Baptiste," Fox said. "As requested, there is multimedia available to show your photographs. You may now read your statement for these proceedings."

"Thank you." Bakary sipped water, cleared his throat, and opened his binder. He glanced at the solemn faces, notepads, and recording equipment in the room.

"Before I begin, two years ago, our community suffered a mass casualty event and the desecration of our ancestors' gravesite. The return of our ancestral gravestones is crucial to our heritage. As the sole survivor, I bear witness to both the physical and emotional scars from losing my son, Pape, and twelve other men. On behalf of them, thank you for allowing me to represent St. Pierre."

Bakary explained how poverty drove men in his village to seek extra work most nights.

"That night, my twelve-year-old son, Pape, asked if he could go with me, to be a man and help his family. My wife objected, but I promised to keep him safe. Pape was so happy; he jumped up and kissed his mother … for what turned out to be the last time."

A couple of spontaneous gasps caught Administrator Fox's attention. He stared around the room at the interruption.

Hands shaking, Bakary started his slideshow. "This is my son, Pape, with his mother, my wife, Saruba. It was his graduation day from elementary school."

The room became solemnly quiet. All eyes in the room stared at the photograph.

"That night, we were picked up by my friend, Filipe. I noticed a man in the front seat with a black hat, a mustache, and a deep scar running down the left side of his cheek. He said his name was John. We stopped outside the old peanut processing plant. John selected twelve of the strongest men for a two-hour work session, which would pay each of them one hundred dollars. The men pushed and shoved each other. My son told me, 'Papa, we'll work side by side, and I'll be a man.' And then he thanked me for bringing him."

Bakary momentarily hung his head and murmured, "If only I'd gotten off the truck, Pape would still be alive."

Bakary described the rainy night, huddling in the back of a flat-bed truck, and driving forty minutes before stopping at a closed fish and tackle store outside town. The men were told to grab a shovel, head down to the dock, and get into a boat.

"My son and I got into a boat with two neighbors. There were two other men in the boat. That's when I noticed they had guns. Four vessels of men quietly floated past Shell Island, eventually pulling into an embankment. We were led up a hill; three men with guns walked in front, and three men with guns walked behind. They carried large flashlights to light the way. We stood at the top and looked down, realizing we were on Impie Island.

"We stared in silence at our oldest graveyard, over four hundred years old. An eerie feeling came over us. We were afraid and started to back away. John saw our reaction and shouted, 'You dig, or no money.' One of my friends told him we weren't grave robbers. But, John yelled, 'Don't worry, you ain't diggin' up bodies. I want the grave posts. Start digging.'

"We knew John was a foreigner and did not understand. My next-door neighbor bravely told him it was forbidden; no one was allowed to touch the sacred gravestones of our ancient tribal elders, especially these stones. John aimed his gun at his face and said, 'Either you start digging, or I'll blow your head off. I'll blow all your heads off.' One man threw his shovel to the ground and walked away. We heard a muffled popping sound and saw the man fall to the ground. Then John aimed the gun at the rest of us. None of us wanted to die. All I could think about was keeping my son safe. So, I'm ashamed to say, we started digging."

Bakary paused, head bowed. Still ashamed. Everyone else in the conference room was stunned and silent. Bridget glanced at Adama. She knew his blood boiled at the brutality and disrespect by foreigners. The commission waited while Bakary composed himself. He displayed before-and-after pictures of the graveyard. Photos showed a disheveled area, with broken pieces of granite and empty, muddy holes where gravestones once stood.

"The base of each stone lay three feet underground. The rain made it difficult to remove the stones. We worked in the dark for hours. John's men stood guard, yelling to us to dig faster, or we wouldn't get paid. None of us cared about the money. We were so ashamed; we believed our ancestors could see us destroying the graves. We knew our community and children would learn about what we had done. We could barely look at each other. I knew they all felt the same, praying for the night to end. We just wanted to go home, so we worked as fast as we could."

Mr. Fox interrupted Bakary. "Excuse me, Mr. Baptiste. Would you please provide more context about the gravestones? Perhaps a description and their significance."

Bakary acknowledged with a nod. He noticed everyone staring. Adama gave a slight smile. Bakary collected his thoughts, adjusted his posture, and leaned forward.

Bakary nodded. "Of course. These gravestones signify our ancestry and heritage. They represent more than four hundred years of tribal knowledge. Ancient ancestors carved them from granite. They stand six feet tall, two feet wide, and weigh over one hundred pounds. When a tribal leader passed, a shaman directed the stonecutter to carve our sacred symbol at the top. These particular stones have the Kanijugu symbol and were isolated on Impie Island. It was forbidden to touch those stones."

"Thank you, Mr. Baptiste," Administrator Fox said. "Please continue."

"We dug up twenty grave posts, but only thirteen survived intact. We carried them to the shoreline and placed them into large wooden crates filled with straw. John's men put the lids on and nailed them shut. Once all thirteen stones were loaded, there was no room for us. John said the boats would come back. My friend Filipe left with John in a boat. I never saw him again.

"Four men stood guard and moved us back up the hill to wait. That's when I saw the four boats headed out to a cargo ship on the horizon. Pape and I sat on the wet ground. He was shivering, and I put my arm around him. He hugged me and cried, 'Papa, I want to go home.' My heart ached for Pape.

"After John returned, we were ordered to stand. I remember feeling relieved and thankful that we were finally going home. Two men appeared with automatic rifles. We looked at each other, confused, not knowing what to do, but we knew we were in trouble. There was barely time to react.

"What–what happened next was terrifying. A strange clacking sound echoed; I grabbed Pape's shirt and shoved him to the rear. I yelled, 'Run, Pape, Run!'" Bakary abruptly stopped talking. "It was the last time I saw my boy alive."

Reliving the experience overwhelmed Bakary. He covered his face. Adama leaned forward, wanting to comfort his brother. Soft murmurs filled the room.

"Order," Administrator Fox said. "Mr. Baptiste, do you need a minute?"

Bakary did not answer. Instead, he raised his head high, feeling a duty to those lost. He summoned strength, hearing Adama's voice, "Dëgëral—be strong." Bakary continued.

"It all happened so fast. They opened fire on us. I heard popping sounds. Men panicked, screamed, and bumped into each other. Bullets riddled our bodies. A bleeding friend toppled onto me, and we fell to the ground.

"Blood filled my eyes—I didn't know if it was mine or someone else's—and I couldn't see. I was pinned under two men. I heard moaning and men crying out in pain. After the gunfire stopped, they searched for survivors. I heard men beg, 'Please, I have a family,' and 'Please, my wife and children,' then pop.

"They randomly fired into us. One bullet tore through my right arm. I lay still and quiet, thinking of my wife, Pape, and our family. One of the gunmen hit me in the side of my head with the butt of his rifle, most likely to see if I was dead. I felt a horrible pain in my head and left temple. Then I passed out."

Bakary instinctively touched the scar.

He scrolled through numerous police photos. The room fell silent at the images of bodies—grimaced faces, tangled limbs, soaked in reddish-brown blood. Bakary cleared his throat.

"The next morning, I woke up buried under several dead friends and neighbors. After freeing myself, I remembered telling my son to run. I searched frantically, hoping he had gotten away. But I found his body twenty yards away; he was lying face down. His favorite jacket was soaked in blood—he had been shot in the back."

Bakary showed one distant photo, preserving his son's dignity. "I held my son, and wept. Then carried him home to his mother." Teardrops fell onto his papers. "It was all my fault. I killed my son." Bakary's voice tapered off.

Tears fell around the room. Everyone wiped their eyes. Adama brought him a box of tissues. The administrator looked around and saw everyone wiping their eyes. He addressed Bakary.

"Mr. Baptiste, would you like to take a short break?"

"Thank you, sir. I would like to use the restroom."

"We'll take a ten-minute break." Mr. Fox ordered.

Adama saw Bridget wiping her red eyes, along with others, as he had done. The image of his dead nephew was now permanently etched in his mind. *I never got to meet him.*

Noting that Bakary had returned from the restroom and was seated calmly, Mr. Fox said, "We are back on the record. Mr. Baptiste, please continue."

"Thank you." Bakary blotted new tears that had pooled on his face.

"Based on what I witnessed and what they saw, the police determined what happened that night. They found eleven bodies on Impie Island, and my friend Filipe was in his truck with a gunshot wound to his head. With a pistol in his hand, police initially ruled it a suicide. But, my brother, Adama, arrived and assisted with the investigation and proved that Filipe was murdered."

Everyone glanced at Adama. Bridget knew he was trying to control his emotions.

"All the boats were tied up at the dock. No fingerprints were found. Though investigated, the police never found the killers or our thirteen missing stones.

"Days later, I attended my son, Pape's, funeral, with my wife, my daughter, my mother, my brother, and the community. Separately, we buried our twelve friends and neighbors. Good, decent men who only wanted to make a little extra money for their families. Our community remains broken over this horrific event."

Bakary displayed funeral photos and fresh gravesites behind his community church.

"We repaired most of the sacred broken gravestones on Impie Island, but we ache for the rest of our stones to be returned. These aren't just carved rocks—they embody centuries of our ancestral heritage and tribal history. They play an important role in our culture. They belong to us, the people of the ancient tribes of St. Pierre."

Bakary shared photos of the damaged and repaired gravestones. Fresh red earth contrasted with the older brown soil.

"In closing, and as a representative of the community of St. Pierre, thank you for this opportunity to present my statement. I am happy to answer questions. With great respect and gratitude, we thank you."

Administrator Fox acknowledged Bakary. "Thank you for your statement, Mr. Baptiste. We appreciate how difficult this has been for you. We will admit your statement as part of the record for this investigation. This panel will ask questions related to your statement."

For three hours, Bakary answered the commission's questions about the event. He provided police reports, research, and documentation from notable historians about St. Pierre, Senegal, as well as newspaper articles and "before-and-after" photographs of Impie Island, including police crime scene photos of the full exploitation.

Administrator Fox thanked Bakary for his explicit and emotional statement, as well as his cooperation, and closed the proceedings. He and his colleagues gathered up their items and left the room. The cameraman and court reporter packed up their equipment.

Bakary looked for his brother, who was already approaching. The two brothers embraced long, while others kept a respectful distance.

"How was it? Did I do well for our people?" Bakary asked.

"You were fantastic. Je suis fier de toi, mon frère." Adama held his brother tightly.

Bridget appreciated Adama telling Bakary, "I am proud of you, my brother." Her eyes welled with tears at the sight of these two men. *Thousands of miles may separate them, but their hearts are filled with love.*

Bakary kissed Adama's cheeks. "Thank you so much for finding our stones."

"You're welcome, but it wasn't just me." Adama glanced at Bridget.

Bakary walked to Bridget. "Thank you for everything. Adama said your connections and research made this possible. I don't know how to repay you."

"No need. Your testimony is invaluable. I hope you find peace and the remaining stones properly returned to your community."

"Vous êtes un être humain tout à fait excellent," Bakary said, with intensity that conveyed profound gratitude.

"Oh, Bakary." Bridget's eyes widened, and appreciation and humility washed over her. "You honor me beyond words." She crossed both hands over her heart.

They hugged and kissed each other's cheeks, exchanging the newly formed trust and a shared understanding of their cultural heritage.

The court clerk, gathering equipment, overheard the French statement. Seeing Bridget's reaction, she quietly asked Adama, "What did he say to her?"

Adama smiled. "He said, 'You are a most excellent human being.'"

"Oh, wow, what an amazing thing to say."

Adama watched his brother and Bridget. "And that she is," he whispered.

After everyone left, Adama unexpectedly kissed Bridget on the cheek, conveying warmth, trust, and appreciation.

"What was that for?" Bridget asked.

"For being you."

She smiled and touched his cheek. "Thank you."

"Listen, I'm going to take Bakary back to my place. We're both exhausted, and he needs to call his wife. We'll spend the rest of the week together before he leaves. Can I call you in a few days?"

"Of course." Bridget turned to Bakary. "Enjoy your stay in New York and time with Adama. It was nice meeting you."

Bakary kissed her cheek. "And you as well." Then he leaned in and whispered, "Take care of my brother." He pulled back and winked.

Bridget flushed. "It would be my honor. Take care, Bakary."

Adama raised an eyebrow in silent question. Bridget nodded reassuringly, mouthing, "It's all good."

With dimples pronounced from a broad smile, she waved goodbye as the two brothers disappeared through the doorway.

Chapter 52: A City Restored

Once the legal documents were approved, confiscated gravestones would be returned to St. Pierre, Senegal. Senegal's Ministry for the Preservation of Cultural Artifacts approved a security and transportation fund for the safe return of the stones. The six wooden crates would be sealed and loaded onto an airplane in two weeks. Adama would escort the stones and attend the ceremony, where each gravestone would be restored to its original placement. He looked forward to visiting with his family.

Dr. Betty Pearson concluded her forensic and pathological findings regarding the cause of death for the billionaires. Her subsequent autopsies and the official cause of death for each victim were based on forensic science. Her analysis of the stones revealed that each was contaminated with a rare fungal organism. Tests showed that once exposed to air and touch, the fungus released a toxin that induced temporary psychosis. This information would be used for political purposes and media narratives. Regarding Gerald Decker, an overdose of multiple drugs caused his heart to stop. For Thomas Miller, the cause of death was cardiac arrest caused by an accidental overdose of an opioid.

Bridget wrapped up her NYPD assignment. Based on the results, New Scotland Yard reopened the London cases. She obtained the autopsy reports for Colin Taylor, Susan Baker, and Ahmed Senusret, the only person who touched the stone at the Taylor gallery. London's medical examiner found a distinctive "tattoo-like mark" behind Senusret's left ear. No marks were found on the other two victims. Bridget worked with authorities in London to return the confiscated stone to Senegal. She brought Margaret Taylor the good news that the false murder-suicide label about her husband, Colin, had been cleared, bringing closure and relief to her dear friend. She also promised to visit soon.

Adama and Detective Ricky Burke met with the Brooklyn District Attorney's office about Captain Ricci. They coordinated with the FBI, presenting facts and evidence to the DOJ. The captain had been arrested and charged with aiding and abetting in the commission of a federal crime, as outlined in Title 18 U.S. Code Section 2. In addition, the State of New York charged her with obstruction and tampering in the Vanhorn case. Both cases are ongoing.

Henry Miller was at the memorial service honoring his deceased son, Thomas Miller-Chevalier. Jacqueline Miller gave a moving eulogy that brought tears to a full congregation at St. Patrick's Cathedral on 5th Avenue. Thomas's remains were buried in a private cemetery next to his mother, Violet Chevalier, in the family's ancestral plot.

Adama's neighbor, Mark Dawson, who had personally "scooped" the deaths of William Vanhorn, Daisy Hunter, and Henry Miller, penned several articles for the Manhattan Gazette. Dawson also wrote an article regarding the outcome of the billionaire deaths in Manhattan. His boss, Jason Walker, personally edited the article, which was factually correct but lacked specific details to preserve public confidence.

PRESS RELEASE – Dormant Super Fungus Kills Billionaires – Follow Up Story

> By Mark Dawson
> Investigative Reporter
> Manhattan Gazette
> May 29, 2023

> The City of New York may rest assured there is no cause for concern or alarm related to the deaths of four billionaires, William J. Vanhorn, Daisy Hunter, Dick Betrug, and Gerald Decker, who died while visiting Manhattan during the first week of May.

> The City's Chief Medical Examiner, Dr. Betty Pearson, determined the deaths were directly related

to a deadly super fungus called prototaxite coccophagus. The extinct fungus is believed to date back to the Late Devonian period and was discovered in 1633 by Christian Siegfried Kepler, a German scientist.

Roberta Bilham, a renowned pathologist and expert in mycology, oversaw the process that eradicated the fungus, which produces deadly neurotoxins. Despite the objections of a world-renowned mycologist, the destruction by fire ensured its eradication. Extensive laboratory tests confirmed the fungus is officially extinct.

Mark Dawson was promoted to a journalist position and received a substantial raise. He would cover high-profile cases under the tutelage of Jason Walker.

The Office of the Medical Examiner provided no context or report regarding the quarter-inch symbols found behind the ears of William Vanhorn, Daisy Hunter, Dick Betrug, or Gerald Decker.

Within the special task force, a quiet manhunt was underway for a mysterious man in a black hat.

In the meantime, other meetings and plans were taking place in the city.

Chapter 53: The Ultimatum

Henry Miller arrived at Gracie Mansion at ten in the morning. His limousine pulled through the private drive and parked outside the entrance. A cane assisted him in walking up to the steps of the famous 1799 structure. Waiting to escort him up the steps was his boyhood friend and New York City's mayor, Gryffin Tait.

Over brunch, they sipped tea from antique Russian teacups and discussed the front page of the Manhattan Gazette. Henry folded the paper and set it aside.

"That reporter, Mark Dawson, has chops. Better keep an eye on him," Miller said.

"Yeah, he had our city on edge for weeks. Thank god his boss, Jason Walker, is on our payroll," Tait said. "So, which do you think got our comrades, the fungus or that African curse?"

"Who gives a shit? It's over," Miller said. "We've got bigger fish to fry."

"Oh, you're ready to get down to it. Good. But first, everyone sends their regards; we're glad you're feeling better. We thought we'd lost you, buddy."

"Me too. It was touch-and-go for a while. The doctors say my ticker is good to go, so I'm working part-time to assist Jacqueline. She's been a mess since losing Thomas. My children were very close. I don't think she'll ever be the same."

"Yes, very sad. I'm sorry for your loss, my friend." Tait paused, deliberately choosing his wording. "And thank god your cover wasn't blown while you were in the hospital." He took a sip from his beautiful Russian teacup.

Henry understood the comment—a warning shot across the bow.

"Don't even fucking go there. I'm safe. In fact, I'm better off. Everyone thinks of me as the poor widower and man who lost his son. Business is booming." Miller grinned.

"Awesome! Then let's discuss business, yes?"

"Let's do it," Miller said.

"I understand you have questions about Dr. Jeeves and what happened with Thomas."

"Yes. One question: where is he? That old fuck killed my son, and I'm going to tear his heart out. I want blood. I'll make him suffer for hours, torturing him myself." Henry's face contorted with anger.

Tait knew all too well what Henry Miller was capable of, having seen his brutality personally. The mayor pushed his plate away, lit a cigar, and puffed a small white cloud upward.

"Henry, you and I go way back. We owe each other a lot. And it pains me to say, nothing will bring your son back. You know that."

"Yeah, so, what's your point?" Henry was bewildered by the change in topic.

"You have a decision to make, my friend." Tait took another puff and then laid his cigar in an ashtray.

"Oh, really? What's that?"

"You must leave Jeeves alone."

"You can't be serious!" Henry said. "I'm not going to forget about it! Are you cracked in the head? I will make that weasel of a man wish he'd never been born." Steam emanated from his nostrils.

"You can pursue Dr. Jeeves, or you can let sleeping dogs lie, which, for the sake of everyone, is the preferred choice. I urge you to choose the latter." He gave Henry a warning look.

"What the fuck does that mean? Jeeves killed my son. It wasn't an accident. He must pay!"

"I understand, and I empathize. Truly." Tait patted the back of Henry's hand. He searched his face for a concession while puffing his cigar.

Henry's eyes slowly grew larger, his eyebrows raised, and his facial muscles dropped; his ire was replaced with shock. He finally understood. "Oh my god, Jeeves did it on purpose!" He leaned forward, begging for understanding. "But why?"

"Henry, I'm sorry to tell you this. Simply put, your son didn't follow the rules. He opened one of the boxes, *saw inside, and* reached out to touch it, for Christ's sake. Jeeves was given a directive; he had no choice in the matter. So unfortunate." Tait waited for Henry's reaction.

"A directive? Fuck, he was my son! Who do they think they are? I'll kill them all."

Tait had anticipated this response. "Henry, you know the rules—no loose ends. Now I know you're having a bad reaction. I encourage you to calm down and think about the consequences."

"Fuck! Fuck! Fuck!" Henry stood and stomped around the room. Tait watched.

"Come sit, my friend. You don't need another heart attack." Tait guided Henry back to his chair. "You know what you have to do."

Henry's head hung, and tears welled. Distraught, he shook his head. "That stubborn, stupid kid of mine. God damn it! The one fucking time he takes initiative, and it gets him killed."

"Yes," Tait agreed. "Now that you understand, I beg you, don't pursue Jeeves. For your sake, for your daughter's sake." Tait's eyes narrowed as he leaned forward.

The ultimatum hung in the air, like the smoke from Tait's cigar. Henry felt the blood drain from his face. *No! My daughter. Fuck. They'll go after Jacqueline.* As the threat crystallized, fear consumed his body—his heart rate spiked, and his stomach turned. He clasped his hands to control the trembling. His body's reflexes had kicked in—fight or flight?

He was a man who'd learned how to compartmentalize fear. With practiced discipline, Henry swallowed hard, lifted his chin, and stiffened his spine. He willed his facial features into a mask of acceptance. The corners of his mouth slowly turned upward.

"No. You're right, my friend. I won't pursue Jeeves. Please let them know that I didn't understand the circumstances. And I'm one hundred percent on board." Henry exhaled quietly.

"Excellent. I'm so glad. They'll all be glad. I told them you'd see the light. You always do whatever it takes, and that's what we all love about you, Henry."

Painful as it was, Henry had no choice but to surrender. He coughed and cleared his throat. "Well, then, shall we get down to business?" Henry used his napkin to dab beads of sweat off his forehead.

Tait smiled gratefully. "Yes, let's."

"What about the money?" Henry's tone was sober.

"That's my Henry! Gotta scratch that itch." Tait smiled broadly. "I've been informed that one million had been distributed to Thomas. However, it was retracted, and his account was closed. We couldn't leave a money trail, you understand."

"Of course," Henry said. "But, since my gallery was used, I believe compensation is due."

"On that we all agree," Tait said. "Now that we understand each other, the full ten million shall be deposited into your Swiss account."

"I appreciate that, Gryffin. Thank you."

"No problem. They will be very pleased to accommodate you."

"Great." Henry cleared his throat. "So, with that settled, can you tell me what you've heard about Daisy Hunter's replacement? Has the council decided about my taking her place as Provincial Leader for the North American Province?" Henry's mood shifted from self-pity to egotism.

"Her demise was most unfortunate. An announcement is forthcoming. But it'll cost you." Tait's voice was melodic, teasing, and singing the last part.

"What, a hundred million buy-in? Chump change," Miller said.

"Well, sir, you've got my vote."

"Thank you, Gryffin. I knew I could count on you. And what of our two loose ends?"

"All taken care of, as of this morning." Tait puffed on his cigar.

"Good to hear. I don't want anything coming back on me or the gallery."

"Not to worry, my friend. We've taken measures. This morning, I was informed that Gunter Maximilian and Ling Chen had a mishap. Prisons can be hazardous places."

"Turncoats. They're both despicable. I'm glad I didn't sponsor them." Miller sipped his tea.

"True. So, shall we review the transcript of the story that Dr. Jeeves told the Manhattan group? I'll read it, and we can see what we're up against. Come on, Henry, you must admit, Daisy Hunter and Dr. Jeeves did a great job."

"Fuck him," Miller said.

"Understood. But we must be clever and upstage Daisy's event. Had she lived, the bonus would have been enormous. We'll create an even better event and story." Tait thought Henry looked tired. "Say, I need a break. Why don't we stretch our legs and regroup on the veranda?"

"Sounds good," Miller said. He welcomed the time to recuperate, having spent mental and emotional energy regaining his composure after the ultimatum. He wanted to bring his A-game.

Chapter 54: LeGalére

The voice on the other end of the line was calm, throaty, and commanding. She spoke confidently and clearly, befitting the world's wealthiest woman and Supreme Leader of LeGalére, an exclusive syndicate of multi-billionaires.

LeGalére's hierarchy consisted of a Grand Council with one Supreme Leader and five Provincial Leaders overseeing Europe, Asia, Africa, South America, and North America. The exclusive membership had expanded rapidly to three hundred twenty billionaires from around the globe. LeGalére's charter was simple—"creative equilibrium." The euphemistic doublespeak masked their true purpose: orchestrated chaos and exploitation. Each event generated unique and unprecedented narratives, told exclusively to members. Each experience promised both exhilaration and exorbitant profits.

The Supreme Leader's assistant was a wimpy little man, but incredibly competent. His name was Simon Finch, though the Supreme Leader called him Simp. He possessed the traits most endearing to her: loyalty above all, then submissiveness, greed, and intelligence—in that precise order.

"I only have a few minutes, Simp. Give me an update," she said impatiently.

"Yes, madam. We lost six members in the U.S.A. and one in London. All died unfortunate deaths related to the gravestones."

"That's unnerving and not good for business. We don't kill our membership. Now tell me, where are the other six gravestones?"

"No one knows. Dr. Jeeves had them in cold storage in one of Spain's freeports. He said the locker had been broken into, and they disappeared."

"Ridiculous incompetence." Supreme Leader's voice filled with controlled anger. "Find them!"

"Yes, madam." Simp shuddered at the sound of her elevated voice. "And may I add, now we understand what happened, and after they've been located, we'll know how to manage them, and offer them up to mitigate our losses."

"Negative, Simp. Return them all discreetly. That should stop the authorities and the vile press from pursuing the issue. We'll absorb the loss. Now tell me, what is the temperature of our membership?"

"Well … at first blush, understandably nervous. But the fungus story brought comfort."

"Good, I want happy investors. And about Daisy Hunter—have we secured the contents of her secret safe?"

"Yes, all documents have been recovered. I'll have them by tomorrow."

"What was the outcome with Henry Miller?"

"Tait reported no problems. Miller is one hundred percent on board."

"Good man. Still, such a shame about his son." Supreme Leader sighed into the phone.

"Tait revealed that Miller wants revenge on Jeeves."

"Of course he does, who wouldn't?" she said. "Going forward, change all Dr. Jeeves' names to Dr. Higgins for future events. Any event still in play will keep the name, Dr. Jeeves."

"Yes, madam."

"Now, what about recruits?"

"We've identified and confirmed seven excellent candidates."

"That only gives back the seven we lost. I'm asking about additional recruits."

"Of course," Simp said. "We've identified ten potential targets, two for each continent—all properly vetted. A dossier about each prospect is being prepared for the council's approval."

"Good. Get it on the agenda. We'll finalize the selection at the next meeting, along with Miss Hunter's replacement for North America."

"Consider it done."

"Now tell me, who's in charge of the next event?"

"Gryffin Tait and Henry Miller in New York."

"Oh my, it should be spectacular. Gryffin is enviably our most creative member."

"True," Simp agreed. "Also, he is anxious to be POTUS. He's ready to run in the next election."

"Yes, it's time. What about contributions and election manipulation plans?"

"Funds are streaming in. And we've secured a competent individual who can intercept and manipulate the results, if needed."

"Outstanding." Supreme Leader paused. "Now, one more thing— Bridget Murphy. Is she safe from that ridiculous excuse of a tormenter?"

"Yes, madam. We orchestrated a skiing accident in the French Alps. He died of severe head injuries after falling several hundred meters. He's no longer a bother to Miss Murphy."

"Good. Miss Murphy must be protected at all costs. She has proven herself a formidable adversary, and being a woman adds a certain charm and intrigue for our membership. The feedback is very positive. Not to mention, she's attractive. Our council finds her antics and high-strung personality stimulating. Bridget is crucial for our art, antiquities, and archaeology needs, as well as creative equilibrium. As a new addition, we must ensure everyone in the chain understands how important she is to our charter."

"I'll see to it." Simp snickered to himself. *Haha, equilibrium events—I love how she intellectualizes our exploitative events.*

"Now tell me, how much does Miss Murphy know about LeGaléré?"

"Only what we've allowed, which, of course, is pure conjecture," Simp said. "She doesn't know our name but suspects a syndicate exists. We're a giant puzzle for her abstract and passionate mind. We feed her the pieces needed while we intercept, inject, distract, and exclude enough to keep her following our breadcrumbs. So far, she's been the perfect marionette."

"Splendid, ensure her brick road is safe and continually twists and turns. Understood?"

"Absolutely, we'll keep her safe and on track."

"Good. Now, if there's nothing else, I'd like to visit with my grandchildren."

"Certainly. Enjoy your evenin—"

The phone went silent.

Chapter 55: Past and Future Exploits

Gryffyn Tait and Henry Miller had moved outside to a lovely flowery veranda. They continued their meeting to understand the full magnitude of the story Dr. Jeeves told the six, now deceased, billionaires at Miller Antiquities just three weeks prior.

"So, I've got the transcript of the story that Jeeves read. We'll learn from it and create a better chaotic event and story."

"Okay, but just go over the juicy parts—we already know most of it."

"Will do. I've circled the colorful parts. It looks like Daisy had one hell of a lead man—a former Russian special task force commander and elite combat unit member known for his brutality. He goes by the name John QT. The guy is six-three and two hundred pounds of muscle—a lean and mean son-of-a-bitch. He's got over one hundred kills in combat. Used to be a sniper and evidently, he has physical scars from years of combat, including the remnants of several gunshot and knife wounds."

Miller interjected, "I love John. That guy is old-school and diabolical. Maybe we can use him."

"Maybe," Tait said. "Let me scan this for a moment. Ooh, this is good…"

The story read at Miller Antiquities contained details from John's comprehensive diary. Miller and Tait enjoyed the diabolical plan—the location, John's men, the graveyard, the date, and luring poor people with money.

Tait shared how John had executed the plan flawlessly, including the timing, the weather, stabbing a taxi driver with a black, double-edged dagger, severing his spinal cord.

"Does it say what weapons were used?" Miller asked.

"Oh yeah, listen to this," Tait said. "John drew his Russian Army PL-15, with a striker trigger for a fast, short reset. He executed a dissenter as a deterrent. Pretty cold-blooded with a man pleading, 'No, please! I have a family.' John put a bullet between his eyes. John had hoped for an instigator, kept the rest of them in line."

"God, he's good. No mercy, excellent. Obedience is key." Miller was riveted. "I'll bet Betrug and Decker loved it; those guys were psychos. And don't forget Daisy, I heard she cut another worker's ears off in front of his team to keep him in line."

Tait continued searching for brutal scenes. "I think it's coming to an end, but let's see. Okay, listen to this: 'John had them gather the men together. Two of his men stepped forward, each carrying a Russian AK-47 Kalashnikov Model 1947, a gas-operated, rotating-bolt design. Without warning, shots rang out, and hot, burning gases exploded from each muzzle, like fireworks streaming outward. The men screamed and bumped into each other as they scrambled to get away. It was the ultimate chaos of men, shoving, hitting, and fighting each other to stay alive.'"

"Purely primal. Men are willing to sacrifice others to live." Miller shook his head.

Tait said, "Hang on, there's more. 'Two guards emptied their metal jackets, reloaded, and fired again. The bullets tore bodies to pieces, shredding tissue, shattering bones, severing nerves and blood vessels, causing massive bleeding. One man after another dropped to the ground. No one survived.'"

"Except one did!" Miller said. "Good thing John covered his tracks."

Tait was grinning ear to ear. "Here we go, the coup de grâce. 'During the massacre, John saw a boy running away—five yards, ten yards, and fifteen yards. At twenty yards, John took careful aim with his AK-12 Avtomat Kalashnikova 2012 Russian gas-operated assault rifle. He locked the twelve-year-old in his sight and aimed center mass at the boy's heart. When he pulled the trigger, the bullet exploded from the gun. The boy's arms flailed outward, his chest jutted forward, and his head jerked backward from the force of the impact. He fell to his knees, landing face down, dead on the ground.'"

"Hell, that's brutal," Miller said. "I wish we could have attended that event."

"You were in the hospital, buddy. Besides, you know the rules. The next chaos team cannot attend an event within six months to ensure originality. Let me finish." Tait searched for tidbits. "Let's see. After the shooting stopped, men moaned, and a few begged for their lives."

"Yeah, I read it. Pathetic," Miller said.

"Oh, you gotta love this part. 'John looked upward. The rain had stopped, and the skies cleared. Moon streaks shone on the pile of bodies. Blood flowed like capillaries and shimmered in the moonlight. With one foot extended on a rock, John fired his gun into the air, like a mighty warrior. His men whooped and cheered.'"

Tait wrapped up the overview. "Looks like the rest of this is tying up loose ends."

"It sounds so delicious," Miller said. "I hate what Jeeves did to my son, but you have to admit, the man knows how to set a table of intrigue."

"There's a bit more. Jeeves included an endnote for the group." Tait read it. "Blah, blah, blah; oh, this last part is good: 'We do hope you feel that your itch has been scratched—until next time.'"

"Solid gold. We need to find someone like him to tell our story," Miller said.

Tait got up and stretched. "Let's take a break, get more tea, and move into the library."

"Sounds good. And thanks, I feel better." Miller patted Tait's back.

"No problem, Henry. I'm glad you made the right decision. I'd miss your ass if you were gone. Let's go."

———

After a bathroom break, a light dessert, and more tea, the two men retreated to the library. It was a handsomely decorated room, old-world dark antique furniture, wall-to-wall books, a world globe, and four large, overstuffed armchairs. The two men lit cigars and relaxed.

"Okay, it's our turn to create an intriguing story, so let's put our heads together," Tait said.

"Yes, and I'm thinking Armistice Day, November 11th." Miller smiled broadly.

"Excellent choice. That's a seductive and infamous date. Ideas?" Tait asked.

"Caves, the ones with the handprints. Did I tell you I had an exclusive tour in a real one?"

"Extremely provocative selection." Tait sat in an overstuffed armchair.

"What about you? Any fun ideas?" Miller asked.

"A couple. I was thinking about vineyards in France."

"Ooh, that's exhilarating. And it would crush the region. Such a shame though, all those grapes and delectable champagne and wines." Miller rubbed his hands together.

"Stock up, my friend. The price of both would skyrocket. Regardless, either of our deeds would fetch a handsome fee."

"Yes, an obscene fee for the pleasure of purely exploitive greed. I love it." Miller beamed.

"The membership can afford it. They always come back for more."

"They'll get their fill. Nothing beats a great story and a collector's item to make a man feel alive."

"We aim to please!" Tait said. "LeGalére exists to create excruciating chaos, fantastic profits, and pitiful deaths, all wrapped up in a great story. It's a thing of beauty, isn't it, buddy?"

"Indeed!" Henry puffed his cigar, knowing he should not be smoking. "Well, whatever we choose, it must surpass Daisy's deed. Her idea was brilliant, except for the hiccup." Miller leaned forward, grinning. "What a clusterfuck that turned out to be."

"So, was it the fungus that killed the four billionaires or that curse that Bridget Murphy identified from an ancient gravesite? According to her and that ridiculous curse, our friends were triggered into facilitating their own deaths. Vanhorn, dead from deviant sex, Daisy through gluttony and self-loathing, Betrug by cheating, and Decker from drugs. Jesus, that's tantamount to suicide." Tait stirred his tea and took another sip.

"Who cares? There's nothing we can do about it now." Miller's tone was cavalier.

"Those poor bastards. Damn shame, we lost some good cohorts."

"Yes. LeGalére's Council was quite upset about losing four of our own. But, thanks to your influence and control, we got away with it, and that's all that matters," Miller said.

"We've also been charged with finding six replacements. Got anyone in mind?" Tait asked.

"I have a couple of prospects to discuss."

Miller and Tait spent the next two hours brainstorming chaotic events and dates, including Armistice Day, focusing on exacting revenge on anti-fascists in Europe. They strategized how to create maximum chaos, an acceptable number of deaths, and the perfect team to execute carnage and devastation through the utter destruction of famous landmarks and artifacts.

The two men created an outline and agreed to meet several times to finalize their presentation for approval by LeGalére's Grand Council. The mayor neatly tucked their notes into his secret safe.

"Henry, my man, I'm so glad you recovered. I wish you all the best and hope you're selected as Provincial Leader for the North American Province."

"Thank you, my dear friend and colleague. And, may I add, POTUS awaits you. Having you as the most powerful man on the planet ensures we control everything in North America."

"Ah, President of the United States! I've waited long enough. I'm ready."

"Here's to chaos and never-ending stories," Henry said.

"And here's to the sleeping masses who have no idea who is running this world and the calamities to come."

"A toast to LeGalére!" Henry raised his antique Russian teacup.

"To LeGalére, cheers!" Tait raised his cup.

The two men grinned like Cheshire cats, lounged in their comfy chairs, and contemplated the deadly exploits to come.

Chapter 56: Heart to Heart

The City of New York had been on edge for weeks, shaken by a bizarre string of deaths, including six billionaires—four by a mysterious fungus and two killed while awaiting arraignment at the prison. Multiple newspaper articles and talk show hosts helped bolster confidence and soothe New Yorkers, business owners, and tourists. Police Commissioner Xavier Prawda held a press conference and congratulated the officers in the special task force for their exceptional work in solving the cases.

At NYPD headquarters, Adama commended his team for a job well done. Gathered in the bullpen, they proposed a celebratory drink as was customary after closing a notable case. Adama declined but encouraged them to raise a glass and to stay safe. As he bid them goodnight and walked out, Bridget followed him into the hallway.

"You're not coming with us?" Bridget's voice echoed with disappointment.

"No. But you should go. It's an honor they invited you and not something you should dismiss. We'll touch base later."

"Okay, well, goodnight, then." She half-smiled and reluctantly went back inside.

"Goodnight, Bridget." He watched her walk away. *Just like music.*

———◆———

After a quick change of clothes, Adama felt lighter as he jogged along the Hudson. When he got to Pier 84, he slowed—this was the spot where it all began. He jogged in place and decided he didn't feel like going to Battery Park. On his way home, he stopped at Serafina's. While sitting at an outside table drinking wine, his phone buzzed; it was Bridget Murphy.

"Hey there, what's up?" He grinned.

"We missed you. You should have come. You know your team is nuts, right?"

"Yeah, they can get that way after an investigation."

"I wanted to thank you for everything you did with the investigations and for me."

"Just doing my job."

"I don't believe that for a minute. You're like me. It's not a job, it's a calling."

"You're right, as usual, Bridget."

There was an awkward pause of silence. They both waited for the other to say something.

"Um, can I buy you dinner or a drink?" she asked.

"Actually, I'm sitting outside at Serafina's as we speak."

"Oh, I'm sorry." She took a leap. "Are you alone?"

"I am." Adama held his breath, then asked, "Would you like to join me?"

"I would. I'll be there shortly." *He's at our first place!*

"See you soon." He picked up his glass, and a huge smile spread across his face. *Here's to joy.*

Adama delayed his food order and stood when Bridget arrived. They greeted each other with kisses on the cheeks. Bridget melted at the sight of his athletic physique—his warm brown skin, muscular legs, chiseled biceps, and broad shoulders. She averted her eyes to hide her thoughts. *His suit hides all those good parts.*

Bridget draped her black jacket over the chair before she settled into her seat. Her white blouse caught Adama's eye with its graceful, scooped neckline—the subtle hint of her breasts broadened his smile. Bridget ordered a glass of prosecco with ice on the side. Adama thought it endearing.

"Were you surprised I called?" She dipped a piece of bread in herb-infused olive oil.

"A little. I thought it was great of my team to invite you; I'm glad you went. They like you, Bridget."

"Well, they're a great team, and I enjoyed working with them. And they sure respect you. Burke's wife called and wanted him to come home, so he left after one beer. One of Gates' kids called and asked him to bring home some ice cream. The rest of the team had a couple of beers and, one by one, left the bar. Oh! And Sanchez offered to fix me up with one of his brothers."

"Seriously?" Adama laughed.

"Yeah, can you believe it?"

"Actually, I do."

The server brought their drinks, and they clinked their glasses.

"So, what did you tell Luis?"

"That I had my eye on someone else." She smiled and looked away.

"Hmm. Are you hungry?"

"Famished. Your team knows how to drink but not eat."

"Yeah, that's typical. They prefer home-cooked meals."

Bridget and Adama took their time with dinner and spent the next two hours talking, eating, drinking, and laughing.

"It's already nine o'clock." She closed her eyes and took in the warm evening.

"What are you doing after dinner?" Adama asked.

"Are we finished?" She felt a twinge of insecurity.

Adama was reflective and took a sip of wine. He did not look away from her but responded after what seemed an eternity. "I'm not."

He tilted his head, looked into her clear blue eyes, and smiled reassuringly. Bridget relaxed.

"Would you like to take a walk, grab coffee, or go for some ice cream?" Bridget asked.

"Ice cream doesn't interest me, but a walk does."

"Great." Bridget smiled.

Adama paid the tab, and they began walking down the sidewalk.

"Wait a second." Adama hustled back to retrieve Bridget's jacket.

"Thanks. I forgot all about it." Bridget reached for her coat.

"I'll carry it."

"Thanks." She smiled at him.

The cherry blossoms created a blanket of pink and white petals that filled the air with sweetness and beauty. Riverside Park bustled with people enjoying the warm evening. Adama and Bridget strolled, deliberately dragging the evening out. They meandered past the river's edge, basketball courts, and playgrounds. They shared stories about their families and life in general. Familiarity had resurfaced. Once again, they found themselves in a comfortable place, seeking to rekindle what time and distance had dimmed.

By the time they emerged at Riverside Drive and W. 106th Street, the magic between them had been reignited, leaving both wanting more.

"I'm just around the corner; would you like to come over?" Adama looked deeply into her eyes.

"Sure," Bridget replied. She fought to hold back her anticipation.

"It's still on the fourth floor." Adama looked up.

"I remember." Bridget's heart skipped a beat.

They climbed the stairs and went into Adama's apartment. He hung Bridget's jacket on the back of a chair. Their eyes locked, the magnetism impossible to resist. Adama's strong hands found her waist, drawing her close with gentle persuasion. He leaned in as she rose onto her toes to meet him. Their first kiss was slow, deep, and the culmination of four excruciating months of longing and separation. In a single breathless moment, they found themselves as one.

Adama suddenly pulled back. "Hey, I need a shower. If you don't mind."

"No, go right ahead."

"You can wait here; sit on the couch or outside if you like."

"Or, maybe I could join you." She gave him a come-hither look.

"Or you could join me—great idea." He grinned.

Adama unclipped his holster and put his gun away, then came back to Bridget. She kicked off her shoes while Adama untucked her blouse. After she lifted the T-shirt over his head, his arms came down around her. They kissed—long, deep, and slow. Bridget unzipped her pants and watched as Adama hurriedly removed his shoes and socks. She let her pants drop to the floor and flicked them away with her foot, while Adama dropped his jogging shorts; then came her blouse.

He waited, admiring her in her blouse and underwear. Shadows in the apartment contrasted with her golden hair, creating a mystical quality in the room. Then he approached. He started at the bottom, slowly lifting the delicate fabric, eyes locked, running his fingers along the sides of her body. She delighted in the slight tickle and enjoyed the sensation as he pulled upward, drawing out the moment until it flowed over her face and hair.

Then he pulled her in close, reached his warm, strong hands around, and unsnapped her bra. She stood back and let the straps fall from her shoulders, exposed, vulnerable yet confident. As he took in her bare breasts, a broad smile engulfed his warm face. "God, you're beautiful," he said softly. She seductively walked over and pressed against him.

Adama took her hand and led her into the bathroom. He turned on the shower, and steam billowed upward. They both dropped their underwear and stepped into the small space. Body parts were lathered in between kisses. Adama turned the water off and wrapped a towel around Bridget. He led her into his bedroom, and they lay on the bed. He peeled strands of damp hair away from her face and leaned into her.

They spent the next hour making love, caressing, soothing, pleasing, and loving each other. Both lay back, panting. Bridget nestled close under his arm. They held each other for a long while. Once again, they felt the release of pent-up tension, as if a weight had been lifted from their shoulders. Adama got up and pulled on his briefs. He retrieved a knee-length, red-and-white-striped cotton robe from a hook and brought it to Bridget. She slipped it on while he went to the kitchen. Upon returning with two glasses of water, he stopped in the doorway.

"Can we go to the living room and talk?" he asked.

"Sure, I'd like that."

Bridget got up and followed him to the living room. Adama set the glasses on the coffee table. Sitting on the couch, they reflected for a few moments. Bridget could see that Adama looked concerned; it made her feel nervous. Adama hoped what he needed to say would come out right.

"I need to say a few things." He momentarily glanced away. "And I'm not sure where to start."

"Maybe I can help by telling you a few things," Bridget offered.

Adama put his hand up. "Just give me a minute to get this out." Adama reached for her hand and lovingly looked into her eyes. "You know I love you, right?"

Bridget's heart raced, and she felt surprised, relieved, and joyful. "I do. I hoped." She squeezed his hand. "I felt we were falling in love. But after how badly I behaved …" She searched his eyes. "Can you forgive me?"

"There's nothing to forgive, love." Their clutched hands seemed to bridge the months of silence they'd both endured. He moved closer. "I'm sorry about my recent behavior. Call it self-preservation. I was shocked and angry, yet very happy to see you again. I didn't know what to think. But I need to understand what happened to move forward."

"Of course," she said.

"We fell in love, and I wish to god I had told you. I regret that, so I'm telling you now. I love you, Bridget." Adama's gaze never left her eyes; his genuine affection was evident.

Bridget saw his vulnerability and melted. "And I love you."

"Love, that last phone call haunted me," he said. "You asked for space, and I understood. But something in your voice changed. I didn't recognize you anymore." He swallowed hard. "I spent these last couple of months convincing myself that nothing about us was real."

Tears streamed down Bridget's face. She hastily jumped in. "Adama, you didn't do anything wrong." She wiped tears on her sleeve. "What I did was actually for you."

"For me? What are you talking about?"

"Oh, Adama, where do I start?" Bridget collected her thoughts. "Okay, you knew about my divorce. But what you didn't know was…well, my ex-husband threatened you. And I believed him."

"A threat to me? How?"

Bridget briefly closed her eyes. "He hired a PI. He had photos of us, here in your apartment, and mine. He threatened to expose us and destroy your career at the NYPD. I couldn't let that happen. He has friends in high places."

"Jesus, Bridget." Adama leaned back, hands behind his head, processing her words. "That bullying, cowardly …" He checked his anger and stayed calm. "He was the reason?" *I'd like to kick the shit out of that guy.* He hunched forward. "I wish you'd told me."

"I wanted to tell you. I wanted to call the police, but I had no proof, recordings, or written demands—all just innuendo. He showed me details about you, your schedule, the names of your staff and bosses, even your family." Bridget hung her head. "I'm so sorry about him."

Adama stood and paced around his living room, lost in thought. He turned to Bridget. "Was that all?" He sat next to her. "How did he threaten you?"

"It doesn't matter now. I made a deal—to give him everything if he promised not to harm you. So, I sold my house, cashed in my 401(k), gave up my mother's inheritance, all my savings, and agreed to alimony. I was happy to do it, to save you." She looked down. "Then I made a plan to take away all his leverage."

"Oh, no!" Suddenly, Adama understood. "You broke up with me. No relationship, no leverage." He grabbed her. "Oh, Bridget. That's why your house was empty. And why you turned cold and told me to go away."

"Yes." That single word carried the weight of months of solitary suffering. "And you were so sweet, and supportive, and persistent. I didn't know what else to do. I had to convince you." She sobbed in his arms.

"Oh, Bridget. Honey, I'm sorry." He pulled her close, encircling her in his arms. For several minutes, they held each other, breathed together.

"Love, it's okay," he whispered against her hair. "I promise, he'll never hurt you again. And you don't need to worry about me." He pulled back to look in her eyes. "Did you think I couldn't take care of myself?"

"I couldn't take the chance." Bridget wiped her nose on the sleeve of Adama's robe. "Anyway, he can't hurt us anymore."

"What do you mean?"

"He died in a skiing accident, in the French Alps. It happened a couple of months ago."

"How did you find out?" The news shocked him.

"The police in Lyon, France, notified me. Everything changed overnight. It's over." Saying the words out loud caused Bridget to collapse into the couch—it was real.

"What about the evidence? The pictures?" Adama's detective mind—always at work.

"That's the strangest part. I received an envelope containing everything. An anonymous delivery with a note saying the case was resolved and no paper trail."

Adama nodded at the news, but his eyes showed he wasn't convinced.

"There's more," she said quietly. "Shortly after that, my dad passed away. I moved into my parents' home and managed their estate." She took a deep breath for the rest. "And then Colin was killed in England. These past few months …"

"Oh, Bridget. I wish you'd called." He reached for her hand. "I'm sorry. You've had so much to deal with by yourself."

"I wanted to; I picked up the phone so many times. When I arrived in New York, I hoped to explain everything to you, but—"

"But I wouldn't let you." Adama touched her face, brushing a tear away with his thumb. He raised her lowered chin and looked into her watery blue eyes. "I love you, Bridget. Very much, and I want us to be together. Do you want that too?"

She threw her arms around him, feeling free, feeling blissful. "Yes! I love you too." Their lips met, gently at first. Then she softly said, "*Very* much." They kissed again. She lay her head against his chest, and they held each other.

Whispered words of love had dissolved the last threads of tension. Adama and Bridget had found peace. It enveloped them like a warm blanket. Exhausted, emotionally, and physically, they found their way to the bedroom and crawled under the covers.

"Sweet dreams, love," Adama said.

"You too, my love," Bridget whispered in his ear.

They kissed each other goodnight. With bodies pressed together, they drifted off to sleep.

———◆———

The next morning, streaks of sunlight brightened a brand-new day and a fresh beginning for Bridget and Adama. Their fingers intertwined as they strolled to a nearby café, claiming a small bistro-style table with worn cane-backed chairs.

"I'd love a latte and quiche this morning." Contentment radiated from her eyes.

"Some things never change," Adama said, eyes crinkling with affection.

Everything tasted better to them: golden crusted Quiche Lorraine, sweet berries, crispy home-style potatoes, and lattes crowned with white foam and a fancy heart design.

"What should we do today, love?" Adama asked, reaching for her hand.

With a wordless proposition, she bit her lower lip slightly. "How about …" Bridget inclined toward him and whispered, "… we just hang out in your apartment." She tilted her chin into her left shoulder and raised her eyebrows in an amorous glance.

Adama eagerly nodded and tossed his napkin on the table. "Check, please!"

Their laughter mingled in the space between them. Bridget savored the warm sunlight bathing her as they waited for the bill. She closed her eyes and tilted her face upward. When she opened her eyes, Adama was watching her with a tender and nostalgic gaze.

"What?" she asked softly.

"I thought I'd lost this," he said simply. "Lost you." The moment hung suspended; they both reached their hands across the table.

It only lasted a minute before Bridget's phone buzzed.

"Ahh, who could that be?" She dug it out of her pocket and saw the caller. "It's New Scotland Yard."

"Really?" Adama's eyes sharpened, curious. He nodded once.

"Hello?" Bridget answered.

Adama watched her eyes widen, brows arch, and her spine stiffen. Her smile faded, and her face turned pale. "I understand. Thank you." Bridget's voice turned hollow, professional. With careful deliberation, she closed her phone.

A cloud slowly moved to block the sun, casting a shadow across their table. The warmth diminished, matching the chill that had settled between them.

Adama waited patiently, knowing something dire had happened. He moved closer, her voice barely audible, as Bridget shared the news. "That was the Yard. Three billionaires were found dead." Her eyes revealed a mix of surprise, dread, and determination. "They want me to work the case." She leaned back, shoulders curved inward; her voice cracked. "It's not over."

Around them, the café maintained its rhythm—laughter, clinking cups, the hiss of the espresso machine. But at their table, time seemed suspended.

Adama squinted, and his jaw muscles hardened as he clenched his teeth. He leaned back in his chair; it squeaked under the pressure. He folded his arms as his thoughts raced, compiled, and backtracked. He beckoned her inward, gaze unwavering. "Well, love. Looks like we're going to London."

As he spoke, the cloud drifted past the sun. Warmth returned to bathe them, and Bridget's smile resurfaced with it. She beamed and nodded wholeheartedly. Once again, their thoughts had merged into perfect alignment.

"Looks like it," she echoed.

The End

About the Author

Janet Boydell is an American author and former businesswoman. Upon retiring in 2022, Janet decided it was time to focus on writing the multiple stories she has developed during the past thirty years.

Raised in Southern California, she earned her Bachelor of Science in Business Administration with an emphasis in law and finance from California State Polytechnic University at Pomona.

Beginning her career in accounting, Janet worked in the field of corporate finance until 1991, when she pivoted to executive-retained search. She eventually founded her retained search firm called "A Hire Connection, Inc.," specializing in C-suite functions. During that time, Janet wrote two books related to strategic management and best hiring practices. Based on her two books, she traveled the United States, presenting half-day workshops to CEO groups. She concluded her corporate career as a partner in a firm that provided structural design, sustainability, and code-related services, where she successfully managed and grew a multi-million-dollar staffing division.

Janet wrote and published two business books while she was still working. She co-authored *You're NOT The Person I Hired!: A CEO's Survival Guide To Hiring Top Talent* (Oct. 2005); and wrote and published *A Hire Connection: How to Make Your Next Hire Your Best Hire* (Oct. 2007).

Outside of her success in the business world, to her family and friends, Janet is known for her imagination and storytelling. Her children and grandchildren are delighted with her mysteries and whimsical stories about people and places. She turned that giftedness into her first fiction, *Deadly Exploits*, published by Berry Powell Press.

Janet lives in Southern California and has two grown children and two grandchildren. She enjoys traveling and attending writers' workshops. She spends a lot of time developing her stories, and is already working on her next book—possibly the second of a series.

To contact Janet visit *www.janetboydell.com*.

Note From the Publisher

We at Berry Powell Press are incredibly proud to introduce a stunning new novel written by Janet Boydell. We expect that this will be one of many works of Janet's fiction to come, as she has already demonstrated her exceptional writing capabilities as a nonfiction author. The book, intriguing and compelling from the first word, is not only remarkably well-researched, but the author has also used a breadth of imagination to create a world that is both alluring and complex—sure to engage the most "who-dunnit" mind. We are proud to publish a book that showcases the author as one who has honed her writing skills, is meticulous with detail, and provides a resolution that will leave readers begging for more.

But even more important to us as a publisher committed to publishing stories based on the highest ideals, the book serves up a heavy dose of justice in ways many of us wish would be more directly and blatantly impactful. In this story, those who have hurt others horrifically and stealthily open themselves to payback, coming from a most unexpected place. *You will reap what you sow* is the satisfying theme of this story, and the reader will feel it deeply.

Likely, Janet, whose mind is teeming with intricate stories full of suspense and intrigue, isn't finished with Adama and Bridget, two strong and lovable characters. We can't wait to see what's next!

If you have a message that needs to become a book—either fiction or nonfiction—please visit our website.

www.berrypowellpress.com.

Berry Powell Press is a hybrid publishing house that publishes authors with transformational perspectives on timely personal and societal challenges. We provide our authors with in-depth mentorship and collaborative assistance to create life-changing books. Additionally, we assist them in building book-based businesses that can impact the largest audience possible. We publish fiction and non-fiction for children through adult audiences.

www.ingramcontent.com/pod-product-compliance
Lightning Source LLC
Chambersburg PA
CBHW071152020726
47502CB00002B/383